MW01027104

Peach Blossom Debt

◇◇

Da Feng Gua Guo

ISBN 978-1-956609-05-9 (print)
ISBN 978-1-956609-07-3 (ebook)

Translation by XiA
Editing by Demi Guo
Proofing by Lori Parks
Cover Illustration by 侑橋 (AtsumuBa)
Cover Design by Lucid Chen

Printed in the USA

Published by Peach Flower House LLC 2023
PMB # 2718
1050 Lakes Drive
#225
West Covina, CA 91790
Visit www.peachflowerhouse.com

Learn how to pronounce the character names here!

https://www.peachflowerhouse.com/
pronunciation-guide/peach-blossom-debt

Table of Contents

CHAPTER ONE	1
CHAPTER TWO	3
CHAPTER THREE	9
CHAPTER FOUR	25
CHAPTER FIVE	51
CHAPTER SIX	75
CHAPTER SEVEN	95
CHAPTER EIGHT	119
CHAPTER NINE	129
CHAPTER TEN	155
CHAPTER ELEVEN	167
CHAPTER TWELVE	181
CHAPTER THIRTEEN	193
CHAPTER FOURTEEN	203
CHAPTER FIFTEEN	215
CHAPTER SIXTEEN	235
CHAPTER SEVENTEEN	247
CHAPTER EIGHTEEN	259
CHAPTER NINETEEN	279
CHAPTER TWENTY	289
CHAPTER TWENTY-ONE	311
CHAPTER TWENTY-TWO	323
CHAPTER TWENTY-THREE	345
CHAPTER TWENTY-FOUR	359
CHAPTER TWENTY-FIVE	377
CHAPTER TWENTY-SIX	389
EXTRA: THE LIVING IMMORTAL	399
AFTERWORD	411

Chapter One

"Young Master." Chief Wang was watching me. He had two, maybe three, bumps on a face burned dark by the sun, and beads of sweat wobbled on the ends of his beard, ready to fall.

Although it was now the beginning of autumn, the midday sun was still no less scorching than the hottest days of summer. Autumn cicadas chirped at the top of their lungs, while the ground could scorch one's feet.

"Young Master, our humble selves have been lying in ambush here for the entire morning on your orders. What exactly is our mission? Please give us your instructions."

I crushed a mosquito that was feeding on my cheek, wiped away a handful of damp sweat, and flashed a knowing smile.

"Your Young Master is abducting a person who will pass through this road today. As soon as the horse carriage appears, mask yourselves and charge. Make certain to take this person alive."

Chapter Two

I was originally a carefree immortal without an official post in the Heavenly Court, one who had humbly received the nominal title of Guangxu Yuanjun. As my title was quite a mouthful to pronounce, the immortals in heaven all call me Song Yao Yuanjun.

Song Yao was my given name before I became an immortal.

Even as a human in the mortal world, I was long established as a carefree person who lived in leisure. I spent the prime of my youth, swaggering around town a free spirit.

The concept of "Dao," or the Way, had been a world far removed from mine at the time, until the day Taishang Laojun lost his grip while opening his furnace, and dropped one of its golden elixir pills into the mortal world below. This golden elixir just so happened to drop into a pot of soup in a marketplace noodle stall. The stall owner, thinking it was simply a bit of bird droppings that had fallen from the sky, stirred the pot with a big ladle and scooped up a portion of noodle soup into a bowl to serve.

That unfortunate customer who ate the noodles—
That was me.

Even now, I marvel at the intensity of the ravenous hunger that blinded me then. Just like that, I gulped down a golden elixir the size of rat poop along with the soup.

And so, on that very night—when the golden crow descended in the west and the moon palace rose in its place—my essence, energy, and spirit merged as one, auspicious clouds surged beneath my feet, and I ascended.

From then on, I became an immortal.

When the heavenly envoy led me to the Lingxiao Palace to pay my respects to the Jade Emperor, the Jade Emperor said, "Immortals each have their own immortal root. Some cultivate it, some are born with it, and some chance upon it."

There were no titles to bestow upon immortals who became immortal by chance, so the various gentlemen in the Heavenly Court all called me by my name, Immortal Song Yao. After enough time had passed for the land to turn into the sea and back many times over, the Jade Emperor graced me with his favor, bestowing upon me the title of Guangxu Yuanjun.

My fellow immortals had long since grown accustomed to calling me Immortal Song Yao, and when they saw this face of mine, they could not bring themselves to say the words Guangxu, so they all called me Song Yao Yuanjun. As time elapsed, even I myself had forgotten about this title.

One certain day, Donghua Dijun hosted a tea banquet and issued a genteel invitation to respectfully request Guangxu Yuanjun's presence. Holding the invitation in hand, I said to the azure bird delivering the message, "Who is Guangxu Yuanjun and why did you mistakenly deliver this invitation to my Song Yao Yuanjun's residence?"

There was a common saying in the mortal world, "to be

as carefree as an immortal," and in the Heavenly Court where immortal friends were aplenty, time was as ephemeral as drifting clouds.

Days passed, one after another, until a certain day when Taibai Xingjun came to this immortal lord's residence and said that he was here on the Jade Emperor's orders to relay a secret decree to me.

In a spot in the back garden of my residence where floating clouds drifted, Taibai Xingjun told me that Tianshu Xingjun and Nanming Dijun had been declared guilty of engaging in an illicit affair. The Jade Emperor had already severed their immortal roots at the Immortal Execution Terrace and banished them down into the mortal world.

Such a rare incident had been unheard of for thousands upon thousands of years, so this immortal lord naturally had to do a double take first before asking the most important question. "It's an illicit affair between Tianshu Xingjun and Nanming Dijun... not them both seducing the celestial maidens...?"

Jinxing said nothing.

This immortal lord smiled awkwardly. "So they are what the mortal world calls the cut-sleeves..."

This was common, and in itself, nothing rare. What's unusual was that it actually turned out to be Tianshu Xingjun and Nanming Dijun.

Tsk, tsk.

Nanming Dijun always carried himself with an air of solemn aloofness far removed from the masses, while Tianshu Xingjun could be described as refined and untainted by worldly affairs. Both gentlemen were exalted lords who had never thought much of an immortal like me who ascended by pure luck. So how could such a thing happen?

That said, however, they were quite the perfect match when put together.

"Still, we cannot close the books on the sins of both lords

just yet," Jinxing said. "The Jade Emperor is merciful, and he has given them a chance to atone by sending them to the mortal world to undergo a lifetime of love trials. If they can see through their inner demons and realize the errors of their ways, they may once again cultivate to immortality and return to the Heavenly Court. For that reason, the Jade Emperor has issued a decree to ask that you, Guangxu Yuanjun, make a trip to the mortal world too."

I was astounded. "Why?"

Jinxing stroked his beard and smiled. "The Jade Emperor thought about it and decided that the task of setting up the trials to punish them in the mortal world would be best handed to you."

Now, I understood. This immortal lord had some past grudges with Nanming Dijun and Tianshu Xingjun, and Old Man Jade Emperor must have liked me for this.

I furrowed my brows and sighed. "I have been acquainted with both lords for thousands of years. How could I have the heart to set trials as their punishments?"

Jinxing said, "The Jade Emperor has shared with me that once you return to the Heavenly Court after your descent to enlighten your fellow immortals in the mortal world, he will personally draw up a decree and bestow upon you the title of Guangxu Tianjun in recognition of your contribution."

Then he stroked his beard again and smiled. "Tianshu and Nanming will start as immortals with no official post when they return to the Heavenly Court. They will still need Tianjun to guide and enlighten them then."

The Jade Emperor's terms were pretty good. Descend to the mortal world once, and this immortal lord could earn the title and rank of an exalted lord. As they said, to be an immortal was to discard all desires and worries from one's mind and let nature take its course. So rising from a superficial rank to a meaningful one once in a while could be considered a cause for rejoicing.

I sighed again. "Very well. To be subjected to a lifetime of suffering for love, yet enlightened in the supreme art of cultivation. As their fellow immortal, I have no choice but to endure my heartache, and reluctantly oblige."

Six or seven days later, the Jade Emperor sent Mingge Xingjun to instruct me on what I must do upon my descent.

When the Jade Emperor banished the two lords to the mortal world, he had prepared a body there for me. The role I was going to play was that of the insurmountable mountain straddling Nanming and Tianshu's road to love, the mother of all rods wrecking the lovebirds' relationship.

In this life, Nanming Dijun was a man of great valor, while Tianshu Xingjun was a delicate, refined young master. Yue Lao, the deity of marriage and love, ran a thread of fate as thick as a finger between their names and secured it with a huge, impeccably tight knot. Deeply in love since their youth, both had mutually exchanged a solemn pledge of everlasting love until the end of time.

This immortal lord was responsible for getting in their way. When they trade messages, I intercept, and when they reunite, I tear them apart. They would not see each other in life, nor would they be together in death.

I mulled over this lousy script in my heart, and no matter how I looked at it, I felt like I was the one who should have been sent to the Immortal Execution Terrace.

Several more days passed, and the time for my descent arrived. My fellow immortals saw me off to the Southern Heavenly Gate. Outside the gate, I took Hengwen Qingjun's hand. "I'll be back in a few days. Do save some of the residence's exquisite wine for me."

Hengwen Qingjun's eyes curved into a smile. "Don't worry. I'll be sure to leave some for your homecoming feast." He patted my shoulder and came closer. "Always stay true to the core of your very essence and hold steadfast to the integrity inherent to you as an immortal. You must never relinquish your immortal roots while sleeping in the same bed as Tianshu Xingjun every night."

"What?" I blurted, dumbfounded.

The smile on Hengwen Qingjun's refined features betrayed the rotten nature beneath. "Still playing dumb. Everyone in heaven knows that the son of a vassal prince you are about to become has to pretend to take a fancy to Tianshu Xingjun. To punish him so that he'd have no time to even pine for his love, the Jade Emperor has ordered you to strand him in your residence, keeping by his side every day and sharing his bed every night."

The Jade Emperor duped me!

Mingge Xingjun didn't say a word of this to me at all!

I made to leave, but Hengwen intercepted me with a raised sleeve. "What are you doing?"

I sidestepped him. "To look for the Jade Emperor. I'm not doing this anymore!"

That geezer Jade Emperor duped me into sleeping with Tianshu!

Hengwen responded with glee at my misfortune, "At this stage, it's too late for you to back out. The decision is already out of your hands."

A gust of strong wind struck me, and this immortal lord lost my footing, tumbling headfirst off the heavenly gate.

Chapter Three

On the second day of the fifth month in the year of the fire rat, this immortal lord rode down Shangchuan City on an auspicious cloud. A light breeze rose. The passersby raised their heads for a look, then shrank back into their shells and dashed off, while street vendors scrambled to pack their wares.

This immortal lord heard a distant shout. "The sky's overcast; it's going to rain. Quick, pack up and hurry home!"

Peasants are obtuse. This immortal lord would do well not to quibble with the likes of them.

Mingge Xingjun led me until I was floating over the manor of the Vassal Prince of Ningping of the Eastern Commandery. He pointed at a spot in the back garden of the prince's manor and said, "This is your mortal body."

There was a reclining chair in the back garden, where two young children had surrounded and now clambered over a prone form. This motionless one was Li Siming, the youngest young master of the vassal prince—and this immortal lord's to-be self. I sized him up carefully. His gaze was vacant; his expression, blank and wooden. The top of his head was even adorned with flowers and plants, courtesy of the two young children.

"This person… seems to be a dimwit."

Mingge Xingjun gave a dry laugh. "Ahem. This mortal flesh was specially prepared for you. It's naturally soulless before you take possession of it, and can presently only eat, drink, urinate, and defecate. The time has come. Yuanjun, enter the body. Posthaste, if you please."

Without waiting for this immortal lord to say another word, he started reciting the incantation. With a flick of his finger, a golden light materialized within my vision, and soon the incantation had propelled me into the garden.

A sense of familiarity from thousands of years ago spread throughout my body. Thus concluded this immortal lord's successful possession of the body.

After being a weightless immortal for thousands of years, it all came rushing back—the sensation of my feet on solid ground, the familiar weight of my limbs, the mess of sensations in my chest, the worldly sounds flooding my ears. They were, unexpectedly, reassuringly endearing. Something squirming and heavy clambered on my body. I opened my eyes, and the first thing that greeted me was a tiny face covered in smudges. A pair of round eyes swiveled in their sockets, and a mouth missing two teeth bared in a highly irritating smile. Dirty little paws raised a handful of black mud toward my mouth.

"Heh heh, Little Uncle, be a dear and eat this. Be a dear and eat this."

I smiled kindly and raised a hand to pat his head. "Sweetheart, get down from your Little Uncle now and go back to your parents."

Those round eyes blinked twice, and he cocked his little head to look at me. I turned aside and picked up another child poised to scramble up my knees to stick flowers on this immortal lord's head. "Sitting upright and walking properly are the fundamentals of human conduct. Did your tutor not teach you this?"

Another pair of round eyes stared right back at me. This child was brighter than the one earlier. He puckered his mouth—and with a *waaah*, burst out bawling. "Mother—Mother—Mother—Grandfather—Little Uncle's scary!!!"

He created such a din that his cries drew the maidservants who yelled for servants, who in turn called for the steward and the wet nurses, who then helped the madams out of their chambers. Two loyal servants, both strong men puffed up with the imposing air of Wu Song heading up the mountain to fight a tiger, plucked the two little young masters from my side.

I smiled genially at both of them, and both men retreated to the walkway with a terrified look. Head after head peeked out from some distance away, looking at this immortal lord like they had seen a ghost.

The sheer ignorance it took not to recognize a real immortal. This immortal lord would not quibble with the likes of them either.

Several armed guards crowded around an approaching man. He was adorned in a reddish-purple robe embroidered with a fierce tiger motif. He had graying temples, a beard, a broad forehead, a square jaw, and worn, weathered features. Needless to say, this was the Vassal Prince of the Eastern Commandery in the flesh.

This immortal lord would have to play the part of his son for quite some time, so I had to establish some rapport during our first meeting.

I approached slowly, my hands lowered as I adopted a humble stance and greeted him with the utmost respect.

"Father."

A strange light glinted in the Prince of the Eastern Commandery's tiger-like stare as he gazed at this immortal lord. One could only imagine how rife with emotion he was now that his dimwit son was suddenly lucid. His excitement was so palpable that his face was now deathly pale, and he was trembling uncontrollably.

Then, those black eyes rolled up, and he passed out.

Thus, I successfully concluded my transformation into Li Siming.

The folks of the Prince of the Eastern Commandery's manor trembled at the mere sight of me for the entire day. It was on the day after the Prince of the Eastern Commandery woke up, that he invited a Daoist priest to invoke a great deity before me. Holding a sword made of peach wood, the priest danced for a bit, then chanted incoherently for another bit. I greatly enjoyed the show he put on, as though he really had summoned the deity into his body. Just as the performance reached a climactic high, the priest's eyes suddenly blew wide to gawk at this immortal lord. He fell to his knees, kowtowing so hard that we heard the thuds. "This humble Daoist respectfully welcomes the high immortal."

That startled me. I had not concerned myself with mortal affairs for many years now. Given that there had been no newly ascended immortal in the Heavenly Court of late, I thought the art of Daoism had fallen into decline. Never did I expect there to be someone in the streets who had cultivated with such proficiency that he could tell this immortal lord's real identity at a glance.

The priest continued to kowtow in trepidation. "This humble Daoist's cultivation is too shallow to recognize Baihu Xingjun's venerable self at a glance. Please forgive me for my offense!"

Baihu Xingjun—the White Tiger Star? There were seventy-two lunar mansions and eight star lords in the Heavenly Court. Since when did a tiger come to be an exalted lord? The Heavenly Court did indeed have a few white tigers, all of which were raised to guard the heavenly gates, but since when did one come to be called a lord in the palace itself?!

The priest turned on his knees to kowtow to the Prince of the Eastern Commandery. "Congratulations, Your Lordship! This humble Daoist shall boldly venture to divulge heaven's secret. The little young master is an incarnation of Baihu Xingjun of the heavenly realm. Your Lordship is a man of great fortune, and this is a blessing from heaven for the immortal affinity forged."

The Prince of the Eastern Commandery looked at me, still trembling a little. "Master priest, are you telling me the truth? This son of mine has been dull and ignorant of the ways of the world since he was a child, but suddenly, he's lucid and literate. This is truly..."

The priest rose. "Your Lordship, the little young master is an immortal incarnate. Naturally, he differs from the common person. As the ancients say, a crouching tiger is like a boulder. Xingjun has been lying dormant for several years, and the common people, being ordinary, could not have known."

The Prince of the Eastern Commandery was so very pleased with the explanation—that his son was the tiger star who had descended to their mortal world—that he even believed the nonsense like his youngest was a dimwit because the tiger star had been sleeping for a while. He looked again at this immortal lord, no longer trembling, but with a face radiant with happiness.

"But master priest, if what you say is true, and this son of mine has been in a dormant state for so many years, why has he suddenly woken up?"

I plucked a teacup from the table and moistened my throat.

With an enigmatic pose—one hand behind his back and the other stroking his beard—the priest said, "The secrets of heaven cannot be divulged."

What a load of rubbish!

From then on, this immortal lord lived very comfortably in the Prince of the Eastern Commandery's manor.

The Prince wasted no time telling the entire household that his youngest son, Siming, was a tiger star; I ended up being secretly gawked at for several days. I gradually became familiar with the people in the prince's manor. When I wandered around the prince's manor surveying the place, servants would pretend to pass by, and attempt to strike up conversation with their little young master.

The Prince of the Eastern Commandery had ill luck with his wives. He successively married ten or so wives and concubines, all of whom he jinxed to death. Including Li Siming, this immortal lord's now mortal flesh, he had a total of three sons. His eldest son, Sixian, and his second son, Siyuan, often vied with one another, both overtly and covertly, to be his heir.

After talk of the tiger star spread, both elder siblings sought out the novelty that was their little brother. They went to extra lengths, preparing a feast with wine in the garden of a side compound. It was here that we admired the scenery and chatted the night away.

It had to be known that I, Song Yao Yuanjun, had spent my several thousand years roaming all over heaven, drinking tea, sampling wine, playing chess, and expounding the Dao. In the realm of immortals, no one save Hengwen Qingjun could out-talk me. I had just begun to touch on the topic when, before I knew it, it was morning. In contrast, my two elder brothers slept the entire ensuing day, further cementing the notion that this immortal lord was indeed the tiger star.

Several days later, I more or less got a grasp on Nanming Dijun and Tianshu Xingjun's current circumstances through the marketplace, teahouses, and prince's manor.

Mingge Xingjun once told me that Nanming Dijun's name in this life was Shan Shengling, while Tianshu Xingjun's reincarnation was called Mu Ruoyan. It was only after several days of inquiries that I learned both were fairly renowned in this secular world. Especially Tianshu Xingjun, who was really one trouble magnet, which came as a surprise to this immortal lord. Plastered all over the walls in every alley in the city were arrest warrants for Mu Ruoyan, along with a large, half-body portrait.

It was said that the Shan and Mu clans had been high-ranking officials of the Imperial Court for generations. Both clans had known each other just as long, and their friendship ran deep. More than a decade ago, Nanming Dijun's paternal grandfather had offended the emperor, and the entire clan was executed. The Mu clan secretly rescued Shan Shengling and brought him into their residence, where they raised him to adulthood. Nanming Dijun was an imposing figure in the Heavenly Court, and even when he was banished to the mortal world, he was not a person who could suffer humiliation in silence. These were turbulent times, when vassal princes in various lands possessed massive military force, whittling imperial power down to almost nothing.

Shan Shengling threw in his lot with the Vassal Prince of the Southern Commandery. And just a month before, he had incited the Prince of the Southern Commandery to openly stage a revolt with the intent to usurp the throne.

The emperor flew into a rage, and when investigations revealed it was the Mu clan who saved the life of this scourge, he had the entire clan sentenced to death.

Of course, the Jade Emperor could not let Tianshu Xingjun fumble into an execution and have it all end here. So, the servants of the Mu clan risked their own necks to protect their little young master, Mu Ruoyan, as he fled for his life. He was presently in hiding, drifting through the world at large.

The Mu Ruoyan in the wanted poster had a pointed face and thin eyebrows; it was extremely unlikeable, and this immortal lord sighed a few times, gazing at that portrait.

While in the Heavenly Court, Tianshu Xingjun dressed in white and wore a jade hairpin—looking charmingly refined and indifferent. Such was his aura, untarnished and ethereal.

It was plain abhorrent of the Jade Emperor to arrange such

a body for him after banishing him to the mortal world. After all, this immortal lord still had a love script to enact, and on the orders of the Jade Emperor himself, no less. At least leave him a fraction of the exalted lord's looks. How could I bring myself to utter sweet nothings to a face like this when I get my hands on him?

At night, I adjusted my qi and regulated my breathing. I was hoping to shift my primordial spirit back to the Heavenly Court and negotiate my lot with the Jade Emperor, but I could not. It was as if my spirit had been nailed into this body. Only then did I remember the words of Mingge Xingjun, that old scoundrel, telling me that my immortal skills would be barred from me on my descent, save for at the most crucial junctures. He must have kept the truth from me, knowing I would quit had I known.

Left with no other options, I spent several idle months in the manor, drinking tea and sleeping the days away.

The Prince of the Eastern Commandery was unusually affectionate to this suddenly lucid tiger star son of his, and he specially allocated a whole courtyard for me to live in. I often drank wine and played chess with both of my elder brothers; we even went to the entertainment quarters together to listen to the songs there. Our relationship improved with each passing day.

Three months later, Mingge Xingjun finally returned to the mortal world. He released this immortal lord from Li Siming's body in the middle of the night and told me—midair above the prince's manor—that the show was about to start.

Tianshu Xingjun, having recuperated from his wounds whilst in hiding, had been spirited away by his attendants to his lover's side in the Southern Commandery. The little young master of the Prince of the Eastern Commandery, Li Siming, was to come charging at this time and abduct Mu Ruoyan back to the manor.

On the day after tomorrow, before noon, Mu Ruoyan's

horse carriage would pass the foot of the mountain outside Shangchuan City.

As the Prince of the Southern Commandery assembled his army and proclaimed himself emperor to boot, the Prince of the Eastern Commandery grew restless too. The two territories bordered each other; armed conflicts would be inevitable. These days, the Prince of the Eastern Commandery and his eldest son inspected the military camps at the border garrison, under the jurisdiction of the commandery. The second son, Siyuan, remained in the prince's manor as its administrator, while simultaneously guiding his younger brother—this immortal lord— through internal affairs.

The first morning, I claimed to have received a tip-off from the Eastern Commandery's spies, and asked for twenty to thirty sturdy bodyguards to lie in ambush by the mountain path outside the city.

Who could have known we would not even catch a glimpse of the carriage, even after waiting from morning to noon?

The mountain path was completely empty. No carriages. No passersby. Not even a wild hare.

Such a scenario was an impossibility. Tianshu's passage through this road was personally arranged by Mingge Xingjun, and it was all recorded in his book. Tianshu Xingjun was now a mere mortal, unable to escape the fate heaven had decreed for him. Besides, Old Man Mingge had clearly told this immortal lord it would happen in the morning, so why had he yet to appear at noon?

Dozens of bodyguards' clothes were drenched in sweat. Li Siming's stomach growled. This immortal lord was burning with hunger. Should I go somewhere secluded on the pretext of relieving myself and nab a local earth deity to make inquiries? Just as I was considering it, a voice breezed past my ear.

"Tianshu Xingjun's carriage has run into bandits on the road one kilometer from here. He has already been abducted back to their mountain stronghold. Go now!"

My fury blazed when I heard this voice. *Mingge, that old geezer, is he playing me?!*

The most pressing matter at present was to get Tianshu back in my hands. Thus, I summoned Chief Wang before me. "Is there a bandit stronghold on this mountain?"

"To report to the young master," Chief Wang answered, "there are indeed one or two gangs of vermin hiding on the mountain."

I waved a sleeve. "Have our brothers fall into rank. We'll head up the mountain to round up that gang of vermin."

The bodyguards from the Prince of the Eastern Commandery's manor were all well trained. Although Chief Wang looked uncertain, he said nothing further and gave his order. The bodyguards immediately rose from the thick undergrowth of grass and charged up the mountain.

It might be called a mountain, but in truth, it could only be considered a hillock; it did not even have a proper name, although the folks from Shangchuan all called it the Great Slope. A trail, worn down by woodcutters, meandered up the sides of the hillock. This immortal lord was stealthily leading my bodyguards up the mountain, having made it halfway when an ominous chill gusted past, and two men sprang from the woods. "Who goes there calling on our Heifeng Stronghold?!"

These two vermin were disheveled and shabbily dressed. Clearly, this no-cost business was not going well for them. Before they could even stand firm on their feet and announce their names, the bodyguards had swarmed and knocked them to the ground. They trussed the men up into two bundles and discarded them by the side of the road before continuing their upward charge.

There was only a dilapidated mountain deity temple at the top, with a banner raised before the temple, inscribed with two words as large as the rim of a bowl—Heifeng Stronghold.

Inside the temple were only about ten to twenty shabbily dressed bandits and a burly man—the self-proclaimed bandit chief. The bodyguards charged into the mountain deity temple, and in less than an hour, all the bandits were tied up on the ground. I personally conducted a careful search of the mountain deity temple, but did not catch any sight of Tianshu. Uncaring of which, I dragged forward one of the bandits and asked, "Where did you lock up the man in the carriage you robbed today? I'll let all of you go once I find him."

The bandit chief and his pack of minions pricked up their ears at the demand, and craned their necks up. That bandit I was interrogating immediately grinned. "So, you're looking for that invalid? The mountain deity statue is hollow, and the incense burner is a switch. Turn it to the left to open a secret door. The man you want is inside."

One bandit shifted, and said in a small voice, "We only managed to rob one today in the last ten days or so. We thought it'd be a big haul, given the horses and carriage and even the escorts. But there was only an invalid inside, and it's earned us nothing but misfortune."

This immortal lord played deaf to his murmuring. I turned the mechanism, circled behind the mountain deity statue, and strode through the secret door.

Within the chamber, a few vaguely human shapes were half lying in the pitch-darkness, likely having been drugged by the mountain bandits.

I silently recited the incantation to sight immortals.

In the darkness, I saw a faint layer of silvery light wholly envelop a person. Clear and frosty—that was Tianshu Xingjun's immortal glow. No doubt this person was Mu Ruoyan.

I was dying to know what Tianshu Xingjun looked like now. I picked him up, and carried him out of the earthen statue and turned him over for a look. His face was filthy with mud, and his hair was a disheveled mess. I could not tell what he looked like other than that he was unkempt. With no other choice, I shouted for Chief Wang. "Tie up the rest of them and find a stretcher for this man. Bring him back to the prince's manor."

Before leaving, however, I untied the bandits and begged their pardon for the offense. This immortal lord has always been merciful. In such turbulent times, it was not easy making a living out of any trade.

And so it was without a hitch that this immortal lord brought Tianshu Xingjun back to the Prince of the Eastern Commandery's manor.

But how did I go from abducting this person to rescuing him instead?

I told Li Siyuan that the tip-off had made these people out to be Southern Commandery spies, but an investigation turned up nothing. Li Siyuan was up to his neck in the prince's manor's affairs, so he said, "I'll leave this matter to you, Third Brother; investigate as you deem fit."

And so Tianshu was justifiably carried into this third young master's exclusive courtyard.

Per Mingge Xingjun's arrangement, once Mu Ruoyan woke up, this immortal lord would claim to have taken a liking to him. Looking at this face on the stretcher in the courtyard, I sighed twice, then instructed the attendants to give him a thorough wash from head to toe.

When I entered my bedchamber and bolted the door, there was a flash of red light, and then Mingge Xingjun was standing beside the table, his old face crinkled in laughter as he cupped his hands in greeting. "Song Yao Yuanjun, congratulations on successfully concluding your first mission!"

I pulled a glum face. "Xingjun, you played me. You clearly said to abduct him on the mountain road in the morning. How did it go from that to rescuing him from a mountain stronghold?"

Mingge Xingjun said with a dry laugh, "I might have simplified it when I wrote it down. It won't affect the overall situation. Not at all." He then fished out the book of fate and flipped to a particular page. He handed it to me for a look, and shockingly enough, written in the book were the words:

Mu Ruoyan is abducted from the mountain road at the morning hours of chen; Li Siming receives Mu Ruoyan.

So that was how it was.

This lazy, corner-cutting old man! His writing sure is spot-on!

Seeing this immortal lord's hostile look, Mingge Xingjun tucked the Book of Fate back into his sleeve and put on an earnest expression. "Everything occurs on its own unique variables, and so does fate. With the way this event has played out, Tianshu now owes you a favor, and that is in itself a good thing."

"Oh?" I said, unmoved.

Mingge Xingjun tucked his hands into his sleeves. "You are acting on the Jade Emperor's order to let Tianshu's reincarnation suffer a lifetime of love trials. To a man genuinely and deeply in love, there is no greater sorrow in the world than a broken heart. Love hurts. Without the love, where could the hurt come from?"

A shudder ran through my heart. "Are you telling me to feign affection and coax Tianshu into falling for me?"

"That's one way of doing it," Mingge Xingjun replied meaningfully. "Whether it is to ride the clouds or to ride the winds, the decision is up to you, Yuanjun."

My face twitched. That this immortal lord bore a grudge against Tianshu Xingjun was public knowledge among the immortals. Surely the Jade Emperor must have thought I would be ruthless. It did not matter whether Tianshu Xingjun was determined to love only Nanming Dijun or if he was coaxed into falling for Li Siming. This immortal lord only needed to be concerned with unleashing every trick up my sleeve, however unconscionable it might be.

After Mingge Xingjun left, I paced a few times in my

chamber. Then I pulled the door open and walked out.

A maidservant came to report that the man was now cleaned and settled in an empty side chamber.

I strolled to the chamber door and pushed it open. Making my way over to the bed, I froze for a moment.

The man lying on the bed was the Tianshu Xingjun that this immortal lord knew in the Heavenly Court. His facial features were exactly the same, except that his complexion was sallow on top of the paleness. He was a tad thinner, and looked unwell.

Although his portrait had made me apprehensive, this sight immediately felt like a lucky break. The Jade Emperor might be abhorrent, but he had not been excessively so in this respect.

His pitch-black hair was still a little damp as it fanned over his shoulders and across the pillow. To the side of this pillow, someone had set a piece of jade. I picked it up for a look. It was smooth and lustrous, as though someone caressed it often. Could this be a token of love from Nanming Dijun?

Tianshu Xingjun, from now on, this immortal lord has a job to do, so don't blame me. I, Song Yao Yuanjun, am not a person who would abuse the power of my office to avenge a private grudge. This is what the Jade Emperor has decreed; I don't have a choice. Even if it's not this immortal lord, the Jade Emperor will still send another immortal down. You are meant to suffer for all of this lifetime.

I set the ink-black jade back beside the pillow.

The breathing of the person on the bed shifted slightly, and his eyelids fluttered. I braced myself, ready in my position by the bed.

His clear gaze, laced with a hint of doubt, landed upon this immortal lord's face. I smiled suavely at this refined face I had known for thousands of years.

"Young Master Mu, are you awake now?"

His perplexed expression underwent a slight change, and his pallid face turned a few shades paler. I tugged at the corners of my mouth, widening my smile even more.

"This humble one is Li Siming. My father is the Prince of the Eastern Commandery, Li Jutang. I have admired you for a long time. I discovered by chance that you were passing through this small commandery, so I'd like to extend a special invitation for you to stay in my humble abode."

It was on Mingge Xingjun's command that I confessed my feelings to Tianshu upon waking. We call this dealing him a heavy blow before he could regain his bearings.

Besides, I would have to do this sooner or later. So, I steeled myself, going for broke as I curbed my suave smile and replaced it with a lascivious one.

"Several years ago, I dreamed an immortal had a one-night tryst with me. It was only when I saw Young Master Mu today that I realized the immortal in my dream is right before me." I grabbed hold of Mu Ruoyan's wrist, which was so bony that it jutted uncomfortably against my hand.

"Ruoyan, I'm going to keep you by my side for life, never to let you go, ever."

Chapter four

It was now dusk. As the sun set, dazzling golden-red rays broke through the window. Given that it was the end of summer and the beginning of autumn, the evening breeze was cool, with a lingering touch of lotus scent from the small pond. Such was the charm of this scene.

Mu Ruoyan fixed his eyes on me, his expression a basin of rippling clear water that now stilled like a mirror. As expected, the reincarnation of Tianshu was still as composed as he had been in the Heavenly Court, carrying himself with an air of aloofness. His heart may have been in turmoil, but he kept up appearances and committed to his role as an invalid.

Mu Ruoyan spoke, his voice mild and gentle. His first words surprised me. "Is Young Master Li the legendary little lord of the Eastern Commandery? The incarnate of a star lord of whom they speak?"

Rumors sure spread fast. I released Tianshu's hand and flashed a smile. "The tiger star's descent to the mortal world is merely the nonsense of a charlatan. How could there be such a rare, mystical phenomenon in the world?"

The real reincarnation of a star lord is the one sitting on the bed—you, Exalted Lord, who dragged this immortal lord into this drudgery of a job with you.

Mu Ruoyan stood up from the bed. "This humble one heard of it by chance while passing a rural inn." He smiled. "Please pardon me if I have offended you in any way, Young Master Li."

I moved closer to Mu Ruoyan and looked down into his eyes. "You are already mine now. There's no need for such politeness between us."

Tianshu Xingjun, please brace yourself when you hear these harsh and sudden words.

Mu Ruoyan's face sallowed further. The refreshing evening breeze made its way into the chamber, sending the thin fabric of his single robe fluttering. It looked ready to blow him over.

Still that mild, courteous smile remained upon his face. He maintained his refined bearing.

Sighing internally, this immortal lord watched his pale lips part and close as he said to me, "It's this humble one's privilege to set foot within the compound of the Prince of the Eastern Commandery's manor today. Presumably, you must have long known my whereabouts for my entire journey. I'm eternally grateful to you for saving my life on the mountain outside the city—"

I interrupted him. "Don't give me the spiel like, 'you are unable to repay my kindness.' You will be with me for a long time to come; you have all the time in the world to repay me any way you please."

Mu Ruoyan's sallow complexion blanched even more. He covered his mouth with his sleeve and coughed a few times. With a forced, bitter smile, he said, "An honest man does not speak in riddles, so I shall be frank. I, Mu Ruoyan, am a wanted fugitive. In bringing me to the Prince of Eastern Commandery's manor, Young Master Li must have your own arrangement. This humble one, however, is a man at the end of his rope, and my life and death are at the mercy of heaven. I'm not deserving of the great effort you have expended thus."

Such was the bitterness in his tone.

Having stared at his figure faltering on the verge of collapse for so long, this immortal lord simply had to reach out to support him. Mu Ruoyan, unable to step back in time, stiffened.

Tch, this immortal lord was just buttering you up. It's not like I'd really do anything to you.

But I had to play the role of this villainous character to the hilt. Partially supporting and partially hugging Tianshu, I said, "Ruoyan, you are an intelligent man, so I won't keep the truth from you. When I captured you, I had originally meant to escort you back to the capital. But I fell in love with you at first sight and couldn't bear to do so. After thinking about it, I decided to keep you in the manor. On one hand, I can be close to you all the time. On the other hand," I brushed away a lock of his hair, which had been hanging on his shoulder, and gave a sinister smile, "that General Shan of yours is truly a great man of untrammeled spirit. It'd be wonderful if I could make his acquaintance through you."

Without waiting to see Tianshu's expression, I flicked my sleeves, turned around, and laughed out loud. "You must be tired. Take a nap. When the moon is shining clear and bright, this young master shall be back to spend the night."

I strode out of the chamber. The evening sun was half-submerged in the horizon, and the rosy clouds were brilliant.

I instructed the young maidservant, "Bring some soup and tea snacks to Young Master Yan."

I swiftly returned to the bedchamber and downed two cups of tea. I touched my right arm, the one I had wrapped around Tianshu. A strange, indescribable feeling came upon me.

Out of the corner of my eye, I saw a little head poking out from the bottom of the doorframe, peeking at me. It grinned at me with two missing teeth; it was this immortal lord's little nephew, Li Sixian's son, Li Jinning.

The mere sight of this trickster of a child was cause for a headache for everyone in the prince's manor. However, this immortal lord had scared him and Li Siyuan's son, Jinshu, in the courtyard from the get-go. Subsequently, I was established as the tiger star incarnate. So every time he saw me strolling through the prince's manor, Jinshu would run from me, only daring to poke half a head out from his pillars and corners. This one, however, would diligently follow me. At first, following was all he did. Then, the little sneak started to throw pebbles at my turned back.

There had been a day where I was sitting in a pavilion in the back garden when he rolled out from the undergrowth of grass and pounced on my knees. With round eyes, he very solemnly asked, "Little Uncle, they all said you're a white tiger spirit. Is that a lie?"

"White tiger star, not white tiger spirit," I had clarified. It was one thing for this immortal lord to have become a tiger star. What immortal dignity would I have left if I was downgraded to a tiger spirit instead?

Li Jinning puffed out his cheeks. "Saying that Little Uncle is a white tiger spirit must be a lie! A tiger's face is round. Little Uncle's face isn't round. Little Uncle isn't a tiger!"

Tears brimmed in my eyes. How insightful was this child? To think that from top to bottom, no one in this manor compared to a child seven or eight years of age!

I reached out to pet Li Jinning's head. He immediately flashed his two missing upper teeth and scrambled up my knees. "Little Uncle, you're not a tiger spirit, but can you tell stories of tiger spirits?"

I smiled benevolently. "Yes, not just tiger spirits. Your Little Uncle can tell you stories of fox spirits, black bear spirits, spider spirits, and river deer spirits."

Li Jinning clutched the front of my clothes. "Black bear spirit! I want to hear about the black bear spirit!"

This immortal lord cleared my throat and began the story. By the halfway mark, Li Jinning was already all sprawled on me, sleeping soundly, his saliva drooling all over my robe.

Left with no choice, I carried him back to the inner courtyard and handed him over to the wet nurse. From then on, Li Jinning glued himself to me, making his way to my courtyard once or twice daily.

Presently, upon realizing I'd spotted him, Jinning immediately covered the distance between me and the threshold of the door. He clambered up this immortal lord's knees. "Little Uncle, I want to eat grilled bird eggs."

My head ached. "There're no grilled bird eggs here. Go back and ask your mother for them. Have the kitchen grill quails for you."

Jinning shook his head. "Not grilled quail. There's a bird nest on the tree in the backyard. Little Uncle, let's knock the bird's nest down, and we'll have bird eggs."

This little brat sure knows a lot.

Dealing with Tianshu Xingjun earlier had already sapped me of energy, so how in the world would I have the strength to humor a child? I pulled a stern look. "Bah, 'knock down,' my foot. What if you fall?! Go back to your room and practice your calligraphy!"

Jinning pouted, his little paws still tightly gripping my robe. "I'm not going back. I want to hear the story of the lizard spirit. Tell me, Little Uncle!"

All right, then. In any case, this brat would definitely fall asleep midway into the story, and once he slept, this immortal lord could get my peace. Lizard spirit... How to go about spinning a yarn about a lizard spirit...

As expected, Jinning fell sound asleep midway through the story. I carried him out of the chamber. The wet nurse from the eldest branch of the family, having gotten accustomed to this ritual, was already waiting in the courtyard. She curtsied and greeted me with a smile. "So he's gone pestering Third Young Master again." Then she took Jinning and returned to my eldest brother's Shen Court, and I finally got myself some peace and quiet.

At the first sign of night, the lanterns sprang to life with their light.

I finished my dinner, bathed, and changed my clothes, then summoned the maidservant from the side chamber to ask after the young master there. Seeing as it was almost time, this immortal lord ought to go and sleep with Tianshu.

The maidservant answered, "The young master is in poor health; he only took two sips of tea in the evening, coughed for a spell, then passed out; he has just woken up, so this humble servant stepped out to warm up the tea for him."

I made a sound of acknowledgment and trod lightly as I made my way to the side chamber. Upon hearing an object falling to the ground, I shoved the door open. In the dim yellow light, Mu Ruoyan was hanging from a ceiling beam, a strip of his white silk sash wound tightly around his neck.

My heart dropped. I had not expected Tianshu Xingjun to be so fragile in the face of humiliation. I had merely shot off a few words in the afternoon, and that was all it took for him to harbor the intent to die. I scrambled to release him, bearing his body back to earth. If Mu Ruoyan died, how was I to explain this to the Jade Emperor?

Mu Ruoyan lay limp and light in the crook of this immortal lord's arm, his eyes tightly shut, his complexion spotlessly pale. Tentatively, I held a finger under his nose. No breathing. No matter what I did—from pinching his philtrum to patting his back—it was to no avail. How abominable that those old men in heaven did not even consider this critical juncture; at this crucial moment, I still could not use even a fraction of my powers. Left with no choice, I steeled myself, and moved my lips to channel a breath of immortal air to him.

Our mouths connected. Tianshu's lips were icy cold, but surprisingly soft. When I touched his lips, there came a prick at my conscience; this was quite the advantage I had taken of Tianshu Xingjun. Oh, well, just consider it his repayment to me for saving him twice.

I pried Tianshu Xingjun's teeth apart with my tongue and channeled a breath of immortal air within. When finished, I raised my head to wipe my mouth; if Hengwen Xingjun were to learn of this matter, I would never hear the end of it.

Tianshu drew in a breath, and his eyelashes fluttered. I thumped his back a couple times, and while his eyes opened slowly, he promptly broke into a coughing fit.

I smiled savagely at him. "Seeking death right under my nose? I went to such efforts to drag you back here. How could I let you die so easily?!"

The Jade Emperor was not pulling his punches when it came to the first twenty years of tormenting. It did not take me much effort to pick him up and toss him onto the bed.

Mu Ruoyan glared at me, eyes cold and harsh. Then, with the fleeting hint of a bitter smile in the corners of his lips, he shut his eyes.

This immortal lord felt immensely heavy-hearted and miserable. Everyone said it was hard to be a good person, but in truth, it was even harder to be a villain. I could not bear to see Tianshu in his present state.

Several thousand years ago, when I had first ascended the Heavenly Court, the heavenly envoy led me to call on the various immortals. It was among the floating clouds of the Nine Heavens that I first met Tianshu Xingjun.

He had just stepped out from the Beidou Palace. The other

six mansions of the Beidou Qixing—the seven stars of the Big Dipper—followed behind him. In the silvery glow, I saw a poised, elegant figure with white robes and a jade hairpin. It was a sight one would not dare to gawk at, but could not help but want a glimpse of either. He was truly the finest specimen among the immortals.

At the advice of the heavenly envoy, I turned to the side and waited respectfully. Then I kneeled and prostrated in greeting. "This humble immortal is Song Yao, a newcomer to the Heavenly Court. Greetings to Xingjun."

A gaze as clear and cold as stars stopped on me for a mere instant. He nodded and returned the greeting, and went on his way without exchanging a single pleasantry. Even the Jade Emperor did not put on that much air.

The Tianshu Xingjun at that time was all lofty and aloof. Who would have thought he would be reduced to such a state now? What's more, it was this immortal lord who had caused this wretched sight before me now.

Oh, what a sin. This immortal lord is committing a sin. The Jade Emperor is forcing this immortal lord to sin...

It was with a deep bitterness that I continued to address him so ruthlessly. "To think the young master of Prime Minister Mu's manor would find a rope to hang himself like a woman. Did you know? The tongues of hanged men will stretch at least three centimeters out, and their bowels will empty. The servants of my prince's manor would have to scrub the floor for half a day alone just to collect your corpse for you. Do you want your grandfather, uncle, father, and mother to see you as a hanged ghost in the underworld?"

Mu Ruoyan was as stupefied as wood.

I removed his shoes and socks, shifted him to the inner side of the bed, and covered him with a thin quilt. Then I opened the door and called for another set of pillows and bedding.

As two young maidservants entered carrying the bedding,

the color drained from their faces at the sight of the still-hanging sash. Putting on a frosty look, I instructed them to offload the bedding and remove it. The young maidservants, daring not to speak more than necessary, left with their heads lowered.

I discarded my outer robe and shook open the quilt. To Tianshu, who looked to be dozing against the wall, I said, "Starting tonight, you'll sleep with me. Over time, you'll surely come to see me for the good person I am."

The oil lamp went out, and the chamber fell dark. I lay on the bed and closed my eyes. The breathing of the man beside me was barely perceptible as he lay there, motionless.

I thought Tianshu would have a hard time sleeping.

The bandits had knocked him out for half a day in the mountain stronghold. After I spirited him to the Eastern Commandery manor, he had slept for yet another half day. Then, after his failed hanging attempt, he passed out again. All in all, he had slept the entire day away.

I yawned and rolled over to face the room. Whether or not he could sleep was none of this immortal lord's concern. After all the muss and fuss today had been, this immortal lord's upper and lower eyelids yearned only to meet again. I knew only the stilling of my mind and evening of my breath. Then a mosquito-soft voice calling from overhead, "Song Yao Yuanjun... Song Yao Yuanjun..."

I batted at the air, then covered my head. Only sleep mattered...

A numbness spread from my chest to my limbs as I began to float. I opened my eyes just a crack, and was greeted by a golden glow. Floating in midair, I hurriedly averted my gaze to the world below. Two dimly visible figures were motionless on the bed. I rose, higher and higher, passing through the roof beams and tiles before halting on the rooftop.

Mingge Xingjun stroked his beard under the moonlight,

beaming as he greeted me. "Song Yao Yuanjun."

Half propping my eyelids open, I sniped at him rather blearily, "With one book, you hold in your hands the fates of all beings. And yet, you still have the leisure to fuss over my mission and lift me out for chitchat. Song Yao could not be more astounded by your divine skills. What gifted knowledge do you have to be summoning me at this hour?"

Old Man Mingge beamed so hard, his eyes curved into slits. "Isn't it because you are only available at this time? When you return to the Heavenly Court, I'll send you a bed of clouds as an apology for disrupting your sweet dreams. Yuanjun, I saw all that happened in the evening."

Oh, did Mingge Xingjun see Tianshu hanging himself, or did he see me channeling a breath of immortal air into him? I heaved a long sigh. "Just as well that you saw it. I was just about to bring this up with you. May I trouble you to pass on a message to the Jade Emperor? I beseech the Jade Emperor to assign another immortal to these heavenly tribulations. This humble immortal is unable to undertake this responsibility. Tianshu has a feisty nature, and he seeks death each time he is tormented. I may be acting on the Jade Emperor's orders, but who will be held responsible if Tianshu dies due to a momentary oversight? I'm not doing this anymore."

"That's precisely why I asked Yuanjun yourself out tonight," Mingge said. "The Jade Emperor has already cast a spell on Mu Ruoyan. Until he goes through all his love trials, he can't end his life. You can have your way with no holds barred and no misgivings."

Good heavens! The Jade Emperor was another level of abhorrent if he prevented Tianshu from dying by his own free will. All he had done was have an illicit affair with Nanming Dijun, didn't he? Why punish him to such an extent?!

I returned to the chamber from the rooftop and repossessed Li Siming's body. Tianshu was still motionless beside me. What if this immortal lord were in his shoes? I shifted to the edge of the bed so that he had more space to himself. Then I faced outward, and fell into a sound sleep.

The next time I opened my eyes, it was bright.

I rose and flipped aside the quilt. Beside me, Tianshu was lost in slumber, his breathing was long and even. No doubt it was from his steadfast attempts to keep his eyes open until dawn, when his efforts only exhausted him further. I peered at his sleeping face. His expression was serene, his eyes closed in repose, his long brows relaxed.

Having come this far, it had not been easy for him to get a good night's sleep. Gingerly, I left the bed and opened the door. Once the maidservant had brought water, I washed up and headed to the small hall for breakfast.

It was hardly noon, and my bedsharing tryst with the frail young master I had abducted must have become common knowledge. While pacing in my courtyard, I noticed the young servants, maidservants, and wet nurses gathered in twos and threes, whispering furtively and occasionally sneaking glances toward the east wing of Han Court. The moment they saw me, they immediately dispersed.

I just pretended not to have seen them. Homosexuality was nothing uncommon. Before this immortal lord's ascent, plenty of wealthy men and noble heirs kept male lovers; what's more today? There was no point in hiding it; I took the initiative to find Li Siyuan.

"Second Brother, a handsome scholar was brought here the day before yesterday. Your little brother took a liking to him on sight, and would like to keep him in my courtyard. What do you say?"

This must not have been Li Siyuan's first time hearing this, as he looked at me, his smile reserved. "So, Third Brother swings *this* way."

"I didn't know at first either," I said. "But for some reason, I couldn't resist wanting to tie him down the moment I saw him. Your little brother knows his origins are dubious. Although I'll keep him by my side, I'll also be sure to keep an eye on him and not forget to investigate him."

"Could you bear to kill him if you really did uncover something?" Li Siyuan asked.

I twitched my face, then said with a soft sigh, "Second Brother knows my weakness well. If my investigation turns something up... I'd like to ask you to show mercy, and hand him to me so I can deal him a quick death. Don't... don't torture him."

Li Siyuan laughed, and came from behind his desk to pat my shoulders. "I never expected you to be a tender-hearted romantic! I investigated the rest of the guards yesterday and found nothing of significance. Just keep him. When our father returns, I'll put in a good word for you."

I hurriedly thanked him in delight. "Thank you, Second Brother! Thank you so much!"

"Don't just thank me," Li Siyuan said. "How about treating me to a round of wine?"

You do me a favor at no cost to yourself, yet you still want to fleece me out of a round of fine wine.

I called all my servants and maidservants attending before me and said it plain. "From today onward, the Young Master Yan in the east wing is my man. Wait upon him as respectfully as you treat this young master. There must be no lapses. If I find out that you have uttered so much as a disrespectful word to Young Master Yan—whether to his face or behind his back—or if you have been neglectful in serving him..." I smiled coldly and released my grip on the cup. It fell to the ground and shattered into smithereens as I finished, "You'll end up like this cup. Do you understand?"

My servants shook like leaves and prostrated themselves at my feet. "Your wish is our command."

Satisfied, I rose from my seat. This immortal lord was getting more and more adept at playing the villain.

Of course, I did not forget to torment Tianshu Xingjun with this matter.

This immortal lord swaggered into the east wing chamber, where Tianshu was standing by the window. Old Man Mingge had commended me for channeling air to him—a cue, I realized, that I should go all out. So I strolled over and half wrapped Tianshu in my embrace. With a lascivious smile, I said, "Everyone in the prince's manor now knows that you're mine. I've already instructed the steward to swap in a big bed in the principal chamber. From now on, sleep with me in the main quarter."

Mu Ruoyan's stiffened body quivered. He partially closed those clear, cold eyes of his. He gave a bleak laugh. Then all at once, he broke into a coughing fit and hacked two mouthfuls of clotted blood onto my sleeve. It was only after shoving me, staggering, that he said in an uneven voice, "I, Mu Ruoyan, was born a real man imparted with the teachings of wise men... I would rather die than be subjected to the humiliation of scoundrels like you..."

To my surprise, he moved to slam his head against the wall. Knowing that the attempt was futile, I was slow in reacting to this suicide attempt, maybe slower than I should have been. I grabbed his sleeve, but his forehead had already made contact. Fresh blood spilled onto the ground, and he passed out.

Once more, I had gone too far...

I shouted for the servants, who summoned the physician, who applied medicine to the patient and issued a prescription for more.

Utter chaos all around.

This immortal lord squatted by Tianshu's bed, feeling very despondent. It appeared that the Jade Emperor had not sent me down to torment Tianshu, but for Tianshu to torment me.

Case in point: Right now. Tianshu, in his unconscious state, was clenching his teeth so tightly that he could not take in the decoction. This immortal lord could only drink a mouthful before feeding him through our mouths. Tell me, was he the one who got the short end of the stick, or me?

Mingge Xingjun, that old geezer, had said that Tianshu could not die—easy for him to say! It would have been convenient if Tianshu died; just find a coffin to put him in, bury him, and that would have been that. When he fainted instead of dying, he was confined to his sickbed, waiting for *me* to wait on him. *If you're so capable, why don't you, old geezer, try?*

This immortal lord did not dare to curse the Jade Emperor, so I released this barrage on Mingge Xingjun. For every time I cursed him—"old geezer"—I fed Tianshu one mouthful. A look askance revealed human figures through the door seams and paper windows; no doubt I had an audience of maids and young servants. Mere days ago, everyone in the prince's manor looked at this immortal lord, and saw an ill omen. After today, it was with eyes full of understanding, sympathy, and admiration.

Admiration, for being the lovestruck romantic I was.

Fearing that Tianshu would go banging his head against the wall again when he woke, I sprawled at the edge of his bed to sleep. The next day, I was a disheveled sight, looking neither human nor ghost. Several maids and young servants coaxed me to wash up and have my meal. With some effort, they tidied me up so that I looked halfway human.

I made sure to feed Tianshu his medicine before noon. It was midway through that he woke up, and the revelation of how he was being fed filled him with such shame and resentment, he tried to commit suicide again. This time, it was by biting off his tongue.

I had only just finished feeding him a mouthful of medicine.

I barely had time to even raise my head, but I grasped his jaw, and in a moment of desperation, I stopped him by planting my mouth on his. My hand slipped, and his teeth clamped down firmly on my tongue. Blood spurted. The pain almost tore me apart.

For several days, I lived with a swollen tongue and slurred speech. I could only drink cool tea; not even hot soup was an option. Perhaps Tianshu had let off some steam injuring this immortal lord, or perhaps he realized after several attempts to bite his tongue off that it was hopeless, but there was no further commotion from him.

I was secretly rejoicing when the maidservant came in with the report: Young Master Yan was not taking his medicine, eating a grain of rice, or drinking a drop of water.

Good grief. He was on a hunger strike again.

I rubbed my temples and slurred, "Let him starve. He won't starve to death anyway."

That might have been the case, but Mu Ruoyan had been skin and bones to begin with. A few more days of this, and he would look like a skeleton. Heaven forbid he get fresh air in the courtyard at night, scaring everyone to death.

So, I applied some cooling medicine to my tongue and made my way to the east wing again.

Mu Ruoyan was breathing feebly, his face having lost so much color it was a sheet of paper. He had found a spot in a chair where he pretended to meditate when he saw me enter the chamber.

I tried my best to enunciate my words. "You have a death wish, but why can't you find a better way to die? A hunger strike, is it? This young master heard ghosts who starved to death don't pass into the underworld. They become wandering souls that devour other souls or the life force of other beings. Reuniting with your kin and General Shan a century later will be but a pipe dream."

I turned to leave, and Tianshu suddenly spoke. "Young Master Li knows quite a lot about the supernatural."

I turned back and grinned. "Rumors have it that this young master is the tiger star incarnate. Of course the tiger star would know a lot about the supernatural."

The mere sight of Tianshu brought my tongue nothing but pain. There was no fun in saying more, so I threw a last quip and strode out the door. "If you don't believe me, go ahead and starve to death."

Come nightfall, the maidservant Luoyue told me that Young Master Yan was eating.

This immortal lord was also having my meal then. On hearing the good news, I forgot to blow on my soup. I took a spoonful into my mouth, and it hurt so much that my face soon became a mask of agony.

Luoyue stood by my side as I suffered. With reddened eyes, she said, "Young Master, everyone can see just how well you treat Young Master Yan. This humble slave believes that as long as he is not a hard-hearted man, he will come to understand your sincere feelings for him."

This immortal lord almost wept.

"My feelings for him."

Oh, Jade Emperor. Was it really Tianshu you had sent me here to torment?

Young Master Yan ate his meal. Young Master Yan took his medicine. This immortal lord's tongue healed. Young Master Yan's scars faded.

Unable to seek the death he wanted, Tianshu was no different from a walking corpse. His eyes were hollow, and his expression, wooden. He did not cry, laugh, or speak: instead, he put himself at others' mercy, letting them do as they wished to him. I shifted him into my bedchamber, where we ate and slept together. He did not eat much, and I did not force him.

At night, we each slept on our own side of one large bed. He lay motionless on his side, and I paid him no attention. This went on for several days, and all this time, Mu Ruoyan was like a puddle of stagnant water, making neither waves nor ripples. Once, I saw him pluck up the pendant hanging on his chest, and it was only when he was looking at that piece of jade that there came a spark in his eyes.

His emotions might have been as flat as still, rippleless water, but I had waves to make. The Jade Emperor had sent this immortal lord down to inflict him with trials of love, not to wait on him every waking moment. These days, I could be found spouting sweet nothings as I held Mu Ruoyan in my arms. Mu Ruoyan, on the other hand, did not seem to be fooled. I spoke, he listened. He was about as responsive as he had been before.

There was a day I sat Mu Ruoyan in the back garden's lakeside pavilion. Knowing he disliked being perceived, I dismissed the attendants, instructing them to stay away unless the matter was important. Still, Mu Ruoyan was like a log. No matter what topic I broached, he remained silent and wooden. It was extremely boring. I spent half the day speaking to this wooden stake of a man until it parched me, but with no one around to attend to us, I had to go searching for tea myself.

I returned with a teapot in hand, but stopped on a narrow path amid the flowering shrubs. It gave me a look into the pavilion from afar, where Mu Ruoyan was staring blankly at that piece of jade.

This immortal lord was delighted. The moment to torment Tianshu was here.

This immortal lord strode into the pavilion and set the teapot heavily on the stone table. In a frosty voice, I said, "What were you looking at just now?"

Mu Ruoyan looked up at me. A hint of panic flashed across his face, and then he turned back into wood as he mildly replied,

"The scenery."

Letting out a savage smile, I yanked his left hand up and forcefully pried it apart. Holding the jade pendant by its string, I raised it high. "What is this?"

"A common pendant and my family heirloom," Mu Ruoyan answered.

I palmed the pendant as I held it behind my back. "A common pendant?! You mean the common pendant Shan Shengling gave you, right?" This immortal lord had never heard the outrage of a cuckolded husband catching his wife in the act, so I gave my best approximation.

I grasped Mu Ruoyan's frail shoulders and shook my head with a bitter grief. "In what way am I, Li Siming, inferior to that Shan person? After all this young master has done for you, why are your heart and eyes filled with only that Shan Shengling?!"

I admit these words were really a tad too gross, but at this moment, this immortal lord could think up no other tricks.

I released my grip on him, took a step back, and spat venom. "I can't tell which of your words are true and which are lies. Since this piece of jade is just a common pendant—" I raised my hand and flung it toward the lake. The black dot arced through the air, and kicked up a spray of water.

Mu Ruoyan's face turned deathly pale. He stood and laughed, bitterly. "This humble one can't tell which of Young Master Li's words are true and which are lies either. You keep me captive in your esteemed residence, but I can hardly hazard a guess as to your motives."

I abducted you to torment you, and that is Heaven's secret. Of course, you can't guess.

"Regardless of the intention you seem to harbor, you always act contrary to it. This humble one is merely a wanted fugitive of the Imperial Court, a worthless person much akin to rotten wood beyond saving. What is it about me that is deserving of such unrelenting and painstaking effort on your part?"

Oh, Tianshu, the unrelenting one making such painstaking efforts is His Venerable the Jade Emperor. This immortal lord is merely acting on his orders. It's tough for me too.

Not breaking eye contact, Mu Ruoyan suddenly smiled. "Young Master Li, you do not like men, right?"

"Huh? You—" This immortal lord blanked out for a moment. Did he see through my act? I calmed myself. That was impossible. This immortal lord had been going all out playing this show; no way there could be a slip-up.

Mu Ruoyan never once looked away as he leaned against the railing. His sleeves fluttered gently in the breeze, just like—

Just like the high and lofty Tianshu Xingjun standing amidst the silvery clouds the very first time I went to the heavenly palace of the Nine Heavens.

"Young Master Li, is there anything in particular to be said about ghosts who drown to their deaths?"

Before I could return to my senses, Mu Ruoyan had already leaped over the railings and thrown himself into the lake.

Oh, good heavens. Don't tell me Old Man Mingge is sabotaging me behind my back? Why must Tianshu try to take his life every time I make my move...

I stared at a lock of gradually disappearing black hair on the water's surface and thought, *why not just let him have a soak? He will find out he can't die, then there will be no next time.*

Suppose I fished him out of the water. Suppose that after that, Tianshu Xingjun tried out Eighteen Ways to Commit Suicide for a trial run, and after slicing his throat, jumping off the cliff, and consuming poison, he still did not die. My body and spirit might very well just disintegrate from the ordeal.

The first immortal skill this Immortal lord learned in the Heavenly Court was the art of parting water.

Because, actually, this immortal lord has a phobia of water...

I stared at the water's surface, feeling a little dizzy. It would not do to leave Tianshu down there either.

This immortal lord, having attained the Dao so many years ago, had ventured the firmament up above and the yellow springs down below. What was there to fear in one lake?

I flung off my outer robe and dove into the water. The lake water unceremoniously gurgled up along my nose and mouth, choking me until I felt dizzy and my vision blurred. I considered whether to stretch out my hands or my legs first. This was such a big lake, and I did not know where Tianshu had sunk.

The roar in my ears grew louder, and my head felt heavier.

Oh no. Li Siming could not hold out any longer!

A thin voice shouted in my ears, "Song Yao Yuanjun, Song Yao Yuanjun, Tianshu Xingjun is here…"

All at once, my body became light. The lake water around me parted, opening up a large expanse of space in all directions. An old turtle at the bottom of the lake greeted me with a bow of its head. "This humble deity, Shou Zhen, is the steward of the creatures of this lake. Greetings to Yuanjun."

I had not expected the prince's lake to be inhabited by a water deity.

More than that, I did not expect that I, the great Song Yao Yuanjun, would nearly drown to death in this lake without my divine powers.

Beside the old turtle, Mu Ruoyan lay with his eyes shut. The old turtle said, "Xingjun has swallowed two mouthfuls of water. He has passed out, but he'll be fine after going ashore and catching his breath. This humble deity was a little tardy in saving him, and for that, I beg your pardon."

I cupped my hands in greeting and said with an apologetic smile, "Elder Zhen, you're too polite. If not for you, even I may have lost my life in this lake. Please excuse me for making a mockery of myself."

"Yuanjun, you can't fully deploy your divine powers; that's why you are afraid of water. This humble deity has a water-parting pearl here. If you don't mind this humble gift, please accept it, and you'll be able to come and go freely in the water."

I said my thanks and put away the water-parting pearl, after which I picked up Tianshu in my arms and opened up a path to return to the banks. Then, supporting Mu Ruoyan's head in my palm, I began to channel a breath of immortal air in the way I was now too familiar with.

I had only just pried his teeth apart with my tongue and transferred the second mouthful of breath when a voice suddenly piped up beside me. "Little Uncle, what are you doing?"

I jerked my head up, my face burning a little.

Jinning sucked on his finger, his black, round eyes blinking as he stared at me. Jinshu, on the other hand, hid behind him, only half of his little face peeking out.

I coughed once. "This uncle fell into the water. Your Little Uncle is channeling air to him."

Jinning tilted his head. "Channeling air? What's that? I've seen Dad do that to Mom. Eldest Uncle said it's called kissing, and you can only do it after getting married. Is Little Uncle married to this Uncle? Why do you have to kiss? Why is Little Uncle calling it channeling air?"

This immortal lord laughed dryly. The thick skin I had cultivated for several thousand years nearly cracked. "Ahem, about that... What Little Uncle did might look very much like kissing, but it's actually meant to save people. Only a man and a woman can get married, so how can Little Uncle and this uncle get married? So, this is called air channeling, not kissing." I raised a hand to stroke his head. "Don't say a word of this to anyone else."

Jinning's eyes shone. He puffed up his little chest and said, "Little Uncle, don't worry. I won't tell anyone. I get it now. It's called kissing between a man and a woman. Little Uncle and Uncle are both men, so it's air channeling."

I choked on my saliva and nearly fainted.

Jinning squatted down by my side. Smacking his fingers, he

45

stared at Mu Ruoyan and said in all seriousness, "Little Uncle, I want to help channel air to this uncle too. Can I?"

This immortal lord almost choked with exasperation. I pulled a stern face and said solemnly, "Air channeling is a form of martial arts. You're still young, so you can't train it or use it. You'll naturally understand when you grow up. Little Uncle is going to take this uncle back. Behave yourself and play here with your big brother."

Picking up Mu Ruoyan, I scurried back to my courtyard. When I turned the corner of the trail and looked out the corner of my eye, Jinning was still standing in the same spot, looking at me with puppy eyes.

Mu Ruoyan coughed out two mouthfuls of water on the bed in the bedchamber. After catching his breath, he finally came to.

Sitting on the edge of the bed, I gazed into his eyes and pulled the quilt up for him. "Ghosts that drown have bloated stomachs and swollen heads. They are the ugliest ghosts."

Mu Ruoyan's eyes were pitch-black and bottomless.

I continued, "Ghosts that cut their own throat regenerate another mouth in their necks. Gruel that enters the regular mouth exits from the mouth in their neck. They cannot enjoy their offerings. Ghosts that jump off a cliff lose their four limbs and can only wriggle on the ground. Ghosts that consume poison have their faces scorched black. Blood trails from their seven orifices. They cannot speak, and all they swallow and spit is miasma. Ghosts that burn to death retain their scorched look. Then, there are also ghosts that swallow gold..."

I smiled. "So, if you want a smooth ride to see Yanwang—the King of the Underworld himself—Buddha, or the Jade Emperor, you can only follow heaven's will and behave yourself while you wait for the ghost guards to come calling."

Tianshu stared unblinkingly at me, and I said in all earnestness, "No more of this, all right?"

Mu Ruoyan was still looking at me in silence, a curious

expression on his face.

Being scrutinized in such a manner sent an unexpected pang of guilt through this immortal king. I could not help but say, "Don't worry, I…"

The door suddenly slammed open, and something lunged over. "Little Uncle—"

I closed my eyes, dispirited. *Why is this little brat here?* "Didn't I tell you to go back to playing in the garden? Where's Jinshu? Be a dear, won't you? Little Uncle is in the middle of something."

Jinning pulled at the front of my clothes, wailing miserably. "Little Uncle, it hurts…"

I pressed my throbbing temple. "Where does it hurt? Did you knock against something in the garden? Be a good boy and go look for your mother. Get her to call for the physician."

Jinning pulled up my hand, using it to open his mouth wide. "Here, the tooth's shaky. It hurts."

I felt the shaky molar. "You're growing out your milk teeth now. Once this one drops, you'll grow a new one in its place. How can changing out your milk tooth hurt?"

Jinning clambered up my knees. "It didn't at first, but Dad said Grandfather and Uncle will be returning today, and there'll be wild deer meat to eat. I want to eat wild deer meat, but my tooth's shaky. It feels terrible. I want to pull it out!"

I thanked my lucky stars for attaining the Dao and ascending in my youth. Had I gotten married and sired such a child, I would have lost ten years off my life just from how much he pissed me off.

Jinning twisted around on my lap. Meanwhile, Mu Ruoyan lifted the quilt and sat up, and Jinning immediately turned to him. Blinking his eyes, he greeted, "Uncle."

Mu Ruoyan raised his eyebrows, and a hint of a smile actually materialized on his face. Jinning immediately took to him like a fish to water and struggled to get off my lap. "Uncle, my tooth hurts."

Mu Ruoyan asked in an affable voice, "Does it hurt a lot?"

Jinning threw himself at the bedside and nodded his head vigorously. I caught the shine in his eyes as he looked at Tianshu, the way he seemed ready to crawl onto him, and was instantly alert. Mu Ruoyan's current body seemed like it had just been glued together. How could he withstand this brat's chubby body?

Jinning's little paws crawled up Mu Ruoyan's knees. Blinking his watery, puppy eyes at him, he gaped his bloodthirsty mouth wide in an ingratiating grin. Between his teeth, there was even a silver thread of saliva. "My tooth hurts... Uncle, channel air to Jinning to cure it..."

I covered that disaster of a mouth. Expression frosty, I picked this harbinger of calamity up by the collar and lifted him out of the door. Jinning kicked out with both legs and yelled shamelessly, "Little Uncle's a bad egg! Little Uncle won't let uncle channel... mnm, mhmph..."

I dragged Jinning to the yard. The little brat wailed aloud, his snot smearing all over this immortal lord. The maidservants on the walkway barely concealed their laughter. I pretended not to see and growled, "Where's the wet nurse? Men, send the little young master back to his room!"

Two purse-lipped young maidservants came to coax the little scourge away. Someone hurried into the courtyard and kneeled beside this immortal lord. "Third Young Master, His Lordship and Eldest Young Master are back. They have brought along a distinguished guest and are in the main hall right now. His Lordship has instructed you to head for the main hall immediately."

This immortal lord hastily changed my outer robe and hurried to the main hall. Sixian and Siyuan were both standing to the right of the main seat. A gentleman in an azure outfit was sitting on the guest seat, his ink-black hair half secured with a jade crown and half cascading down the sides of his shoulders. He was the very picture of carefree elegance.

I strode across the threshold, and the Prince said, "Why are you so late? That's just being a poor host to our honored guest. Here, let me introduce you. This Young Master Zhao is an advisor in my employ. He will be living in the manor from now on. You must treat him with utmost respect. See that he is well attended to."

The young master in azure stood.

The sight both startled and delighted me, like the brilliant bloom of three thousand peach blossom trees sweeping in the spring breeze.

His smile was soft amidst the magnificence of the three thousand peach blossom trees.

"This humble one is Zhao Heng. Greetings, Young Master Siming."

Chapter five

This immortal lord was like an old tree battered by the snow and frost, one whose branches could not help but bloom with flowers at the first touch of a spring breeze.

Simply put, I was over the moon.

In my unadulterated joy, I stared at the man opposite me a tad too long, and without realizing it, my smile had widened. Li Siyuan's "*cough, cough, cough*" behind me jolted me back to my senses. I had been making to grasp Zhao Heng by the hands, but the coughing intensified.

The Prince of the Eastern Commandery looked a little worried. "Yuan-er, you are coughing non-stop. Did you catch a cold?"

"I'm fine," Li Siyuan said. "I might have choked on my saliva earlier..." Then he joked, "Third Brother must really be taken with Young Master Zhao's looks. He's forgotten to even greet him, haha..."

This immortal lord snapped out of it. I cupped my hands and greeted, "It's an honor to meet you. This humble one is Li Siming. Young Master Zhao, please don't stand on ceremony."

After thousands of years of fair-weather banter up in heaven, we still had to feign civility before the others. *Interesting, interesting.*

The Prince said, "This father of yours had to persistently invite Young Master Zhao for several days before he was willing to join us as an aide. The three of you must treat him with the utmost courtesy. You will only call him Mister Zhao in the future."

For days? It must have been a trick. He waited for you to invite him, putting on airs but actually dying to sharpen his head and drill his way in here.

"Mister Zhao" played his part with a smile. "Your Lordship is too kind. Zhao Heng is not deserving of it."

"Not at all, not at all," the Prince of the Eastern Commandery said, and instructed the servants to tidy up a chamber for Mister Zhao, attend to him as he bathed and changed, and prepare a feast to welcome his guest.

Seeing as Mister Zhao would be surrounded by servants at all times, I returned to my courtyard. I was on pins and needles as I shared some stories with that wooden stake, Tianshu, partially in conversation with him and partially with myself.

"... After Jiang Ziya arrived in Xiqi..." Yuanshi Tianzun had spoken of his disciple's achievements several times, but this immortal lord could not remember them at this moment. "Ahem. When Yang Jian cleaved Mount Hua, heaven and earth underwent a kaleidoscope of changes, and the stars shook in their wake. That black bear spirit sprang out from the mountains and said, 'Daoist Priest Zhang. I have never harmed a single human while cultivating here. Why do you insist on taking my life?!'"

"Young Master Li." It was the first time Mu Ruoyan took the initiative to talk to this immortal lord. For a moment, I was flabbergasted, unable to wrap my mind around it.

"Are you sick of hearing the sound of my voice? If that's the case, I'll take a stroll in the courtyard. You should rest."

"It's fine." A tiny smile materialized on Mu Ruoyan's face again, looking for all the world like glorious sunlight on water. "*Guan Yu battles Qin Qiong* is a good book. Jiang Ziya, the deity Erlang, and Daoist Priest Zhang's valiant battle against the black bear is truly a fantastic tale."

I coughed, self-conscious. "You caught a cold after falling into the water today, so you should lie down and warm yourself up. I—*cough*—this young master will instruct the servants to boil you some ginger soup."

I spent the last hours of the day strolling through the courtyard. Mu Ruoyan and I exchanged a few words of pleasantries at the welcome feast for Mister Zhao, and returned to our respective chambers once it ended. After my nighttime routine, I lay down beside Mu Ruoyan.

When the night was deep and all was still, I heard soft laughter overhead. "Song Yao, are you intoxicated with bliss yet, sharing the same bed as Tianshu Xingjun?"

Restrained in Li Siming's mortal flesh, I could not return fire, so my only response was to rise from the quilt. The voice overhead asked, "What are you getting up for? It won't do to alarm Tianshu with a sudden motion. Lie down. I'll release you."

My mind cleared, and my limbs relaxed. Breaking free of Li Siming's body, I raised my eyes for a look around, then passed through the door.

Standing under the moonlight, the speaker said, "Fortunately, there is an art for cloaking immortals. If someone were to see you and me in this state, nonsensical rumors would fly."

After enduring it for half a day, this immortal lord could finally close that distance between us. "Hengwen!"

Hengwen Qingjun fanned that worn folding fan of his. "I saw you embracing Tianshu and acting intimate with him from the Heavenly Court, and couldn't help but descend for a look. The view from afar is not as vivid as watching from the front seat."

Don't tell me this immortal lord's hard time on earth is being watched by my fellow immortals from the clouds?

My face twitched. "How did you see it?"

"The days in the Heavenly Court are laid-back and carefree, and it's inevitable that one feels lonely," Hengwen said. "Mingge has a Mortal Realm Observation Mirror that allows one to see ongoing events in the mortal world. Occasionally, he would take me to view with him."

To think Old Man Mingge still had such an object in his hands. Who knows who else he had asked along to watch the mirror other than Hengwen? At the thought of all those eyes in heaven were watching while I was hugging, channeling air to, and feeding medicine to Tianshu, my face burned.

"Since you saw it from the mirror, you should know the kind of life I've been leading after descending here. Is your trip down this time on the Jade Emperor's order or in private?"

Having been friends with Hengwen for thousands of years, this immortal lord knew his temperament well. Despite his mean words, he must have seen how tragic a sight I was in the mortal world, and so descended exclusively to lend me a helping hand.

"Mingge Xingjun has so many trifles to attend to that he has no time to concern himself with what's happening here," Hengwen said in a leisurely tone. "Nanming Dijun is a formidable man in this life. The Jade Emperor fears you can't defeat him without immortal skills. You would need someone to assist you. All in all, I am the only one in the immortal realm who has the free time, and you and I are comparatively more familiar with each other. So, he sent me down."

Hengwen went on to tell me that after descending, he had encountered the Prince of the Eastern Commandery and Li Sixian under the pretext of being on the way back to Shangchuan City from a border town. The meeting turned into conversation about military strategy at a tea booth.

Who was Hengwen Qingjun, you ask?

He was an exalted lord in the Heavenly Court who oversaw the world's knowledge. With just a few words, he had beguiled the Prince of Eastern Commandery so that the latter, dizzy with amazement, called him a gentleman of outstanding talent and repeatedly invited this great god to his residence.

As of late, this immortal lord held no shortage of pent-up resentment against the Jade Emperor, but I had misjudged him: Although the Jade Emperor committed the occasional abhorrent act, he was still immensely virtuous, wise, and benevolent. Sending Hengwen down to the mortal world was like giving the cold and starving a bowl of hot ginseng soup in the snow—that was benevolent. It was like bestowing a pair of wings on a ferocious tiger—that was wise.

I stood with Hengwen by the lotus pond and took him in, my heart full of joy.

Returning my gaze, Hengwen smiled. "This time, I descended using the name you gave me—Zhao Heng."

I gave a silent chuckle and suddenly remembered something. "Where is the chamber they put you up in? Show me so I'll know the way."

Hengwen readily led me over. As it turned out, it was in the principal wing to the left after exiting my Han Court.

Looking into the chamber, I could not make out a thing in the nighttime dark. I felt my way to the bedside, where I took my seat, and could not help but sigh. "I feel like sleeping whenever I see a bed. I haven't been sleeping well."

"If you want to sleep, go ahead," Hengwen said. "In any case, Li Siming is still in bed with Tianshu. I'll send you back before dawn."

This immortal lord did not stand on ceremony with him. I was tormented throughout the day, and at night, I was still painfully conscious of Tianshu beside me, taking care not to crush him when I turned over and not to block my airway when

I slept so that I would not startle him awake by snoring. It was one worry after the other; I had no peace of mind.

This immortal lord rolled onto the inside of the bed and yawned, feeling sleepy.

Hengwen lay down beside me, and I said, "You might as well lift me out every night. Let Li Siming sleep with Tianshu. This immortal lord will find his own bed."

Hengwen said leisurely, "Listen to yourself. You share a bed with Tianshu Xingjun of all people every night, and you're still nitpicking your circumstances. Aren't you afraid lightning will strike you? You seem to enjoy it when you're hugging Tianshu, feeding him medicine, and channeling air to him, so why are you putting up a front before me?"

He moved his head closer to my ear and whispered, "So, is your heart moved, getting Tianshu Xingjun's divine favor?"

I reached out to wrap my arms around Hengwen, propping myself up as I said lasciviously, "Tianshu might be delicate and pretty, but how can he compare to elegant, unparalleled charm that ranks Hengwen Qingjun first in all of heaven? With Qingjun by my side, how could Song Yao have eyes for anyone else? Song Yao has had only one evil design these thousands of years, and that is to have one nighttime tryst with Qingjun. If Qingjun agrees…"

"I agree," Hengwen said in a low baritone. "Now what?"

This immortal lord curbed my lascivious smile and said in all seriousness, "Then the heavenly troops will descend and capture us back to the Heavenly Court. The Jade Emperor will definitely show you mercy, and punish you with detention or a demotion. At worst, you'd be a Yuanjun of the same rank as me. On the other hand, my head will roll on the Immortal Execution Terrace, or worse, my head will roll and *then* I'll be struck by a bolt of lightning that obliterates me clean."

Hengwen knocked me back onto the pillow. "You know the consequences, so when you are with Tianshu, remember not to go too far. You can very well imagine your fate if you, the one who set the trials, end up on the receiving end instead. When that happens, I might not be able to protect you."

So he was afraid that this immortal lord would develop feelings for Tianshu after channeling a few mouthfuls of air to him. I yawned. "Don't worry. When I was a mortal, a fortune teller said I was doomed to suffer a fate of eternal solitude. I'm destined to a hundred lifetimes without a wife, and even if I *were* to reincarnate a hundred times, no one would take a fancy to me. Have I told you? Before I ascended to the Heavenly Court..."

Hengwen mumbled, "Mmhm, you've said this many times...," turned over, and fell silent.

This immortal lord frowned. "I'm not done talking. You didn't even know what I was about to say, and your first response is to tell me you've heard this story before?"

Talk about shutting your friend down!

Hengwen did not even make a sound of acknowledgment. From the looks of it, he—

—had fallen asleep.

I sighed in resignation and rolled over, facing inward.

Perhaps I really had told him about that incident before.

I had probably rambled once—or several times—to Hengwen about all my mortal follies from before my ascension. However, I thought it was still worth talking about, and for good reason.

Because in all my thousands of years of existence—human and immortal—that incident was the only one that had anything remotely to do with that word. It was the one and only time I had fallen in *love* as a mortal.

I was in the prime of my youth then, and I would spend whole days frequenting the brothels for entertainment, thinking myself to be a free-spirited romantic. One day, while on the streets of Chang'an, a sudden look back revealed to me ravishing beauty leaning against a railing, and with this one glimpse, she sealed my fate.

She was a courtesan who sang in the brothel. A song from her would set you back ten bolts of fine silk, and you needed at least a hundred taels of gold to spend a night with her. I generously blew a thousand taels, easily exchanging them for a glorious night with her. Unwilling to make her feign conjugal bliss in bed, I simply sat and chatted with her every night, doing all I could to please her in the hope that she would willingly profess her love for me.

In the end, she did not fall for me, but for an impoverished scholar.

She sold off all the jewelry, antiques, jadeware, valuable ink slabs, and the precious seven-stringed zither that I gifted her to rent a house for the impoverished scholar and sponsor his studies. She also bribed every official involved, so that he could participate in the imperial examination. In the end, that impoverished scholar emerged as the top scholar in the imperial examinations. A pink sedan chair carried her into his residence, where they finally wedded, and she became another man's wife.

And so, a love story for the ages made its rounds on the streets.

And in that tale, I was the sucker who financially helped the lovebirds get together.

One can very well imagine just how crushed this immortal lord was. I drowned my sorrows in wine in the day and lamented my broken heart with poems at night. I could recite every one of the mournful poems and forlorn verses backward—from Li Shangyin's lamentation of the passing of spring to Wei Zhuang's melancholy of autumn to Du Mu's ten-year intoxicating dream of Yangzhou. I was brokenhearted from the ninth day of the ninth month to the fifth month of the following year. I caught her during the Dragon Boat Festival, in the main hall of the temple where she would light incense. I asked her then, "In what way is that scholar better than me?" My love for her was deep and sincere, yet she had given her heart to a *scholar*.

She replied, "Young Master speaks of nothing but love, but in truth, you do not understand what love is. You thought falling for someone meant squandering money, and that loving someone was to give gifts of a precious seven-stringed zither, scented fans, jade bracelets, and golden hairpins. My husband, though poor then, could open up his heart to me and I, him. You might be the young master of a wealthy and powerful clan, but you probably haven't even eaten wonton noodles from a roadside stall. You mistake personal whim for true love. So how can you understand the principle that 'we are one' when a couple is mutually in love?"

Dejected, I left the temple and loitered on the streets. Over a year of pining and heartache, and she made it all out to be a momentary whim worth nothing.

From where I was standing, I spied swirling smoke on the side of the street. Was my love not love only because I had never eaten wonton noodles?

Downcast, I strolled to the source of the spiraling smoke and dragged a small stool before the short table. Then I sat and ordered, forlorn, "Boss, give me a bowl of wonton noodles."

And after drinking that bowl of noodle soup, I became the Immortal Song Yao.

Hengwen had put on a show of comforting me. "Fate. Such is fate. Heaven's will cannot be defied."

Right. This was the derision with which Hengwen had responded to this immortal lord's plight. I had indeed told him of this incident before.

This immortal lord had responded with a long sigh. "Fate decreed that I was doomed to a life of eternal solitude."

Hengwen, lying with his eyes shut by the lotus pond, had responded, "No, no. Fate decreed that you would become an immortal."

In which case, this show about Tianshu and Nanming came

from a similar playbook as my bygone love incident.

Li Siming took a liking to Mu Ruoyan, who was *mutually* in love with Shan Shengling. Li Siming held Mu Ruoyan captive by his side, using every means possible to torture and break the lovebirds up. The Jade Emperor would never arrange a happy ending for Nanming and Tianshu, but Mu Ruoyan and Shan Shengling stayed mutually and unwaveringly in love.

Dare I say that I'm still, in truth, the sucker who helped the lovebirds get together?

Don't tell me I'm fated to play this sort of role in this kind of show?!

Jade Emperor, that abhorrent geezer!!

This immortal lord fell asleep with pent-up grievances, so much that I even dreamed of an armor-clad Nanming Dijun bringing a little pink sedan to the gate of the manor with his blade, demanding I return Tianshu to him.

Even as I was internally screaming, *Dijun, hurry up, hoist Tianshu onto the sedan, and run as far as you can; this immortal lord really doesn't want to attend to him anymore,* I was vehemently saying, "This immortal lord is set on having Tianshu. He's my precious person. No one can snatch him away!"

In my daze, someone dragged me upright and shook me.

I looked at Hengwen, who was grabbing the front of my clothes, with partially opened eyes. "What?"

Hengwen dragged his words out. "Your *precious* Tianshu is on the bed in your bedchamber, coughing out blood right this moment. Stop yelling in your sleep and go check on him."

This immortal lord zipped back into Li Siming's bedchamber. Dawn was breaking, and in the half-light, I saw Tianshu's paper-white face. His eyes were feeble even when shut, and blood trailed from the corner of his lips. A white, bloodstained handkerchief had fallen to the ground. Splotches were also present on the corners of his quilt and where his sleeves opened.

Where did this come from?!

Beside me, Hengwen said, "The object of your affections has already lost blood and passed out. What are you standing around for? Hurry up, take him into your arms and call for the physician."

Then he raised a hand and pushed me into Li Siming's body.

I rolled over and sat up from the bed. Half holding up Tianshu, I wiped the blood at the corner of his lips.

Hengwen had used a cloaking spell, but he had made it just so that Li Siming's mortal eyes could see him. From his seat on a stool, he watched Tianshu slump in my arms with a smile.

Bracing myself, I yelled, "Men!"

The maidservant opened the door with a kowtow. In a trembling voice, I instructed, "Quick, summon the physician. Young Master Yan has coughed up blood."

The manor physician told me that Young Master Yan's pulse was weak and uneven. "The cold, coupled with his chronic ailment, had led to a stasis of blood and a buildup of phlegm," and so and so.

I cut him short with a wave of my sleeve. "This young master is not well versed in the art of medicine, so what's the point of prattling on and on to me? Since you know what ails him, treat him."

The old man assented with a "Yes," and slowly wrote out a prescription. He could only prescribe medicine to stabilize the cough first, he said, implying that Mu Ruoyan's illness could not be wholly cured at its roots.

Could not be wholly cured—wasn't that tuberculosis?

I looked down at Mu Ruoyan. No wonder he was sallow and pale and coughed all day. All this time, he had tuberculosis...

Hengwen, who still had yet to leave, spoke in unhurried tones from the table. "Look how worried you are. Such tenderness. Such heartache."

This immortal lord's heart is spasming because of your barbs; where on earth would it have the time or energy to hurt? Seeing now that no one was around, I said under my breath, "The day has already broken. Isn't Young Master Zhao worried that someone would go looking for the advisor?"

"You're right," Hengwen concurred. "I shall return to my bedchamber, then. Watch over Tianshu."

A flash of silver light, and he vanished. *Finally.*

This immortal lord sat on the edge of the bed. Tianshu had yet to wake up. I placed his hand back under the quilt and tucked him more snugly under it. The Jade Emperor seemed to be especially ruthless toward Tianshu. His entire family was wiped out, he was taken as someone else's lover, and now he was afflicted with tuberculosis. He was made to suffer, hanging there with one foot in the grave. On the contrary, Nanming was having the time of his life as a general in the Southern Commandery. Not once did I hear of any misfortune befalling him.

Tianshu woke up before I could finish feeding him his medicine. I reached with a sleeve to wipe the corners of his mouth. "Soaking in the water only caused your illness to flare up again. Why make yourself suffer?"

Mu Ruoyan smiled bitterly. "Perhaps this body of mine is fated to be at death's door. I'll have to trouble you again."

I said with a feigned smile, "You're my precious person. For you, I'm willing to do anything."

The Jade Emperor dumped you on this immortal lord, making you my responsibility. Whatever this immortal lord has to do, it serves this immortal lord right.

Grumbling to myself did nothing to quell my anxieties. Unable to bear it, I asked, "The physician said your illness is an old ailment. It hasn't been that long since the Mu manor was prosecuted. Prior to that, you were the young master of the prime minister's residence. How did you contract tuberculosis without rhyme or reason?"

Mu Ruoyan said nothing.

I wondered, "Don't tell me it has to do with Shan Shengling again?" As he continued to stay silent, I continued, "Your love for him is more solid than gold. When are you going to tell me your love story?"

I reached out to scoop up a handful of his hair. "Let this young master learn how he won your heart."

Mu Ruoyan remained silent. I toyed with his hair for a long time before releasing it, and left the chamber.

On the front courtyard's walkway, a shape shot at my leg like an arrow. Little paws grabbed and shook the hem of my robe.

"Little Uncle, Little Uncle!"

My eyebrows twitched. Stroking Jinning's head, I asked, "Why are you running around instead of studying?"

I looked askance to see Jinshu in hiding, his little head just visible from behind a pillar. He shrank back when he realized I had spotted him.

This immortal lord prided myself on being charming and carefree, but this child always reacted to me as if to a real tiger spirit. How perplexing.

Jinning wrinkled his nose and gave my leg a shake. "My hand hurts when I write. Little Uncle, I want to go see the uncle in the courtyard. My hand hurts. I want to ask him to blow the pain away."

My face twitched. *This slippery brat.*

From a distance away, Hengwen approached from the direction of the study.

Jinning was bogging down my leg, so I stayed where I was and greeted him with a dry laugh. "What a coincidence. It's Mister Zhao."

Hengwen cupped his hands, all proper-like, as he neared. "Third Young Master." He smiled at the person on my leg. "Is this the little young master?"

That earned another dry laugh from me. Suddenly, Jinning released his grip on my leg and pounced on both of Hengwen's. "Gege—"

His weight actually caused the tall and slender Hengwen to stagger back a step. Jinning got a tight grip on the hem of Hengwen's robe, and swung it from side to side. Lifting his little face, he asked in a cloyingly innocent voice, "Gege, what's your name?"

Hengwen Qingjun was a pure-bred immortal; he had never been part of this world, and so had never seen such a child before. He was momentarily taken aback. Then, in spite of himself, he broke into peals of laughter. "Are you asking me? My surname is Zhao, and my given name is Heng."

This immortal lord strode forward and attempted to pull Jinning off, but the brat wouldn't budge. Unperturbed by my efforts, he said, "Zhao-gege is good-looking. Jinning likes! Hug me, Zhao-gege!"

I pulled my face and dragged him away from Hengwen. "Tch! Who're you calling 'Zhao-gege'? This is Mister Zhao, whom your grandfather invited to the manor. Greet him properly!"

Jinshu, who was sucking his finger, had been shiftily closing the distance between his pillar and Hengwen. As I approached, he shrank back again.

Hengwen, on the other hand, smiled like he was enjoying this as Jinning wriggled for another chance to pounce.

A voice from the walkway yelled, "Ning'er, what are you doing?!"

Jinning immediately became the picture of a well-behaved child.

His father, Li Sixian, swiftly strode over and pulled Jinning over to him by the ear.

Jinshu lowered his little head and greeted him "Eldest Uncle" in a small, housefly-like voice.

Li Sixian reproached the boy sternly, "So ill-mannered before this honored guest! Is this how I raised you?! Return to your room and copy *The Protocol of Proper Conduct and Mindful Speech* a hundred times!"

Jinning's pout quickly turned into a sob and sniffle.

The two wet nurses collected Jinning and Jinshu and whisked them away.

Jinning cried as he walked, but even as he wiped his snot with his sleeve, he did not forget to look back at Hengwen.

Li Sixian cupped his hands. "My son is out of line and has been rude to Mister Zhao. Mister Zhao, please do not hold this against him."

"Mister Zhao" was smiling so widely that his eyes were narrowed to slits, so how could he be holding anything against this child? "Eldest Young Master, you're too polite. The little young master is young and simple by nature, but his speech and insights have a natural intelligence to them. Someday, he will become an extraordinary talent."

Li Sixian demurred this compliment with polite humility, then turned to this immortal lord. "Father is in the main hall. He calls for you to make haste and see him."

Li Sixian's expression was heavy. The matter at hand must have been important. It was with no shortage of anxiety that this immortal lord hurried to the main hall, and was greeted by Li Siyuan near the Chinese parasol tree. Partially covering his mouth, he whispered, "Father found out about you and the man in your courtyard. He's furious."

The Prince of the Eastern Commandery stood at the head seat in the main hall, expression absolutely livid. This immortal lord had barely set foot in the room when he barked, "Close the doors."

The doors slammed tightly shut. The Prince pointed to the dense cluster of memorial tablets on the family altar behind him, and commanded, "Kneel."

I had no choice but to obey.

Tch, old fogeys, this one kneel from me will set your reincarnation back a thousand years. Have fun having your good fortune compromised for three lifetimes.

The tips of the Prince's beard bristled. "Unfilial son. As your father, I have never disciplined you over these ten or twenty years given how dim-witted you were. To think you'd even have a homoerotic fetish and a kept man now! Today, watch how this prince breaks this vile inclination of yours before our ancestors!" He bellowed, "Bring the disciplinary rod!"

A beat—then, a young servant emerged with an iron broom that was bound with wires. The broomstick itself was an iron rod as thick as the rim of a small teacup.

There was no doubt that the Prince came from a martial background. Even his domestic discipline tradition was this violent.

On his orders, the young servant pinned me down to a long bench that was brought in, making certain I could not move. The Prince of the Eastern Commandery rolled up his sleeves and swung the broom onto my back. A heavy thud rang out, and the iron wires pierced my flesh. This immortal lord let loose a tragic cry of pain. Golden light entered my vision, and I abruptly shot into the air.

Hengwen grabbed hold of this immortal lord and whispered, "Sorry, I'm late," as he gently stroked my back. "Were you injured? Does it hurt badly?" He looked apologetic; his gaze, worried.

"How could that one blow hurt my real self?" I said with a smile. "It was Li Siming's mortal flesh that felt the pain. Thanks to you, it only hurt for a moment. If I were unable to count on Mingge Xingjun, who knows how battered I would be?"

Hengwen's expression relaxed. He stayed by my side as we floated and watched as the Prince battered Li Siming, one merciless swing after the other. Li Siming's back was covered in blood.

The young servant said in a sobbing tone, "Your Lordship, Third Young Master seems to have fainted."

Only then did the Prince stay his hand. "Bastard! To think he'd faint!"

The young servant turned Li Siming over, put a hand under his nose, and wailed, "Your Lordship, Third Young Master i-isn't breathing anymore!"

Alarm flashed across the Prince's face. The young servant dashed off to call for the physician. From our spots above it all, Hengwen and this immortal lord observed the hordes surrounding the living body to feel his pulse, administer acupuncture, force medicine down his throat, pinch his philtrum, and apply ice to his person.

I was watching with great interest when I suddenly remembered something: The Prince of the Eastern Commandery's ruthlessness had brought even his son into this condition. Had he laid his hands on Tianshu yet? I hurriedly zapped back to my courtyard.

Not in the bedchamber. Not in the courtyard, either.

I chanted a tracing spell to look for him. As it turned out, he had been dragged to the woodshed in the back garden.

I hurried over in time to see that a burly servant was just delivering the bowl in his hand to Mu Ruoyan's mouth.

The reddish-black decoction in the bowl still had white foam floating on it.

The sight of the bowl thrilled Mu Ruoyan. The tips of his brows and eyes belied only elation as he tilted his head up in anticipation.

Never have I seen you so cooperative when I fed you.

I flew into a rage and sent a small flash of lightning down. The bowl in the burly servant's hands shattered against the ground, and the decoction sizzled on contact, emitting white smoke.

The burly servant looked in the air, his expression one of terror. "H-how can there be lightning in the room in b-broad daylight?! Ghost! There's a ghost!!"

He prostrated over the ground and kowtowed hard. "Please spare my life, oh great immortal! Please spare my life!" Then he scrambled out of the room, wailing, "GHOST—!"

Ghost, my foot. What sort of ghost could send down lightning?

Mu Ruoyan looked down, then up at the sky. With a self-mocking, bitter smile, he lamented, "Looks like heaven is really making a fool out of me."

Well, Tianshu, as long as you know. The one making a fool out of you is the Jade Emperor. It has nothing to do with any other immortals in heaven.

At some point, Hengwen had appeared by my side. "Even if Tianshu drank it, it wouldn't have mattered. There was no need for you to reveal traces of your immortal self."

"He won't die if he drinks it," I said, "but his stomach will still hurt. I'm too lazy to keep attending to him. Even if he survived drinking poison with no one to save him, he'd become a demon in the eyes of these people. That would spell out endless trouble in the future."

Hengwen watched me, but said nothing.

We returned to the main hall just in time to see a group of grunting servants carrying Li Siming back to the courtyard. As the Prince and his two sons sighed with worry before Li Siming's bed, this immortal lord plunged back into the body.

I opened my eyes slightly and cried out feebly, my voice breaking, "Ruoyan… Ruoyan… Even if I die, I can't go on without you…" Looking miserably in the direction where Hengwen was floating, I closed my eyes despondently. Once again, he lifted me back into midair, and so Li Siming went limp again.

With tears in his eyes, Li Siyuan said, "Father, looks like we have no other options. Letting Third Brother keep that man is better than having him turn back into a human piece of wood again, isn't it?"

Li Sixian chimed in as well, "Father, it looks like it's fated."

The Prince of the Eastern Commandery turned his gaze skyward and let loose a long sigh. "What a sin! What evil has this prince done that this little bastard of mine has become like this?" His aged eyes welled with tears, and he shut them with unbearable sorrow. "Forget it. Even a bastard is his own life with his own fate. Let him be." Then he instructed, "Take Physician Guo to the woodshed and see if the man inside can still be saved."

A moment later, three or four people pushed Tianshu in. The Prince looked askance at him, then let out a heavy snort and flicked his sleeves.

Mu Ruoyan was shoved over to my bed, and when he saw just how tragic a sight Li Siming made, his expression wavered a little, making him look more human than the Tianshu of the past.

Li Siyuan said from his place by the bed, "Third Brother, wake up. The one you're pining for is here."

Hengwen put on an artificial smile and patted my shoulder. "Time for you to go back and put on a show." He suddenly struck me with a palm, smacking me back into Li Siming's body.

I stirred and fluttered open my eyes. Feebly, I murmured, "Ruoyan... Ruoyan..." With a trembling hand, I made two weak grabs at empty air. To my surprise, my fingers actually wrapped around a solid object—an icy hand so skinny it jutted against my palm. Mu Ruoyan's hand.

I had merely been putting on a show with these two attempts; I never expected to really catch his hand. Just as I was pondering how to proceed, a golden light flashed before my eyes, and I was in midair once again.

This immortal lord watched helplessly as Li Siming's head drooped back over the bed, his left hand still grasping at Mu Ruoyan's.

Breezily, Hengwen quipped, "Marvelous, marvelous."

Li Siyuan coughed. "Third Brother, rest well. We will visit you again tomorrow." He looked back and signaled Li Sixian with his eyes.

Li Sixian hurriedly chimed in, "Right, right. Third Brother is badly hurt, and the medicine has just been applied. He needs to recuperate. Father, you should return to your chamber for a rest too." Having given that call to action, he turned now to the young servants and maidservants. "Those not involved, you're dismissed. The rest stand guard outside the door. Once the medicine arrives, serve it to the Third Young Master."

The Prince of the Eastern Commandery glanced askance at the bed, sighed aloud, then left with another flick of his sleeves. The others dispersed. Li Siyuan dawdled until he was the last one left, then swiveled back on his heels to the bed and cupped his hands at Mu Ruoyan. "Our father is obstinate and intense by nature, and my Third Brother does make the old man worry a lot. Today, his anger got the better of him, and he did you a great wrong. I hope you can understand." Only then did he leave the chamber.

The door shut, leaving only Tianshu and Li Siming in the chamber. I smiled apologetically at Hengwen. "Can you lift me up again after I repossess the body and have Tianshu release my hand?"

Hengwen tilted his eyebrows. "What's the rush? It hasn't been easy for you to grab his hand, so whatever it is, you should hold it for longer. There's no one around. Let's see how Tianshu treats you, Third Young Master Li."

This immortal lord could only chuckle in return.

Mu Ruoyan stood by the bed, his eyebrows slightly knitted in a frown as he looked at Li Siming, who was now lying motionless on his stomach. Then he bent over to gently pry his hand from Li Siming's fingers. He collected up the thin quilt at the side of the bed and draped it over Li Siming.

Hengwen grinned broadly as he looked at me. "This looks promising."

That look elicited a dry, embarrassed cough from this immortal lord. I laughed. "Tianshu Xingjun was always compassionate to the weak back in the Heavenly Court. This inclination of his hasn't changed one bit even as a mortal."

A moment later, a young maidservant knocked and entered to deliver a calming decoction. Naturally, she handed it to Mu Ruoyan, said, "May I trouble Young Master Yan to feed Young Master? This humble slave shall take my leave," then curtsied and left.

Mu Ruoyan stood there, bowl of medicine in hand. I could not help but crane my neck for a better look. Truth be told, I had actually felt a hint of delight when Tianshu tucked me in. Li Siming was like the living dead in the bed, and I wondered what method Tianshu would use to feed him the medicine.

From behind this immortal lord came Hengwen's insidious tone: "You are craning your neck so far out it's like an arch bridge. Waiting for Tianshu to feed you by mouth?"

Eh? As far as this immortal lord remembered, Hengwen Qingjun had never learned the art of mind reading.

Hengwen dragged his words out. "Dream on." Then he shoved me back into Li Siming's body. "Behave yourself and drink the medicine."

I could only open my eyes and act like I was struggling to wake up. Having possessed Li Siming, I immediately felt my injuries flare up. Feebly, I called out for Ruoyan. I heard Mu Ruoyan's clear and cold voice saying, "Here's the medicine. Drink some first."

Well, that was why this immortal lord was here to begin with. But I had to put on a show first. I struggled to prop half of my body up, speaking haltingly. "Ruoyan... Ruoyan... You're still here... My father, he... he didn't make things difficult for you, did he…"

Wordlessly, Mu Ruoyan brought me the bowl. Propping myself up, I accepted the offering and drank. Once the bowl was empty, Mu Ruoyan offered a hand and set it back on the table. When he opened the door, the young maidservant immediately entered to collect the bowl. Like a man on the verge of death, I rasped, "Young Master Mu is still sick. Take him to the east wing to recuperate. We'll talk again once I recover from my injuries."

The young maidservant assented.

Once again, Hengwen lifted me into midair. Leaving Li Siming lying on his stomach in bed, this immortal lord was free to idle the next few days away. At night, I slept in Hengwen's bedchamber. In the day, I made myself invisible and strolled around the prince's manor, then I changed my appearance to go wander the streets. Several times a day, I woke up in Li Siming's body to take my medicine and meals, and to relieve myself.

Hengwen, on the other hand, was busy. The Prince of the Eastern Commandery held his advisor, Mister Zhao, in high regard. Every day, he would invite him along with his two sons to deliberate over major affairs in the study, discussing strategies based on the current state of affairs in the world. I concealed myself beside Hengwen to listen in once, and it was rather boring. Thus, I very unrighteously abandoned Hengwen and headed out to the streets to listen to tunes. A betrayed Hengwen, bearing a grudge thus, refused to let this immortal lord sleep in his bed that night.

I could only stand at his bedside and smile in a placating manner. "Could Hengwen Qingjun bear to let a fellow to sleep on a tree branch on a windy night like this?"

Hengwen said, face overcast, "There are more than enough unoccupied side chambers in the manor. You can't sleep in one of those?"

I shook my head. "Unoccupied chambers are plenty, but

those with a bed and a quilt are few."

"Then go be Li Siming," Hengwen said. "Such a big bed in that chamber. And then in the east wing, Tianshu's bed is soft with a thick quilt. It's also a good place to go."

I put on a miserable look, said, "My back will hurt as Li Siming, and my head will ache sleeping with Tianshu," then swapped on a lascivious smile, setting a hand on Hengwen's shoulder.

"There may be millions of beds in the world, but this humble one only desires Qingjun's bed."

Hengwen scoffed, "You say this like you aren't afraid of being sent to the Immortal Execution Terrace for it."

Thus, I successfully wormed my way under Hengwen's quilt.

As expected of my incarnation, Liu Siming's injuries healed rapidly. In just four or five days, the bruises faded, and the wounds scabbed over.

His recovery meant that my days of leisure had come to an end. Once again, I reverted back to being Li Siming, sleeping on that spacious bed in my bedchamber, and returning Tianshu to my side.

My innate form had been roaming outside these past few days, during which I drifted for a look at Tianshu several times. He would merely eat a couple of mouthfuls every day, read several volumes of classics and other books, and then pine for Shan Shengling by a little apricot tree facing the pond, playing a few rounds of chess against himself. Ensconced in such a dull existence, it was small wonder he had fallen ill.

I moved Tianshu back into my bedchamber. He still coughed at night. What's more, he would not make a sound. He chose instead to muffle the coughs, covering his mouth tight with his hands. This immortal lord could not but feel compassion toward this choking, frail body. I helped him up and patted his back to ease him, then opened the doors to instruct the servants to brew hot tea, which I then poured for him.

With sincerity, I said, "Don't hold back if you feel like coughing. I'm not afraid of being startled from my sleep."

Mu Ruoyan compliantly drank the tea and lay down. With a sigh, I joined him.

My head was faintly aching when I heard those mosquito-like calls, "Song Yao Yuanjun, Song Yao Yuanjun—"

Old Man Mingge, whom I had not seen for several days, was here.

And in coming here, he must have new abhorrent jobs for me to undertake.

Chapter Six

Sure enough, the first thing Mingge Xingjun when I reached the roof was to hypocritically ask after this immortal lord's injuries. I answered with a smile, "Xingjun, you are the one who arranged for me to receive the beating. Whether or not my injuries healed is in your hands, so why ask such an unnecessary question?"

Mingge Xingjun responded with a dry laugh. Then he cut to the chase. "Five days from now, at the nighttime hour of hai, Shan Shengling will arrive at the Prince of the Eastern Commandery's manor to abduct Mu Ruoyan. He will take a stab wound from Li Siming's sword after blocking a blow meant for Mu Ruoyan, and flee alone."

Oh? Doesn't Li Siming love Mu Ruoyan? How could he bear to strike him with a sword? Even if he wanted to stab someone, it would be Shan Shengling.

Mingge Xingjun weighed his beard in his hand. "Yuanjun, the love of mortals is the most difficult thing to gauge with common sense. Every love is different. There are some who lose regard for even themselves in the name of love, and others who would turn to hatred, and see that love destroyed if they can't obtain it."

Now this immortal lord understood. This one stab was designed to draw out Nanming Dijun's earth-shaking love with this immortal lord's ruthlessness. One stab, and Tianshu and Nanming's love would deepen, while Tianshu's hatred for me would intensify.

Very well, then. Ruthless it is. If he hates me, then so be it. In any case, what this immortal lord was doing was nothing good. I had never expected anything good to come of it.

It was really nice of the Jade Emperor to give me the one chance to stab Nanming Dijun. He must have heard me saying in a fit of pique back at the Heavenly Court that I really wanted to stab Nanming Dijun. Wise be the Jade Emperor.

After I was done listening to Old Man Mingge, I gladly made for my chamber when I suddenly remembered something. "Tianshu's persistent coughs are giving me sleepless nights. Is it possible to treat his illness?"

Conflicting feelings crossed Mingge Xingjun's face. "The Jade Emperor has decreed that no immortals of the Heavenly Court are to interfere with the will of heaven with their powers…"

"If there is a way in the mortal world to cure him, can I do him a favor and treat him?" I asked. "I get a headache every time I hear that sound."

Mingge stroked his beard and considered it for a moment.

This immortal lord added, "The Jade Emperor said before that Tianshu and Nanming are punished this lifetime to suffer all sorts of love trials. His tuberculosis does not count as a love tribulation, so there's no harm in treating it."

Mingge finally relented. "Then so be it. But you mustn't use your powers."

Struck rather speechless, I managed to say, "In my current

situation, it would not be convenient for me to use my powers regardless."

Mingge chuckled. "I admit, these past days have been hard on you."

The old man did this immortal lord a favor and acquiesced on this matter, then asked me to send his regards on to Hengwen Qingjun. Only then did he ride away on the wind, but he had just begun his ascent when he came back down again. This immortal lord was about to return to my bedchamber myself when he yelled, "Song Yao Yuanjun, hold on a moment." Panting hard, he fished out a bronze Eight Trigrams tally that he handed to this immortal lord.

"This object is called the Spirit Detachment Tally. It is a treasure from Taishang Laojun, specially prepared for you. You and Tianshu's reincarnation are both in the Prince of Eastern Commandery's manor, and now Hengwen Qingjun lives here too. I fear mountain spirits and wild monsters will sniff you out, looking for trouble. With this item, you can manifest your true form in an emergency. However, it can only be used three times a month. Yuanjun, use it wisely."

I accepted the tally. "Only three times. That's a tad too little."

But Mingge was unimpressed with this immortal lord's picky attitude, and after explaining how to use it—and no short- age of nagging—he rode a gust of wind back to the Heavenly Court.

I repossessed Li Siming's body. Mu Ruoyan had already fallen asleep. His breathing at night was weak and shallow. It was not easy to grow up without illness or pain, but it was also not easy to grow up with such an affluent life and still be as weak as him. How exactly had he been living these past twenty or so years?

I had not shut my eyes for long when he awoke with another cough. I helped him up and patted his back to soothe his fits, then got off the bed to feel for the teapot on the table. It was still warm, so I poured a cup for him to drink. He slept a little more soundly after falling asleep. I pulled his quilt up and tucked it tightly under the pillow. Only then did I close my eyes for the rest of the night.

The Prince was not in the manor the next day, which made it convenient for this immortal lord to go looking for Hengwen in the morning. Not finding him in his chamber, I scoured the area until I spotted him from afar, sitting in the back garden's octagonal pavilion. A vague shape squirmed at his side, and as I neared, it turned out to be Jinning—squatting on a stone stool, clinging and twisting on Hengwen. I had been wondering why he had not been in my courtyard lately. As it turned out, he had turned to pestering Hengwen.

Jinshu, who was sitting all well-behaved on the other side, boldly tugged on Hengwen's sleeve with a hand.

This immortal lord approached the pavilion, only to hear Jinning asking Hengwen, "... Mister Zhao, if there's any part I don't know when reciting articles from memory in the future, can I ask you?"

Hengwen was still holding a book in his hand. Apparently, he had been reading when the little brats came to pester him.

I took two more steps forward. Hengwen had yet to answer when Jinning continued with a grin, "Mister, I learned a martial art skill, do you want to try it out?"

"You even know martial arts?" Hengwen laughed. "That's very impressive. How about showing me a move?"

Jinshu looked anxious as he tugged at Hengwen's sleeve, while Jinning's little paws felt their way to Hengwen's shoulders. "Mister, I learned this move from Little Uncle. It's called air channeling. Uh..." Just as he moved his face forward, this immortal lord took a sudden stride forward and pulled the little scourge—this close to touching the tip of Hengwen's nose—away and set him on the ground. I growled, "Little Uncle has some business to attend to with Mister Zhao. Go play elsewhere."

Not once in thousands of years had this immortal lord ever taken any liberties with Hengwen Qingjun, and this little brat nearly got his way.

Jinning ran off wailing, while Jinshu reluctantly released his grip on Hengwen's sleeve and followed, his head lowered.

I heaved a long sigh of relief. "Thank goodness they're gone."

Hengwen set down his book and turned his attention to me. "The child's just playful. Why are you trying to split hairs with him?"

I grinned at that. He went on to ask what I wanted from him with a smile; Hengwen must have been in a very good mood today.

"Nothing, really," I answered, and told him about Mingge's latest instructions.

"Mingge Xingjun has the tendency to be lazy and simplify things to make writing in his book easier," Hengwen quipped. "His words don't fully convey his intent, and their ambiguous interpretations may allow for new destinies to unfold. I only hope he will write a little more clearly this time. There'd better be no further complications."

His words reopened this immortal lord's old wounds, and I promptly chimed in. "That's right. Who knows what he wrote in his book? It better not end up with Nanming stabbing me instead. That'd be the grossest injustice!"

Smiling faintly at that, Hengwen replied, "Who knows, maybe Tianshu will be moved when you collapse to the ground bleeding. As you yourself said: Tianshu has always had a heart of compassion for the weak."

This immortal lord shuddered.

Hengwen set his hand on my shoulder. "I was just trying to spook you. Don't worry. I'll be there too, so how would you be hurt?"

"I'm not afraid he'd hurt me," I said with a wry smile. "I'm just afraid that the date Mingge mentioned is not all that accurate. He said it'd take place four to five days later, but it might very well happen tonight."

That very night, this immortal lord lay in bed with eyes open as wide as copper bells for fear that Shan Shengling would make his move. They stayed open until after the third watch of the night, but other than Tianshu coughing, nothing exceptional happened. Unable to hold up any longer, I fell asleep.

For the next two days in a row, this immortal lord sought out renowned physicians who could treat Tianshu. And every night, I retired with the fear that Shan Shengling would burst in ahead of schedule. Living in constant vigilance drained me, but my anxiety-induced wakefulness made it easier for me to soothe Mu Ruoyan's coughs with water. I was feeding him tonics daily to nurse him back to health and his nighttime coughing receded some. His hands, too, grew warmer. One night, after bringing him water, I returned to bed to a soft "thank you" from his spot on the pillow.

For whatever reason, this immortal lord wanted to shed bitter tears in response.

On the third night after Old Man Mingge's update, midnight settled moonless, dark, and ominously windy. This immortal lord heard rustling and unusual movement outside the window.

Was this immortal lord really right about Old Man Mingge, and Shan Shengling had entered the prince's manor ahead of schedule?

I held the copper Eight Trigrams tally in both palms before my chest, and silently recited the incantation. In an instant, my celestial form broke free to hover in the air. Quietly, I snuck out.

Outside, wafts of stench permeated the air along with the wind. In the courtyard, an indistinct human figure drifted among the flowering shrubs. Now and then, a bewitching laughter rang out like the miserable howls of the cold wind—it was the voice of a woman.

So, this immortal lord had guessed wrong.

Old Man Mingge, that jinx of a mouth.

It was not Shan Shengling who had come, but a demon.

And with this stench, it was a fox demon.

The vixen was heading toward Hengwen's bedchamber. She was clearly a little furball with not even a thousand years of cultivation, and she still dared to throw herself into the hands of an immortal.

This immortal lord was disinclined to expend any effort chasing after her, so I simply teleported myself before Hengwen's door and waited for her to deliver herself to me.

The vixen was quick and alert, and as soon as it saw this immortal lord, it said with a charming smile, "Oh, my, there really are a lot of immortals in this courtyard."

According to the rules of the Heavenly Court, these kinds of minor demons could not be instantly killed on sight. We had to first reason with them.

Thus, I proceeded in a quiet voice. "Demon, seeing that you have the heart to cultivate the Dao, this immortal lord shall not beat you back into your original form. If you can abandon the evil path and cultivate the righteous path, you may very well attain the Dao after some spiritual trials and tribulations and enter the Heavenly Court as an immortal."

"Oh, my!" the vixen exclaimed, "I knew old Daoists were naggy, but I didn't think a young immortal like you would be such a nag too. This humble slave only wishes to tryst a night with that immortal lord in there, and imbue myself with some immortal *nectar*. Forget it; it seems I have been beaten to it. I am not wasting another breath on you. Let's not meet again." Then she twisted at the waist and bore south in a black blur.

I raised a hand. A flick of my fingers, and from the black blur came a howl of misery. I had shown her plenty enough mercy. Whether or not she could survive on this last breath of hers depended on her luck.

Hengwen's bedchamber was heavy with demonic energy. I was just about to break down the door when I suddenly remembered: I had left Tianshu alone in our chamber. As the reincarnation of a star lord, there was no doubt he would attract unwanted attention from evil beings.

Hengwen's divine powers far surpassed mine, and there was no commotion in his chamber, so he must have been fine. I said through the seam of the door, "Hengwen, handle it yourself for the time being. I'll come back to help you after I've checked on Tianshu."

I zapped right back to my bedchamber in Han Court. Mu Ruoyan was sound asleep on the bed; fortunately, nothing was amiss. I drew up a divine barrier to secure him further, and only then did I return to Hengwen's bedchamber.

The stench was even thicker now, and the demonic aura before Hengwen's bedchamber was intense. Still, there was no sign of activity within. This could not bode well; I concealed my breathing and entered.

Amidst the glowing red light that bathed me, there stood a figure with Hengwen in his arms. The figure breathed, "Ever since I've laid eyes on you, I've been pining for you day and night, unable to help myself. I know only death awaits a demon like me who encounters an immortal. In coming here, I've no expectation to come out of it alive. I only hope..." The tip of a tongue gently licked Hengwen's ear. "I only hope you can allow me to spend one night. Do you know what exactly the most delightful deed in this world tastes like...?"

Even after hearing all this, I made no move; I was stupefied.

Long hair as silver as white snow. A pair of slanted, bewitching eyes.

It was a white fox spirit.

The white robe the fox wore was wide open at the chest,

exposing perfectly sculpted pectoral muscles.

Devastating.

Even more devastating? This was a male fox.

Despite my stupefaction, I revealed myself. "Furball, what are you doing?"

This fox was a real romantic, treating this immortal lord as invisible as air as he held Hengwen in his arms. He stroked Hengwen with his paws in a display meant for this immortal lord.

Hengwen—Hengwen, on the other hand, looked clear-minded and invigorated. He had not been restrained.

I should have known from the instant I entered that his eyes were fixed on the fox and the fox alone; until I had shown myself, he had looked nowhere else, and let him do as he pleased with his paws and mouth. Could Hengwen have taken a fancy to Furball?

Was all that worth it? The fox spirit didn't look half bad but how could it compare to this immortal lord's elegance?

Fox demons had red phoenix eyes that bewitched whether they were male or female, but there were still differences. On a woman's face, they were the beautiful, bewitching eyes of the red phoenix, ravishing and captivating, the stuff of poems and paintings. On a man's face, they were gallant and glaring, red like the jujube complexion of the Second Master, Guan Yu.

I admired the fox's guts. I did not intend to strike him with such a heavy blow, but as I prepared to give this fox an inch, he took a mile—the more he touched, the closer he came to unmentionable spots. Without a second thought, I recited a lightning spell, and a flash of heavenly light struck at the crown of the fox's head.

The fox, having several years of cultivation under his belt, dodged, and deflected the rest with a charge of demonic energy. He blocked a significant portion, but still staggered back a step;

he coughed out a mouthful of black blood, gasping for breath as he leaned against the table.

I reached Hengwen's side and lit an oil lamp. The fox raised a pair of begrudging eyes at Hengwen before closing them in resignation. "So, you were using me as a front. Never mind. I'm content with having been close to you just this once." He opened them again to look at me. "Go ahead."

Hengwen took a step until he was in front of me. "You are not at fault for this. You may leave. It was I who had the idea to play a trick on this immortal lord earlier; that was why I used you. On second thought, now that I've put myself in your shoes, it was really wrong of me to treat you like this."

The fox wiped the blood from his mouth and slowly straightened himself, eyes sorrowful. "You are teasing me again, aren't you? A demon like me is nothing but a furball in human form, just as the immortal lord said. You must have found those things I did to you vile and filthy. When I came, I never expected to make it out alive. I am content with dying by your hands."

Such moving words. This immortal lord could not help but sigh.

Hengwen took another step forward until he must have been thirty centimeters away from the fox and said gently, "I was actually quite happy when you said all those words to me. For several thousand years, no one had ever said those kinds of words to me. I can't answer your feelings, but it's not because I'm an immortal." He laughed softly. "You've done nothing particularly significant, and for that, I apologize. You should go back and nurse your wounds."

The fox's pointed ears quivered, and he said in a hushed tone, "A few days ago, when you descended to the mortal world, you landed next to the mountain where I was cultivating. It was originally because I coveted the immortal aura on you, but when I saw you up close, I could not forget you, and that was why I tailed you here. I presumed too much tonight. I understand

what you mean by those words you said earlier. It's just that..."
Eyes that brimmed with longing gazed deeply at Hengwen. "If
my cultivation comes to fruition and I become an immortal, can
I meet you again in the recesses of the clouds and have a drink
with you to my heart's content?"

Hengwen nodded. "Yes. You have my word. Be sure to
remember that my title is Hengwen Qingjun."

The fox's eyes lit up. "So you are the Hengwen Qingjun who
presides over the literary arts. May I trouble Qingjun to remember my name, Xuan Li, as well?"

This immortal lord stepped up with a broad smile. "This
humble one is Song Yao Yuanjun. If after you've attained immortality, you would like to seek revenge for the blow tonight, you
can come looking for me too."

The fox's ears twitched. He did not even raise his paws. I
must have wounded him deeply when I called him Furball in
front of Hengwen.

This immortal lord had always been magnanimous; there
was no need for me to come down on this Furball any further.
As he made to leave, I intercepted him with a reminder that
needed to be said. "Furball... oh, right, it's Young Master Xuan.
You are fond of the same sex and so would not harass ordinary
girls nor cultivate the demonic art of harnessing yin essence
to nourish your yang essence. This is a good thing. Perhaps it
was also precisely because of this that you have an affinity with
immortality. But you must never, ever do evil deeds like harassing pretty and delicate men. Did you know that absorbing yang
essence to nourish yang essence would be detrimental to you?
The road of cultivation stresses maintaining a heart pure and
free of worldly desires. To be pure in spirit is to possess clarity
of one's vital energy, and..."

The fox transformed into the wind and left, leaving this
immortal lord's unfinished words buried in the night.

Rarely did this immortal lord expound the Dao, yet he

would not listen to my teachings.

With a raise of his brows, Hengwen quipped, "You spend all day rambling about how you became an immortal by chance, yet it turns out you're quite persuasive when you talk about the art of cultivation."

"That's all I've been hearing for the several thousand years I've been in heaven," I refuted. "Furball has taken enough advantage of you tonight. Add my teachings to it, and that is enough to build off of for the next hundred years or so."

Waiting on Mu Ruoyan had become a habit, so seeing the front flaps of Hengwen's clothing still pried slightly open, I could not help but reach out to close them. "I've been by your side for several thousand years, and now even share your bed every night. Yet a furball beat me to all the acts I have yet to commit with you. That stings."

Hengwen's smiling gaze bore into me. "In that case, how about you and I do something that the fox did not get to do?"

Remaining by my side, his face slowly inched closer. Tender lips suddenly made contact with this immortal lord's skin, and I shuddered.

Good grief, behave. The Jade Emperor and Mingge could very well be watching from heaven right now.

But some things only allow you a fleeting moment of clarity. It was like being submerged in a lake; it did not make sense for the clothes not to get wet.

Hengwen was unfamiliar with this kind of endeavor, and he nibbled and licked as he pleased, looking increasingly alluring. I could not help but embrace him tightly and take the lead. Those soft lips were a deep pool of water that I would willingly drown in. When we parted, Hengwen slightly opened his eyes—misty under the light. Those moist, red lips drew into a smile. All of a sudden, he moved in close to my ear and breathed, "So that's how it tastes like."

These words would really be the death of me. I was about to get as restless as that fox and touch my tongue to his ear. The body in my arms shifted slightly. Fortunately, this immortal lord's years of cultivation won over, and my mind cleared just in time. Grasping Hengwen by the shoulders, I pushed him a short distance away.

Hengwen furrowed his brows. "What's wrong?"

With a bitter smile, I said, "Carry on, and we'd be sent up to the Immortal Execution Terrace."

Hengwen backed off a little. "If that was the case," he argued, "you'd have long been taken back to the Immortal Execution Terrace and hacked into eight pieces considering all those breaths of life you've channeled to Tianshu."

This immortal lord silently poured a cup of cool tea and downed it.

Hengwen sat on the edge of the bed and retrieved his worn folding fan. "It's just a moment of fun. It's not like it's for real. Even if we really did do something, couldn't we say we were performing the art of dual cultivation?"

Silently still, I set down the teacup, and Hengwen continued, "No wonder you always look so dejected whenever you mention your fate of eternal solitude. It turns out that there is no shortage of marvels when it comes to love in the mortal world." He appeared to be fascinated, and this immortal lord was racked with terror.

"Qingjun," I said, "you and I descended to the mortal world to set up love trials for others. On no account must you allow complications to arise, much less end up paying the price for it. If you get involved in such a thing, know that its cost is far more excruciating than suffering from any other brutal torture in the world."

Hengwen's clear eyes were fixed on me. "Don't worry. I was just a little curious and wanted to get a feel for this business. You, on the other hand, talk about it like you are being tormented right now. It couldn't be that while the Heavenly Court's back was turned, you yourself have been moved by mortal love?"

"How could that be?" The laugh I released was dry indeed. "I was merely feeling sentimental over my past."

I bid Hengwen good night, and returned to my bedchamber.

I repossessed Li Siming's body, reckoning that it would not be long before the day broke. Tianshu slept soundly. Perhaps the divine barrier I set up had melded with his immortal aura and calmed his mind.

I rolled over in bed. It would be a miracle if I could sleep after kissing Hengwen earlier.

Let's see. The first time I saw Hengwen in the Heavenly Court. How did that go again?

This immortal lord had been rather nostalgic of late.

When I thought back to the first time I met Hengwen, I recalled having had the feeling that this Qingjun was even more ostentatious than Tianshu Xingjun.

Indeed, Hengwen Qingjun's standing was even higher than Tianshu Xingjun's to begin with.

I had just paid Tianshu Xingjun an official visit and gotten a cold nod of his head in return. The heavenly envoy had guided me away, saying that we were going to call on Hengwen Qingjun. The heavenly envoy filled me in: This Qingjun presided over acclaimed literary figures as well as their works of literature, and was of equal rank with several Dijun, or emperor lords. This humble one had listened with rapt attention and committed it to memory. Just as we were about to arrive at Hengwen Qingjun's Weiyuan Palace, we saw a crowd of immortals heading the other way.

The heavenly envoy had said, "Unfortunately for you, it seems that Hengwen Qingjun has something to attend to out there."

The immortals were crowding around some figures a

distance away. The envoy pointed out a few of them. The two at the sides were the Civil and Military Kui Xing, the three behind were Zhang'an Wenjun and the two immortal lords, Wen Chang and Wen Ming. The one in the middle was Hengwen Qingjun.

I looked ahead and only saw a figure in light purple gradually receding into the distance. Graceful and elegant, the length of his back bore some resemblance to Tianshu Xingjun's, except that I had met Tianshu Xingjun face-to-face, but had not even caught a glimpse of this Hengwen Qingjun.

All I could do was hand my visiting card to an attendant boy outside Weiyuan Palace and continue to call on the other fellow immortals.

Several days later, I was just about done calling on the myriad list of immortals in the Heavenly Court. I ventured out every day to roam and familiarize myself with the paths, and that one particular day, I went to a lotus pond not far from the Peach of Immortality Garden. The lotuses of the Heavenly Court bloomed all seasons, each standing gracefully erect on the water's surface. Clouds drifted by the pond, and the fragrance of lotuses wafted over in waves, drawing one to take one step at a time along the edge of the pond and revel in the sight. When I reached the inner reaches of the clouds, I saw a piece of paper spread out on a large rock. Someone who was partially crouching was wielding his brush, presumably to paint this pond of lotuses.

I moved in closer with an, "Excuse me." The man turned his head aside, the brush whipping around in his hand. He exclaimed in surprise as splotches of ink splattered over my robe. He hastened to his feet and cupped his hands, smiling as he said, "That was careless of me. Sorry, sorry."

I was momentarily dumbstruck, not by the splatter of ink on my clothes, but by the lotus-like elegance of this man.

At the time, he had a youthful air about him, his hair loosely let down behind his head with only a ribbon securing it toward the end. He wore a hemp-colored cotton robe, with the corners tucked in and the cuffs of his sleeves rolled up. I guessed that he was either an attendant under the command of some immortal lords, or an immortal without an official post like me.

He apologized, looking truly contrite. I hurriedly responded, "It's fine, it's fine. I was the one who was rude in the first place and kept you back from your painting." I shook my robe, then continued with a smile, "As it is often said in the mortal world, 'he who is tinged with ink, is endowed with three days of literary scent.' What's more is that this is divine ink. One could consider this the greatest refinement."

His eyes lit up. "Oh? Is that what the mortals say? I've never seen you before. Are you newly ascended from the mortal world?"

"Indeed," I answered.

He smiled. "That's wonderful. I was born in heaven and have never been to the mortal world. Please tell me more about the mortal world in the future."

While calling on my fellow immortals those past days, I had spoken nothing but polite civilities. Finding the words of this younger immortal—whom I could have easily mistaken for an attendant—to be quite amicable, I said, "Of course. However, I tend to ramble on and on once I start, so please do not be annoyed after you've listened long enough."

His smile widened. I looked down at the painting on the rock. Just a few strokes, but already the outline of a lotus flower could be seen. It was charming and vivid.

My praise was sincere. "What a marvelous painting."

He brightened. "If you like this painting, how about I give it to you when it's finished as my apology for the robe?"

"I couldn't wish for anything better," I answered. "I would be reaping a gain."

Seeing him crouch down, roll his sleeves, and prepare the ink to draw again, I said, "My being here will likely distract you from your painting, so I shall take my leave."

When I turned, I heard him calling out for me to hold on a moment. I looked back, and he turned his head to look at me fully. "What's your name?"

"This humble one is Song Yao," I replied. "Song, as from the states of Qi, Chu, Yan, Zhao, Han, Wei, Song; Yao, as formed with the characters 'wang' and 'zhao.'"

I left after giving my name. Never would I have expected that he would appear the next day, in the palace back garden that the Jade Emperor bestowed upon me that very night. With a smile, he greeted me, "Song Yao."

Seeing my astonishment, he pulled a scroll from his sleeve. "The painting has already been mounted. I'm here to deliver it to you. Entering by the front door and having my arrival announced by all those attendants is a hassle, so I just came in through the back garden."

He sure did not stand on ceremony, climbing over my walls the way he did.

I took the scroll. I had just been lamenting over my latest gift, two bottles of exquisite wine from the Jade Emperor and no one to share them with. I invited him to have a drink with me.

He did not decline; in fact, he nodded in agreement. So, I set two plates of heavenly fruits and snacks on the stone table in the back garden, where we toasted each other under the colors of the night.

The night passed such that, out of the blue, I found myself sighing with emotion. "Had this been in the mortal world, we'd be able to see the luminous moon above as we drink. The human figure, illuminated by its light, forms a pair of shadows. Truly a splendid way to spend our time. Now that I'm in the Heavenly Court, I can only run to the entrance of the Moon Palace if I wish to see the moon, and even so, I fear that the other immortals will think that I'm trying to take liberties with Chang'e if I go over one time too many."

"What does the moon look like in the mortal world?" he asked.

I gestured with my hands. "Waxing in the first quarter and waning in the last quarter. It's round only two days, on the fifteenth and sixteenth of every month. It reaches its fullest on the fifteenth of the eighth month of every year; that's why those in the mortal world call that day the Mid-Autumn Festival, or Mid-Autumn. But even at its fullest, it's only as big as this plate. During the Mid-Autumn Festival, everyone in the mortal world would take in the moon as they drink wine under osmanthus trees…"

We drank cup after cup and I spoke bit by bit. He listened with relish, and I spoke with gusto. We drank until we were dead drunk. In the end, we simply rolled onto a stone out in the back garden and fell asleep.

When the sky was bright on the second day—so bright I reckoned Maori Xingjun had already been on duty at the Eastern Heavenly Gate for two hours—I woke up, eyes still bleary with sleep.

He smiled at me with disheveled clothes and hair. "I had a great time, drinking to my heart's content last night."

Still unfamiliar with the comely sight of him, I took a moment to respond. "Indeed, indeed." I smiled. "It has been the first time I had such a wonderful time drinking since I set foot in the Heavenly Court."

He straightened his clothes. "Unfortunately, I have to take my leave now. I didn't return to the residence last night, and they might be looking all over for me."

It was then that I remembered. "Oh, right. I can't believe I forgot to ask your name." Since he mentioned returning to the residence, might he really be the junior to some exalted immortals?

"Oh, yes," he answered. "I forgot to tell you, since you didn't ask. I was born in heaven, so I have no surname or given name, only a title I was born with.

"My title is Hengwen Qingjun. You can just call me Hengwen."

I stood by our bed of stone, dumbfounded.

The sky had tentatively brightened. Once more, I rolled over in bed so that I was lying on my back. *Sigh*, back in those days, Hengwen Qingjun's divine powers were still rather raw at the edge, so his stature was still a little lower than this immortal lord's, and he still had with him the pure and naïve air of a youth. Several thousand years had passed since then. Compared to yesteryear, the Hengwen Qingjun now lying in the side chamber was... Ah, the passage of time, the passage of time.

This immortal lord turned to the side and scrutinized that soundly sleeping face on the pillow. For several thousands of years, Tianshu Xingjun had hardly changed a bit. Even if he had now reincarnated into this illness-wrecked Mu Ruoyan, those calmly shut eyes on that delicate face still belonged to the Tianshu of the past.

As I stared and stared, a headache began to creep up on me.

Nanming Dijun should be here either tomorrow or the day after.

Oh Tianshu, your lover is coming.

I never once got an inkling of their illicit affair in the Heavenly Court. When those exalted lords met in the palace hall, one of them would always be pulling an awe-inspiring expression while the other would be putting on a frosty expression. In truth, however, a tempest had been raging deep in the recesses of both their hearts.

How hard was it for them? How terrible they must have felt.

Gazing at Tianshu's sleeping face, I smiled pleasantly and tucked him in again.

How would it all play out when Tianshu and Nanming met in the manor garden right under this immortal lord's nose?

Chapter Seven

It was overcast the next day, and the soft gentle breeze carried a faint chill. I feared staying in the chamber all day long would be stifling for Tianshu, regressing his illness, so I accompanied him for a breath of air in the yard.

The few maidservants with us were quick-witted. Luoyue presented us with a chess set, and so this immortal lord had a match with Mu Ruoyan on the stone table.

Two games.

Three games.

How dull.

The so-called fun in playing chess was to vie with the other player for the win or loss of one or two chess pieces and the gain of an edge or two in the game. You rejoice, I fume. You smirk complacently, I sneer glumly. You play, at times scratching cheeks, at other times breaking out in cold sweat, hard-pressed to make a move. This was the fun we as players sought.

But when Mu Ruoyan played chess, he was completely expressionless. He was unflappable when I conquered one of his chess pieces, and he was still as impassive when he conquered one of mine. Win or lose, his expression was the same. This immortal lord felt extremely vexed.

This immortal lord had played a few games with Tianshu Xingjun back in the Heavenly Court, but he was not like this at all. When I pushed him into a corner, his brows would furrow slightly while he mulled it over. When I fell into his trap, the corners of his eyes would betray a hint of a smile even if he did not reveal his delight openly. There might not have been much, but there were *some* emotions. Now that I compared them like this, the wooden sculpture of Mu Ruoyan was slightly different from the Tianshu of yesteryear.

I still remembered the time we had met by chance at the Old Man of the South Pole's place. This immortal lord had just played a match with Tianshu, and that game was extremely unfavorable for me; I was held in check everywhere, and even when I did all I could, I could not turn the tide in my favor. So it was with sorrow that I had thrown down my chess piece and conceded defeat with a sigh. Tianshu, who had been tapping against the chessboard with a white piece he was holding between his fingers, smiled upon my surrender. His long, slender fingers retrieved the chess pieces on the board and put them back into their respective baskets. Tianshu Xingjun usually was a frosty one, but with that one smile, he had no longer looked as cold.

I looked at this Mu Ruoyan before me. With this one reincarnation, he had become completely devoid of whatever bit of the warmth that had remained in him. Mu Ruoyan was just like the breeze today—mild and gentle, but cool through and through.

Mu Ruoyan raised his clear eyes to look at me—a gaze that spooked me. I had been so absorbed in my thoughts that it took a moment to register what had happened. Hastily, I said through an embarrassed smile, "I was lost in my thoughts and forgot all about making my move." Then, without thinking, I set down the piece in my hand.

Mu Ruoyan's expression finally underwent a change. "Young Master Li is playing the white pieces. Why did you put down a black piece?"

My face burned slightly. I had won a number of Mu Ruoyan's pieces earlier and had been collecting them when I'd unwittingly been distracted by a stolen glance at his expression. In my confused state, I had put down the one in my hand—a black piece.

My embarrassment only mounted. I picked the piece back up. "I was befuddled."

An unhurried voice spoke from afar, "Not befuddled, but 'intoxicated as the wind, as I view the flowers.'"

This immortal lord let out a cough and watched as that figure in azure walked in.

"Young Master," a maidservant announced. "Mister Zhao is here."

Rubbish, I thought, *Mister Zhao is standing right in front of your young master. How would this young master not know he's here?*

"Mister Zhao" cupped his hands in greeting, "I took the liberty of coming to pay a visit, and entered your courtyard directly. Third Young Master, please do not hold it against me."

I followed suit and returned his greeting, cupping my hands back. "Mister Zhao, please don't stand on ceremony. I'm only too glad to have you here today."

Hengwen must have come over because he could not contain his curiosity to see Tianshu Xingjun.

I waved a hand to dismiss those waiting in attendance. Sure enough, Hengwen feigned an uncertain look and looked at Mu Ruoyan. Mu Ruoyan rose to his feet.

I coughed again. "Ruoyan, this is Mister Zhao. Mister Zhao, this is…"

Hengwen politely cupped his hands at Tianshu. "This humble one is Zhao Heng, an advisor from the prince's manor. I hope Young Master Yan will not hold it against me if I intrude and interrupt you from playing chess." His pair of smiling eyes fixated only on Tianshu.

Mu Ruoyan returned the greetings. "Mister Zhao, you're too polite. If you don't mind, you can simply call this humble one Ruoyan. I'm too undeserving of the title of 'young master.'"

Hengwen could tell that Tianshu's words bore no malice, but still, given Tianshu's present circumstance, seeing outsiders would only draw out more of the bitterness in his heart.

A breeze swept past again. Mu Ruoyan let out two light coughs, and must have strained himself to swallow back the rest of them. With some difficulty, he said to Hengwen with a smile, "Please excuse my lack of decorum."

"This humble one has a small issue to confer with Third Young Master," Hengwen said, "so I shall not hold you back from your rest, Young Master Yan."

He stealthily tugged at my sleeve, and I followed him about ten steps away.

"Why are you here?" I asked in a hushed tone.

Hengwen softly said into my ear, "Nanming Dijun is here. Right in the front yard."

This immortal lord was astonished. "Huh?"

"*Shhh*," Hengwen hushed me. "You have to pretend to know nothing of it and go over to the front yard. Tianshu doesn't look good. You should first get him to take a rest in the bedchamber."

I immediately turned back. At the stone table, Mu Ruoyan was sweeping up the chess pieces.

"You should head back in and rest. Read a book. Let the servants tidy up."

Mu Ruoyan ignored me, so I could only leave him in the courtyard and hasten to the front yard with Hengwen.

On the way there, I asked Hengwen, "I can't believe Nanming Dijun is this bold, brazenly coming to the Prince of Eastern Commandery's manor under the name of General of the

Southern Commandery."

"General Shan may be a lovesick one, but he is astute," Hengwen answered with a smile. "How could he commit such a folly? You will understand once you see him."

The scene in the front yard gave this immortal lord a huge shock.

Ten or so people dressed in short jackets were lined up on the open space. The chief steward of the inner courtyard paced to and fro before these people, with one hand behind his back while the other twirled his goatee.

These dozen or so people were the newly recruited servants of the manor, and one of them was a stalwart figure dressed in tattered clothing and straw shoes—Nanming Dijun, Shan Shengling.

I had envisioned countless scenarios in which Shan Shengling would sneak into the manor. Mingge told me he would abduct Tianshu in the middle of the night, which I had assumed would be on a moonless, windy night under the cover of darkness. I had considered all sorts of possibilities, from scaling the wall to breaking down the door to crawling through a dog hole to using his qinggong skills to land on the roof before flitting down… but never had I imagine that he would sell himself as a servant to sneak into the manor, and in broad daylight at that.

Nanming Dijun was really one lovestruck fool.

This immortal lord sighed.

Just like that, Nanming Dijun had entered by selling himself, and just like that, the chief steward of the Prince of the Eastern Commandery's manor had taken him in.

Was the chief steward blind?

Shan Shengling's appearance was not that different from his appearance as Nanming Dijun. He towered at about eight chi tall, with a gallant physique, brows that cut like fine black swords, and a pair of bright eyes, alert like a hawk's. Although his face was filthy and his hair a bird's nest, he stood out among this group of people like a wild boar among a herd of skinny pigs. It took only a glance to tell that he was no ordinary man. Under what circumstances could such a man be sold into servitude?

Don't tell me this was Mingge's arrangement?

The chief steward took out the register of names and began to record their assignments. This immortal lord strolled over, and the chief steward immediately lowered his hands to bow. "Greetings, Third Young Master."

The moment "third young master" left his mouth, Shan Shengling's gaze slashed over toward this immortal lord like a pair of blades. Pretending not to notice, I nodded. "Are these all the new household servants?"

The chief steward answered in confirmation. This immortal lord strolled over to the group and pretended to scrutinize them one at a time. When I came to Shan Shengling, I paced for a moment, sizing him up as I contemplated this situation.

Nanming had fallen into this immortal lord's hands. To live up to the Jade Emperor's expectations, what errand should this immortal lord assign him to? So that he could see Tianshu but not touch him, and the two of them would be mutually tormented?

Those chopping firewood, lighting fires, and guarding the doors usually could not enter my Han Court, and Nanming was too imposing to be a young servant lad. After some deliberation, I decided there was only one errand that would allow him access to my courtyard and his lover.

Once I was done pondering it over, I said to the chief steward beside me, "For the time being, let him clear the night soil in the various courtyards."

At night, I held Tianshu in my arms. "It's cold these days. I'll sleep with you under the same quilt."

Once I was done washing up the next morning, I pretended to visit the back garden for some morning air, hiding as I dodged into Hengwen's chamber. I unabashedly had him lift my real form out of Li Siming's body. Hengwen did so readily, and gladly returned to Han Court with me, where we concealed ourselves in midair to watch the show.

In a corner of the courtyard, Shan Shengling, all dressed in servant attire, was making an inventory of the chamber pots. The instant he reached out to lift the chamber pots, he inadvertently looked up, just in time to see the frail figure in the walkway. As if sensing his gaze, the figure turned around. The moment the two pairs of eyes met, heaven and earth froze.

Cue the meeting between the Butterfly Lovers, Liang Shanbo and Zhu Yingtai.

When this immortal lord was still a mortal, a poor scholar—who repeatedly failed the imperial examinations—had asked someone to deliver several heart-wrenching poems to me as a demonstration of his talents. I had yet to fall out of love then, and for a time amused myself reading those resentful poems and sorrowful verses. I remembered two lines in particular. They spoke of the eyes of a woman in her lady's chamber, a woman long parted from her husband:

"Like autumn waters up close and mountains afar;
the crabapple blossoms weep in the dark of the night."

Reading it shook me greatly. Eyes that looked like water when viewed up close and looked like mountains when viewed from afar, and when viewed in the middle of the night, they resembled two crabapple blossoms shedding teardrops of dew. Imagine just how terrifying it would be to see such a pair of eyes on a person's face?

I had truthfully conveyed my thoughts. The person who delivered the poem left without saying a word and repeated them verbatim to the poet. Allegedly, the poor scholar spread the poem manuscript open and let loose three hysterical laughs, then coughed a mouthful of fresh blood onto the paper and left with a flick of his sleeves. And—allegedly again—he had gone into a remote, forested mountain to cultivate the Dao or turned to Buddhism.

Thinking back on it now, I had indeed wronged him. Because of my ignorance and incompetence, I had forced such a great literary talent deep into the mountain forest. How insightful those two verses were! Just look at how fitting they were for the scene playing out now.

Tianshu's eyes were just like autumn waters seen up close, while Nanming's eyes were the barren mountains seen from afar. One brimmed with unspeakable misery, sorrow, pining, delight, and never-ending tenderness, while the other teemed with deep longing and bare, naked love.

A gaze—that's all it was, a mere gaze.

Shan Shengling picked up the chamber pots and left the courtyard without so much as an expression, while Mu Ruoyan feigned composure and turned back, although his face had inevitably blanched a little whiter, and as he took a step, his body quivered.

"The little lovebirds being battered apart are indeed pitiful," Hengwen commented.

"And the rod battering the lovebirds is detestable, right?" I quipped.

Hengwen yawned. "Nanming Dijun has no right to blame you. When he was the rod in the past, his blows were far more merciless." He looked at me from the corners of his eyes. "You're still bearing a grudge over what happened to Qingtong and Zhilan, aren't you?"

I let out a grim laugh. "How could I forget?"

Qingtong was a messenger boy under the command of Donghua Dijun. Donghua Dijun had been on good terms with

Hengwen Xingjun, so he often extended the invitation for chess or tea to me as well. It was always Qingtong who delivered the messages, and after some back and forth, we became familiar with one another. Qingtong was bright and quick-witted. As his job involved delivering messages, he was able to travel to the various areas of the Heavenly Court. Who could have expected him to begin an illicit love affair with a junior celestial maiden at Pixiang Palace over the course of frequent contact? Touched by secular love and desires, they did something they ought not to do in the Heavenly Court. One day, during a secret rendezvous, they were unfortunately caught red-handed by the heavenly soldiers on duty, who sent them right to the Jade Emperor.

Originally, with Donghua Dijun, Hengwen, and me to intercede on their behalf, the Jade Emperor seemed inclined to have them cursorily punished and banished to the mortal world, but Nanming Dijun just had to step forth and said that the Heavenly Court had its own rules, so we could not condone the act because of personal sentiments; they had to be strictly punished in accordance with the laws of heaven. Nanming asserted his opinion with such upright righteousness at Lingxiao Palace that the Jade Emperor handed the matter over to him to handle.

Under Nanming's instructions, Qingtong and Zhilan were taken to the Immortal Execution Terrace, where their immortal roots were severed, and they were cast to the Path of the Beast to be reincarnated as animals. If Qingtong were to be born as a wily rabbit, Zhilan was certain to be born as a fierce tiger; if Zhilan was an ant, Qingtong would be a pangolin; and if Qingtong become a shrimp, Zhilan was bound to be a fish that ate shrimps. Only in this way of mutually killing and living at odds against each other for nine lifetimes would they be able to reincarnate as humans, and even so, they would still be each other's mortal enemies, fated to never be together.

Nanming Dijun had not dared to offend Donghua and Hengwen at that time, so he slapped a charge against this immortal lord on Lingxiao Palace—the crime of inciting and abetting. He said that I did not have any cultivation, and my mortal root had yet to be severed, which implied to the Jade Emperor that it was this immortal lord who had instigated Qingtong to flirt with Zhilan.

Who would have expected it would be the same Nanming Dijun who would have an affair with Tianshu Xingjun? Now that he had been reduced to such a state, this immortal lord had only this to say: karma.

Nanming, your stolen glance with Tianshu is indeed touching. But when you gave the command back then to have Qingtong and Zhilan thrown into the Path of the Beast, did you ever think that this day would come?

"Whenever I think of Qingtong and Zhilan, I feel that the Jade Emperor has been pretty fair in punishing Nanming Dijun the way he did," I said. "But Tianshu had never done such a wicked thing before, yet he suffers so much more than Nanming. That makes it unfair."

"You aren't afraid the Jade Emperor will hear you saying that, huh?" Hengwen said.

With one in front and one behind, we swung back to Hengwen's bedchamber, and this immortal lord became Li Siming again. Hengwen had to go over to the Prince of the Eastern Commandery to present himself for the morning call, so I returned to Han Court on my own.

Mu Ruoyan was sitting in the chamber with a book in hand, but his eyes were not on the book; he was gazing elsewhere, his mind wandering.

This immortal lord stepped up to him. "Ruoyan, you look to be in a trance. Are you thinking of home, or are you thinking of your lover?"

Lovesickness was written all over Mu Ruoyan's face, but he

answered, "Just lounging around all day, occasionally reminiscing the past."

I stood before him and said cynically, "Oh, the past with that particular old friend of yours, right?"

Mu Ruoyan said nothing. This immortal lord set a hand on his skinny shoulder and took the book he was holding with the other. It was a book of poems by Attendant-in-Ordinary Gao Shi.

Li Siming's bedchamber was split into two sections by a semi-openwork sandalwood partition. A bed canopy had been set up in the interior section, while the exterior, which had some antiques and trinkets, could be used as a study with a writing desk placed within.

After moving Mu Ruoyan in, this immortal lord went to the special effort of placing stacks of tragically sorrowful poems and forlorn prose on the small table by the writing desk to fuel his heartsickness.

I had originally wanted to see Tianshu with a book of poems tucked under his sleeve, gazing tearfully at the drifting clouds outside the window. That would surely be a sight that would evoke feelings of pity in the others, but he did not appreciate my good intentions. Two days ago, he had somehow found a Book of Changes in some random corner and taken a weasel-hair brush to add annotations as he read. What was there to annotate? Which fortune-telling booth on the streets did not have a copy displayed in their stalls? Just seeing the archaic small seal scripts on those pages hurt my teeth.

Let him read since he loves to read, this immortal lord thought. It was better than making a scene and hanging himself or jumping into the river.

The night before last, it was only by the time I was sitting on the edge of the bed that he set down the book and came to sleep. He finally swapped to a book of poems today, but it just *had* to be by the poet, Gao Shi.

I looked at the cover, my brows creased in a frown. It then suddenly dawned on me. That's right, his lover, Shan Shengling, was a general now. That was why he was reading war poems from Gao Shi—taking in verses of beacon fires and blade glints, imagining the man amidst beacon flames and flashes of the blade.

And having seen Nanming carrying chamber pots in the yard earlier, he had to read a few more verses to reacquaint himself with the real and valiant appearance of Shan Shengling.

Some thoughts of yours, I can discern with a glance. I laughed inwardly to myself and returned the book to Mu Ruoyan. "You are already mine. Old flames, old times—those are not things you can think about anymore. From today onward, you can only think of me and us."

"That's easier said than done," Tianshu said.

"What?" Never had I imagined that he would refute me.

Mu Ruoyan closed the book, raised his chin, and turned to face me with those cold but clear eyes. "The heart acts in spite of oneself, much less others. How could I simply stop thinking by just saying so? If I acquiesced, wouldn't that be a lie?"

Such cutting words, and to think it was Mu Ruoyan who had said it right to my face. Love was truly formidable. Now that his lover was here, even his person had changed.

In a display of my magnanimity, I smiled without taking it to heart. I dragged over a chair and took my seat before the table, then poured a cup of tea to drink. Mu Ruoyan looked at this immortal lord's left sleeve with a slightly doubtful expression. It was then I remembered that the solid object in my sleeve was meant for Tianshu. I hurriedly fished it out and laid it erect on the table.

A bamboo tube about fifteen centimeters tall, verdant green on the outside, smoothly polished on the inside.

"Do you like it?" I asked Mu Ruoyan with a smile.

Mu Ruoyan examined it. His expression was reluctant as he answered, "This brush holder is very simple and interesting."

I pushed it in front of Mu Ruoyan. "It's not a brush holder. Take a closer look."

Mu Ruoyan looked even more reluctant as he examined it again and pondered it without saying a word.

With a gentle smile, I said, "I saw you reading the Book of Changes these last few days, so I got this for you."

I fished some copper coins out of my sleeve and tossed them inside the bamboo tube before picking it up to shake it.

"From now on, if you get bored reading the Book of Changes, you can divine some fortunes. Do you like this divination tube?"

Mu Ruoyan stiffened as he looked at the bamboo tube on the table.

I felt pleased with myself. This immortal lord was always right on the money when giving gifts. Looking at Tianshu's reaction, he must have been touched.

I continued gently, "If you also wish to tell fortunes based on the eight characters, I'll fetch you anyone in the manor whose fortune you'd like to read."

Mu Ruoyan opened his mouth and made to speak, but then he covered his mouth with his sleeve and coughed a few times before he said, haltingly, "Th-thank you for going to the trouble... I merely look at it occasionally..."

I got up and stroked his back, then handed him the tea for a few sips. "I only got it in passing. There's absolutely no obligation attached to it. Just treat it as a relief for your boredom if you like it."

His coughing stopped for a bit after a few sips. I put the teacup back on the table. Mu Ruoyan looked at that teacup and smiled bitterly.

I picked up the poetry book that had fallen to the ground and set it on the table. Making conversation to fill the silence,

I said, "I didn't expect you to read this. I thought you'd prefer reading Meng Moji and Meng Xiangyang."

Although this immortal lord had to rely on Hengwen every time we played drinking games in the Heavenly Court—linking verses, dedicating poems, all the things to help with wordplay—I had in fact studied poetry as a mortal. I was able to chat on the topic.

"Although the poems by Wang and Meng speak of indifference to fame and fortune, one of the poets was actually a wealthy idler while the other idly dreamed of wealth," Mu Ruoyan said. "Might as well pursue fame and fortune openly like Gao Shi. How gratifying."

"Right," I concurred. "This gentleman talks big and acts timidly; his poems are powerful and impressive, but he's incompetent on the battlefield. Then again, how many people in this world can truly walk the talk? Most are like Gentleman Gao."

Enlivened, I looked into Mu Ruoyan's eyes and waited for him to continue the thread of conversation, but he avoided my gaze. He spoke no further as he returned the book from the writing desk to its original position on the adjacent table.

Feeling rather hollow, I awkwardly blathered a few more words and strolled out of the bedchamber.

The Prince of the Eastern Commandery had been hesitating between going independent under his own banner and biding his time in the conflict, so discussions over official affairs became more frequent. Hengwen was caught up in them the whole day, with no chance of leisure time. As I wandered around the yard, I would encounter Shan Shengling several times. He was either sweeping the yard or rooting out the weeds. He was unfathomable. He would respectfully say his greetings when he saw this immortal lord, his eyes revealing nothing of his brilliance. Which in turn made me spend the whole day deliberating over where I should stab him with my blade come nightfall.

I finally got to meet Hengwen at near dusk. Looking extremely weary, he lowered his voice, "That commandery prince father of yours is really not your average long-winded. How long do you still have to be here? I fear I might very well strike him with lightning one of these days if we have to continue like this."

I said with an apologetic smile, "Don't fret. I'll slowly return the favor I owe you once we return to the Heavenly Court. Tonight, I'll put on a show of stabbing Nanming to relieve you of your boredom. How's that?"

"You must have been spending the whole day mulling over where to stab Nanming, right?" Hengwen said, and moved in closer to my ear before continuing, "Once night falls today, I'll head over to your bedchamber and wait."

His words stirred up an itch. I whispered back, "So where should I stab Nanming?"

"Wherever you please, I guess," Hengwen said. "You can even stab him in the heart. In any case, he won't die; there's Mingge to see to that, and if that fails, there's still the Jade Emperor. You just need to deal the blow."

Upon hearing those words, this immortal lord felt even more buoyant and practically flew back to my Han Court.

When night descended, I sat at the edge of the bed and glanced at a relaxed Hengwen leaning against it. I gulped down a mouthful of saliva, then braced myself to say to the man, who was currently reading a book under the lamp. "Ruoyan, it's late. Come and sleep with me."

These were the words that Old Man Mingge had instructed me to say before bed every night.

I have no choice either, okay? So, Hengwen, can you not put on such an uncharitable expression?

Mu Ruoyan, on the other hand, was already accustomed to hearing this. He blew out the candle in the outer room and walked woodenly to the bed, where he removed his outer robe, then his crown to let his hair down. His body, clad only in a plain white inner robe, looked all the more thin and frail under the light. He froze a little on seeing the bed, but eventually, he came to slowly lift the quilt and lay down.

There was only one thin quilt on the bed, since this immortal lord was going to sleep under the same quilt with Tianshu starting last night.

Hengwen said from where he was propped against the bedpost, "Aren't you going to sleep?"

I was on pins and needles all over. With Tianshu here, I could not talk to the air. Unable to respond or smile, I thickened my skin and took off my outer robe, then I lifted the quilt and leaned forward to snuff out the bedside candle before lying down again to sleep. I completed each step with much difficulty.

Mu Ruoyan was pining for Shan Shengling, and judging by his breathing, he seemed to be awake and lying with his eyes open. Hengwen lifted me out of my mortal body and quietly, smilingly asked, "So has your love blossomed after sleeping with Tianshu every night, sharing the same bed and quilt?"

I laughed dryly. "Isn't it because Nanming is here that I have to put on a realistic show? This only started yesterday, and after tonight, I reckon there will be no more need for it."

"Those words you said before bed are rather affectionate," Hengwen commented.

"That's what Mingge taught me to say," I said, with a twitch of my face. "I had to say it."

Hengwen probably felt that he had laughed at me enough, so he made no further comment. We both sat down in the chamber, and Hengwen yawned.

"You've been overworking the entire day today, so you should be resting early. How about I lend Li Siming on the bed to you? You can possess him and lie down."

"Forget it," Hengwen said lazily. "Leave that bed for you and

Tianshu to lie in. Let's not cause complications. I fear it might be easy to possess but hard to get out of." Then he propped his head up with a hand on the table to rest.

Toward the hours of midnight, the wind rustled, and a black shadow flitted past the window. A thin blade slipped through the slit in the door and pushed aside the bolt. The door soundlessly opened a crack, leaking in a gust of night breeze.

This immortal lord and Hengwen promptly perked up, watching as that black shadow slinked into the chamber.

General Shan, you are finally here to make your move.

The shadow half crouched as it moved, taking advantage of the moonlight to enter the inner room and approach the bed. The weapon in his hand glinted coldly in the darkness. Hengwen and I stood by the partition, and I could not help but say, "Two people are sleeping on one bed, and it's dark in here. How can he tell which is Tianshu and which is me? Look at him flashing his weapon. Isn't he afraid of injuring the wrong person?"

Just as I spoke, Nanming came to a stop before the bed. Something suddenly glowed in his hand, a night-luminous pearl the size of a pigeon egg. With his other hand, he used the tip of his blade to lift aside the bed curtain. Tianshu was sleeping on the same side where he stood, so Nanming only had to cast the luminous pearl over him and see Mu Ruoyan. Hengwen and I swung over to the bed and craned our necks to look.

Within the bed curtains, Mu Ruoyan seemed to sense something and abruptly sat up. Under the glow of the luminous pearl, the eyes of the lovebirds met, and for a moment, time froze.

Truly, neither of them were afraid that this immortal lord, the Third Young Master Li, who was sleeping at the side, would wake up.

"Time for you to take the stage," Hengwen said. "Aren't you going back in and getting up?"

"No rush, no rush," I said.

111

Shan Shengling grabbed Mu Ruoyan's arm and pulled him off the bed. He lifted the coldly glinting dagger and moved to bring it clean down on the inside of the bed. Mu Ruoyan reached out to stop him. "Don't kill him."

He spoke so quietly, but I heard it clearly.

"Why?" Shan Shengling said, the word so chilling it was like millions of ice blades.

Cut the rambling! Fleeing is more critical, gentlemen.

But these two simply would not flee, and insisted on fussing over details.

"He has not done anything. He's not a bad person," Mu Ruoyan said, his tone extremely mild, as if he was talking about cabbage.

"Oh, Tianshu's feelings for you are *deep*," Hengwen quipped.

"Do you not want me to kill him because you're worried for his life, or because you're afraid of tainting my blade?" Shan Shengling said coldly.

Tianshu said nothing.

Shan Shengling sneered and suddenly raised his pitch. "I made such a commotion by your bed for so long, and although you may have held your breath to conceal your breathing, you in fact woke up a long time ago. Why not get up for a chat?"

Now, this immortal lord could begin the show.

I plunged into Li Siming's body and calmed my breath.

When faced up against a master, one had to keep a steady, imposing presence. So, I *slowly* opened my eyes, *slowly* got up, *slowly* felt for the flint to light up the candle, and *slowly* walked out from the other side of the bed.

And *slowly* wondered where exactly I had hidden my steel blade.

Shan Shengling had already tucked the luminous pearl under the front of his clothes. With his free hand, he gripped Mu Ruoyan's arm. Trading looks with the two people before me, this immortal lord felt delight, concern, and woe.

Given how I treated Tianshu, he actually stopped the blade for me; therein lay the delight.

Given how I treated him, he actually said I was not a bad person, so either I had played my role to perfection, or he was out of his mind; therein lay the concern.

As for that one woe…

"Your blade is inside the big vase in the corner," Hengwen piped up from behind me.

This immortal lord immediately said, "Pardon me for my lack of manners in being tardy to welcome you when you entered my bedchamber in the middle of the night. The menial work of a servant in the daytime is strenuous, filthy, and varied, and it's indeed a great wrong done to General Shan. I'm truly sorry about that. But I wonder what is General Shan's intent in abducting my man from our bed in the middle of the night?"

With my hand behind me and a smile on my face, I strolled to the vase and drew out the long, unsheathed blade.

"I initially did not plan to take your life with this blade and sully it," Shan Shengling said. "But never mind. I'll allow a beast like you to struggle before your death." The brightness in his eyes swept over me, holding so much contempt. "The dozens of guards outside are already down for the count, so it seems like you won't be able to count on them."

"Oh," I said.

Can't count on them? With Hengwen here, I could snatch Tianshu back from the hands of Heibai Wuchang themselves before they brought his spirit to the underworld, let alone those who got knocked out.

So what was there to worry about? "Fight it out in the garden?" I said.

General Shan strode readily out of the chamber. I seized the opportunity to cast a glance at Mu Ruoyan. His expression was pale. He turned and headed for the garden too, never once looking at me.

Under the bright and clear moon in the yard, this immortal lord asked for pardon and then hollered for the guards. Dozens of guards emerged from the darkness and surrounded Nanming and Tianshu. Weapons clashed with a clang, and cold glints intersected.

I stood on the periphery and watched the show. All I could do was wait until Nanming started losing steam before I went right up and stabbed him. All's well that ends well.

Hengwen, who had left my chamber earlier to wake the guards, had returned to the yard, where he stood and watched the battle from a safe distance.

"What a low blow," he quipped to me.

That could not be helped. This immortal lord was now in mortal flesh, so how could I ever win against the valiant general that was Shan Shengling? It was only by wearing him down with the guards, then dealing him a blow with my blade, that I could be assured of victory.

Having received this immortal lord's instructions not to hurt Mu Ruoyan, the guards could only unleash their blades and swords on Shan Shengling, which limited them. Unexpectedly, Shan Shengling alone was more than enough to ward off the various guards. Having already spotted a way out, he fended off the blows and simultaneously retreated toward the exit of the Han Court. With Mu Ruoyan in tow, he darted through the moon gate into the back garden. Behind the rockery stood a wall, and behind the wall lay an empty alley. The guards patrolling the main courtyard rushed in as they noticed the commotion. More and more people came. As Shan Shengling dodged, retreated, and blocked the blows left and right, his strength began to fail him. By the time he made it to the wall, he had already suffered four or five flesh wounds.

Seeing an opening, I gripped my long blade and dashed into the crowd.

With his right hand, Shan Shengling leveled his blade in a move that blocked several spears in midair. With his left hand, he struck against the incoming force from the other side, leaving the front of his chest exposed. Seizing my chance, I aimed the tip of my blade and did him the honor of striking toward his right breast.

Twenty centimeters.

Fifteen centimeters.

Ten centimeters.

Five centimeters…

At five centimeters, the figure before me blurred, and I felt a sudden chill in my chest.

Astonished, I looked down at the long spear, the tip of which was buried in my left breast. A pair of hands held on to the other end of the spear, hands that were long and slender and seemed to lack strength—I had held those hands before, bony hands that jutted uncomfortably against my own.

It was also in this very instant of astonishment that a gust of chilly wind pressed in toward me. Silver light glinted; it seemed to come from Nanming's blade.

The chill was already on my neck.

Mingge—he must have simplified it again in his Book of Fate…

A *clang* rang out, and the chill stopped. Shan Shengling's blade stopped across my neck, because a long sword glowing with azure light was held up against Mu Ruoyan's neck. A pale, azure gown fluttered slightly in the wind.

"Let him go, and I'll let you and Mu Ruoyan leave the prince's manor safely."

Oh, Hengwen. It does not do to be ostentatious. Showing yourself is one thing, but that sword of yours is a tad too bright.

The guards gripped their weapons, undaring to make a rash decision.

Shan Shengling looked at Hengwen with his eyebrows raised. "Could you make such a decision?"

"Of course," Hengwen said, before turning to the guards. "Put down your weapons and retreat from the garden."

Mister Zhao was a hot favorite of the Prince of the Eastern Commandery. The quick-witted guards set down their weapons and withdrew to the moon gate.

The blade retracted from this immortal lord's neck.

Hengwen, too, withdrew his longsword from Mu Ruoyan's.

"Young Master Yan," he said mildly, "the spear tip is already buried in his flesh. Shouldn't you let go now?"

The hands gripping the hilt of the spear unclenched, and Hengwen supported my back with a hand. "Can you hang in there a little longer?" he asked under his breath; in that instant, his expression held nothing but blatant sympathy.

I sucked in a breath of cold air and gasped, "It's just... a tad too painful, *cough cough...*"

Mingge, that g*dd*mned Mingge!!

Shan Shengling narrowed his eyes at Hengwen. "I didn't even notice it when you got close earlier. Amazing skill you have there."

Clearly. He took advantage of the chaos and used his powers to manifest himself instantly. It'd be odd if you, a mere mortal, could detect him.

Putting on airs, Hengwen casually replied, "You flatter me."

Shan Shengling smiled. "I'm in awe of your poise. May I know your esteemed name?"

So Hengwen responded, "It's my honor to be asked by General Shan. This humble one is Zhao Heng."

Surprisingly enough, Shan Shengling cupped his hands. "Thank you, Young Master Zhao, for your guidance today. I hope I will have the chance to spar with you again on another."

Hengwen's hand remained on the back of this immortal lord, holding me upright, so he remained standing, and gave a slight nod of his head. Shan Shengling narrowed his eyes again, trying to read Hengwen. Then, with Tianshu at his side, he turned away. Tianshu looked back. I had not managed to get a good look at his face after he stabbed me. Looking at him now, his face had not become any more readable than before. Those pitch-black eyes looked back as he said, "I'm sorry."

I took a deep breath to brace myself. "It's fine. I deserve it, right...?"

I really did deserve it.

Mu Ruoyan blinked for a fleeting moment; then he turned away.

Shan Shengling took him, and jumped onto the perimeter wall. Then, they disappeared into the night.

I slumped to the ground. I heard the people around me begin to bustle, bursting into a fuss. It was Li Siming's father and two elder brothers who had crawled out from under their quilts after getting wind of what had transpired. I wondered if they had brought the physician.

Hengwen whispered under his breath, "Endure it for a moment. I'll lift you out when I get away from the public eye."

This immortal lord gasped with a bitter smile, "You can't... Given the extent of the injuries... the moment you lift me out... Li Siming... will surely die... I'll just have to stay in here, and hang on."

And Hengwen said to me in a frosty tone, "Serves you right."

Chapter Eight

This was what Old Man Mingge had written in his Book of Fate—

Night. Shang Shengling rescues Mu Ruoyan. Li Siming finds out. A fight ensues. Heavily wounded because of Mu Ruoyan. Flees.

Mingge held his beard in his hand and said to this immortal lord with a smile, "See. It's all very clearly written, isn't it?"

I said nothing.

For what it was worth, Li Siming was already a stiff corpse.

And it was the errand the Jade Emperor assigned me that was being jeopardized.

At any rate, they could not blame me for this mission holdup.

And in any case, I was now in Lingxiao Palace, and His Venerable Jade Emperor could naturally come to a decision of his own.

By a stroke of luck, Tianshu's spear had entered Li Siming's chest and pierced his heart. Even someone who had aimed with that intention would not have been guaranteed to have such accuracy. The heart was made of flesh. If it were pierced by such a large spearhead, causing blood vessels to instantly rupture, how could the result be good? It spasmed twice and went completely dead, relying solely on this immortal lord to suffer through the agony as I hung on for dear life inside the body.

What gave this immortal lord a hard time was that I still could not use my powers, but I had Hengwen with me; even if I had ten hearts that had been stabbed to mush, turning them back into vivaciously beating hearts would only take a breath of immortal air. But Hengwen just had to be Mister Zhao at this moment, and he could not use his powers right in public view.

It took only an instant for the prince's manor servants to swarm over, jostling Mister Zhao to one side and carrying me into the bedchamber. Several physicians took turns taking my pulse—which subsequently scared the living daylights out of them, rendering them speechless from panic, trembling from head to toe.

Those poor things. How many people in this world could come across a living person who had no pulse but was still talking with open eyes?

"How's my son?" the Prince of the Eastern Commandery asked. "Can he still be saved?"

The physicians shook like leaves.

Seeing how they were trembling so pitifully, this immortal lord spoke from the bed, "Father... don't put them in a spot. Let's just leave it to Heaven's will."

"Father, don't you worry," Li Siyuan said, wiping his tears. "Look, isn't Third Brother still here comforting you? Heaven will bless him on account of his filial piety..."

He choked with emotion at the end of his sentence.

Old Li's family huddled together and cried before this immortal lord's bed.

"Bastard, what have I done to deserve this?" the Prince wailed, while Li Sixian and Li Siyuan cried, "Alas, our ill-fated

Third Brother." Even Li Sixian's and Li Siyuan's head wives wept into their handkerchiefs. "Fate is cruel to our Little Uncle."

I was very touched by their tears. In the hustle and bustle of the mortal realm and the secular world, a personal touch of humanity was still quite heartwarming.

Speaking of which, why wasn't Hengwen here to treat me? Wasn't it a tad uncharitable to watch on indifferently while I was hurting and suffering here?

Just as this thought occurred to me, my entire body suddenly made a slow ascent. I was greatly alarmed. *This is no joking matter! Does he want Li Siming to die, lifting me out right now like this?!*

I was just about to struggle when a low, muffled voice overhead said, "Song Yao Yuanjun, this humble immortal is the Deity of Daytime Patrol. The Jade Emperor has decreed that I am to lead Yuanjun back to the Heavenly Court."

It turned out that the fates were *so* erroneously and outrageously wrong this time that Nanming had actually managed to rescue Tianshu, and thus the Jade Emperor, slightly furious, had hauled this immortal lord and Old Man Mingge to Lingxiao Palace for questioning. Hengwen was at the side as a witness.

"How did it come to this?" the Jade Emperor asked.

This immortal lord stood calm and composed in the hall. Reason was on my side. "The Jade Emperor is wise. When Song Yao descended to the mortal realm this time, I did everything just as instructed, but everything turned out different from instructed. My sufferings are of little significance, so I shall not mention it. The Jade Emperor is wise and omniscient. Right or wrong, you will surely be able to come to an impartial judgment."

I looked askance at Mingge. Wiping his sweat, the old man immediately confessed to his mistake to the Jade Emperor with fear and trepidation. He also opened up the Book of Fate to show this immortal lord, smiling appeasingly as he apologized.

Being the reasonable one I was, I did Mingge a favor. "Jade Emperor, there is a saying in the mortal world that 'trifles are tough to avoid, and fates are tough to determine.' Mingge Xingjun is in charge of countless fates, a job that is tedious and complicated, so one or two oversights are only understandable. Nanming has merely abducted Tianshu. Both are but mere mortals, so there's is no major setback to tearing them apart. We'll just have to see how to play it next."

The Jade Emperor contemplated it for a moment and nodded. "You're right. We'll see how to play it next." His lips spread into a smile. "Song Yao, I'll wait to see how you'll play it next."

I said with an apologetic smile, "Jade Emperor, this humble immortal is not very reliable in carrying out my duties. It was mostly due to this humble immortal's incompetence that Nanming could abduct Tianshu. Could the Jade Emperor possibly…" I glanced at Hengwen from the corner of my eye as a hint to back me up, "… choose another talent?"

Before Hengwen could make his move, the Jade Emperor said from above me, "You've done a great job in the mortal world. Every time I chat with the Queen Mother, she praises you for being thorough. Once you return to the Heavenly Court in triumph after assisting your fellow immortal through the secular world, your rank and salary will surely be increased by another grade."

I hurriedly deferred to his compliment. Before the words were fully out of my mouth, the Heavenly Inspector came to report to the Jade Emperor on some other matters, and elbowed us out of Lingxiao Palace.

This immortal lord grasped Mingge, stopping him in his tracks. "Xingjun, from today onward, you must do a better job writing about me in the Book of Fate."

Mingge Xingjun smiled so widely that the wrinkles on his face all gathered in one spot. "Definitely, definitely. I owe it to Yuanjun for putting in a good word for me today. It's just that one day in heaven is one year on earth. You've been held up for so long. If you still don't hurry back, I fear…"

All at once, I halted in my tracks and pulled Hengwen with me as I rushed toward the Southern Heavenly Gate.

Despite being dragged along with me, Hengwen said without a trace of a hurry, "What's the rush?"

With a bitter smile, I said, "If we don't rush, Li Siming's grave is going to be overgrown with grass."

In the end—

This immortal lord and Hengwen rushed our way down with some haste.

Not so late that we would see a grave mound with verdant grass.

The soil on Li Siming's grave was still damp, and his tombstone, still brand new.

We had just passed the seventh official day of mourning after his death.

Hengwen circled slowly around the grave mound. "He's already been placed in the coffin and buried. What now?"

"We have no choice but to wait until midnight to dig the grave open and see if Li Siming has already rotted," I answered, "and if he still can be used."

In the middle of the night, when the moon was bright, this immortal lord and Hengwen called up the local earth deity to part the grave so we could pry open Li Siming's coffin. Li Siming lay in the coffin, wearing top-quality silk and satin robes, buried with loads of gold and silver antiques.

Bodies tend not to last long in the warmer days of autumn, and although Li Siming had not rotted, a few insects were crawling in and out of his nostrils and ears. The moment there was a breeze, the stench of the corpse permeated the air.

I covered Hengwen's face with my sleeve. "Filth, such filth.

Quick, turn away."

Hengwen lifted aside my sleeves and said with a smile, "He was once you too, and there's nothing about his appearance now that I find offensive." After moving the coffin lid back in place, I thanked the local earth deity for going to the trouble and closed up the grave mound.

Li Siming could no longer be used. We had to return to the Heavenly Court and think of another way.

I touched the tombstone in front of the grave. A small stone platform was inlaid at the foot of the tombstone, where offerings were placed. Displayed on the platform was a set of wine pot and wine cup that had yet to be removed. The cup was still brimming with wine, so clear the bottom could be seen. It was as if it had been newly poured today. Li Siming sure was popular after his death.

Hengwen and I rode the clouds back to the Heavenly Court. I looked down at the earth while in midair. The place where Li Siming was buried was the Prince of the Eastern Commandery's ancestral graveyard, densely packed with grave mounds.

This immortal lord could not help but sigh with emotion. "Had I not chanced upon and eaten an immortal elixir back then, I'd have also ended up in a coffin and grave mound like this many years later, with insects crawling all over me as I rotted in the mud. My soul would have returned under the charge of the Yanwang and undergo lifetime after lifetime of reincarnation. I wonder what I'd have been reincarnated into by this lifetime."

Hengwen looked askance at me and sucked in a breath. "So broody."

On returning to the Heavenly Court, this immortal lord dashed right for the Western Gate.

Of the Four Gates of the Heavenly Court, the Southern Gate led to the present realm, the Western Gate to the past realm, the Eastern Gate to the future realm, and the Northern Gate to the mundane realm.

Once at the Western Gate, this immortal lord intended to return to the time when Li Siming was still bedridden for diagnosis and treatment. I wanted to repossess the body at the very instant the Daytime Patrol Deity lifted my real body out and Li Siming breathed his last. Hengwen would then restore that utterly ruined heart to its original state. All's well that ends well.

Marshal Gong Zhang, who was on duty before the Western Heavenly Gate, stopped this immortal lord. "Yuanjun has just returned from Lingxiao Palace. Haven't you heard that Heavenly Inspector Cao has already reported to the Jade Emperor that the Western Gate has collapsed and is undergoing repairs? It cannot be used for the time being."

So, I had no choice but to turn to the Northern Gate, which connected to the various realms; it could be considered a backup for when the other three heavenly gates were being repaired.

A gaggle of divine generals surrounded the Northern Heavenly Gate too, making a din as they traipsed around.

To my surprise, Taibai Xingjun was among them.

I went over to say my greetings and craned my neck to see that the Northern Heavenly Gate was tightly shut.

"Song Yao Yuanjun, are you going to pass through the Northern Heavenly Gate too?" Taibai Xingjun asked. "You can't use it now. The key is gone."

"How?!" I exclaimed in shock.

Jinxing let loose a long sigh and explained that when Bihua Lingjun was passing through the Northern Gate yesterday, the divine general standing guard was in the midst of playing chess, so he had taken the key to unlock it. The divine general had locked the gate after he left, only to remember that the key was still in the hands of Bihua Lingjun, who was now on the other side. Bihua Lingjun's destination was the Western Paradise, where the Dipankara Buddha was holding a doctrine banquet. We would have to wait for the banquet to conclude before Bihua Lingjun could begin the journey back—first to the mortal world, where he would transfer to the Southern Gate that would return him to the Heavenly Court. Only then could this Northern Gate be opened.

I asked approximately how long it would take, and Taibai Xingjun's words brought me to despair. "Ten to twenty days, I suppose."

Ten to twenty days. That meant ten to twenty years. Nanming and Tianshu would practically be an old couple living in conjugal bliss.

With a sigh, I said to Hengwen, "Fate. This is fated to be. Let's report to the Jade Emperor. Then we can wash our hands of this matter and return to our residences to sleep."

Hengwen yawned. "Sure. I'm a bit tired too. Do we drink and sleep at your residence or mine?"

That was what we said, but would the Jade Emperor actually spare me and release me from this assignment?

Mingge Xingjun was already waiting when we were midway to Lingxiao Palace. "Qingjun, Yuanjun, the Jade Emperor is already aware of what happened in the mortal world. Tianshu and Nanming have already left Shangchuan City and are on their way to the Southern Commandery. A few days later, there will be a surge of heavy waves in the Yangtze River, and their party will be stuck at the Riverfront Inn at Zhoujia Ferry Crossing. There is currently a body available, an itinerant Daoist priest staying for the night at a Daoist Temple in Shangchuan City. He has reached the end of his life, and his soul has gone to the underworld, so his body is available for Yuanjun's use. This matter brooks no delay, so please descend through the Southern Heavenly Gate posthaste."

At the break of dawn, when the sun was warm, this immortal lord opened my eyes on a bed built out of wooden planks to a drab, plain room with a crooked, half-rotting door and window.

Just then, someone rapped loudly at the rotting door.

"Guangyunzi! Guangyunzi! The thirty-fifth-day ritual assembly for the third young master of the prince's manor is about to start! If you don't go now, you won't be able to make it in time!"

Oh, so this short-lived Daoist priest was called Guangyunzi. One character of his name was even similar to this immortal lord's title—Guangxu Yuanjun.

Chapter Nine

Guangyunzi did not seem to be even fifty years old, more likely in his forties. The instant I opened my eyes, I first caught a whiff of something rancid, so much that I felt dizzy. This man had not washed up in a very long time.

I reached out to feel myself. There was a fairly long beard under my chin, which felt sticky to the touch. I picked it up for a look, just in time to see a bug scurrying through the dense gaps as if foraging for food. I could not bring myself to continue.

Hengwen tossed me a word from where he was in midair. "What a stinky, unkempt Daoist priest. Don't expect me to stick around you. I'll come again when you've cleaned yourself up." Having said that, he vanished.

Seriously, is this Daoist priest more unkempt than Li Siming's corpse? You sang such pretty words while we were at the coffin, but look at you now.

There was nowhere on me that was not itchy. I reached behind my neck to scratch it, rubbing out a considerably sized gray lump of dirt. I flicked it away, rubbed again, then flicked again; quite interesting.

The top of my head was itching terribly, and I could vaguely feel something running around. I heard there was a kind of bug called flea, and in all probability, that was the culprit.

The banging on the door persisted. I scratched my scalp and opened the door even as one of my hands was rubbing around a ball of dirt. The person outside was also a Daoist priest. He had a slightly oval face, and looked rather stocky and good-natured.

"You're finally awake," he said at the top of his voice. "I thought you had gotten immortalized in there."

Wasn't that exactly the case? First, he breathed his last, and then this great lord came to immortalize him.

"Right," I said. "I toured thousands of mountains inhabited by immortals, then it suddenly turned into a dream. I've practically forgotten all affairs of the secular world; I don't even remember you."

"Then you have to remember it, Immortal Guangyun," the Daoist priest said. "This humble Daoist is Chang Shan, the errand-runner of Mingyue Temple. Don't forget to look out for me when you become an immortal." He chuckled merrily as he rubbed his hands. "You told this humble Daoist to remind you this morning not to oversleep, so I came to call you earlier. This day is like none other. It's the princely manor's ritual ceremony. We are severely lacking in people in the temple. It hasn't been easy to get the nod from the master and let you fill in and make up the numbers. The least you could do is to wash up and change into something more decent."

My eyes lit up at the words "wash up." "Where is the water?"

"Amazing," Chang Shan quipped as he led me to the backyard. "You usually say you won't bathe for fear of getting ill from excessive water. To think you'd actually come to your senses today."

There was a wooden shed in the backyard, with a well in the shed, a bucket and a large wooden basin beside it.

I bolted the door to the shed, filled the basin full of water, and craned my neck out for a look. A shaggy head came into view. This immortal lord remained by the side of the well, drawing several basins of water and using more than a catty of soap before my hair and beard smoothed out, and my skin was scrubbed of grime to reveal a normal complexion.

Chang Shan prepared a set of brand-new clothes for me to change into. After my hair was secured and my beard neatly combed, I felt light all over. It was only then that Hengwen drifted over. Taking advantage of the absence of possible onlookers, I dusted my brand-new Daoist robe and asked, "Do I have the aura of Immortal Lü of the Eight Immortals?"

"If I play along and say yes, Lü Dongbin will no doubt destroy my Weiyuan Palace," Hengwen said.

I let out a wry laugh. "Don't I look a lot more handsome than I did this morning?"

After a moment of silence, Hengwen answered with sincerity, "You look human now."

I followed the Daoist priests from Mingyue Temple and arrived at the Prince of the Eastern Commandery's manor.

Striding across the threshold, I was overwhelmed with emotions.

Just a few days ago, I was family to the people across this threshold. Although Li Siming was not as suave as this immortal lord, he was, at the very least, a handsome and youthful young master. But now, he was rotting in his coffin, and in exchange, this immortal lord got a middle-aged Daoist priest with a complexion that resembled a wind-dried persimmon skin.

Did Mingge and the Jade Emperor expect me to seduce Tianshu with *this* face?

The ritual ceremony for the thirty-fifth day of Li Siming's death was ostentatiously done up, with a total of eight Daoist temples and sixty-six Daoist priests reciting the scriptures. It was among this crowd that I shook a bell.

I saw the Prince of the Eastern Commandery, as well as Li Siyuan and Li Sixian. This immortal lord understood they had a deep bond with Li Siming, but no matter how deep the feelings ran, or how many tears had been shed, the tears would have all dried up by the time they cried to the thirty-fifth day after his death.

So, when they were burning paper offerings before his spirit tablet, everyone was wailing with dry eyes.

Only one statement uttered by the Prince roused this immortal lord's spirits.

Before the spirit tablet, the Prince of the Eastern Commandery stuffed an offering of paper money into the fire basin, and declared, "Ming'er, rest assured, knowing that Father will definitely gouge out that Shan Shengling's heart and sacrifice it to you!"

As we collected the payment for our services, Chang Shan whispered into my ears, "From what His Lordship said today, our Eastern Commandery will surely clash with the Southern Commandery. Alas, what a sin. To put it bluntly, it could be said that the little young master's death was fated, and that he was asking for it. Once war breaks out, the commoners will suffer." Lowering his voice even further, he whispered, "Do you know how that little young master died?"

No one in the world knew better than I.

Chang Shan continued, "I heard that this little young master was originally a dimwit, but for some reason, one day, he suddenly became lucid. And when he did, goodness me, he immediately kept a young lover of unknown origins in his courtyard. I heard he pampered this gentleman a lot. But not two days later, His Lordship invited another young master to the residence as his advisor. They said that advisor was quite the extraordinary character, like an immortal. When the little young master saw him, he immediately discarded the young lover in his courtyard and gave all his heart to the advisor. The one in the courtyard, stewing in jealousy, then hooked up with his old flame, and after stabbing the little young master, the pair jumped over the wall and fled. Interesting, don't you think?"

My beard twitched a teensy bit. "Interesting."

Chang Shan added, "And even better yet, that old flame of the young lover actually turned out to be the great general of the Southern Commandery, Shan Shengling. After the little young master died, the advisor vanished too. This whole farce is straight out of a play, only this turned out to be a tragedy. He lost his life, and now the commoners have to suffer for it."

Despondent, I said nothing.

Jade Emperor, Mingge, this is all on you.

I covered the two strings of copper coins under my sleeve and followed the crowd out of the residence. From afar, I saw Jinning and Jinshu, wearing mourning sashes, weaving their way in and out of the crowd. Jinning eyed the offering platform, as if having design on that plate of pastries placed up as offerings.

I had inquired Mingge after the fates of these two children. The Prince of the Eastern Commandery would die of a stroke five years later. Three years after that, Li Siyuan would meet with a sudden death, and another year later, Li Sixian would meet his end on the battlefield. Jinning would become a commander-in-chief in his youth and emerge victorious battle after battle. However, the one who would take the helm of the Eastern Commandery actually turned out to be Jinshu. This timid Jinshu, who tagged along behind Jinning all day, would go on to become the founding sovereign of a new dynasty.

The world truly was ever-changing and volatile.

I had been standing before the funeral awning for a long time. Jinning's swiveling eyes stopped on me, and he waddled over.

"Hey, old Daoist priest with the long beard. What are you looking at?"

As usual, Jinshu followed behind him.

Jinning would be quite the philanderer in the future. This immortal lord looked at him, imagining him relishing in the embrace of dozens of beautiful concubines. What a worrisome child.

I took out two little jade gourd pendants from my sleeve and bent over. "This humble Daoist sees that both little young masters have auspicious faces that bode good fortune, so I'm giving this pair of jade charms to both of you, so you may establish an affinity with the Dao."

Jinning reached out to take them, but Jinshu tugged on his sleeve and looked up at me. "You're a Daoist priest of unknown origin. Is there something you want in exchange for giving us things?"

I laughed. "Since this humble Daoist is able to come here to partake in the ritual ceremony, my origins are naturally verified. How else is a common person able to enter the Prince of the Eastern Commandery's manor? These two pieces of jade are merely to establish an affinity with the Dao; there are no other motives. If the little young master really wants to reward this humble Daoist with a small something..." I stroked my beard and looked at Jinning's hand, "then you may give this bamboo tube to me. How about it?"

Jinning looked at the bamboo tube in his hand, as if he was loath to part with it, then he looked back at the jade gourds in my hand and hesitated.

Jinshu blinked, looked at Jinning, then said to me, "Then I'll give you this, but can you give us the gourds and not take the bamboo tube?" He felt in his belt with his little hand, then held out a fist before me and spread his palm.

I looked at that piece of jade, delighted. What a stroke of luck, having it all delivered into my hands without needing to expend further effort.

"Thank you, little young master." I picked up a pendant and handed it to Jinshu.

Jinning yelled, "Hey, we agreed on two, so why only one?"

I shook my head. "This little young master's gift is only enough to exchange for one. One thing for another of similar value, isn't that only fair?"

"You said earlier that it was free!" Jinning retorted.

I stroked my beard again. "I did, but I've changed my mind now."

Jinning scrunched his nose and glared at me.

Jinshu stuffed the pendant into Jinning's hand. "Forget it, don't waste your breath with him. I don't care about this, anyway. Here, take it."

Jinning shook his head hard and held the bamboo tube out to me. "Here you go. Give me that!"

This immortal lord beamed. "Thank you, little young master. May heaven's blessings be with you."

I took the bamboo tube and handed Jinning the other pendant.

"You like the bamboo tube, so why give it to him? I don't want this pendant," Jinshu said.

Jinning stuffed the pendant into his hand. "You exchanged your item to give me, and I exchanged mine to give you. The two things we gave him were both taken from Little Uncle's room without permission, anyway. If our dads recognize them, we'd have to take a beating from the broom."

Only then did Jinshu take the gourd and tuck it into his sleeve.

This immortal lord left with the two items, triumphant.

On returning to the Daoist temple, I gave Chang Shan a string of coins and thanked him for taking care of me.

A big smile bloomed on Chang Shan's face. "Fellow Daoist Guangyun is truly too courteous. If you visit Shangchuan again in the future, you must come seek me out at the temple."

That night, I admired the bamboo tube and jade pendant, feeling smug. Standing before the bed, Hengwen remarked, "Do you have peace of mind now that you have coaxed and swindled both items out of the children? So how about it? Do you think of him when you look at them?"

How could this immortal lord do something as shady as swindling children? Those two jade gourds were treasures on which I had cast a protective spell. It would ensure that no evil or demon could get to them, and keep them safe and sound at that.

I smiled obsequiously at Hengwen. "Do you want to lie down on the bed?"

"Forget it," Hengwen said. "That bed of yours is no cleaner than the shroud Li Siming was buried in."

The next day, I took my leave from Mingyue Temple and left Shangchuan City.

Guangyunzi was of mortal flesh, so this immortal lord could not ride the clouds. I could only walk the entire way to Zhoujia Ferry Crossing, which was four or five days on foot.

After I was a long way from Shangchuan City, Hengwen materialized and accompanied me on foot. Although he manifested himself, he still wore Mister Zhao's looks, unwilling as he was to accommodate me in the form of a Daoist priest himself. The entire way we went, passersby all cast sidelong glances at us, finding this duo combination to be quite strange.

Five days later, I stood in the evening before Riverfront Inn.

Dark clouds hung overhead, making it extremely dim. The high waves of the Yangtze River slapped against the riverbanks, while the inn's banner meant to beckon customers flapped in the wind.

With a bamboo pole in my right hand—bearing the words "Ironclad Fortune-telling" on a black banner—and a thin horse-tail whisk swinging from my left, I strode into the inn.

The waiter initially cast a sidelong glance at me and could hardly be bothered as he made to turn away, but then he saw

Hengwen entering, and his face turned positively radiant.

When they realized that Hengwen and I were fellow companions—and when I fished out the silver—the smiles on the waiter's and innkeeper's faces widened even more. They very solicitously arranged for two deluxe rooms upstairs, and just as solicitously prepared the best seat in the hall downstairs, where they served their best wine and dishes.

After the dishes were served, a waiter came to pour the wine with infinite hospitality, and started a conversation with me: "Daozhang, you have the divine demeanor of an immortal. I can tell at a glance that you're a great master."

"Not at all, not at all," I answered modestly. "My cultivation is meager, and my knowledge in the arts is superficial. I can merely read faces to predict one's fortune and future prospects."

The waiter's eyes shone with admiration.

So, I continued, "This humble Daoist also has a smattering knowledge in reading fengshui, observing astronomical phenomena, and the divination art of Qimen Dunjia."

The admiration in the waiter's eyes brimmed even more.

So, I continued further, "Actually, this humble one can also take a look to see if there are any occurrences of demonic possessions, supernatural hauntings, and even dubious, tricky illnesses that cannot be cured."

The waiter's face lit up with pleasant surprise. He promptly set down the wine jar and bowed. "Daozhang, you're a blessing straight from heaven! We do have a patient with a tricky illness in our humble inn. Could I trouble you to grant us some compassion and take a look at him?!"

The innkeeper personally led Hengwen and me up the stairs. Several more waiters scurried about, doing their utmost to serve.

According to the innkeeper, an esteemed master had come to the inn with an entourage. They had initially intended to cross the river, but the waves on the river were too strong, which made it impossible for them to pass, so they had stayed in the inn. A gentleman from the group was down with illness. Several days later, the master seemed to have some urgent matter to attend to and left with half of the party, leaving the other half to take care of the sick man. But the sick man simply would not get better, and the remaining people trickled out for their own important matters. Eventually, only the invalid remained.

"Before the last one left, he left a huge sum of money and said they would be back in a few days. He instructed us to take care of the sick gentleman. He even went as far as drawing his sword to hack off a corner of the table to intimidate us, saying that this was what would happen to us if we did not take good care of him." The innkeeper's tone was greatly distressed.

"But that gentleman's health deteriorated by the day. We looked for every physician we could find to see him, and they all said that he couldn't be cured. All he does now is lie on the bed and cough out mouthful after mouthful of blood. He's only barely hanging in there by a thread. I beseech you to think of every way possible to save his life. How are we going to explain it if he dies and that group of people returns…"

The innkeeper pushed the door open to reveal the bedridden invalid breathing his last.

The oil lamp was not very bright, but it was enough for me to see that supposedly dying man on the bed.

Having gotten a clear look, I immediately said to the innkeeper, "Don't worry. No matter what happens, he won't die."

The innkeeper grabbed me, a drowning man clutching at straws, his hands trembling as he said, "Daozhang, you're truly a living immortal who understands the secrets of the universe with a glance. With your word that he won't die, I can rest assured knowing my head will stay intact!"

I took one step at a time into the room and walked over to the bed.

The man on the bed suddenly opened his eyes, a pair of black orbs that appeared abnormally bright under the light.

He stared at this immortal lord, and opened his mouth to very clearly say—

"Li Siming, are you here to make me pay for your life?"

This immortal lord got a fright and took a big step back.

Oh, dear me, Jade Emperor. Don't tell me Tianshu has suddenly attained enlightenment? To think he could recognize me at a glance!

"Daozhang, don't be surprised," the innkeeper said. "This gentleman is severely ill, and in his delirium has been dropping this phrase on everyone he sees. When the master was still around, he would step out of their room and head downstairs to smash the tables. Too many of our tables have already been destroyed by him."

The innkeeper heaved a long, weary sigh. I calmed myself. So, he was delirious with fever. If that was the case, was Tianshu still feeling guilty over stabbing this immortal lord?

I walked over and sat at the man's bedside. Mu Ruoyan's bright, shiny eyes were still fixed on me. I smiled affably back, and picked up one of his hands to put on a show of reading his pulse.

The few grams of flesh I had so painstakingly nursed back onto Tianshu's body had all burned off. At that time, he had been all skin and bones, and now even that layer of skin covering the bones on his wrist was so thin, it looked like there was practically nothing. I set two fingers on his bone and partially closed my eyes, putting on the look of a master.

Hengwen stood beside the table with the small, lit oil lamp and coughed once, a move that complemented the innkeeper's sigh.

"Daozhang is a great master, as expected. Even the way you feel the pulse differs from the others," he marveled.

"This is my own unique way of taking pulses," I said leisurely. "In fact, I'm even better at reading pulses with silk threads."

I retracted my hand. On the bed, Mu Ruoyan coughed four or five times. A few drops of blood splattered from his mouth.

Having very tragically cultivated a habit from all my time attending to him in the Prince of the Eastern Commandery's manor, I reached out and wiped off the blood for him with my sleeve.

With eyes both shut, Mu Ruoyan spoke, his words breaking up, "Li Siming, what kind of ghost… do you think I'll turn into this time?"

"Benefactor," I spoke up, "this humble one's Daoist name is Guangyunzi. Don't worry. With me here, I'll surely cure you of your illness and restore you back to health."

Mu Ruoyan's emaciated fingers grasped my sleeve. He made a pained sound in his throat. "I harmed you, cost you your life, yet you want to preserve my life and make me suffer. Forget it. This is the retribution… I deserve…"

Oh, looks like my words aren't falling on deaf ears.

Hengwen yawned. "Daoist Master, take your time on the diagnosis and treatment. This humble one is going to bed first." Having said that, he turned and left.

I shifted, pulling my sleeve from Tianshu's grip, and stood from the edge of the bed.

"How is it?" the innkeeper asked, impatient.

I stroked my beard and shook my head. "Not too good. This gentleman is afflicted with a chronic illness on top of his emotional distress. I shall have to return to my room first and meditate on it, so the prescription can only be ready tomorrow morning. May I ask if your esteemed inn has bird's nests available? You can decoct a bowl for him to take first."

"That master did bring along several kilograms of bird nests when he came," the innkeeper said. "There are still some left."

The quick-witted waiters immediately left to decoct it.

The innkeeper respectfully saw this immortal lord to the guest room, where he ordered a brand-new wooden bathtub to be carried out and for bathing water to be prepared. He even gave us two complimentary plates of dried fruits as a late-night snack.

Before I stepped out of Mu Ruoyan's room, I cast a look back at him. The pallid figure lying in the dim light of the oil lamp looked not unlike a paper figure.

I stepped out the door, and he did not say a word more.

The guest room next to mine must have been Hengwen's, and the door was closed. I took a look, and told the innkeeper to send the brand-new wooden bathtub and bathing water to the gentleman in the other room, as well as to change the bedding and pillows in his room. This gentleman was a distinguished personage, and everything he used must be the newest and the cleanest. At any rate, he could afford to pay for it.

The innkeeper, naturally, acknowledged my instructions in the affirmative. When I was done washing up, I blew out the oil lamp and lay down on the bed, holding the copper Eight Trigrams tally in my palms as I extracted my true form.

At each stop of our journey here, we would always book two guest rooms—one for Guangyunzi, and one for Hengwen and me. Since he did not come to lift me out, I could only go looking for him.

The lights in Hengwen's rooms had been extinguished too. I felt for the bed in the darkness. The person on the bed turned over and asked, "Done with the consultation?"

I let out a wry laugh. "Yeah."

Then I rubbed my hands. "Move over inside and make room for me."

Hengwen scoffed and shifted a little. I took advantage of the space to lie down and pull a corner of the quilt over myself.

"Tianshu is severely ill," Hengwen remarked. "Seems to me like he's hanging on to life by a mere thread. I doubt mortal methods could cure his illness, and the Jade Emperor doesn't allow us to heal him with our divine powers. I wonder what miraculous remedies Guangyunzi Daozhang has to treat him with?"

"I'll deal with it as needed. If all else fails, then just leave him hanging," I said.

Hengwen chuckled. "Could you bear to do so? It took just a few words from Tianshu, and you've already forgotten that one stab, right? You say to leave him hanging, but you already have a plan in mind, don't you?"

I did not dare to respond to that. Hengwen's appraisal of me was correct. I did indeed have a plan.

Outside the window, the wind stirred indistinctly. I was very familiar with this movement; it had followed us this entire journey.

"Is this what you are planning?" Hengwen asked, voice hushed.

There was the sound of the wind, a slight rustling, then all was silent. Two hours later, I softly opened the door, and sure enough, there was a bundle of neatly secured lingzhi lying by the threshold. This species was also called the jinluo lingzhi. Although it was an extremely valuable divine herb, it grew in the mortal world. I had only seen it a couple times back in the Heavenly Court.

This bouquet of lingzhi was meant for Hengwen, and its sender was that dauntless, homosexual romantic of a fox who had been yearning for him.

That said, this fox had been furtively following us the moment Hengwen and I left Shangchuan City. Furball was quite the resourceful one. He could always sneak into the inn where Hengwen and I stayed in the middle of the night, where he could linger and fix his gaze outside the room before putting down a handful of jinluo lingzhi.

Jinluo lingzhi could purge impure vital energy and

nourish the primordial spirit. The fox was probably worried that Hengwen, being dragged through this corrupted world of the mortals, would be tainted with the ills of the secular world, and so he gave him these.

This immortal lord was a compassionate one.

Alas, the world abounded with lovesick romantics; I would treat this matter as one as ephemeral as floating clouds.

After Hengwen took the lingzhi, he would always keep them away in his sleeve with a smile, feigning ignorance to his sender. And so, to this date, the fox still thought that he had concealed himself well.

This went on, day after day.

Holding the lingzhi, I returned to the bed and flashed Hengwen an obsequious smile. "Would you mind sharing a piece or two of this with me?"

"I knew it. You are thinking of using it to save Tianshu," Hengwen said lazily. "Take it if you want it, but let me just remind you again that you descended to the mortal realm to set up trials, not to save him from hardships and suffering. It looks like you are veering from the script, from breaking up the lovebirds to falling for the beauty. Rein yourself in and remember not to go too far."

I tucked the lingzhi in my clothes and lay back on the bed. "Although Tianshu Xingjun and I would clash after the fact, he still saved me once, after all. I have to repay him for this debt of gratitude somehow."

I, Song Yao Yuanjun, was the most averse to owing others debts of gratitude, especially Tianshu, with whom I would eventually fail to see eye-to-eye.

Many years ago, when I had just been promoted to the title of Guangxu Yuanjun, there had been a day when Hengwen left for the Western Paradise, the Buddha realm, for a doctrine dialogue. Feeling lonely in the Heavenly Court, I went to Bihua

Lingjun's palace. To relieve my boredom, I had tea and a look at the celestial beasts he was raising. It had just so happened that there was a one-horned dragon that strayed while cultivating to be an immortal, and had gone berserk. With sword in hand, this immortal lord fought the dragon. Unfortunately, that beast spewed smoke into my face and, with a sweep of its tail, sent me flying several meters away.

I was utterly disgraced. And heavily injured.

Coincidentally, Tianshu Xingjun was also at Lingjun's residence. Although he was usually indifferent to those around him, he treated my injuries. I owed him a debt of gratitude ever since.

Several hundred years later, when we ended up confronting each other at Lingxiao Palace, I still thought of that moment as an unreal dream. The same Tianshu Xingjun who had once saved me, the Tianshu Xingjun who was cold and aloof, now actually wanted to plant a trumped-up charge against me and have me exiled to the mortal world, never to return to the Heavenly Court.

"When Tianshu pressed his charge against you back then, he had some evidence to back it up. So it can't be said that he wrongly accused you," Hengwen said. "But I can't figure out why he would do so. Tianshu would never do such a thing, given his character, yet he did. There has to be a reason."

"I can't be bothered to know the reason," I said. "In any case, I've repaid my debt and done what the Jade Emperor has instructed me to do. He failed to frame me back then, so I'll treat it as if it never happened. When he returns to the Heavenly Court, we will still be fellow immortals who smile when we see each other."

I, Song Yao Yuanjun, am a magnanimous immortal.

The next day, I woke up early in the morning and prepared to inform the innkeeper to decoct a bowl of lingzhi for Mu Ruoyan. When I headed downstairs with Hengwen, however,

I saw a bunch of waiters rubbing their hands together as they gathered around a cage.

One of the waiters greeted us jubilantly. "We caught a rare beast last night. Do the two of you want to come over for a look?"

I readily agreed and leaned over.

It turned out to be an old friend in the cage.

A silvery-white furball crouched in the cage, all huddled up with its head drooping, looking forlorn like a hero at a dead end—Xiang Yu the Conqueror at Wujiang River.

Fox, how did you get caught?

Hengwen, too, was taken aback. The fox peered up at him, its eyes glistening as though filled with tears, and lowered its head to crouch in the corner of its cage.

The waiters were all very excited.

"The stray cats and weasels have been making a lot of commotion of late, so we set up a live trap under the eaves, hoping to catch those animals, but we didn't expect to catch this beast. Daozhang, you are experienced and knowledgeable. This fox's coat color is rare and extremely valuable, right? I wonder if we would be able to sell it for ten taels of silver if we skin it alive?"

This immortal lord held up a palm and recited a Daoist mantra before saying, "What a sin, what a sin. It may be a beast, but skinning it alive is too brutal. Heaven decreed that it is to meet its end here. On account of this humble Daoist, at least give it a quick end before skinning it."

The fox jerked its head up and glared sharply at me, then it looked miserably at Hengwen and lowered its head again.

I saw what appeared to be bloodstains on its right front paw. It seemed to be a recent injury and not at all minor.

As expected, Hengwen declared, "This humble one shall offer ten taels of gold. Sell it to me."

He set the gold ingots on the table, and the waiters broke out into radiant smiles, looking very much like a cluster of brilliant sunflowers.

One said, in an attentive tone, "We will immediately skin this fox for you."

"It looks very rare," Hengwen said, "so I'll keep it alive for now."

"Benefactor, aren't you afraid of the fox's odor?" I asked.

The fox glared hatefully at me again.

Hengwen opened the cage and carried the fox out in his arms. "I don't smell a thing. Let's keep it."

The fox thrust its head deep into Hengwen's bosom and nuzzled against him.

Back in my room upstairs, I closed the door. The fox lay in Hengwen's lap and huddled into a ball, looking very cozy.

I leaned against the table. "Furball, you looked like a stud, well-defined chest and all, the last time this immortal lord saw you. You could be said to be a man, but look at you now, so frail and delicate."

The fox immediately jumped off Hengwen's lap and rolled into human form. In a display of his dignity and honor, he coldly said, "This humble one is Xuan Li, and it seems like you know that." He twitched his ears and did not look at me; instead, he gazed at Hengwen like a man besotted. "Thank you, Qingjun, for saving my life."

"You're seriously injured. Jinluo lingzhi is a divine object that you can't take, and if you do, you have to show your real form. Why take this risk?" Hengwen said gently—of course, Hengwen had always been a good-tempered person who was gentle with everyone and everything.

"For Qingjun, it's worth it even if I lose my life," the fox said. "I am willing."

Oh, so mushy.

Hengwen stretched out a hand, offering him an elixir pill. "Take this elixir first; it might benefit you."

The fox palmed it in his paw and gazed at Hengwen in a

manner that I found very nerve-racking. It was quite a while before he delivered the pill to his mouth and swallowed it.

It was inevitable that this immortal lord gave a pointed cough. "The wound on your arm looks extremely odd. How did you get it?"

The fox initially treated me as though I was invisible, but Hengwen was looking at him too, so he answered in a muted tone, "I was wounded by a mortal."

That greatly surprised me. Furball had at least a thousand years of cultivation. Which mortal was tough and fearsome enough to injure it?

Hengwen had the same question. "What is this person's origin? I'm surprised he was able to injure you."

"I don't know his origin," the fox answered insipidly. "He actually came to my cave to steal the lingzhi, so I struck out at him to teach him a lesson, but in a moment of carelessness, I ended up slightly injured. I locked him up in my cave. It seems like his surname is Shan."

So, Nanming Dijun was not a heartless cad who had discarded his lover after all, but had been caught by the fox while stealing medicine for Tianshu.

Oh, this immortal lord was somewhat touched by Nanming's love for Tianshu.

He had been aggravatingly ruthless back when he was breaking up lovebirds, and now that he was lovestruck, he was even more aggravating.

Love. Oh, such is love.

But, come to think of it, how had he known to steal the divine lingzhi, planted by a demon, to treat Tianshu?

Who had pointed him in that direction?

"What did you do to the lingzhi thief after catching him?" I asked the fox.

"Locked him up," the fox answered.

"Just locked him up?" I wondered. "He stole your lingzhi and injured your arm. Didn't you torture him or break his limbs for fun?"

The fox cast a glance at me and answered in a cold voice, "No. I've never been one to split hairs with mortals. I only broke one of his arms and tied him up in my cave."

He retrained his gaze on Hengwen. "I've never hurt a mortal."

The fox was laying out his lofty character for all to see. He gazed at Hengwen, his eyes sincere, while the tips of his ears trembled ever so slightly.

Hengwen smiled at him, earning an instant beam of delight. The fox looked very much like he had the intent to revert to his original form and jump back onto Hengwen's lap.

As chance would have it, there came the sound of footsteps outside the door. The fox immediately reverted to its original form and bounded onto Hengwen's lap. This immortal lord caught it by the scruff of its neck and lifted it up. Furball twisted its body around and bared its coldly glinting fangs.

The waiter knocked on the door. "Gentlemen, your breakfast is ready. Please make your way downstairs for your meal."

I tucked the fox under my armpit and held it there. With my free hand, I opened the door and uttered a Daoist mantra. "We'll be right down. Thank you."

I closed the door again. The fox leaped to the ground and rolled into human form. Hengwen and I got ready to head downstairs, where our meals were waiting. Before we left, this immortal lord even asked the fox out of the kindness of my heart, "Do you want me to bring back a steamed bun for you?"

The fox answered defiantly, "Nope."

As we returned after breakfast, I crossed my fingers that the fox had already returned to its lair. But the moment I opened the door, I saw a white furball huddled up contentedly on Hengwen's quilt, taking a little nap.

The fox would not return to its lair. It argued with conviction and logic. Hengwen Qingjun had brought it in full view of the public. If it were to vanish all of a sudden, it would surely rouse suspicions. So, in order to spare Hengwen Qingjun further trouble, it decided to stay for the time being.

Perhaps moved by Furball's devoted love, and also probably because he found it an interesting situation, Hengwen tacitly allowed it to stay.

The fox was ecstatic, but this immortal lord was a little worried. I had also fallen into unrequited love in the past, and I knew this sort of thing would be even harder to extricate from the more it dragged on. Tianshu and Nanming were a poignant example, right in front of us. While Hengwen was different, he had a shortcoming, and that was that he enjoyed trying things out for the novelty and fun of it. If he were to get a taste of love with the fox on a whim…

I shuddered.

Moreover, Tianshu was still in his room, barely hanging in there by half a breath as he waited to consume the lingzhi. Jinluo lingzhi was a gift from the fox to Hengwen. With the fox staying here, how could this immortal lord swallow my pride and ask Hengwen for it?

There was no use in sitting here and worrying about Hengwen and the fox, so I went to check up on Tianshu.

Two waiters were meticulously cleaning up Tianshu's room. They said since last night, Tianshu had coughed out several more mouthfuls of blood. The innkeeper also made his way into the room and looked at me expectantly. "Daozhang, you said last night that you'd definitely have a prescription today. Do you have the medicine?"

This immortal lord coughed. "I do, but…"

Two knocks on the door, and a waiter entered the room, a bowl of dark green soup in his hands. "Daozhang, this humble servant has arrived with the medicine."

I was astonished.

Hengwen strode into the room. "I noted the time and had it decocted beforehand. Let him drink it, and we'll see if it works."

Two waiters eased Mu Ruoyan up and pried his teeth open. This immortal lord fed him the medicine, one spoonful at a time. Mu Ruoyan took to the jinluo lingzhi well, and the medicine went down smoothly. After being settled back on the pillow, he remained still.

The innkeeper hemmed and hawed. "Daozhang, this gentleman..."

Mu Ruoyan's breathing was even and shallow, and the distressed expression on his face receded some too. Only when he was sleeping soundly could he look like this.

Knowing this, I said, "He's fine. Let this benefactor rest quietly for now. Hopefully, his illness will take a turn for the better when he wakes."

Mu Ruoyan slept for an entire day and night.

The innkeeper and waiters worried that this immortal lord had actually poisoned him to death, so they would go in and out of the room to check on his breathing. The waiters lay in wait by the front and back doors, beneath the windows, and before the staircase on the ground floor, fearing that I could flee when I saw my chance. So I simply moved a chair to sit by the table in Mu Ruoyan's room when I was not sleeping, saving the innkeeper and waiters from having their hearts in their mouths all the time, and played chess with myself to relieve my boredom.

When night fell, I returned to my room, extracted my real form, and went to look for Hengwen. The fox was in his original form, sleeping on a pillow on a chair. I picked it up and pointed next door. "The body this immortal lord uses in the daytime is lying on the bed in that room. You can move him to the floor and have the bed to yourself."

The fox hugged the pillow tightly with his paws. "Why won't

you let me sleep in the same room as Qingjun?"

This immortal lord did not mince words. "You have feelings for Hengwen Qingjun. This immortal lord is afraid something might happen if you are in the same room as him."

The fox transformed into a human and said with a cold smile, "Song Yao Yuanjun has a filthy mind. I admire Qingjun, but I would never force him if he was unwilling."

Yeah, I thought, *but that's not what I'm worried about to begin with. This Hengwen Qingjun is not so easily coerced. Even I myself have no hope of success if I so wished, much less you with your little bit of cultivation.*

On the bed, Hengwen did not stir even the slightest. Presumably, he was having a blast, listening to the commotion here.

So I steadied my tone and reasoned it out with the fox. "Qingjun and I descended to the mortal world with a mission, and there are fellow immortals up in Heaven watching our every move. The rules of the Heavenly Court are strict. I fear it will incur suspicion if the conversations and actions between you two are too intimate."

The fox sat on the chair with his arms folded before his chest, his eyes flashing with faint, green light. "Forgive this humble one for disagreeing with Song Yuanjun's reason. Song Yuanjun sleeps on the same bed with Qingjun every night, and I heard that you often mooch food and wine from Qingjun's residence back in the Heavenly Court. It seems like you have never been punished by the laws of Heaven, so if you ask me, the rules of the Heavenly Court are not as strict and rigorous as the rumors make them out to be."

This mongrel actually went as far as to make inquiries about this immortal lord and Hengwen! And where in the world did he hear of untrue gossip, saying that this immortal lord often sponges off Hengwen?!

The fox continued, "Is Yuanjun going to say next that I

can't do what you can do just because I'm a demon and you are an immortal?" He straightened his robe and stood up. "I said before that I'd never cause trouble for Qingjun. Since Yuanjun has reminded me of that, I'll go over next door to sleep. It's just that…"

The fox walked to the wall, then looked back out of the corner of his eye. "I may be a demon now, but I only have to pass a thousand and five hundred years of heavenly tribulations, and I'll be able to ascend to immortality. It remains to be seen how things will turn out when we are in Heaven."

With a flick of his sleeve, he stepped through the wall to sleep in the next room.

When I dragged a chair over and sat, Hengwen spoke up softly, "I've never seen you take the rules of the Heavenly Court so seriously. Did what happened to Tianshu and Nanming make you see the light?"

"More or less," I answered with a dry laugh, and stood to walk over to the bed. "By the way, it was fortunate you sent over the bowl of lingzhi decoction today. Thank you, thank you."

"Just remember, you owe me a drink," Hengwen said lazily. "Actually, I wanted to see what else you can do further down the line after repaying your so-called debt to Tianshu."

"Of course, I'll be doing whatever the Jade Emperor instructs me to and whatever Mingge arranges," I replied.

Speaking of which, there had been no sign of activity from Old Man Mingge these few days. Strange.

Hengwen moved inside the bed to make way for me, and I lay down on my side. Suddenly, I remembered something. "Oh, right. Isn't Nanming still being held captive in the fox's cave? Since the fox isn't leaving, Nanming must be starving in there. Given that I've already saved Mu Ruoyan, should I commit another act of kindness? Get the fox to release him, so that he can have his theatric reunion with Mu Ruoyan?"

Hengwen chuckled beside me.

"What are you laughing at?" I asked.

"Nothing," Hengwen said, "I just find your words interesting."

When the day broke, I went to sit in Mu Ruoyan's room again to assuage the innkeeper's panic.

A waiter found a chess set, and Hengwen played with me to relieve my boredom. The fox crouched on the chair beside Hengwen, while the waiters looked back and forth at it.

In the thousands of years I had played chess with Hengwen, I had never beaten him once. I suffered yet another depressing defeat today.

The innkeeper, with great attentiveness, instructed the waiters to deliver lunch to the room, which included five dishes and one jar of wine, along with one pot of hot soup.

A waiter placed the pot of soup on the table and lifted the lid. The instant a mist of piping hot steam escaped, Mu Ruoyan, on the bed across the veil of mist, moved.

Chapter Ten

I had been chewing on a strip of dried bean curd, and now I watched blankly as Mu Ruoyan propped himself up and looked dazedly over.

The innkeeper, standing beside me personally pouring wine for Hengwen and me, froze in stupefaction.

It had to be known that Mu Ruoyan had been lying bedridden for far too long, so when the innkeeper saw him sitting up by himself, it was like seeing Chang'e ascend the moon with his very own eyes. It worked him up till he trembled all over. After a while, he fell to his knees with a thud and cried, "Daozhang is truly a living immortal! Truly a living immortal!"

I stroked my beard and smiled, first at the innkeeper, and then at Mu Ruoyan. When I opened my mouth, I realized I had yet to swallow the dried bean curd. I did so with composure, then smiled again.

First, I said to the innkeeper, "It's nothing; no need to stand on ceremony."

Then I affably asked Mu Ruoyan, "Young Master, are you feeling a little better now?"

Mu Ruoyan fixed his eyes on me, still looking a little dazed.

"Young Master," the innkeeper said, "you've been so sick these few days that you fell unconscious. It was all thanks to this Daozhang's divine medicine. How do you feel right now?"

The dazed expression on Mu Ruoyan's face gradually receded. His mind must have cleared up. He straightened himself, his face awash with a weariness that was part self-derision. Then he schooled his expression and lifted the quilt. Jinluo lingzhi was potently effective, and to my surprise, he managed to stand on his first attempt. Taking over his outer robe from the waiter to drape over himself, he looked at me and said, "Please pardon me for my slovenly appearance. I heard it was all thanks to you for saving this humble one."

I rose to my feet and raised a palm. "It's just some medicinal remedy this humble Daoist came across while roaming the world out there. As long as it helps to restore your health."

"I am but a mere scholar," Mu Ruoyan said. "I have nothing to thank you with, so please accept my kowtow as an appreciation of my thanks."

I was stunned when he bent his legs. To think Mu Ruoyan actually wanted to kneel to me? He who had no wish to live kneeling down to the person who saved his life—*if that's not a joke, I don't know what is.*

Despite this thought, I found that my legs had strode forward, and I reached out to stop Mu Ruoyan from completing his kowtow.

The clatter of a wine cup being set on the table rang out; I released my hands and stepped back. Raising my palm again, I said, "Benefactor, that is too much of a kowtow for this humble Daoist to accept."

"Since the Daozhang isn't willing to accept my kowtow, then please accept my bow," Mu Ruoyan said, and bowed deeply.

Left with no other choice, I could only raise my palm and return the gesture, bowing deeply at the waist.

"In the future, when I am able, I will surely repay your kindness to me," Mu Ruoyan said. "I go by the humble surname of Yan, and my name is Zimu. May I ask for your venerable name?"

My, my, was Tianshu something else, even in the mortal world. He had only just returned to consciousness, and here he was, instantly conjuring a fake name without batting an eyelid.

I raised my palm in greeting again. "That's putting it a bit strongly, benefactor. I truly don't deserve this. This Daoist's humble name is Guangyunzi. The others all call me Daoist Priest Guangyun."

After going on and on for a bit and mutually trading some more civilities, I said, "Your health is just starting to show improvements, so you still need to recuperate in quietude for a few more days. Don't catch another cold. It'd be better to rest in bed."

"Thank you, Daozhang." Mu Ruoyan looked at the table. "Please accept my apologies for disrupting your meal."

I laughed dryly. We were clearly the only ones eating in his room, and yet he was still being so polite.

Hengwen, sitting with his back to the bed all this time, turned to give him a sidelong smile. "Don't worry about it, Young Master. We are the ones who've imposed on you."

Mu Ruoyan instantly froze, as if he was at the summit of a frigid mountain, and a basin of icy water had been poured over his head.

His gaze was astonished, and his complexion, ghastly pale.

Hengwen leisurely rose to his feet. "Looks like you still remember this humble one."

The innkeeper looked left and right. "So both young masters actually know each other. No wonder Daozhang went to such efforts to cure the young master. Haha, haha, turns out all of you are old acquaintances. You must have an affinity with one another indeed if you have met in my humble inn, haha."

This Daoist priest had to play an outsider, so I remained standing where I was.

Mu Ruoyan looked at Hengwen and said in a hoarse voice, "You..."

"It is truly an affinity that has brought us together here," Hengwen said. "Bouncing back to health after a severe illness is like getting a new lease on life. Since everything that occurred is in the past, let's just treat it as history of a former life. Forget about it all, and live well in the future."

Cupping his hands, he then said to the innkeeper, "May I trouble you to move the dishes downstairs? The Daozhang and I shall have our meals in the hall. Let this young master rest."

The innkeeper acknowledged the request, and the waiters nimbly tidied the plates away. The fox jumped off the chair and slipped into Hengwen's arms.

Beside me, Hengwen whispered, "Are you going to stay here or dine downstairs with me?"

Mu Ruoyan's gaze followed over, his eyes glinting. Something about them looked very different from earlier. I felt a chill run down my spine. Raising a palm, I said, "Benefactor, please have a good rest. This humble Daoist shall take my leave." I followed Hengwen out the door, and in the instant I turned, I saw Mu Ruoyan's cheerless eyes.

The potency of the fox's jinluo lingzhi was extremely good. I was beginning to regret curing Tianshu.

At dusk, while Hengwen and I were dining in the brightly lit downstairs hall, Mu Ruoyan came out and wandered around.

He wore a long, light-blue gown, walking very quietly but steadily. His gown fluttered around his body. It was clear at a glance that he had not merely recovered from a severe illness, but had bounced back to his feet.

Mu Ruoyan came down the stairs and headed for the hall. I stood, raised my palm, and asked after him. Meanwhile, Hengwen nodded his head. After Mu Ruoyan returned the greeting, he seated himself at a table beside ours. A waiter attended to him as he placed his order.

Hengwen was not particularly talkative, so this immortal lord was a little glum. I sat opposite Hengwen, while Furball crouched on a chair next to him, looking the very picture of guilelessness as he ate the scrambled egg Hengwen fed him.

Hengwen picked the chopped green onion out of the egg, and used his chopsticks to move the pieces to fox's plate one at a time. The fox ate them, one mouthful at a time, and after it was done, it licked its whiskers. It looked up at Hengwen, wagging its tail.

This immortal lord watched nonchalantly, and ate my porridge with indifference.

From time to time, I picked at the autumnal garland chrysanthemum leaves in my food.

The waiters stood to the side and watched too. "Young Master, you're too amazing. This beast is so obedient before you. The way it eats is so interesting."

I sneered to myself, *It'd be even more interesting if it transforms into its human form and exhibits its pectoral muscles—imagine, a fully grown man wagging his tail with his head lowered.*

There were a few guests staying at the Riverfront Inn. Everyone in the hall was looking at the fox, as was Mu Ruoyan.

At a table in the corner, one of several rotund men—merchants, they looked like—said, "Do you two gentlemen have a miracle-working method to taming a wild creature into such an obedient animal?"

Hengwen smiled mildly, while I answered, "Oh, no, you flatter us. It's actually just a small trick."

The fox glanced very disrespectfully at this immortal lord out of the corner of its eyes.

I added, "It's actually easy to tame wildlife. All you need is a bowl of water blessed with the ashes of a talisman from this humble Daoist, and their wild nature will be immediately eradicated."

159

The others from that particular table all addressed the rotund man who spoke as "Squire Dong." Squire Dong eyed this immortal lord skeptically and said, "This humble one has traveled over most of the world, yet I never knew that the Daoist arts could still be used in such a way."

I held my beard and said nothing. Not speaking at the appropriate time was the hallmark of a great master.

Immediately, a waiter chimed in, "Squire Dong might not know this, but this Guangyun Daozhang is indeed a great master. Look at the young master at this table. Guangyun Daozhang was the one who cured him using only a dose of medicine. He is truly a miraculous physician, capable of bringing the dying back to life."

Squire Dong and his fellow rotund men were instantly filled with deep reverence, and repeatedly apologized for the lack of manners. Likewise, I repeatedly deflected their praises with humility.

Then Squire Dong said, "Daozhang has such a brilliant air, like that of an immortal, so you must also be adept in the art of subduing evil and resurrecting the dead."

Seeing as it was straying far off track, I could only say, "Occasionally, when there is unrest in a residence haunted by evil beings, this humble Daoist could muster my meager abilities to expel them. As for resurrecting the dead, I wouldn't dare to boast of it. Life, death, and fate naturally fall under the jurisdiction of the underworld. This humble Daoist has yet to break free of the six paths of existence to attain immortality, so how could I dare to talk big about life and death?"

Squire Dong, admiring this immortal lord's humility, sighed in appreciation.

Hengwen idly pointed around the plate with the tip of his chopsticks. He had fed the entire plate of egg to the fox, and all that was left were the black fungus mushrooms, chopped green onions, and ginger that he had picked out earlier.

As I reached my chopsticks out toward the black fungus mushrooms, I heard Mu Ruoyan say, "As they say, karmic affinity begins at birth and perishes at death. But then, where do those souls that come to collect their debts, and those spirits with fury and resentment, come from? Or is that just a rumor?"

I picked up the black fungus mushrooms to put into my bowl of porridge, considering how to respond when Hengwen suddenly chimed in, "It's really hard to say when it comes to such matters. Whether it's a rumor or not remains to be seen. Living in this world can be likened to a person staying in a house. When the house is not livable anymore, that's when death and the extinction of affinity are imminent. But even if your affinity with this house has ended, you might still have some affinity with another house." He pointed the chopsticks at me. "For instance, this Daozhang said he won't come back from the dead, but perhaps he might swap over to another house to live in."

Hengwen, are you trying to tear down my façade and sabotage me?

All at once, Mu Ruoyan's eyes latched onto this immortal lord. I let out a dry laugh, "Young Master Zhao's joke is so witty, this humble Daoist is at a loss as to how to react."

Hengwen set down his chopsticks, and the fox sprang onto his lap and yawned. Then Hengwen excused himself, and swaggered up the stairs with the fox in his arms.

Thus, I also returned to my room.

In the hallway, I hesitated whether to return to my room or head to Hengwen's. After a moment of pondering, I went to Hengwen's room, and pushed the door open. Hengwen was seated at the table, drinking tea. I joined him. Hengwen lifted the teapot, and I picked up a cup and held it before the spout.

"You want to save even this bit of energy?" Hengwen quipped.

"Pour a cup for me, and I will refill the remaining tea for you," I said with a smile.

Hengwen scoffed, and filled the teacup in my hand to the brim.

I glanced at the fox lying on the bed. "Furball, I have a matter to discuss with you. Lead the way tonight. Qingjun and I will make a trip to your cave, and release the Shan person whom you've locked up."

The fox jumped to the ground, transformed into its human form, and stood leaning against the bedpost with a frown on his face. The wound Shan Shengling had inflicted on his arm was still there. The fox must still be feeling indignant, and his face turned livid on hearing that I was telling him to let his prisoner go.

"Qingjun and I descended to the mortal world for official business on orders," I explained, "and the person you've locked up just so happened to be a key player. Truth be told, this immortal lord has some feud with this person. If not for Heaven's decree holding me back, this immortal lord would even be willing to build a fire to roast him for supper, if you so wanted."

The fox folded his arms, reticent until Hengwen said, "Song Yao Yuanjun is telling you the truth. Although this is unfair to you, we still hope you can help us."

The fox immediately answered meekly, "Since Qingjun wishes to release him, I'll let him go tonight." He looked like he was willing to lay down his life for him.

And so, in the middle of the night, the fox and I set off for its lair. Hengwen lifted my real form out and said he would not be going since his present appearance was similar to his real looks, and he feared that it would complicate matters if Shan Shengling were to find out.

On hearing that Hengwen was not going, the fox pulled a glum face. He led this immortal lord to his mountain stronghold, saying nothing the entire way.

The night was dark, and the wind, swift. There happened to be a tailwind when we set off, so riding the wind and the clouds took us only a little more than a quarter of an hour to arrive at the fox's mountain home.

The fox and I landed halfway up the mountain, lush with tall tree shadows and thick, long grass. I asked the fox for the name of this mountain, and the fox answered me in a frosty tone, "Mount Xuanqing."

Xuan as in Xuan Li, Qing as in Hengwen Qingjun.

This immortal lord cringed for a moment. "What was this mountain called before you gave it this name?"

"Mount Kuteng," the fox answered resentfully. After walking a few steps with his head lowered, he asked, "How did you know I changed the name?"

I did not answer.

Geez, when this immortal lord was out of love and reciting poems in the mortal world, you were still out there somewhere stealing some households' chickens.

The fox's cave entrance was concealed within the vine leaves climbing all over the mountain cliff, along a long and narrow stone path that meandered its way inside. This was a fox that knew how to live it up. He had dug a channel of water across the road ahead, with a stone bridge above it. After crossing the bridge, we rounded the edge of a stone screen. The fox raised his sleeve, and flicked forth a flame that lit up torches on the four walls, revealing another scenic abode: A fairly spacious stone cave that had been decorated to resemble a furnished hall. There were fruits and vegetables, wine and snacks displayed on the stone table, and the stone chairs were padded with satin and brocade cushions. To the right, there was even a screen with a colored glaze, inlaid with cowries.

I was just about to praise the fox's stone lair, but the fox, standing in the center of the hall, frowned and muttered, "Something's amiss." He then strode to the other side of the screen.

This immortal lord followed suit. There was another stone path with countless forks behind the screen. The fox moved swiftly ahead, and I was close behind. After turning several bends, he opened a stone door and entered yet another cave. The fox raised his hand to light up a torch. There was only a bare pillar in the cave, and broken pieces of chains lay scattered at the foot of the pillar.

From the looks of it, the fox had locked Shan Shengling up here.

I looked at the scattered chains with a frown. Who would have known Shan Shengling was brave and strong enough to break free and flee?

The fox ground his teeth, and hissed something hatefully before dashing from the cave. He turned seventy or eighty bends along the stone path before opening yet another stone door. A gust of wind from outside blew its way in. I raised my head, and to my surprise, was able to see the dark sky. This place was a fissure in the mountain, which the fox had made into an inner courtyard.

A small, black figure sprang from the shadows and leaped straight toward us.

A whimper of a sob followed as the figure buried itself into the fox's arms and squirmed for a bit. Then it transformed into a young, innocent boy who wrapped his arms around the fox and bawled, "Oh, Great King! You're finally back!" A sob. "Someone powerful came and rescued the guy locked up in the cave! Honghong, Qiujiu, Huahua, Xiaoqi, and the others... that person put them all in a cage..." *Sobs.* "I-I-I managed to hide myself, though it wasn't easy. I was so afraid," *sob, sob,* "oh, Great King..."

The boy burrowed his head into the fox's arms, crying and

smearing his tears and snot as he recounted what had happened.

When he finally stopped, the fox led the both of us back to the stone hall. The boy shrank into a chair, still sobbing and sniffling while sneaking glances at this immortal lord. He had a pair of lush green eyes, and the two pointed ears at the top of his head still had grayish-brown stripes. So it seemed that this child had originally been a mountain cat spirit.

The little mountain cat spirit was unclear in his speech, speaking incoherently. He stammered for a long time before he managed to give a rough account of what had happened.

Supposedly, someone with a horsetail whisk had barged into the cave this morning, abducted Shan Shengling, and captured a dozen or so of the demons and spirits residing here. There were pretty vixens and other minor demons whose cultivation was not high enough. The mountain cat's cultivation was the shallowest, and his demonic aura was the weakest. It was only by burrowing into a crevice in a corner that he got to preserve his little life.

The fox's expression was livid, and his gaze, harsh. This immortal lord knew that he and Shan Shengling were now sworn enemies.

The little mountain cat could not clearly describe the appearance of the guest with the horsetail whisk who had saved Shang Shengling. After some back and forth, all he said was that he "had no beard," "looked like a Daoist priest," and "wore blue clothes." Then he aggrievedly extended his two injured front paws to show the fox.

This immortal lord listened and looked, but I had to say, "Since the man in the cave is already gone, my matter here is considered done. It's late now, and I have to return to the inn." I looked at the fox and the little mountain cat. "What are your—both of your plans?"

The fox said nothing. The little mountain cat huddled up and shrank back in the chair.

The fox's tiny mountain stronghold of demons and spirits was now empty, and he looked rather miserable as he sat there with his head hanging.

There was no knowing if the powerful guest with the horse-tail whisk would come barging back in. The fox and this little mountain cat were both in peril.

This immortal lord was actually an easily soft-hearted person. Seeing such a sight now, my heart could not help but soften a *tiny* bit.

Just this *tiny* bit, and by the time I returned to Hengwen's room, I had behind me a fox and a gray-striped mountain cat.

The fox jumped onto Hengwen's lap, let out a whimper, coiled itself, and lay down, downcast.

Hengwen stroked the top of the fox's head. The fox looked up and licked Hengwen's hand.

The little mountain cat leaped onto the corner of the quilt at the end of the bed and lay there, smacking its lips and licking its injured front paws.

I truly regretted this *tiny* softening of my heart.

Chapter Eleven

Mu Ruoyan and Shan Shengling would meet on an afternoon when the wind and waves raged and the rain poured in torrents.

By the next day, I had brought the fox and the mountain cat cub to settle down in the inn.

Hengwen and I happened to be in the hall downstairs having our lunch when someone rapped hard on the inn's tightly shut doors. The waiter opened the doors a crack, and the gale blew the rainwater into the inn, sending splatters of froth onto the stir-fried vegetarian dish before me.

A drenched figure wearing a bamboo hat strode across the threshold, just as a sudden clap of thunder detonated in the sky.

This fellow with the bamboo hat took off that bamboo hat, raising the fox's hackles.

This sharp-eyed immortal lord moved swiftly to hold down the fox.

Shan Shengling stood tall and proud in the hall, and surveyed his surroundings with his bright eyes. His eyes fell upon this table and landed on Hengwen.

All at once, his eyes narrowed, and his eyebrows twitched almost imperceptibly. His expression, however, did not change in the slightest, never once betraying his feelings.

Hengwen politely flashed him a half-smile. Nanming Dijun was indeed something. After returning Hengwen's smile in kind, his electric gaze immediately swept over to this immortal lord's face.

This immortal lord initially meant to raise a palm in greeting, but both of my hands were occupied with the struggling fox, so I could only give a nod. Shan Shengling's gaze passed nonchalantly over the fox.

Just then, the innkeeper rushed over, bowing at the waist. "Master Chen, you're finally back. We will prepare hot water and a change of clothes for you right away. Would you like a jar of wine first to warm yourself up?"

This innkeeper is really so clueless, currying for favor with bath water and warming wine, I thought. *Other than that frail scholar who's his lover in the room up there, is there room for anything else in his heart right now? Yet of all things you could have brought up, you just had to omit him.*

As expected, Shan Shengling spoke, "How has that Young Master Yan upstairs been these few days?"

It was then the innkeeper suddenly saw the light. As he answered, "Good, good," he had the waiter lead the way. He then apologized for the unsatisfactory service, saying they had been a poor host to that other young master, so would Master Chen please forgive them?

Shan Shengling took big strides up the stairs. He had only just reached the midway mark when he braked to a stop and looked straight ahead.

Mu Ruoyan stood at the end of those stairs, gripping the railing tightly with one hand. Two pairs of eyes locked as they gazed at each other.

Such a sight was immeasurably touching.

And incredibly mushy.

So mushy that even the fox could not stand it. He twitched beneath my hands and went still.

After trading gazes in silence for a moment, Shan Shengling asked Mu Ruoyan, "Are you feeling better these days?"

"Much better now," Mu Ruoyan answered.

Shan Shengling uttered an "Oh," strode up the stairs, and returned to the room with Mu Ruoyan. The rest of their conversation was inaudible.

We returned to the room after our meals, and as soon as the door was bolted, the little mountain cat lunged over. "Great King, Great King! I-I saw the man whom you locked up in the cave… That man, he…"

The fox shifted into his human form, voice icy. "I've already seen him." His fists were clenched tight, and his eyes had a murderous gleam in them. The enmity brought on by the capture of the demons and spirits from his cave ran as deep as the sea. He must be itching to spring over next door and flay Shan Shengling alive.

This immortal lord had no choice but to advise Furball to keep calm. Shan Shengling had returned alone to the inn, and we still had no idea who the person who had captured an entire cave of demons alive was. Nanming had quite a few good friends in the Heavenly Court. Could they possibly dare to defy the Jade Emperor's decree to help Nanming down here in the mortal world? So I said, "We still don't know where your lair of demons is locked up. If you act without careful consideration and hurt Nanming, your little demons might very well end up losing their lives. Let's not act rashly for the time being."

Furball clenched his fists so hard that they cracked. He stood still by the table.

I opened the door and shouted for a plate of fried crucian carp—lunch for the mountain cat. The waiter clicked his tongue and marveled, "Daozhang, you sure have a good appetite. You just had your lunch, and now you want a snack."

I laughed. "Just something to aid digestion."

In the afternoon, Shan Shengling came knocking on this immortal lord's door. He had already taken a bath and changed into a set of dry, fresh clothes. His cheeks were slightly sunken, no surprise given his days of captivity in the fox's cave. Still, he was full of spirit and energy.

On entering the room, he cupped his hands and said, "Daozhang, I have already heard of how you've miraculously saved Yan Zimu from death. Yan Zimu is this humble one's sworn brother, and so I've come to offer my thanks."

His gaze that was as cutting as blades coolly sized up this immortal lord. With both hands, he held out a red paper envelope. "This is but a modest token of gratitude. Please do not turn it down, Daozhang."

I raised a palm, and said, "Benefactor, you're too polite. It was merely some herbal prescription. As a Daoist, this humble one ought not to accept money from the material world. But seeing as you're sincere, this humble Daoist shall regard it as your donation to the art of Daoism and accept it for the time being." I did not stand on ceremony at all as I accepted it and squeezed it in my hand. It was heavy, perhaps a gold bar.

"It seems to me that Daozhang and that young master next door are fellow travelers?" Shan Shengling asked.

I smoothly made up a story. "That's right. The young master is very fond of the art of Daoism. He wishes to find a quiet spot to cultivate, so he travels with this humble Daoist. We often study the art of elixirs together."

"So the Daoist master is skilled in the art of concocting elixir pills," Shan Shengling said.

"Not exactly," I said. "Actually, this humble Daoist is more adept in divining the future and reading fengshui. The middle of your forehead is full, and your bone structure is refined. It's the face of a comfortable and distinguished station in life, and one with such a face is blessed with ancestral blessings and a peaceful, carefree life. Benefactor, would you like this humble Daoist to divine a fortune for you and read your luck in recent days?"

Shan Shengling retracted his gaze. "This humble one is a little tired today. Perhaps on another date." He turned to leave.

I took a large, dramatic stride forward. "Benefactor, do you really not want me to tell your fortune? This humble Daoist's divination art was personally imparted by Taishang Laojun himself in a dream. One telling costs only ten coins. Since this humble Daoist is acquainted with your sworn brother, then just eight coins will do. I can additionally read a character to tell your fortune. What do you think?"

Shan Shengling answered that he would surely have his fortune read another day and strode away.

I heaved a long sigh and closed the door.

Behind me, a voice said, "I'll fork out twenty coins. May I ask of Daozhang to divine my fortune?"

I turned. Hengwen was all grins as he sat by the table. I dragged over a chair to sit beside him, and picked up the teapot to pour his cup to the brim. "Do you want King Wen's divination with copper coins or Guiguzi's divination with eight characters?"

"Is it not Song Yao Yuanjun's divination?" Hengwen asked.

Finally, I could not refrain from laughing. "You sure are a carefree one. Instead of watching Furball in the room, you come and watch the show here."

"Those few words of yours had quite the impact on him. I don't think he will act rashly," Hengwen said. "The entire lair of demons had been taken captive. Both of them looked so pitiful, I left them in the other room to calm down. Shan Shengling just so happened to come knocking, and I couldn't resist the urge to come and watch." He drank a mouthful of tea. "Your act as a Daoist priest is quite convincing. You are looking more and more like a cultivator."

"Of course," I said smugly. "I had my fortune told all day long when I was in the mortal world, having them read from countless fortune-telling stalls, so much that I can do better than those who had just joined the trade. If I were to violate the rules of Heaven someday and get banished back to the mortal world, I'd really go and be a fortune teller. Business is guaranteed to be good."

Holding his cup, Hengwen shook his head. "More like you've gotten addicted to playing a Daoist priest. I've heard that all mortals love fortune-telling. Like how you used to have your fortune told all the time back then. What did you ask about?"

"Didn't I tell you before?" I said. "When I was seven years old, my father invited some master from the mountain to divine my fortune. That master said I had great luck and would get to enjoy a very rare blessing, but that I was doomed to a fate of eternal solitude. I refused to believe this, so I went all over to have my fortune told. And yet, there was nothing to be said at all whenever it came to my marriage."

Bringing this up made me sigh again. This immortal lord had been seven years of age and already cognizant of many things. I still remembered Steward Xu's daughter, Fang-niang, a little maiden about twelve or thirteen years old at that time. I had liked her very much. I was just planning to tell my father that I was going to marry her as my wife after I grew up, when the old Daoist priest dealt me a blow so hard I saw stars.

But that Daoist priest's jinx of a mouth did indeed prove accurate, and Fang-niang married the son of a merchant at fourteen. Indignant, I had run to ask her why she forgot all those affections I had showered on her—osmanthus cakes, puff pastries, and walnut cookies. Fang-niang petted the top of my head and said, "Young Master, you are still ignorant of the ways of the world. And besides, how could a person like me dream of climbing the social ladder by associating with you?" I had watched helplessly as Fang-niang got into the red sedan and was carried away with great fanfare.

My father had also arranged a betrothal for me. She was the precious daughter of a minister. The matchmaker said she was a ravishing beauty, and her eight characters and almanac readings were extremely compatible with mine; she and I were a match made in heaven. In the end, she fell in love with the Third Prince's heir, and one moonless, windy night, the both of them brazenly eloped.

I got engaged again, this time to the daughter of the emperor's brother-in-law. She eloped with her older cousin.

Another engagement to the Commandery Princess of a Commandery Prince. The emperor took a fancy to her and acquired her for his harem.

To make it up to me, the emperor bestowed upon me the hand of his younger sister, the Eighth Princess. She had an illicit affair with a young vice minister, and even got pregnant with his child.

I had loitered around the pleasure quarters and fell in love at first sight with the top courtesan. I poured all my love and sincerity into it, but how did it turn out? She still ended up becoming lovers with a poor scholar.

It was completely by a fluke that I became an immortal and indeed got to enjoy a blessing that the common people would never get to experience.

Every prediction of the old Daoist had proven itself to be true. So one could not help but believe in this thing called fate.

Hengwen yawned. "All right, all right. I get it. I get how miserable and forlorn you are. I've been listening to you for so many thousands of years, my ears have become callused. Can't you change your wording? You are always harping on and on about how you are doomed to a fate of eternal solitude. Are you not happy being an immortal in heaven?"

"I am," I answered. "But you were born an immortal, so you don't know the power of this thing called love. Once you have a taste of it, you'll never forget it. Why else would Tianshu and Nanming next door be reduced to such a state today instead of being their exalted lordships?"

"Oh, that makes sense," Hengwen said as he turned the teacup. "Interesting, how interesting. If the Jade Emperor were to hear you, he would surely take it as you have still not rid yourself of your mortal roots and expel you back to the mortal world."

But I was really regretting blabbing on so much. I grabbed Hengwen's sleeve and said, "Whether the Jade Emperor hears me or not is of secondary importance. I was merely just spouting nonsense. Don't you think of finding someone to try it with just because you find it interesting."

Hengwen patted me on my shoulder and reassured me with a smile. "Don't worry. I won't find someone else to try it with."

It was getting dark. When we went downstairs for our meals, I casually asked about Mu Ruoyan and Shan Shengling. The waiter replied that they had already eaten and gone back to their respective rooms.

The fox and mountain cat were still stricken over their fellow demons, so we simply left them in Hengwen's room to grieve, while Hengwen and I moved to my room. I pondered it over in my mind, but I still could not figure out who rescued Nanming. Then it occurred to me—Nanming would surely tell Tianshu the whole story now that he had gone and returned. It was likely he would not keep Tianshu in the dark about these matters.

I conferred with Hengwen about spying in Nanming's room.

Shan Shengling's room was at the end of the corridor.

Tianshu's room was beside it, and this immortal lord's room was right next to Tianshu's. Hengwen lifted my real form out. Concealed in midair, we headed for our destination, but we never expected to take the long way round to Nanming's room only to find it empty. He must be in Tianshu's room.

So Hengwen and I entered Tianshu's room.

And what a sight greeted us.

Mu Ruoyan and Shan Shengling were entwined together, about to, *cough*, stir up a storm under the sheets.

Mu Ruoyan's back was pressed up against the bedpost. All that remained on his body was a thin robe partially opened at the bosom. His eyes were partially shut, and he was gasping slightly. Meanwhile, Shan Shengling gnawed on Mu Ruoyan's neck even as one of his hands slowly removed the latter's robe, and his other hand wandered down...

Amitabha. This immortal lord has really been an immortal far too long. To think I had forgotten about the most inopportune time to come calling.

"Huh, they're so enthusiastic with their dual cultivation, aren't they?" Hengwen remarked.

I hurriedly dragged Hengwen Qingjun away and crashed back into our room. "What a sin, what a sin. Mortals who see this will get styes in their eyes for sure."

"This lord here is an immortal," Hengwen said. "Besides, you and I entered purely by coincidence, and we only had just the one look."

I sat down silently in front of the bed.

Hengwen waved his worn folding fan. "There's nothing to feel uncomfortable about. Don't tell me you never did it as a mortal."

I let out a dry cough. "I have, but it was all with women... which is slightly different from this sort of, *cough*, cultivating..."

"Mm, yeah," Hengwen concurred. "I've seen illustrations in

the books. They are indeed a little different."

Shocked, I jumped to my feet. "In the books? What books?! Why would you be looking at them?!"

Oh, good lord. If the Jade Emperor were to discover that Hengwen Qingjun had returned with his mind choked full of obscene stuff after this one trip to the mortal realm, he would surely send a flash of lightning right onto my head and obliterate me to ashes.

"Why are you so startled?" Hengwen said. "Since I'm in charge of the instruction of literary ethics in the world, I naturally have to look at all kinds of books. Back then, when I was at Dongjun's manor, I had nothing to do, so I went to the marketplace to buy a few illustration books and flipped through them, wanting to see how dual cultivation was done."

He felt around his sleeves and fished out a tiny object in his palm. In an instant, the object enlarged into a stack of books with ink-blue covers. He lifted them and patted each before setting them on the table.

I reached out for one of the books to flip through, and saw stars—it was erotica.

What's more, it was homoerotica of men thick in the act.

Back when I was a mortal, I had seen my fair share of erotica. My closest friends and I often commented on the books and appreciated them together. We even traded our rare editions.

However, enticing Hengwen Qingjun to look at erotica was a crime that was no joking matter in the Heavenly Court. I was still comfortable in my role as an immortal, and I had no wish to be escorted up the Immortal Execution Terrace to be struck by lightning.

I broke out in a cold sweat looking at the books.

"It was only after looking that I realized that dual cultivation was indeed an art that calls for careful study," Hengwen remarked in a particularly relaxed manner. "A pity the illustrations weren't well drawn and were a little of a turnoff."

"That's because you bought the common ones on the market," I could not help but say. "Those kinds are all crudely drawn. There's nothing novel about them. The real, rare editions cannot be bought from the marketplace bookshops. You have to go through special channels to get your hands on them. The illustrations in *those* are what I'd call fascinating."

"Oh?" Hengwen said with great zest.

I felt like smacking this damn mouth of mine.

Nanming and Tianshu, having not seen each other for a long time, were thick in the throes of passion, and by the time Hengwen and I blew out the lamps to go to bed, the sound of activity next door was reverberating over in bursts.

The creaking bed board.

Mu Ruoyan's intermittent moans.

The sounds of which made this immortal lord feel restless of mind and unsettled of heart. Fortunately, Guangyunzi's body was lying ramrod straight on the ground, putting the brake to many a number of sinful desires.

Staring at Guangyunzi, I calmed my nerves and breathing. Beside me, Hengwen asked, "What are you doing, craning your neck and poking your head out from bed?"

"Lust is in the air," I said, "and Hengwen Qingjun lies beside me. I fear my immortal roots will waver, and I will commit a great sin. So I'm looking at Guangyunzi to still my mind."

Hengwen chuckled. "The sight of the old man lying on the ground does indeed have that calming effect. Keep on looking, then."

I heard him roll over and moved no further. He had probably fallen asleep.

Looking at Guangyunzi gradually exhausted me, and I, too, fell asleep.

And then I had a dream.

I rarely dreamed after I became immortal, and this dream was exceptionally different.

In my daze, I stood amidst a grove of peach blossom trees. The blooming brilliance of the peach blossom surpassed that of heaven's rosy clouds. In the inner reaches of the mist, an indistinct figure stood, and as I approached, he turned his head back, stupefying me.

What an immortal dreamed was his true desire. I understood I was in a dream right now, and when I saw him, I understood that this dream was my one true desire.

I could smother this want, but I could not deceive myself. What I was unsure of was when I started to even have this kind of desire.

Perhaps it all began several thousand years ago, when I saw him from afar in the heavenly palace of heaven. Distinguished and refined, he was so near before my eyes, yet so far beyond my reach.

And yet, I could not help but want to get closer.

For several thousands of years, I had lived a carefree life, filled with gratitude toward Heaven. I had originally been doomed to a fate of eternal solitude, unable to seek what I so willfully sought. But I got to see him often, and for that, I was content.

In any case, I was an immortal who had become one by a fluke, and I had excuses even if I was unable to break clean of my mortal roots. It was just like the time before my ascension, when I clearly knew that I could not have the moon in my hands, and yet there were times I really wanted to pluck it from the sky.

And the dream, at this moment, was a reflection of my filthy heart.

Since this was a dream of my true desire, I could let myself go, to my heart's content.

I hugged the person before me and kissed him.

What were dreams for? They were for kissing lips I did not dare to kiss, removing clothes I did not dare to remove.

Doing deeds I could never do as an immortal.

It was all worth it, I thought the very instant I lifted his waist. Even if the Jade Emperor were to reduce me to ashes with a strike of lightning, it was all worth it.

Even though this was only a dream, I had no regrets.

Before I woke, I could remember feeling immensely completed. As I embraced him in my arms under the rosy clouds—like peach blossoms—I told him I had, in truth, liked him for several thousand years.

That I had been thinking of him for several thousand years.

As he leaned against my shoulder, he softly said, "I, too, have been thinking of you for several thousand years."

And then, I woke up.

The moment I opened my eyes, I saw the canopy of the bed. I turned my head to the left, saw the empty quilt and pillow, then turned my head to the right and saw Guangyunzi lying on the ground.

Hengwen, rested and refreshed, was waiting in his room to have breakfast with me.

Furball was crouching gloomily on the stool, while the mountain cat was lying sorrowfully by the bed.

"What sweet dream did you have last night?" Hengwen asked. "When I left, you were grinning like a fool, and you wore an obscene expression."

I let out two dry laughs. "I dreamed that the Jade Emperor gave me a promotion."

Chapter Twelve

It had been a long time since I had last seen Mingge Xingjun. I missed him very much.

After several days of strong winds and heavy rains, the sky surprised us by clearing up. The blue dome of heaven that had been washed by the rain for several days shone bright, the fiery, dazzling sun hanging high up above. It was cloudless and windless.

I opened the window and complimented on what a fine day it was, and the waiter who entered to refill the tea added, "Right? It has been raining continuously, and the sky finally cleared up. Quite a number of guests have checked out of their rooms this morning to head to the ferry crossing. Even that master who had just returned yesterday and the gentleman whom you've cured have just gone to check out of their rooms."

This immortal lord anxiously went to confer with Hengwen, bringing along my thoughts of Mingge.

"Old Man Mingge used to come and check on me two or three times a day when I'd just descended to the mortal world. He was so diligent then. Why has he been slacking lately? There's not even a glimpse of him to be seen. Shan Shengling has fled with Tianshu. Do we follow them or not?!"

"The Heavenly Court is about to hold the Taiqing Doctrine Dialogue, and the key to the Heavenly Gate has not been found," Hengwen offered, "so perhaps Mingge Xingjun is busy with these matters, and overlooked what's happening on earth."

Hengwen's point enlightened this immortal lord. Right, Old Man Mingge loved to perform meritorious deeds before the Jade Emperor. With how busy Heaven was now, he would definitely wait for his opportunity to grab whatever merit he could amass. He would leave this immortal lord out to dry for the time being.

I looked at Hengwen, still feeling a little worried. "Don't you need to return to the Heavenly Court if there's a Taiqing Doctrine Dialogue?"

The Taiqing Doctrine Dialogue was a gathering to discuss the doctrines of Daoism and Buddhism. Taking place once every sixty years, the Heavenly Court and the Western Paradise of Tathagata took turns to host it. It was only sixty years ago that I had the qualifications to attend this meeting, and even so, I had been there as one of the immortals to observe from the side and make up the numbers. On the other hand, Hengwen Qingjun was a key participant of this gathering. In the past, whenever Hengwen would attend, I, being lonely in the Heavenly Court, would head over to the Moon Palace to drink with the woodcutter Wu Gang. After I started attending the gathering myself, Wu Gang probably only had that Jade Rabbit to drink with.

The doctrine dialogue sixty years ago had been held by the Fanjing River in Western Paradise. The scenery was a magnificent, blissful sight to behold. The sand on the riverbanks was golden, and the Bodhi trees had leaves made of jade and fresh fruits ripe for picking within reach.

The Jade Emperor was unable to attend, so the congregation, led by Taishang Laojun, was comprised of Hengwen Qingjun, the four Dijun, the eight Xingjun, and the other immortals like this immortal lord. All rode auspicious clouds in a grand procession, their sleeves billowing in the clear breeze, presenting quite the imposing sight.

Tathagata Buddha, Bhaisajyaguru the Buddha of Medicine, Maitreya the Laughing Buddha, the Virtuous and Beneficent Buddha, Buddha of Great Compassion, and the other buddhas and bodhisattvas sat upright and orderly on their lotus seats, their halos radiant.

The dialogue went on for forty-nine days. This immortal lord ate fresh fruits and listened to both sides as they engaged in discussion. It was all very interesting. Hengwen Qingjun and the Buddha of Great Compassion discussed the doctrines for three days and three nights in a brilliant display of exchange amidst a deluge of heavenly flowers. Laojun stroked his beard, while Tathagata Buddha held a flower in his hand, both smiling.

Eventually, Hengwen had emerged victorious. He cupped his hands and returned to his seat. With a wave of his sleeve, he brushed away the mountain of fruit kernels beside me and sat down breezily.

"Impressive," I had complimented in all sincerity, and Hengwen lifted the corners of his lips in mock modesty.

Nanming Dijun and Tianshu Xingjun had also attended the dialogue. Five days after Hengwen, it was Tianshu's turn to engage with the Venerable of Wholesome Dharma. Tianshu's expounding and debating of the doctrines were as gentle as water, and his discussion with Venerable proceeded slowly and gradually, without so much as an interruption.

This immortal lord had eaten one too many fresh fruits, and I was feeling slightly bloated. I rubbed my stomach to the slow lull of their tones, and as I did so, I fell sound asleep. But unfortunately for me, Hengwen Qingjun was sitting right beside me. He emerged victorious from every bit of discourse, earning from time to time a pleased glance from both the Buddha of the Western Paradise and the immortals of the Heavenly Court. In doing so, they also glimpsed this immortal lord's closed-eye repose.

When we returned, the Jade Emperor's rage at this immortal lord's disgrace of the Heavenly Court was palpable. With Nanming Dijun taking the lead, the others urged the Jade Emperor to punish me severely. Hengwen, Donghua Dijun, Bihua Lingjun, Taibai Xingjun, and some others interceded on my behalf, so the Jade Emperor summoned Tianshu Xingjun before the steps to his throne and asked, "Song Yao Yuanjun was fast asleep while you were expounding the doctrines. So in your view, how should he be punished?"

At that time, I stood in the hall, feeling rather delighted. The Jade Emperor clearly wanted to show me mercy and was trying to give me an out. By asking in such a way, even those who had a feud with me would likely do me a favor, even Tianshu.

But this immortal lord never expected Tianshu Xingjun to solemnly say to the Jade Emperor that *while sleeping during the dialogue is a small matter, this small matter is known to all the immortals in all of the heavenly realm and all the buddhas in the Western Paradise, thereby making a disgrace of the Heavenly Court. Moreover, Guangxu Yuanjun became an immortal by mere chance, but has never cultivated his Daoist nature in depth and built a firm foundation off his immortal roots. He often speaks of the secular world with longing and sentimentality. In truth, he is not suitable to be an immortal in the Heavenly Court...*

As before, he still spoke slowly and gently, like the murmuring of waters, but it gave me a chill to listen to him.

The Jade Emperor then said, "In that case, in your view, what sin should Guangxu Yuanjun be declared guilty of, and how should he be punished?"

Tianshu bowed at the foot of the jade stairs and slowly answered, "Back then, in the Pure Land of the Western Paradise, there was a venerable one whose mind wandered for a moment while Buddha was expounding the Dharma, and he was cast to the mortal realm for ten lifetimes to endure every suffering there is in the cycle of life. Today, Guangxu Yuanjun's lack of decorum before the various immortals and buddhas disgraced the Heavenly Court, and on top of that, his worldly desires have yet to be fully eradicated. In this humble immortal's view, he should be banished back to the mortal world, never to set foot in the Heavenly Court ever again."

His words were like five strikes of lightning crashing down right on my head, each blow so hard that it rendered me dumbstruck and frozen stiff.

Hengwen strode a step toward the front of the hall. "To *think* it is such a great sin. In that case, this perpetrator has to step forth and confess to my wrongdoing, lest the Supreme One wrongfully punish Song Yao Yuanjun."

The Jade Emperor naturally had to ask why, and Hengwen grinned as he lowered his head and answered, "It was all my fault. Before the dialogue, I had a bet with Song Yao—I mean, Guangxu Yuanjun. I've always made light of Guangxu Yuanjun for chancing on immortality and his lack of proficiency in the art of Daoism. Meanwhile, the doctrines of Daoism and Buddhism are all extensive and profound. To put it blasphemously, I occasionally find them dry and dull each time I listen to them. For that reason, I made a bet with Guangxu Yuanjun that he surely could not refrain from falling asleep during the dialogue. Guangxu Yuanjun's expression was solemn as he told me, 'The dialogue is an excellent opportunity to comprehend the art of Dao. In allowing me to participate, the Jade Emperor has bestowed upon me great kindness. This humble immortal can't even begin to relish every sentence I listen to, so how would I fall asleep?!' So he bet thirty jars of osmanthus wine that Yuezi personally brewed. Donghua Dijun was present then. He is our witness."

Donghua Dijun held up his sleeve to cover a cough. "To

report to the Jade Emperor, this humble immortal is indeed a witness. Oh, Jinxing, I remember you were there too. You also witnessed it, right—?"

Taibai Xingjun nodded indiscriminately. "Right, right. This humble immortal witnessed it too. I'm a… *cough*, witness too."

Hengwen continued, "Guangxu Yuanjun looked so sanctimonious when he placed the bet with me, and it left a sour taste in my mouth. I didn't expect him to sit erect with his eyes shining during the dialogue. I'm afraid I don't have that great of a prestige to ask for thirty jars of Yuezi's osmanthus wines, and in a momentary desire to win…" He coughed once and put on a pained look as he continued, "Seeing Guangxu Yuanjun having such a merry time eating the fruits, I dredged up two sleep-inducing bugs and flicked them into the flesh of his fruits, and so…"

When he spoke to this point, he turned around and bowed to me. "I'm truly sorry. I never expected I would cause Yuanjun to be slapped with such a serious crime. I'm very, very sorry."

Seeing Hengwen shouldering all the blame for me, I almost shed tears. Where in the world would I still be able to utter a word?

Nanming Dijun, Tianshu, and the rest all went silent. With Hengwen Qingjun stepping forth to take the blame and Donghua Dijun and Taibai Xingjun bearing witness, to refute was to accuse these three exalted lords of lying to shield me. If they were to argue any further, no doubt the situation would deteriorate.

Just as we were at a stalemate, the Queen Mother emerged from the rear hall and said, "He merely slept during a dialogue. While it is admittedly a breach of decorum, I don't think it is that serious of a crime. The doctrines discussed during dialogues are profound; even I occasionally find it tiring, let alone Song Yao. Those of us who cultivate immortality stress being true to self and going along with the flow; it is distinctly different from those who study the teachings of Buddha. As they say, we shall cultivate our carefree Way, and they shall sit in their meditation. I don't think we have to mete out punishments according to their precepts. The Jade Emperor is wise. He naturally has his own impartial judgment."

The Jade Emperor was indeed wise. In the end, he judged Hengwen to be guilty of the crime of erroneously confessing to his sin and deceiving his superiors. Subsequently, he sentenced Hengwen to a forfeit of two month's salary and a month of self-reflection on his own sins. Donghua Dijun and Taibai Xingjun were guilty of covering up for me and deceiving their superiors, so they had half a month of salary forfeited. Meanwhile, this immortal, having breached decorum by falling asleep during the dialogue, had to self-reflect for two months.

The Jade Emperor said, "Considering that you would have wiped out your money paying the penalty for Hengwen and Donghua Xingjun, I shall not forfeit your salary."

I extolled the Jade Emperor aloud for his wisdom and magnanimity.

The Queen Mother drawled with the ghost of a smile, "Hold on. I have heard that a certain immortal had also claimed by the Fanjing River that Tathagata was truly generous to allow his fruits to be eaten as one pleases, unlike the Queen Mother in the Heavenly Court, who was so stingy she even had the heavenly soldiers guard a few peaches. I wonder if you have heard of this, Song Yao Yuanjun?"

I let out a dry laugh.

And so, this immortal lord watered the peach trees in the Queen Mother's Peach of Immortality Garden for half a year.

"The dialogue, huh," Hengwen said. "We'll talk about it again when the time comes. One day in heaven is one year on earth. By the time the dialogue rolls around, perhaps our business here would already be done, and we would have returned to the Heavenly Court."

I considered the point and sighed in agreement; a moment later, I reconsidered, and my alarm returned. "It would be terrible if Mingge became too preoccupied. He could forget all about us for four to six hours!"

Hengwen yawned. "It's nothing to worry about. Just do as you please."

"Right," I concurred. "If anything goes awry, I can just plead ignorance and say I had no other option, since Mingge didn't tell me a thing. In any case, I don't have to take responsibility."

The fox looked up from the chair at the corner of the table, cast a glance at me from the corner of his eyes, and let loose a disdainful snort.

This immortal lord shall not quibble with the likes of him.

I stood and looked out the window with my hands behind my back, pacing a few steps.

"You better follow Nanming and Tianshu," Hengwen suggested. "You still have to tail them whether Mingge returns or not."

And so, half an hour later, I hoisted my entire set of fortune-telling Daoist priest getup over my shoulders, and strode out of the Riverfront Inn with Hengwen in tow.

Hengwen set a gold ingot on the counter—pulling a smile from the innkeeper that was as bright as the sun on the hottest days of summer—as he very solicitously and personally saw us to the doorway.

The fox and the mountain cat both wanted to tag along. Feeling compassionate toward the weak, this immortal lord allowed it. The mountain cat lay on the rattan rack on my back. I initially intended to leash the fox to a rope and lead it along, which I felt was appropriate, but the fox glared at me with bloody red eyes, looking all imposing like a gentleman who would rather die than be subjected to humiliation.

Seriously? You sure didn't remember you were a man earlier when you were shamelessly gazing at Hengwen with veiled intent.

In the end, after some mediation and compromise, the fox ended up lying on the rattan rack on my back as well, with the mountain cat taking the first shelf while the fox took the second.

Two demons, both of which almost broke the tired old waist of this immortal lord.

The Riverfront Inn was less than a kilometer away from the Zhoujia Ferry Crossing. As we rushed over before the crossing began, we caught sight of the distant figures standing at the pier. The clothes of one of the tall, slender figures fluttered in the wind—Mu Ruoyan.

A white, vast expanse of water stretched far in the distance. Several small boats drifted like reed leaves.

A decade of good deeds in a past life, a shared boat in this life. So the saying went. I had been fellow immortals with Nanming and Tianshu for who knows how many decades. Of course I had garnered enough affinity with them to share their boat.

As I dashed to the pier, Shan Shengling's as-cutting-as-blades eyes immediately shot past the crowd and swept past me to land on Hengwen. From the corner of my eyes, I saw Hengwen give a polite nod. It was Mu Ruoyan who looked at me instead. I raised a palm. "What a coincidence, Benefactor."

As we were speaking, a few boats pulled up. This immortal lord's legs were agile, and seeing Shan Shengling and Mu Ruoyan step onto a boat, I immediately took a huge stride over.

"Daozhang," the boatman said, "this boat of mine is meant to specifically ferry these two gentlemen to the Pingjiang Ferry Crossing in Luyang. Please find another boat if you're heading elsewhere."

I waved my horsetail whisk. "What a coincidence. This humble Daoist is heading for Luyang too." Seeing the boatman look at me with some doubt, I hurriedly pointed my horsetail whisk behind me. "This humble Daoist is traveling with this young master. Please collect the boat fare from him."

The deck behind me made a sound as Hengwen came to stand beside me. In a soft-spoken manner, he asked, "May I be so bold as to ask the old gentleman how much for the fare to Luyang?"

The boatman's demeanor changed, and he hurriedly bowed and nodded. "No hurry, no hurry. Young Master, please take a seat in the cabin first. You can pay me at your discretion when we arrive at the place."

I stood by the cabin to let Hengwen go first, then bent to enter. The interior of the cabin was very simple, with makeshift side benches made by two planks and a worn-out wooden table in the middle.

Shan Shengling and Mu Ruoyan were seated on one side, so Hengwen and I went to the other. I rested my black banner against the table, and was just about to set down my horsetail whisk when I saw movement out of the corner of my eyes. Hengwen was making straight for the wooden plank. I reacted instantly, crying out for him to hold on. I wiped the surface of the wooden plank and lifted my hand for a look. Contrary to expectation, it was not dirty, but the wooden plank was hard, so how could I let Hengwen sit on it?

I set the rattan rack on the tabletop and took out a cloth bundle—actually a prop—from beside the mountain cat. I opened it up, laid aside the clothes and objects within, then rewrapped the outer layer into the shape of a cushion. I set it on the wooden plank and made a show of putting my palms together. "Please have a seat, Young Master."

Young Master Heng's eyebrows rose. Looking like he was enjoying this, he put on an ostentatious show of sitting down. Then, making the very picture of dignity, he pointed with his folding fan and said, "Take a seat too."

I put my palms together in a show of grace, and said, "Thank you, Young Master," then eased myself slowly onto the wooden plank. Shan Shengling and Mu Ruoyan had already taken their seats opposite us. I looked at the fox and mountain cat somewhat worriedly, fearing that these two demons could not refrain from lunging at Shan Shengling in vengeance. Fortunately, they were still able to keep their cool. The mountain cat curled up in a huddle in the rack, while the spine of the fox heaved a little.

After a moment, the fox suddenly arched his back. This immortal lord was on the alert, but the fox merely shook its fur and scuttled over onto the wooden plank between Hengwen and me. It ended up curling up on itself at Hengwen's side.

And so, Hengwen and I, and Shan Shengling and Mu Ruoyan, looked at each other from across a worn-out table.

Chapter Thirteen

There were five men maneuvering this boat: the boatman from earlier helmed the bow, and a pair of young lads rowed at the bow and stern, respectively. The boat sailed briskly, its hull swaying.

A breeze carried the damp river air into the cabin. Mu Ruoyan sat upright on the wooden plank, his clothes fluttering slightly, but his expression was a little strained.

Nanming really was inhumane. The rocking of the bed had persisted for almost all of last night, and then he had dragged Tianshu in a rush to catch the boat today. It would have been a wonder if his expression weren't strained.

I finally understood why Mu Ruoyan could be in such ill health, even as the young master of the prime minister's residence. In all probability, he had Nanming to thank for tormenting him thus.

Then again, it was *because* Tianshu loved to be tormented by Nanming that he ended up in this state. I would liken this pair to Zhou Yu and Huang Gai. One was willing to give a beating, and the other was willing to receive it.

Mu Ruoyan and Shan Shengling—these two names were connected with a red thread of fate as thick as a finger, so how could Tianshu not be willing to be tormented by Nanming?

Shan Shengling's voice suddenly said, "Are this fox and mountain cat both reared by the young master? The two seem to be rare beasts indeed."

Shan Shengling, feeling lonely during the journey, had started to strike up a conversation.

Hengwen smiled, and I said, "Thank you."

Shan Shengling continued, "Is the young master also heading for Luyang?"

"That's right," Hengwen answered. "I heard the scenery in the Southern Commandery is beautiful, and so wish to have a look."

"The situation was pressed the day before in the Prince of the Eastern Commandery's manor," Shan Shengling said. "If the young master doesn't mind after arriving at Luyang, please do me the honor of coming to my humble residence for a chat and allowing me to play the host."

"That's very kind of you, Benefactor Shan," I said.

Although Furball was all huddled up as it listened to Shan Shengling and Hengwen's exchange, the hackles on its neck were raised. Hengwen patted it on the head, and only then did the fur on its neck smooth back down. Taking advantage of the opportunity, it climbed onto Hengwen's lap.

The fox maintained itself well. Its body was plump and tender, and its fur, sleek and shiny. Snowy-white fur ruffled slightly at the mere nudge of a breeze. The tips of its pelt even seemed to carry a silvery glow, making Mu Ruoyan fix his eyes closely on it. Looking a little hesitant, he softly remarked, "That's a snow fox, right? Its fur is really beautiful."

"That's right," Hengwen replied.

"We bought it while at the inn. Who knows what it is?" I added.

The fox on Hengwen's lap twitched its ears, and Mu Ruoyan could not help but ask, "May this humble one... possibly touch it?"

"That, you'd have to ask it," Hengwen replied unhurriedly.

Mu Ruoyan got up and stretched out his hand tentatively as he came over. But the fox was a proud and unyielding one, and intentionally posturing like this at this time was likely its idea of taking liberties with Hengwen in another way to alleviate its homoerotic yearning. Moreover, Mu Ruoyan was his enemy's lover. So just when Mu Ruoyan's hand was about to touch its head, the fox defiantly cocked its head aside.

Mu Ruoyan's hand froze in midair. With a smile, he said, "Looks like it's not willing. I have been too presumptuous."

Despite those words, he could not help but reach out to the fox again. This time, the fox did not dodge him, and could only let Mu Ruoyan stroke the top of his head. Its ears twitched, then it abruptly shook its head.

Mu Ruoyan, though, smiled in delight as he retracted his hand and sat back. The fox relaxed back onto Hengwen's lap as I looked coolly on. Tugging the corners of my lips into a smile, I marveled, "Amazing. Does Benefactor Shan want to have a go and touch it too?"

The fox gave a start and rolled over, its hackles raised as it bared its sharp fangs and jumped off Hengwen's lap. With a snort, it found a spot on the wooden plank and lay down, seething with resentment.

The oars creaked as the boat swayed along at a leisurely pace.

The boatman told us we would only arrive at the Pingjiang ferry crossing come evening. Hengwen put on a show of rummaging through his sleeve as he conjured a book to read, while Mu Ruoyan, who looked unwell, sat with his eyes closed in repose. That left me and Shan Shengling to only look at each other. He fixed his gaze on the scenery over this immortal lord's head, and this immortal lord, too, looked at the scenery over his head.

Suddenly, Shan Shengling said, "I heard Daozhang is fond of divination. I wasn't able to consult you while at the inn. Would you possibly do a reading for this humble one now?"

This immortal lord braced himself. "What would you like to have read?"

"Please read my palm, Daozhang," Shan Shengling said, "and tell me about my past and future." He stretched out his left hand, and I held it by his wrist to read. His past and future had long been written in the Book of Fate by Old Man Mingge, all of which this immortal lord had committed to memory.

I closed my eyes partially. "Benefactor Shan's palm lines are peculiar. There are many things in your life that differ from the common person. Separation from parents and siblings at an early age. Much hardship in your youth. You are destined to drift from place to place all your life. In addition—" I cut myself off midway and put on a hesitant look, hemming and hawing.

"If Daozhang has anything to say, please just say it," Shan Shengling said.

"Benefactor," I said slowly, "you have an ominous fate; it's a fate that will jinx others and bring them down. Your parents and siblings, your friends and kin, all of them will be implicated. On top of that, you are destined to have no descendants. There will be no marriage in this life, only a doomed relationship."

Mu Ruoyan, who had been sitting with his eyes closed, suddenly furrowed his brows, and his body seemed to tremble.

I continued, "In addition, there will be a great calamity in store for you in the near future. Signs of it are already vaguely showing. This is no catastrophe to bat an eye at. Benefactor, you must tread with caution."

It would be a miracle if a calamity personally arranged by the Jade Emperor turns out not to be a great catastrophe. And the one creating this adversity for you is this immortal lord.

Shan Shengling's eyes gleamed. "Oh? Then does Daozhang have a way to avert this?"

For an instant, my compassion was evoked, and I decided to imitate the ways of the buddhas in the Western Paradise: Give Nanming a chance to pull himself from the brink while he still could. Let him repent for possible salvation. "Benefactor, if you are able to lay down your blade now and head into the mountains alone to cultivate the Dao, it would still be possible to ward off disaster before it's too late. After several decades of cultivating the Dao, you may be able to see the light at the end of the tunnel."

Shan Shengling laughed long and hard. "Thank you, Daozhang, for your advice." He raised his brows. "If I may be so bold as to ask after Daozhang's honorable age and where you have been cultivating the Dao all this while?"

I stroked my beard. "This humble Daoist is forty-eight years of age, and has been roaming the world all this time with no fixed place to call home."

Shan Shengling set an ingot of silver on the table. "This is the monetary reward for the divination, a token of appreciation for troubling Daozhang."

I rested my eyes on that ingot of silver and plastered on a fake smile. "Benefactor Shan, there's no need to be so polite. It's due to our good affinity that we are all traveling on the same boat. The reward is not necessary."

"Daozhang, please don't decline," Shan Shengling said. "It's only right and proper to pay for the reading. Please accept it."

I let out two dry laughs. "In that case, thank you." I then reached out to grab the silver ingot, and kept it in my sleeve.

After going on and on for so long, I was a bit parched. I fished out a water gourd from the bottom of the rattan rack, and was about to uncork it when I looked up to see Mu Ruoyan looked deeply fatigued, his lips blanched white and dry. Nanming had made Tianshu catch the boat and be on their way without clean water or dry rations. He could endure it, being the strong man he was, but how could Mu Ruoyan hold up to such a torment? Inwardly, I shook my head. Sooner or later, the body that I had nursed back to health was going to crumple apart from Shan Shengling's torment.

Holding on to the water gourd, I hesitated for a moment, but eventually, I could not bear to see him in such a state. "This humble Daoist has some clean water here. Would both benefactors like some?"

Shan Shengling voiced his thanks and asked the boatman for a teacup. He poured half a cup and took a sip first before handing it to Tianshu. Tianshu took a few sips, color returning as he thanked me. I hastened to deflect his thanks, and took up the gourd to pour myself a mouthful. Suddenly, Tianshu's face froze over, eyes fixed on the rattan rack between us.

I lowered my head for a look and got a little fright too. The mountain cat was hugging the bamboo tube for divination-telling, the very same one this immortal lord had once given to Mu Ruoyan.

I always kept that bamboo tube in my traveling bag, and upon arrival at the inn, had conveniently set it on the table. For some reason, the mountain cat spirit had taken a fancy to it. It would not do for this immortal to be staring daggers at a child over a bamboo tube, so I had simply turned a blind eye whenever the mountain cat hugged and played with it.

The mountain cat was so taken with the bamboo tube, it had refused to let go. Subsequently, it had stuffed half a tube of dried fish in it. It was perhaps out of hunger and boredom from our half-day's ride that it had dragged the tube out of the rack. It was now partially cradling it—lying flat on its side—under its stomach with its left front paw pressing down on the tube. Its right front paw, on the other hand, was digging out the dried fish it had hoarded.

Surprisingly enough, Mu Ruoyan recognized that bamboo tube. His body slowly started to relax after the initial shock; despite a distinct lack of expression on his face, he continued looking at that tube.

Seeing his unwavering gaze on itself, the mountain cat spirit shrank back and timidly cried out with a meow.

Mu Ruoyan's eyes seemed to twinkle.

The mountain cat hugged the bamboo tube to its bosom and whimpered twice more. Mu Ruoyan stood, and slowly walked to the table, where he gingerly reached out a hand to pet it on the head.

The moment his finger touched the mountain cat's head, it shrank back, but Mu Ruoyan was the reincarnation of Tianshu Xingjun, and he had the aura of an immortal which all spirits just so happened to love. The mountain cat lay still, and let Tianshu pet it a few more times, then whimpered twice more before taking the initiative to nuzzle the top of its head against Tianshu's palm.

Tianshu's hand trembled.

This immortal lord looked askance at Shan Shengling, who was watching nonchalantly. Something about this scene felt amiss; so, frowning, this immortal lord watched as well. Tianshu's expression returned to normal. The mountain cat cooed as it let him pet it.

"This cat is interesting." Tianshu asked, almost off-handedly, "Does it have a name?"

"Yes," I blurted without thinking. "Its name is A-Ming."

Hengwen rolled up the book in his hand and tapped it against his palm.

It suddenly dawned on me. *Tianshu... couldn't be... treating the mountain cat as Li Siming, could he...?*

His imagination wouldn't stretch that far, would it...?

With a dry cough, I said, "This mountain cat was caught by the waiters when it was stealing dried fishes at the inn. We redeemed it together with the fox, haha…"

Mu Ruoyan uttered an "oh," and petted it on the head again before returning to his seat on the wooden plank.

Once again, he closed his eyes.

The mountain cat mewed once, and continued to its bold dig for fish.

As the setting sun cast its red hue over the river, the boat docked at the Pingjiang Ferry Crossing.

The banks of the crossing made a grand sight: A squad of fully armored soldiers and horses standing guard kneeled to Shan Shengling, welcoming their general with the utmost respect.

This was the General Shan of the Southern Commandery's territory.

A soldier led a fiery red steed to the great general, and, kneeling, asked him to mount it. The great general politely cupped his hands at this immortal lord and Hengwen, and flipped onto the horse. Shan Shengling's subordinate had some conscience at least, having brought along a horse carriage for Mu Ruoyan to sit.

Mu Ruoyan very politely bade his farewell along with an "until we meet again."

I raised my palm in farewell, bidding Benefactor Yan to take care, with the promise that we would meet again, fate willing.

Mu Ruoyan then said, "Daozhang should already know that this humble one is Mu Ruoyan, so there's no need to address me by my fake surname in the future."

And so I once again told Benefactor Mu to take care, that we would meet again should fate decree.

Mu Ruoyan turned and climbed into the carriage, and the entire procession of people and horses galloped away, leaving trails of billowy dust in their wake.

Standing at the intersection, I said, "I wonder how far it is from here to Luyang City."

Fanning himself, Hengwen said, "There's a tea booth ahead. Let's go over for a cup of tea and ask about it."

"After sitting in the boat for an entire day, you... must be tired." I asked Hengwen in a hushed tone. "Can you still hang in there?"

Hengwen frowned, sized me up and down, then tapped me on the shoulder with his folding fan and sighed with concern, "Oh, wake up. Tianshu is long gone."

The laugh I gave him was wry.

We asked for directions at the tea booth, hired a horse carriage by the roadside, and entered Luyang City after dark.

The horse carriage went all the way to the best inn at Luyang. We dismounted and booked two of the most deluxe rooms. By the time we were done washing up, the beds in the rooms had brand-new pillows and bedding all spread out, and the brand-new pot on the table held the finest tea, all brewed and ready. I threw Guangyunzi's body to the other room and had Furball and the mountain cat keep him company while I took my pillow and quilt to the room next door. Hengwen was drinking tea at the table. I spread out the quilt and said, "You should be tired. Go to bed soon and get some decent rest."

Holding on to the teacup, the corners of Hengwen's lips twitched. "Your mind must have short-circuited, sitting in the boat the whole day with Nanming and Tianshu. Look at how mushy your words are."

I could only let out another wry laugh. As soon as it had left my mouth, a sudden laugh—clear and loud—entered the throng. "Exactly, exactly, so mushy I'm cringing."

Golden light sparkled where the voice had landed, and two figures flashed into being.

The one in the lead wore a robe of cloud-pattern brocade, with a beautiful jade crown at the top of his head. He was all smiles as he greeted, "Hengwen Qingjun, Song Yao Yuanjun. How have you fared on this trip in the mortal realm? I just so happened to be passing by, so I came to see you both."

My eyes nearly welled up with tears when I saw him. It was like seeing Mingge.

This was an old friend of this immortal lord, the exalted lord who had taken the key to the Northern Heavenly Gate and thrown the Heavenly Court into mayhem—Bihua Lingjun.

The one behind him, however, gave this immortal lord a bit of a headache.

He was dressed in a prim and proper official outfit the color of rosy clouds, his hair tidily secured with a hairpin. Keeping a straight, fastidious face with nary a hair out of place, he first greeted this immortal lord, then bowed to Hengwen. "Qingjun, this humble immortal has come to the mortal world because there are important documents for Qingjun to personally read over."

The various immortal officials under Hengwen from the two Kui Xing to Wenqu Xing and Wuqu Xing were all pretty decent. Only the immortal in charge of files and archives, Lu Jing, was a pain to deal with.

Chapter fourteen

To paraphrase Donghua Dijun, in the entire Heavenly Court, there was no immortal more idle than me, Song Yao Yuanjun, no immortal more flashy than Bihua Lingjun, and no immortal more straitlaced than Lu Jing.

The Jade Emperor made the best use of his resources. Of the immortals in charge of literary texts, Lu Jing was in charge of the rules of language as well as the organization and verification of official correspondence. Every one of Lu Jing's movements, from standing to lying to walking to sitting, was a rule in itself.

In truth, Lu Jing was good at heart. For example, this immortal lord must have been quite the eyesore to him, going in and out of Weiyuan Palace and Wensi Hall all day long, but not once had he gotten indignant or criticized me; instead, he simply tolerated it with magnanimity. When Nanming Dijun had found fault with me, he had also spoken up and put in a good word or two for me. He had my thanks for it.

Each time I went looking for Hengwen at Wensi Hall, Lu Jing would greet me with a smile before his desk. When I saw him smile, I could not but wonder how anyone could smile so primly. Then, considering I was there to look for Hengwen Qingjun to drink, attend banquets, and stroll around, I could not help but feel guilty for it.

Hengwen had once told me, "There's nothing for you to feel guilty about. If we were to swap places in the future, where you'd be sitting in that spot of mine, watching him stand at his desk like a pole every day for eight hundred or a thousand years, you'd naturally grow to be on friendly terms."

And now, with the three of us unrivaled immortals of the heavenly realm in one place, this simple, mortal's inn room teemed with divine aura.

The great and ever-dazzling Bihua Lingjun, made himself extremely at home, taking a seat and pouring himself a cup. Taking a sip with his eyes half-closed, he nodded. "Tea of the mortal world is unrefined, but tasty."

Lu Jing presented a neat, square cloth bundle wrapped around an equally neat, square stack of official correspondence within. He set the pile before Hengwen, conjured a brush and inkstone, rolled up his sleeves, and prepared the ink. All this so Hengwen could read the official correspondence now.

Bihua Lingjun flicked his cup and sized up the guest room. "The buildings in the mortal world are simple, but they have their own charm. I ought to descend more frequently, try them out."

Hengwen set the teacup in his hand far aside, straightened his clothes, sat upright, and picked up one official correspondence at random. Dragging out his words in a drawl, he said, "By all means, go ahead and try them in the mortal world. Did Lu Jing not tell you, by the way, that the Heavenly Court is now in mayhem because the Northern Heavenly Gate can't be opened?"

"A day or two on earth is merely a blink of an eye in Heaven," Bihua Lingjun said. "There's no need to rush. I have always been one to value friendships, so I surely must make the detour to drop in on my two fellow immortals."

"Thank you, thank you. I'm honored," Hengwen said with a laugh. He opened the letter and focused on reading it. With his right hand, he picked up the fine brush and dipped it in ink.

I could no longer hold myself back from saying, "It's late today. You should sleep first. Can't you read it tomorrow?"

"Yuanjun," Lu Jing said, "these letters must be read and reviewed before the scheduled hour. Each and every one of them affects the literary pulse in the mortal world. It must not be delayed."

He said it so sternly and solemnly that all this immortal lord could do was shut up.

Hengwen lifted the brush and wrote a few lines on the letter. After a brief pause, he set the brush back down and closed the letter. He picked up the second one.

"There are dozens of official correspondence," I said. "By the time these are all reviewed, it'll be dawn. As Bihua said earlier, a night on earth is merely a blink of an eye in Heaven. Just how long of a delay can it be if he sleeps for a night before continuing?"

Lu Jing pulled a serious look, not in the least convinced. Embarrassed to be making a din while Hengwen worked, I could only pick up the teapot and pour myself a cup.

Suddenly, Bihua Lingjun spoke up, "I passed by the room next door earlier and saw the body of a bearded Daoist priest on the floor. That's the body you're using now, right? Mingge Xingjun sure has good taste."

Despondent, I said nothing. Bihua Lingjun drank a mouthful of tea and continued, "The two demonic beasts at the side are pretty decent too."

Bihua Lingjun had a very bad habit of collecting rare beasts. Could he have taken a shine to the two little demons next door? In all likelihood, he had set his eyes on the fox.

With a wry laugh, I said, "It was all by chance that they tagged along with us. That fox is a snow fox, but its cultivation is average. A snow fox is not a rare species—or is it?" This immortal lord remembered that Bihua Lingjun's residence had plenty of foxes, from one-tailed to nine-tailed, in all kinds of coat colors.

"The color of that snow fox is fairly pure, but it's indeed not a rare species. That mountain cat seems decent to me." He set down the teacup. "I feel I may like to bring it back to the Heavenly Court."

This immortal lord was astonished. I knew Bihua Lingjun's tastes had always been distinctive, but I had never expected them to be this particular. With a feigned laugh, I said, "If you want one, you can ride a cloud out now to any random mountain and get your pick of something similar."

With eyes half-shut, Bihua Lingjun shook his head. "You've no idea. You have no idea at all."

"Hm?" I inquired.

"I can't tell you. I can't," Bihua Lingjun answered in a faraway tone.

I stared and said nothing. Each time Bihua made a trip to the Western Paradise, he would speak enigmatically like this for several days, but once the whiff of the Buddha on him had dissipated, he would naturally revert to himself.

Lu Jing was standing solemnly before the desk. I suddenly had a thought, and asked him, "Have you heard in the Heavenly Court of any immortals descending these days?"

"Other than Qingjun, Song Yuanjun, and Bihua Lingjun, the various immortals have been present for the morning call at Lingxiao Palace every day," Lu Jing answered.

"In that case, are any of the non-attending or non-salaried immortals missing from the Heavenly Court of late?" I pressed.

"This humble immortal doesn't know about the ones who don't attend court sessions."

I was not expecting to hear any *I-heard-that* rumors from Lu Jing's mouth, so I had little choice but to drop it.

The immortals who attended the court sessions at the heavenly palace were all present. Then who among those non-attendees or non-salaried immortals could have saved Nanming?

Meanwhile, Hengwen was already done looking over several official documents, although there was still a tall stack left to go. I refilled the tea in his cup.

Bihua Lingjun, on the other hand, covered his mouth to yawn, then looked all around him. "Song Yao, which of these two rooms is better to rest in? It has been many days since I last had a moment, and seeing the bedding and curtains in this room is making me a bit sleepy."

Bihua Lingjun put on a phony act of asking, but his eyes had already drifted to the large bed behind Hengwen, where his gaze lingered. This immortal pretended to ponder the request, and said nothing. Eventually, Bihua Lingjun said, "Or this lord could just rest on this bed. I won't take up space when I sleep, so I'll sleep inside. Qingjun, once you're done reading the official correspondences, you can just sleep on the outside. As it happens, there's another bed in the room next door for Song Yao and Lu Jing to sleep on." He yawned again and made to get up.

"Bihua," I spoke up. "You have not slept for many days, and both of them are here reading official documents with the lights blazing. I fear you won't get a good rest."

"It's fine," Bihua Lingjun said. "I often rest in Maori Xingjun's residence when I go looking for him to play chess with, so I've never feared the brightness."

"But this room is not as quiet as the room next door," I said. "Besides, that mountain cat is there too. Don't you want to go and take a look at it?"

Bihua Lingjun beamed. "As expected, Song Yao knows my heart like a soulmate!" In high spirits, he passed through the wall to the room next door. I could only follow him, but before that, I turned back and nudged Hengwen's teacup toward him. "Drink some tea while I go and keep an eye on Bihua Lingjun. I'll be right back."

"All right," Hengwen said, without even looking up. The tip of his brush paused, then he set down the brush, closed the letter, and started on the next one.

I passed through the wall to the next room. The fox was coolly eyeing Bihua Lingjun with its body half-raised. Meanwhile, the mountain cat was huddled into a ball, sleeping soundly against the fox's back, a pillow under its belly. Bihua Lingjun stared covetously at the mountain cat, who, surprisingly, remained totally oblivious. The fox arched its back, stood, shook its fur, and leaped to the ground, where it transformed into its human form.

The fox discerned the situation. The immortal aura on Bihua Lingjun was overpowering, so he instantly knew that this was an exalted lord. He respectfully lowered his head and greeted, "This humble demon is Xuan Li. May I know which of the exalted lords in the Heavenly Court your esteemed self is?"

The commotion woke the mountain cat. It opened its drowsy eyes and looked blankly around. Upon spotting Bihua Lingjun, it gave a start and shrank into a ball, trembling.

Bihua flashed an affable smile. "Don't be afraid. This lord is Bihua Lingjun of the Heavenly Court. I just so happened to have finished a job, and dropped by to pay my fellow immortal friends a visit. I'm not here to subdue demons." He approached the bed as he spoke. Acting natural, he set his hand on the top of the mountain cat's head. The mountain cat trembled all over and shrank into a smaller ball. Petting it, Bihua smiled. "How obedient, how obedient." The obscene expression on his face made his "fellow immortal friend"—*this* immortal lord—sweat a little.

Seeing the mountain cat trembling so pitifully, I finally yielded to my conscience. "Bihua, it's probably shy with strangers and a little afraid of you. Keep your distance first. Don't scare the child."

Bihua Lingjun petted it some more, loath to part from it, but he finally withdrew his hand and stepped away. The mountain cat immediately scampered down to the ground and rolled to take on the appearance of that young, naïve boy before cowering behind the fox.

The fox subconsciously moved before the mountain cat to shield him from view.

Bihua Lingjun took a few graceful steps back. "You've already cultivated for nearly two thousand years, correct? Your cultivation's pretty good."

"Thank you for your high praise," the fox answered softly.

Holding his hands behind his back, Bihua Lingjun smiled. He veered suddenly toward this immortal lord's direction and a few words as soft as the murmurs of mosquitoes wafted into my ears. Bihua was using telepathy to communicate with me covertly. "Song Yao, are the fox and mountain cat from the same den?"

I could only reply the same way. "Yes, the fox is the mountain cat's king. Of its entire lair of demons, only this mountain cat is left. So, if you are harboring designs on this mountain cat, please pardon this friend of yours for not being able to help you."

Bihua Lingjun, still standing with his hands at his back, smiled with an ethereal air of an immortal.

Suddenly, he said, "Come with this lord for a moment," and floated out of the window. Momentarily taken back, the fox hurried to catch up.

Meanwhile, the mountain cat, seeing this immortal lord as his backer, looked pitifully at me. I petted him, and followed them out of the window to watch the show.

"That child is from your den?" Bihua Lingjun asked the fox under the bright moon. "This lord wishes to bring it back to the Heavenly Court. Are you willing to let him go?"

The fox was struck dumb for a moment before saying, "It's his blessing to have caught your eye. But while he might be from my den, I have never imposed any restrictions on the demons in it, and they are free to come and go as they please."

So Bihua Lingjun returned to the room once more and asked the mountain cat spirit, "Are you willing to return to the Heavenly Court with me?"

The mountain cat grasped onto the front of the fox's clothes and clung close to him. He shook his head.

Bihua Lingjun gave a small sigh. "Never mind, forget it. This is all fated. Just that—" he brushed his sleeves and swept his eyes casually across the fox and this immortal both, "you better not regret it a few days later if you fail to persuade it otherwise."

He walked over to the bed, and brushed the surface with his sleeve before rolling onto it to sleep.

The fox looked uncertainly at Bihua Lingjun.

I thought, *Furball, you don't know this, but this Bihua Lingjun has just come from the Western Paradise, and still has yet to pull himself out of that mindset.*

After Bihua Lingjun lay down, he looked askance at the ground. He shook his head, "Song Yao, oh Song Yao. Although this Daoist priest's body looks like Lü Dongbin's Second Master while he was in the mortal world, you have used him for quite some time. Isn't leaving him on the ground a tad too wretched? At least give him a wooden bench for him to lie on."

"You wouldn't know it, but a bench is narrow and uncomfortably hard," I explained. "Might as well put him on the level and smooth ground."

Bihua took a moment to consider my words. "That makes sense, but I heard the ants, insects, and mice of the mortal world are all pretty impressive. Watch him carefully, lest he gets gnawed on."

"Bihua, you can sleep without a worry," I said. "Ants and mice wouldn't eat this thing."

Only then did Bihua Lingjun bid me goodnight and enter dreamland.

The mountain cat, however, cowered behind the fox, still

trembling as he looked at Bihua Lingjun. This immortal lord thought of bringing them over to the room next door, but Lu Jing was in that room standing ramrod straight in that solemn way of his, and Hengwen would not be done with his official correspondence until morning came around. That left this immortal lord with little choice but to remain, sitting in silent repose. Only then did the mountain cat dare to jump onto a chair beside me and curl up to sleep. Probably figuring that it was hopeless to look for Hengwen tonight, the fox, too, found another chair further away to lie on.

Until daybreak.

It was only after morning light that Hengwen finished his official documents. Lu Jing wrapped up the correspondence neatly, and returned to the Heavenly Court with Bihua Lingjun.

Before Bihua left, he even put on a show like he was loath to depart. "Gentlemen, take care. I shall take my leave to the Heavenly Court, where I can return the key to the Northern Heavenly Gate. When I have the time, I'll come and see you again."

Hengwen and I cupped our hands in farewell, watching with glad relief as the pair of figures vanished after the golden light faded.

Having read through an entire night of official correspon-dence, Hengwen looked exhausted. He drank two mouthfuls of the tea and shook the quilt open. Before lying down, he said, "I've already told Lu Jing to drop Mingge Xingjun a reminder when he returns to the Heavenly Court. Mingge Xingjun had better not have really forgotten all about this mission."

I tucked him snugly under the quilt. "Exactly. Mingge has a heavy workload; it's common for him to overlook things."

Hengwen yawned. "You said you sat in meditation the entire night. Don't you feel like sleeping now?"

I sighed. "The waiters will probably come knocking on the

door later with water and meals. Before I sleep, I'll head down and inform the innkeeper not to serve us."

"It's so early," Hengwen said lazily. "How would the waiters be so undiscerning in attending to the guests? In all the previous inns, they would not knock on the door without a summons, and they would only take the initiative to come and attend to the guests at noon, right? So let's just sleep first."

Perhaps that was the case after all. I lifted the quilt and climbed into bed. How could I have known that my head would not have even touched the pillow, and my eyes would not even have shut for a sixth of an hour, when knocking sounds would ring from the door? "Mister, mister, are you still resting?"

I was enraged. The day had only just broken. Which waiter was so undiscerning and tactless?

With a frown on his face, Hengwen raised a hand from the quilt and waved it randomly in the air. "Send him away. I'll continue sleeping."

Very unrighteously, he turned inward.

I lifted the quilt and went to answer the door. I had only just opened it a crack when I heard the waiter say, "You've finally gotten up. This young master said that he has something to… eh? Eh, eh???"

The waiter gaped wide-mouthed in astonishment, and my heart went cold. Oh no, how muddle-minded was I? To think this immortal lord had forgotten to repossess Guangyunzi's body. To think I had answered the door in my true form.

The waiter sized me up and down, stammering, "M-Mister, th-this humble one remembers that th-this room, and the room next door were booked by a Daoist priest and a young master with the surname Zhao… D-Did I make a mistake… Y-Young Master, may I know who you are…?"

This immortal lord was extremely dejected, for standing behind the waiter surrounded by a few attendants… was Mu Ruoyan.

A pair of eyes stared fixedly at me.

Even in my dejection, I still wondered why Tianshu was here so early in the morning.

I opened the door fully, and flashed a refined smile at the waiter. "You didn't make a mistake. Young Master Zhao is in this room; he's still sleeping."

I looked at Mu Ruoyan and put on a gentle smile. "Is something the matter for all of you to come calling so early in the morning?"

The waiter's voice faltered, "Y-Y-Y-Young, Young Master, you are...?"

"Did you forget?" I gasped in astonishment. "This humble one is Young Master Zhao's elder cousin. I came to this inn looking for my younger cousin in the middle of last night. If I recall correctly, you were the one who led me up here."

The waiter, now befuddled, scratched his head. "This, this humble one doesn't remember..."

I frowned. "Don't tell me it was someone else? I was in such a hurry last night, I didn't get a good look." I reached into my sleeves and conjured out a silver piece. "It was all thanks to you for making concessions and leading the way for me last night, but I was rushing to find my cousin and forgot to give my thanks. Please accept these bits of silver as a little token of my appreciation."

The waiter was no match for this immortal lord's great wisdom, and accepted the silver with a beam on his face. "Right, right, I remember it now that you've reminded me. You arrived, all travel-worn, last night in search of your cousin, and this humble one led you up the stairs with a lantern. You're truly too kind. I was only doing what was expected of me. Anyway, this young master said he has something of importance to discuss with Young Master Zhao and the Daozhang. Why don't you speak to him first? This humble one shall take my leave. Just call for me if you need something."

He retreated with a grin on his face, leaving this immortal lord and Mu Ruoyan looking at each other.

I cupped my hands. "It must be a matter of great importance for you to be looking for my younger cousin. May I trouble you to wait outside for a moment while this humble one wakes him up?"

Mu Ruoyan returned the greeting. "In that case, I shall have to trouble you." A beat; then he added, "This humble one is Mu Ruoyan. May I ask for your esteemed surname?"

"It's an honor to meet you. This humble one is Zhao Heng's elder cousin," I cupped my hands and responded. It was at that moment that I remembered our first encounter—how, several thousand years ago, I had waited at the side to prostrate myself to Tianshu Xingjun on the floating clouds. "This humble immortal is Song Yao, a newcomer to the Heavenly Court. Greetings to Xingjun."

I could not help but answer in a gentle, unhurried voice, "My surname is Song, and my given name is Yao. If Young Master Mu doesn't mind, you can call me Song Yao."

Chapter Fifteen

Feeling a little emotional when Mu Ruoyan said "Thank you, Young Master Song, for your trouble," I retreated into the room to wake Hengwen up. Before I could turn to the side, I heard Hengwen say from behind me, "Is that Young Master Mu? This humble one had yet to wake up earlier and thus was unable to greet you. Please do not hold it against me."

The door creaked. Hengwen was already standing beside me, all done up in a light azure robe. There was no way to tell at all that he had just crawled out of bed.

Naturally, Mu Ruoyan had to answer that it was too presumptuous of him to come over so early in the morning, disrupting Hengwen and my sweet dreams like that. He exchanged a few words of pleasantries with Hengwen, after which Hengwen let him into the room, leaving the few bodyguards to stand by the doors.

Inside the room, they politely offered each other seats before Mu Ruoyan finally settled down at the table. "Is Guangyun Daozhang still sleeping in his room?"

Hengwen picked up his worn folding fan and waved it as he

answered, "That's right. Daozhang is advanced in age, and he's probably a bit tired after taking the boat yesterday, so he retired early to his room. I don't know if he's cultivating in silence or sleeping, so it's not convenient for this humble one to disturb him. If Young Master Mu needs to look for him, you can try knocking on his door."

I stood beside the table and circled twice before dragging over a chair for myself.

This was clearly about me, but I could not butt in. The feeling in my heart was rather indescribable.

"Then I shall not disturb him; it's just the same to tell you," Mu Ruoyan said. "War is impending in the Southern Commandery of late. Martial law has taken effect in Luyang City, with military affairs taking precedence and the military having jurisdiction over the civilians. They have issued a new command yesterday to run a check on the city's population." He frowned, as if deliberating over his next words. "I'm afraid the inns in Luyang all have to be temporarily shuttered."

"While taking a break at a tea booth yesterday, this humble one heard that the two armies of the Imperial Court and the Eastern Commandery are pressing in toward Luyang," Hengwen said. "Presumably, General Shan intends to fight it out to the end on water, and in order to guard against spies, is clearing the city of people who have no business being here."

"They wouldn't even let *us* stay in the city?" I could not help but blurt.

"Guangyun Daozhang saved this humble one's life back at the inn in the Eastern Commandery," Tianshu said unhurriedly, "and I have still yet to repay him for this great kindness. This humble one has a modest residence in the city. If Young Master Zhao and Daozhang do not mind, you may come and stay at my residence for a few days."

Hengwen shut his folding fan, answering with a smile, "Young Master Mu, you are clearly aware that I could still be an advisor of the Prince of the Eastern Commandery's manor, and the Daoist Master Guangyun is such an enigmatic character that he raises suspicions as to his motives, and yet you would still let us stay in your residence? Are you afraid that he," he pointed the fan at me, "the Daoist Master Guangyun, and I would collude with the Eastern Commandery's troops? That we would act from within and without to harm General Shan?"

"Even if these events really do occur the way Young Master Zhao says, you've already revealed it to me," Mu Ruoyan said, "so what is there to worry about?"

Hengwen studied Tianshu, and remarked, "Impressive, impressive."

I almost blurted out those same words. In clearing out Luyang City this time, Shan Shengling undoubtedly wanted to get rid of both this immortal lord and Hengwen, lest he get sick of seeing us. And by inviting us to his residence at this time, one could guess that Mu Ruoyan was a man of noble character who trusted Hengwen and me—or he meant to keep an eye on us under the guise of doing us a favor. Hengwen's interest was promptly piqued. At his side, meanwhile, I gulped. I could almost see in him the little flame of enthusiasm that loved getting involved burst ablaze. Sure enough, Young Master Zhao smiled readily. "Since Young Master Mu extended the invitation, this humble one shall not stand on ceremony. However, the Daoist Master Guangyun is still in bed..."

"The checks will start only after the hours of noon. This humble one shall come to the inn again at the later hours of the morning to meet you. Young Master Zhao, would that work?"

Hengwen immediately cupped his hands. "Then we will have to impose on you. Thank you."

Mu Ruoyan smiled. "There's no need to stand on ceremony."

Those clear eyes turned to this immortal lord's face, and paused. I felt that he was seeing right through me. Guangyunzi was this immortal lord, and this immortal lord was Guangyunzi.

But Mu Ruoyan had now seen Song Yao. What was I to do?

Before my thoughts could overtake me, Hengwen adopted a solemn expression, and addressed me. "That's right. Since they will be conducting checks at the hours of noon, you should pack now and depart the city before then."

Instantly, Mu Ruoyan's eyes became lined with doubts. I could think of no excuse as to explain away such a hasty retreat, so I could only hedge it and say, "No rush, no rush. Although the matter is pressing, it's not that urgent. Noon is not too late a departure time."

Hengwen's eyes narrowed as he smiled, and his voice was deeper than usual as he responded. "That's right. I was so pre-occupied with other matters last night that I didn't get to have a good chat with you. In that case, leave at noon."

Mu Ruoyan stood. "This humble one still has some other matters to attend to, so I shall not impose on you any further. Let's meet again in the late morning time."

Hengwen and I stood up and saw him to the door. The guards outside the door swarmed over.

It was at this moment that there came a shout beside us: "Excuse me, excuse me... Please let me through..."

A waiter carrying a basin of hot water turned sideways in an attempt to pass us. Hengwen and I stepped back, while Tianshu moved to the side. The waiter tottered through, his back bent with the burden of his load. Perhaps it was the bright gleam from the bodyguards' weapons, but just as the waiter reached Tianshu, his hands trembled, and he faltered on his feet. A bodyguard threw a flying roundhouse before the hot water could splash Tianshu, sending both waiter and basin flying. Water splashed all over the floor, and the basin clattered onto the ground, while the waiter went crashing heavily—

Right into the next room.

The door slammed open, and the waiter let loose a string of

tragic cries as he tumbled in.

This immortal lord's heart missed a beat.

Oh no!

Beside me, Hengwen let out a wry laugh.

The bodyguards surged forth, a forest of spear tips bristling at the waiter, and then all at once, paused.

The room held a fox and a mountain cat, not to mention quite a few rare objects. However—

"Captain, there's a Daoist priest lying on the ground."

Guangyunzi, oh Guangyunzi. I have let you down. I've borrowed you for my own use, and should never have thrown you aside like, sleeping like a corpse...

Mu Ruoyan's expression underwent a change then. He swept his gaze over Hengwen, over me, and strode into the room.

I had placed Guangyunzi in a spot with excellent geomancy last night. Anyone who looked in the room would spot the body lying stiff and hard on the ground.

"Look, Young Master Mu, Captain," a bodyguard addressed them both. "The way this Daoist Master is lying is so strange."

Their interest piqued, Mu Ruoyan and a big, burly man who must have been the captain made for a closer look. I dashed to the door, a smile meant to please plastered across my face. "This Daoist Master Guangyun is a great master with profound cultivation, and the actions of a great master are not what us mere mortals could fathom. Perhaps he is cultivating some secret and profound technique of a certain sect, and needs to lie on the floor to absorb the essence of the earth."

The head bodyguard stroked his chin as if enlightened, but Mu Ruoyan knitted his brows into a slight frown. "We are on the second floor here. How is Daoist Master Guangyun able to absorb essence from the earth?"

Hengwen looked at me resignedly out of the corner of his eye. I held a fist to my mouth and coughed. "This humble one

was merely saying; it was a guess. Daoist Master Guangyun...
he's a great master, after all. How masters go about their business is beyond what common people can fathom. Haha..."

Mu Ruoyan's frown deepened even more.

I continued, "The Daozhang is cultivating and likely would not appreciate being disturbed. Young Master Mu said yourself earlier that you still have important matters to attend to, so don't let these trivial matters bog you down. You should hurry back first."

The head guard moved closer to Mu Ruoyan and whispered, "Young Master Mu, if I may: This person seems evasive with his words, as if he's hiding something. It's rather suspicious."

Is there a problem? Is this immortal lord's thousand-year elegance and poise not enough to send you mortals to your knees? When the head guard saw the cold gaze this immortal lord directed at him, he lowered his voice even more. "Besides, this person comes from questionable origins. He's dressed like a dandy, but his clothing is in disarray, and he's such a slick talker. If I may, he's *very* suspicious!"

Hengwen looked at me, again with helpless resignation.

This immortal lord was miffed. Before my ascension, I had been considered a refined and distinguished young master in the capital city. The capital city counted all sorts of young masters among its stable, occasionally creating a ranking, and this untalented one even placed first once.

This thick skin of mine had endured the vicissitudes of life and weathered thousands of years of hardship; it was not what it used to be, but surely it had not deteriorated to this low of a point?

My expression frosted over as I straightened my back, adjusted the front of my clothes, and stood with hands by my side.

The fox and mountain cat crouched on the bed—likely having taken the initiative to move there after this immortal lord and Bihua Lingjun left this morning. The mountain cat cowered behind a pillow at the corner of the bed, its green, round eyes wide open, while the fox remained curled up, looking nonchalant.

The captain used his eyes to signal the bodyguard still standing by Guangyunzi. The bodyguard caught the hint and immediately squatted down.

The fox on the bed peered at the scene through its eyelids.

Mu Ruoyan entered the room. The bodyguard extended a finger under Guangyunzi's nose for a moment, then pressed down on his chest, feeling for his pulse. He held down the side of his neck and lifted his eyelids before he turned back and announced, "Captain, this Daoist priest is dead."

"Oh," Hengwen blurted in astonishment and grief, "don't tell me Guangyun Daozhang has passed into immortality?"

My face twitched. "Or perhaps Daozhang is emulating Li the Iron Clutch of the eight immortals, and his soul has left his body to go wandering on the astral plane?"

Mu Ruoyan stayed at Guangyunzi's side, looking down at him without expression. With what seemed like a sigh, he said, "Looks like we have to ask both of you to make a trip down to the local prefect's office."

An hour later, Hengwen and I stood in the main hall of the prefectural office of Luyang. Guangyunzi had been placed on a stretcher, which the bodyguards bore to the office. He was laid out in the main hall as material evidence, right beside Hengwen and me.

This immortal lord and Hengwen Qingjun could have simply fled on a gust of wind at the inn, but without accomplishing the mission handed us by the Jade Emperor, we did not dare expose our identities so soon. It would be bad if we manifested our true forms, displayed our abilities in broad daylight, and ended up scaring this crowd of ignorant civilians witless. So, we concluded, we might as well take a walk to the prefect's office and see what they could try on us.

The fox had taken advantage of the chaos in the inn to make its escape. The mountain cat, on the other hand, did not manage to flee in time given its low cultivation, and Mu Ruoyan, having caught sight of it, had petted it for a moment before picking it up. The mountain cat seemed to have taken to Mu Ruoyan on the boat, and it cooed and nuzzled against him, letting him carry it onto the horse carriage.

Hengwen had quite the interest in the prefectural offices of the human world, and he sized up the place left and right, up and down. But I was afraid that he would admit to the crime during the interrogation just to satisfy his interest in the inner workings of a prison.

The office runners were all yawning and the prefectural prefect had yet to hold court. It was then that I whispered, "So much for friendship. You left me to explain by myself just now without even helping. "

"You were speaking to Mu Ruoyan with such a glib tongue," Hengwen said. "How could I steal your thunder?" He shook his head, as if rueful.

This immortal lord was poised to respond when a loud noise sounded in the hall, signifying that the court trial was about to start.

A person dressed in the blue attire of a civil official—supposedly the prefect—emerged from behind the screen to stand before it, but held his head low and hands down at his sides. He was immediately followed by another person from behind the screen. This time, it was an acquaintance—

Nanming Dijun, Shan Shengling.

General Shan, in a gallant manner, settled down on the old-fashioned wooden chair at the left. Only then did the prefect dare take his seat, beginning the court session. He slapped down the wooden block that served as a gavel and said, "The audacity of you criminals! Why are you not kneeling in the presence of this official?"

This immortal lord and Hengwen remained standing at leisure. Shan Shengling was seeing this immortal lord's real body for the first time, and he feigned nonchalance as he assessed me. The prefect smacked the wooden block down again. "How dare you! To remain indifferent when this prefect is asking you a question! I ask again. How did you murder this Daoist priest? Confess now!"

This immortal lord really could not watch any further. "General Shan, don't you people from the Southern Commandery's prefectural office examine the body first before you hold a court trial?"

Shan Shengling's gaze sharpened. "You know me?"

I held my hands behind my back and smiled enigmatically.

Shan Shengling waved his hand. "Summon the coroner to examine the body!"

His eyes then shifted from me to Hengwen, where it fixed into a stare, so much that this immortal lord became very displeased. Was staring at Tianshu all day still not enough for Nanming, that he had to stare at Hengwen too?

The coroner came and examined Guangyunzi's body left to right.

Using our telepathic technique, Hengwen said to me, "The officials in the mortal world are so muddle-headed. No wonder the commoners in the mortal world offered so much in incense and offerings to the Heavenly Court. It's indeed not easy for them to live."

I replied the same way. "There are decent officials too, but there are always more incompetent or corrupt officials. The common folks indeed have a hard life. That's why the Heavenly Court considers banishment to the mortal realm a punishment and tribulation."

"Why are there so many corrupt officials?" Hengwen wondered.

"You have a role in this too, Qingjun," I said quietly. "Take the prefect in this hall, for example. He had to pass through the imperial examination and emerge as a successful candidate at the highest level of imperial examination before he could become this fourth-grade prefect. The rise and fall of scholars' literary ethics and outcomes of the imperial examinations must first pass through the desks of your Wensi Hall."

Hengwen fell silent. After a moment, he said, "When I return to the Heavenly Court, I'll personally sort out the files on literary ethics and write off all these messes."

"I was just making a dig at you earlier. Don't take it seriously," I said. "Actually, there is a saying in the mortal world which puts it pretty well: 'Thirty percent predestined; seventy percent man-made.' Take your desk and Old Man Mingge's desk, for example. How many books can the desks take? People come and go, live and die in the mortal world. There are countless human births and deaths taking place in just an instant. How can anyone interfere in every single one of them? You can indicate in the books for an ethical, wise, virtuous man to take up the mantle all you want. However, if he still can't win the favor of the emperor and officials in power after passing the imperial examinations, he would still be unable to be an official and put his talents to good use. That is why dynasties through the ages rise and fall, prosper and decline in turn."

"To think there are so many principles of truth in the mortal world. You do really speak like an immortal now. How rare, how rare," Hengwen remarked.

"I've been in Heaven for several thousand years," I said. "Have I ever said anything that did *not* sound sagely?"

Hengwen clicked his tongue.

The coroner, finally finished with his examination of Guangyunzi, reported as he trembled, "To report to General Shan and Your Excellency, there is nothing abnormal with this Daoist priest's body... This humble one did not see any traces of murder."

"These two bits of good-for-nothing scums must have used some special means," the prefect said. "Men! Bring out the torture instruments!"

"Looks like you and I will have to ride like the wind," I said to Hengwen, through our technique.

"Let's wait for them to bring in the torture instruments. It still won't be too late to leave after I've taken a look," Hengwen said.

The prefectural runners carried in a set of clamping rods, then ignited a basin of fire and thrust a branding iron into it. Hengwen shook his head.

The prefect let the wooden block meet the table again. "Apply the torture!"

The prefectural runners lifted the clamping rods and advanced.

Just as Hengwen and I were about to breezily make our escape, a cold voice rang from outside the hall.

"Hold it."

A person strode across the threshold, and with a wave of his sleeve, swept away the prefectural runners who had gone over to stop him. He strolled into the hall and stood before Hengwen to shield him.

"Who dares touch my young master?" he said, his voice ice.

Furball had picked the opportune time to appear before Hengwen.

The fox, thinking himself a charming romantic, had draped a long, white robe around himself. He had hidden away his fox ears and turned his silver hair black, presenting an ethereal sight as he stood before Hengwen.

Meaning no offense, but this immortal lord could destroy his tiny bit of cultivation with just a snap of my fingers, what's more Hengwen? There was simply no need for Furball to come.

The prefect flew into a rage, and the hall descended into

chaos. Shan Shengling, however, narrowed his eyes at the fox. "You seem to be an old acquaintance."

The fox stood in cold silence, only saying after a while, "It's ludicrous for General Shan to frame my young master of murder, and even using torture to extort a confession. How many lives have been lost by General Shan's hands? And yet I don't see anyone arresting him."

The fox raked a sinister gaze across the prefectural runners and prefect. He continued, still in that cold voice, "Speaking of which, General Shan and Young Master Mu have yet another life on their hands recently in the Eastern Commandery, yes? Do you know why your Luyang City is currently besieged on all sides with two great armies pressing in toward you?"

He looked again at the prefectural runners and the prefect, then glanced at Shan Shengling out of the corner of his eye. "In order to save Young Master Mu, a wanted fugitive by the Imperial Court, the General Shan in this very hall snuck into the Prince of the Eastern Commandery's manor and killed their third young master, Li Siming. That's why the Eastern Commandery joined forces with the Imperial Court. That's why they have assembled a large army to close in on Luyang. Pitiful be you foolish mortals, who will pay with countless lives just for a feud that started because Shan Shengling killed someone for his own selfish desire."

The prefectural runners all looked panic-stricken, while the prefect slammed the wooden block with a trembling hand. "The-the audacity of you t-to s-slander the great general!"

"Slander?" the fox spat contemptuously. "Ask Shan Shengling, then. Or wait until the Eastern Commandery's army arrives at the gate of Luyang City to ask them."

It was indeed smart of the fox to expose Shan Shengling, to make the people lose faith in him. Shan Shengling's expression remained unchanged as he narrowed his eyes. "So, were there any bone fragments left in your cave when you returned that day?"

All at once, the fox's eyes turned red.

And burned with the fire of hatred.

An ominous wind stirred, and ghostly clouds rose overhead. The fox's black hair fluttered up, revealing its original silvery-white color. A pair of fox ears stood from that hair.

The prefectural runners and prefect wailed and scurried, huddling together.

"Mortal," the fox snapped, "you harmed the lives of those from my lair. I shall settle this blood debt today!"

Shan Shengling rose, laughing for all to hear as he drew his glinting steel blade. "You finally show your true self, demon. I was negligent the other day by giving you reprieve. Watch how I eliminate your beastly existence today!"

I pulled Hengwen back a few steps, outside the eye of the storm. Shan Shengling was a mere mortal, unable to hold a significant advantage over the fox. This immortal lord would sit and watch the battle, and if Shan Shengling were to be torn to shreds and meet his end here, the blame would not likely fall on me. If the fox were to kill Shan Shengling, would he be slapped with the crime of murdering an immortal? Even if he did not, harming a mortal would make it all the more difficult for him to achieve immortality later. Should this immortal lord reach out and stop the fight?

Hengwen was already worrying for the fox. "Perhaps we should stop this fight first. It's not good if innocents are hurt in the crossfire. And besides, Xuan Li might get charged with a crime if he wounds Shan Shengling."

"In that case, I'll put a stop to this," I answered. "Stand here and don't do a thing."

Hengwen smiled at that. I released his arm, and was just about to cast a spell when a faint voice wafted down from above. "Song Yao Yuanjun, Song Yao Yuanjun. Hengwen Qingjun—"

This voice... Is this not Mingge?!

This immortal lord looked up with joy, as if encountering a welcome rain after a long drought. Concealed among several rays of golden light, Mingge Xingjun hurriedly cried, "Song Yao Yuanjun, quick, break up Shan Shengling and the fox!! They can't fight!! The fates as decreed by Heaven naturally have their own plans in store for them!"

D*mn, now you're shouting about heaven's decree. Where was heaven's decree all these days this immortal lord was waiting for it?!

But in the heaven up above and the earth down below, the Jade Emperor's decree was the most absolute of all. I rose in the light and waved my sleeve in midair, stirring up a great gust of divine wind that blew away the fox's demonic clouds. Then I dropped a flash of heavenly lightning to split both men apart. Once the fox had been forced into its original form, I grabbed it by the scruff and vanished.

I landed on a mountain far beyond Luyang City. Hengwen was already waiting on a cliff. I set down the fox, and he begrudgingly shifted into human form, looking mightily grieved and defiant as he lowered his head and said nothing.

"I know Shan Shengling hurt everyone from your lair, and you want to kill him to take revenge," Hengwen said, voice kind. "However, if you wish to cultivate to immortality, you can't hurt humans or take their lives. Shan Shengling will get his just comeuppance someday as fate decrees. You can't injure him now. That's why Song Yao Yuanjun stopped you. I hope you can understand and not blame us."

The fox's head was still lowered, his ears drooping with inconsolable grief and indignation.

Hengwen continued, "And thank you too, for what you did back there. Actually, Song Yao Yuanjun and I can deal with this matter. You shouldn't have taken such a big risk."

The fox raised his head to look into Hengwen's eyes as he softly answered, "I know Qingjun's divine powers are immense, and you don't need me to save you, but Qingjun, I hope you also remember that I will always step forth when you are in trouble, even if this paltry cultivation of mine is not of much use. This is the extent of my feelings toward Qingjun."

His tone was so thick with sweetness, it hurt this immortal lord's teeth.

The fox continued with feeling, "Perhaps in the eyes of the immortal lords, demons and spirits are the lowest of the low. When a mortal kills a demon, it's considered a merit, but when a demon hurts a mortal, it's an unforgivable sin. But if all I have is this insignificant life and my meager demonic powers, I will protect someone I want to protect to the very end, even if I were to be completely obliterated..."

This immortal lord sucked in a breath of cool air and cut him off, "Qingjun is surely aware of your feelings to him, but you should know that the one listening a few meters away with his ears perked is Mingge Xingjun. If the Heavenly Court were to find out about your homoerotic feelings for Hengwen Qingjun, you would not be the only one obliterated. If you do not want to implicate Qingjun, revisit this kind of talk another day."

The tips of the fox's ears trembled as he raised his head, then lowered it again. "In that case, I shall take my leave and stop holding you up." He gazed at Hengwen, again with feelings so deep this immortal lord's hair stood on end. Only then did he turn into a gust of wind and leave.

Book of Fate in hand, Mingge Xingjun walked to us from the other side of the cliff. He looked in the direction where the fox had left as the wind. "This snow fox has a good foundation. Perhaps after five hundred more years in the mortal world, we will be able to see him in the Heavenly Court."

"Xingjun, does this also fall under the jurisdiction of your Book of Fate?" I asked.

Mingge Xingjun stroked his beard and smiled. "Those who cultivate have already broken free of the cycle of reincarnation. So, by all reasoning, they do not fall under the jurisdiction of the

Heavenly Court. However—" he pressed down on the cover of the Book, "it is also possible that there's a spot for it in the Book of Fate. This is Heaven's secret. I'm not at liberty to reveal it."

"I hardly see you descending to the mortal world of late," I remarked. "Did you imitate Bihua Lingjun and make off to the Western Paradise for tea? The tune you are singing is the same as his."

Mingge laughed, dryly. "Sorry, sorry, Song Yao Yuanjun, I'm truly sorry. It just so happens that there's a thorny issue in Heavenly Court this lord must attend to, which held me up for a few days. The Jade Emperor is concerned about Yuanjun's trip this time around, and even used my Observation Mirror for a look. He's very satisfied with everything Yuanjun has done over these last few days…"

My heart suddenly skipped a beat, but it was with a smile that I said, "You flatter me. It's all thanks to Xingjun for looking out for me."

Mingge then said to Hengwen, "How has Qingjun been these days? The Jade Emperor asked after you and entrusted me to pass you a message on his behalf. The doctrine dialogue is just around the corner. When will you be returning to the Heavenly Court?"

"I'm truly humbled that the Jade Emperor asked after me and had Xingjun convey this message," Hengwen said. "If the affairs in this world are settled sooner, I'll report back to the Heavenly Court. If not, I'll return to the Heavenly Court when the day comes around and ask the Jade Emperor to send someone else down to the mortal world to assist Song Yuanjun. May I trouble Xingjun to convey my reply on my behalf?"

Mingge cupped his hands. "Do rest assured, Qingjun. I will surely pass your message on to the Jade Emperor."

After all this rambling had concluded, Mingge began to flip through the Book of Fate's pages. This immortal lord, always uneasy at the sight of it, asked, "Xingjun, can you show me the words in your book first? Verbally spoken words are not as clear as the written ones. Only once I've studied them carefully can I do a better job at putting the Jade Emperor's and your mind at ease." The body of the Daoist priest Guangyun was still being held in the prefectural office. I had exposed my immortality there, and now did not know what they would turn me into next to get close to Tianshu.

Mingge Xingjun knew the past few incidents were fresh in this immortal lord's mind. He held his book to his bosom, not wanting to hand it over, yet finding it hard to say no. After this moment of hesitation, he stroked his beard. "Actually, Yuanjun's trip down to the mortal world is about to come to an end."

Come to an end? I had achieved precious little in splitting the lovebirds up, and now it was all about to end?

"Yuanjun may lie low and stay in hiding in the city," Mingge said. "In less than two days, there will be a conclusion to this matter." He showed me a few lines from the book.

Shan Shengling and Mu Ruoyan's lifetimes come to an end. Tianshu Star and Immortal Nanming enter the cycle of reincarnation once again.

Reading this, my little heart trembled. In being born as a human for a lifetime, one would become a life in itself, and yet the Jade Emperor simply proclaimed death on them at the mere drop of a hat. However, I had no idea how Mu Ruoyan and Shan Shengling would meet their end.

Old Man Mingge was unwilling to tell me. He only heaved a long sigh. "It's not that I'm trying to fob you off. We have, after all, all been fellow immortals for several thousand years. No one could feel good learning of this ending. Had I not been the one to write the Book of Fate, I wouldn't have wanted to know either. To know and yet to have to watch helplessly as events unfold is probably something neither of you could do. It will only be for a few days. You will naturally understand once the time comes around." Mingge gazed regretfully at the clouds high above, where the mist was thin.

"I believe I just saw the word 'Tianshu Star" circled by a golden circle in the Book of Fate," Hengwen asked mildly. "What is that about?"

His words gave me a start. A golden circle? How had this immortal lord not seen it?

Mingge Xingjun closed the Book of Fate. He crinkled up his aged face to say with a smile, "Probably a mark I made for fear of writing the wrong word."

"When I was on the boat with Tianshu, I thought I saw a similar thin ring around the little finger on his left hand, like it was tied with a golden thread," Hengwen said. "I know that Yue Lao has secured a red thread of fate between Tianshu and Nanming this lifetime, but since when was there another, golden one?"

Mingge Xingjun raised a sleeve to wipe his forehead. "Qingjun, since you already know everything, why keep pressing me? Every cause has its effect, and every effect, a cause. And sometimes, the seeds one sows and reaps are convoluted and a pain to keep track of."

"Please rest assured, Xingjun," Hengwen said. "This lord will not reignite what the Jade Emperor has quelled and sealed. However—" a smile as he glanced at this immortal lord from the corner of his eye, "Could the golden thread on Tianshu's hand come from the same source as the so-called rumor of the Heavenly Court?"

"What rumor?" this immortal lord tactlessly asked.

Mingge said nothing, and Hengwen continued, "The thread of the immortal bond. Have you never heard of it before?"

I had indeed never heard of it.

Mingge was all sighs as he said, "... Actually, I guess it could also be considered the ill-fated affinity between Tianshu Xingjun and Nanming Dijun…"

"Could you be more specific?" I asked, but on seeing the pair's unfathomable expressions, I sensibly added, "If it's a secret of Heaven, then forget I asked."

Mingge sighed again.

"It's really no secret," Hengwen said. "It has been said that when Tianshu Star and Nanming Dijun were first born, they shone and reflected each other, inextricably connected. Tianshu Star was originally the star of emperors, one who protects and blesses the preordained Son of Heaven with the aura of an emperor in the mortal world, while Nanming Dijun was in charge of the fortunes and destiny of a nation. Both immortals mutually complemented and assisted each other as if they were one. So the legend goes, a thread of immortal bond was later formed between Nanming Dijun and Tianshu Xingjun. Actually, this thread is somewhat similar to Yue Lao's red thread of fate, mutually binding them in an entanglement of immeasurable love, adoration, and tender affection."

So it turned out that Tianshu and Nanming had this deep a past.

"Could the Jade Emperor have banished Tianshu and Nanming to the mortal world this time to sever that thread of love?"

Were setting up love trails, Yue Lao's red thread of fate, and even this immortal lord, all just to sever their love with another kind of love?

Mingge looked back at this immortal lord, still saying nothing.

"It's too late." Hengwen shook his head and said in a heavy voice, "The thread of immortal bond has a slipknot and a dead knot. A slipknot can be undone, but the one on Tianshu's hand now is a dead knot, if the tales are true, cannot be undone unless he is completely obliterated."

I was stunned.

"… Actually," Mingge faltered, "the Jade Emperor made such an arrangement… only because he was also trying to think of a way to undo it… After all… " He sighed loudly, shaking his head. He patted this immortal lord on the shoulder in passing, then cupped his hands to Hengwen. "I still have some trivial matters to attend to in the Heavenly Court, so I shall take my leave first."

Then, riding the wind and the clouds, he returned to the Heavenly Court.

Chapter Sixteen

Gorgeous red clouds adorned the horizon. It was nearing dusk.

There was a woodland on the hillside, an expanse of yellow grass littered with withered, yellow fallen leaves outside. Looking out from this spot, the sky appeared all the more far away.

Hengwen and I found ourselves a seat in this place, taking it all in.

With a yawn, Hengwen remarked, "I really am a bit sleepy." He then closed his eyes and lay down on the grass.

I sat watching the distant sky, unwittingly sinking into my inner poet. So high above, yet so far away, and to think I had spent countless years up there. It was a good hand I had been dealt.

As night fell, Hengwen asked me where we should go to kill time.

"I'm thinking of heading to Mu Ruoyan's residence for a look," I answered.

"Oh—" Hengwen said unhurriedly. "You're going over to see how the mountain cat is?"

"No," I replied, "I'm thinking of checking in on Mu Ruoyan. I feel somewhat ill at ease after hearing what Mingge said in the afternoon. It's really fortunate that Mingge didn't tell me a thing, or I'd already be out spilling the details to him. Now... there's nothing left for me to say... but I still keep wanting to check in on him."

Hengwen sighed. "Right, then go. I'm thinking of taking a stroll around Luyang City in another form, so I won't be going with you. Let's meet on the rooftop of the inn we were staying at."

As we rode the clouds above Luyang City, Hengwen pressed down upon the clouds, and I could not help but call out, "Hengwen."

Under the starlight, Hengwen turned to face me. "What?"

But I did not know what I should say, so I stammered, "Stroll to your heart's content. I'll wait for you on the rooftop of the inn."

Hengwen smiled and answered, "Got it."

This immortal lord took on the appearance of a scholar and made some inquiries on the streets of Luyang. A quarter of an hour later, I was standing on the ridge of Mu Ruoyan's roof.

Surprisingly enough, Shan Shengling kept it all very covert. His residence was in the city's north, and he had settled Mu Ruoyan down in the city's east. The residence was not at all large; flowers and trees were planted everywhere, giving it an exquisite look. From where I stood on the roof ridge, I saw several brightly illuminated side chambers in the rear courtyard.

Just as I concealed myself, setting myself in the middle of the courtyard, I spied a maidservant gliding through the walkway, entering one of the side chambers with a plate in her hands. I could not resist following her in for a look.

This side chamber was tastefully furnished and brightly illuminated, the brocade bedding and embroidered quilt laid neatly out for sleeping. The mountain cat was lying contentedly on the quilt, its little paws toying with that bamboo tube of mine.

It sure looked comfortable there. This must be Mu Ruoyan's bedchamber.

The maidservant set the plate on the table, curtsied, and withdrew, shutting the door.

I looked at what appeared to be tiny snacks on the small plate, all wrapped into cubes. Splotches of oil seeped through the colored paper, giving off a sweet aroma.

Hengwen was not very fond of eating the sugary stuff, but it seemed that was not the case for Tianshu.

I thought of Mu Ruoyan's tragic outcome—still unknowable as yet—that was yet to come in a couple of days, and felt forlorn.

The mountain cat on the bed sat up, nose twitching as it craned its neck toward the plate on the table. It leaped to the ground and kicked off onto the table, where it peered down at the snacks, then picked up one with its mouth, set it down, and began nudging it around with a paw. The snack was tightly wrapped, and would not open. It cocked its head at it, licked its whiskers, and with a few furtive glances around, finally hit the ground, instantly shifting back into an eight- or nine-year-old boy. Gingerly, he walked over to the door to bolt it, then tiptoed back again to the table and peeled off a wrapper before stuffing it into his mouth.

A person strode out from behind the screen—Mu Ruoyan.

As if sensing his presence, the mountain cat looked back. The color drained from his face, and he turned to escape, but Mu Ruoyan grabbed him by the shoulder. All at once, the mountain cat cried out and began to squirm out of his hold. He raised a hand to claw the offending arm. Acting quickly, this immortal lord reached out and calmly lifted his front claw. The mountain cat's hand paused for a moment, the force of his blow weakened, but even so, there was still a ripping sound as he shredded several strips of fabric from the sleeve of Mu Ruoyan's light-colored silk robe.

I recited a binding spell that tied the mountain cat's hands together with an invisible thread. Unable to exert force, his attempts were reduced to writhing and struggling. He lowered his head in an attempt to bite Mu Ruoyan's wrist, but he always missed by just a fraction or two.

"Don't be afraid," Mu Ruoyan said to the mountain cat in a kindly voice. "I won't hurt you. I only wish to ask you a question or two. I won't force you if you don't wish to answer, and after that, I'll let you go. All right?"

Seeing that he could not get any advantage over Mu Ruoyan, the mountain cat blinked his green, teary eyes. With hesitance, he eventually nodded and stood obediently still.

Mu Ruoyan slowly let go of his shoulder and pulled him over to the table to sit. He set a handful of the snacks before the mountain cat, who cowered as he looked at him, sniffling. Then he suddenly burst into tears. "Don't hand me over to that bad guy, Shan—"

Mu Ruoyan raised a sleeve to wipe his round face and said softly, "Don't worry, I'll let you go once I've asked my questions. I won't tell anyone. If I really wanted to hand you over, I could have done so earlier, right? Why would I wait until now?"

The mountain cat choked on his sobs. "P-Promise me..."

"I promise." Mu Ruoyan nodded.

Only then did the mountain cat wipe his snot. He still sniffled, but he stopped crying.

This immortal lord felt a little resigned watching from the table. The fox could be said to be an astute man. Why were the little demons he taught all so silly?

Mu Ruoyan petted him on his head, then removed the wrapper from a snack before stuffing it into his hand.

"You are... A-Ming?" he asked gingerly.

The ears on the mountain cat's head twitched. He nodded.

"It's a lovely name. Who gave it to you?" Mu Ruoyan asked.

"The Great King gave it to me," the mountain cat answered in a small voice.

Mu Ruoyan smiled. "Actually, I just want to ask you where... you got that bamboo tube on the bed?"

The mountain cat answered falteringly in a thin voice, "It belongs to that old Daoist priest whom the immortal Song was disguised as. I took it to play with it."

His words were like a punch so out of left field that it made this immortal lord see stars. From the spot where I was watching, invisible, I was this close to pounding my chest and stamping my foot. Several days of painstakingly building up my identity, only for it all to crumple apart because of this brat's exposé!

Mu Ruoyan's expression changed slightly, his brows now knitted, although his tone still remained neutral. "Are you talking about that old Daoist priest who was with that young master?"

After eating a piece of Mu Ruoyan's snack, the mountain cat grew bolder. "That's the one, the immortal with the other immortal, Qingjun, who was disguised as the young master. The Great King likes that good-looking Qingjun, so he wouldn't let me go to Qingjun for hugs. That Song immortal is so scary when he's disguised as the old Daoist priest. He doesn't like it when the Great King asks Qingjun for hugs, and he's very fierce toward the Great King. That's why he never plays with me. So I took his bamboo tube to play with."

This immortal lord would like to slam myself against the wall now.

Mu Ruoyan hesitated. "Could it be that... the snow fox is your Great King?" he asked.

The mountain cat nodded.

Mu Ruoyan closed his eyes, and said slowly, "All right, that's it. Thank you. If you wish to leave, leave quickly." He withdrew a handkerchief that he wrapped the snacks in, then set it in the mountain cat's lap. He stroked the cat's head one more time. "Don't worry. There's no one powerful in this courtyard now. That... Shan person won't come over either. No one will know if you leave quietly. What other snacks do you like? I'll get someone to bring you more."

With snacks in both hands, the mountain cat looked at Mu Ruoyan with shining green eyes.

"Y-You're a good person," he suddenly said. "I don't want your snacks. That bad guy Shan and a Daoist priest in blue clothes captured all my brothers and sisters. Do you know where they are?"

Mu Ruoyan was momentarily taken aback. "I... have no idea."

Tears trickled from the silly cat's eyes again.

Mu Ruoyan wiped them away with a sleeve. "How about this?" he said gently. "If I find out, I'll definitely think of a way to let them go."

The mountain cat rubbed his snot on Mu Ruoyan's sleeve and sobbed. "You're a human who's been transformed from a good immortal, unlike that Shan person who's been transformed from a bad immortal."

This immortal lord's head was buzzing from listening to him. Mu Ruoyan was momentarily stunned, but in no time, he was laughing. "Child, why are you going around calling everyone an immortal?"

Finally, the mountain cat stopped crying. Mu Ruoyan opened the door for him.

Haltingly, he asked of Mu Ruoyan, "Do you know where my Great King and those two exalted immortals went after leaving the inn?"

"I have no idea where they went after leaving even the prefectural office," Mu Ruoyan answered.

With the bundle of snacks in hand, the mountain cat looked

out the door, his expression somewhat lost.

Seeing this, Mu Ruoyan said, "If you don't know where to find your Great King, why not stay here for a few days? Your Great King knows I took you away. He'll surely come looking for you."

The mountain cat visibly hesitated as he held the snacks in his arms and peered at Mu Ruoyan's expression, pondering. Eventually, he gave a timid nod of his head.

And so, he returned to the chamber, ate two snacks, and transformed back into his original form. Surprisingly enough, it chose to snuggle in Mu Ruoyan's lap, and fell asleep.

This immortal lord could not help but wipe my forehead.

Mu Ruoyan set the mountain cat gently onto the bed, then pushed the door open to leave the side chamber. Perhaps because he always liked to stand alone in the yard, there were no maidservants or young servants around to wait on him.

I followed him to the courtyard, where he stopped to stand in silence by a plantain tree.

This immortal lord pondered it over for a moment, then circled around to the shadow of the tree opposite him. Manifesting myself, I walked out from the shadows and cupped my hands in a greeting. "Young Master Mu."

In supernatural tales, the wandering ghosts always apparated from the night like this. What's more, the breeze was gentle here, and the moonlight dim. The moment this immortal lord walked out, Mu Ruoyan took a startled step back, but after a glimpse, he likely figured me out to be an old acquaintance.

I cupped my hands again. "Young Master Mu, this humble one is Song Yao."

Standing in the courtyard, Mu Ruoyan fixed his eyes on me. "Song Yao... Daoist Master Guangyun... May I ask just who exactly your esteemed self is?"

"I am someone whose fate is intertwined with Young Master

Mu," I said. "In the past, Young Master Mu committed a grave wrong, and now must suffer all your current hardships. Karma is looming right ahead. Young Master Mu, please stop before it's too late. If you sincerely repent now, there may yet be room to turn back."

Oh, Jade Emperor. Even if you are watching me from the Heavenly Court as I tip him off, this immortal lord's earnest exhortations could also be considered as going along with your wishes.

Mu Ruoyan said nothing at first, but eventually intoned, slowly, "Karma. The kind of karma I will receive remains to be seen. But I more or less know what the grave wrong your esteemed self mentioned is. Human nature should be free and unconstrained to begin with. The only mistake in my actions is probably that they run counter to the so-called principles of the world. Thank you for your kind reminder. It's just—"

Mu Ruoyan looked at me and smiled. "I must have ended up where I am today because I was unwilling to turn back and repent in the first place. Since this is where I have ended up, then what need is there for me to turn back again?"

I was struck speechless.

Mu Ruoyan turned around, and walked slowly back to the side chamber.

I took a step after him. "Even if you meet an unkind end in the coming days? Even if you suffer the hardships of reincarnation through several lifetimes without a good ending in any life? You need only to admit a mistake. You... must consider it carefully."

Mu Ruoyan stopped in his tracks, turned only to answer, "Is that so? So, it turns out that I still have an end."

Then went straight back to his bedchamber.

I stood blankly in place for a moment before rising on a cloud.

The wind on the roof of the inn was freezing, but the stars up above were dazzling. The stars of the Big Dipper hung in the sky, shining brightly.

Behind me, a voice with a hint of a smile said lazily, "Now that you are done seeing Tianshu, you're going to gaze at the Big Dipper and mope?"

I saw who it was and stood. "Hengwen."

Hengwen and I sat side by side on the roof.

"I went to tip Tianshu off," I said. "Told him cryptically about his eventual fate in a day or two. I said to admit his mistake and stop before it's too late, but he refuses to."

"I knew that this would be the outcome" Hengwen said. "Tianshu's nature is one that would rather break than bend. He never owned up to his mistake back at the Immortal Execution Terrace, what's more today?"

I could only sigh. Changing the topic, I asked Hengwen about his stroll in the city.

"So-so," Hengwen answered. "Shan Shengling put the city on edge; everyone is in a state of panic. Wails were all I could hear when I walked on the streets. Did you know that after Xuan Li revealed the truth, Shan Shengling killed everyone in the hall after we left to prevent it from leaking out?"

I was shocked. "That's a tad too ruthless, isn't it?"

"Indeed," Hengwen sighed. "Nanming Dijun's ruthlessness has only increased this one trip down to the mortal realm, and he has dragged Tianshu into suffering retribution with him." He lay back on the tiles and drawled, "I wonder what will happen tomorrow."

The tiles on the roof were uneven and bumpy, not level or smooth at all.

"Hengwen, lying here is a touch too hard and uncomfortable," I said. "Why don't we go elsewhere? Or you could lean against me while you sleep? You-you haven't got the chance to rest these couple of days..."

Hengwen sat up at once. Eyes that were like pools of ink

gazed into mine. He chuckled. "What has gotten you so broody?"

I was this close to blurting out the truth. Fortunately, my willpower was strong enough. I could only say, "You... Using your powers is physically taxing. Besides... I..."

Hengwen's eyes came closer and closer into view, his voice a low baritone, "What about you?"

I gulped, and cleared my head with thoughts of the mortal realm observation mirror. "Hengwen, I always felt that being able to ascend to the Heavenly Court, becoming an immortal, was a blessing Heaven just dropped into my lap."

Hengwen raised his eyebrows, withdrawing to sit upright. "That good?"

"Yes," I answered.

The breeze was chill around us; the clear moon outlined a sleeping city in light. On the ridge of the roof, I heaved a long sigh.

Hengwen, you have never been to the human world, so you don't know that here, a hundred years is but a far-fetched dream. Yet in the Heavenly Court, one could look forward to an everlasting eternity.

Hengwen had fallen asleep against the roof tiles. This immortal lord lay beside him, and without realizing it, I too fell asleep.

It was already bright by the time I woke up on a cloud. Hengwen stood at the edge, peering down. "You're finally awake," he said. "Look down. I reckon mayhem is going to ensue soon in Luyang City."

I rushed to get up and joined him in observing the ground. Hengwen lowered the cloud a little more, just in time for me to see soldiers moving on the streets of Luyang, checking the passersby one at a time. Non-residents and street beggars were all rounded up, bound, and strung together with a rope as the soldiers led them back to the prefectural prison, all the while striking and kicking them.

That day, the armies of the Prince of the Eastern Commandery and the Imperial Court arrived at the Yangtze River and clashed with the naval units of the Southern Commandery. The battle was an extraordinarily violent one, and the river flowed with corpses.

Shan Shengling had always been arrogant about his achievements in the Southern Commandery; this battle was an opportunity to knock him down a peg. Shan Shengling had only nine thousand elite troops at his command, and the Prince of the Southern Commandery had given him the order to defend Luyang to his death.

The naval units of the Southern Commandery, being no match for the two armies, were almost completely wiped out. On the second day, the armies of the Imperial Court and the Eastern Commandery went ashore on the opposite bank; they had fought their way to the city gates by dusk.

The armies stood in formation outside Luyang City the following morning. Shan Shengling led five thousand soldiers out of the city to face off his enemies in battle.

Li Sixian steered his horse out from the Eastern Commandery formation, and shouted, "Listen up, soldiers and commoners of the Southern Commandery. Our Eastern Commandery have mobilized troops this time only to seek revenge against Shan Shengling. We have no intention of harassing the common folk. Shan Shengling abducted Mu Ruoyan, a fugitive wanted by the Imperial Court, from the Prince of the Eastern Commandery's manor and murdered Li Siming, my third younger brother and the third son of the Prince. If we do not avenge this feud, our Li Clan of the Eastern Commandery aren't fit to call ourselves humans! Hand over Shan Shengling and Mu Ruoyan, and the Eastern Commandery will withdraw our troops immediately, never again to invade the Southern Commandery!"

A general from the Imperial Court army rode out of the

formation and shouted, "Shan Shengling, a fugitive wanted by the Imperial Court, has been hiding in the Southern Commandery for several years, and now harbors another wanted fugitive of the Imperial Court, Mu Ruoyan. We are here on His Majesty's decree to arrest them both. I hope you can hand them over posthaste. The Imperial Court will naturally offer a reward for them!"

Shan Shengling roared with laughter from his horse. "Do you lowlifes think that by sowing discord, you can mess with my troops' morale?!" He waved his longsword, and the soldiers surged forward. Thus began combat with the armies from the Imperial Court and Eastern Commandery.

Nanming Dijun was of course incomparably valiant as he rode his steed through the enemy's midst, cleaving away at the people like he was slashing grass. However, it ultimately proved hard for his five thousand soldiers to win against tens of thousands of soldiers. In the end, Shan Shengling retreated into the city with only three thousand survivors in tow.

Neither the Imperial Court nor the Eastern Commandery pursued them. Instead, they set up camp where they were, and sent runners to the border of the city to shout for Shan Shengling's and Mu Ruoyan's handover.

That night, along the streets of the city, countless torches materialized to surround the residences of Mu Ruoyan and the general.

I stood on the clouds, watching the crowd bay for the blood of those two treacherous traitors.

Chapter Seventeen

It must have been fate at work. Shan Shengling killed the prefect and all his runners that day to silence them, but he had missed an advisor who managed to flee. When the words shouted at the city border matched with the testimony of the advisor, the commoners rioted, and the army was promptly thrown into disarray. This crowd, already panicking at the massive troops outside with only meager forces within to protect them, swarmed to kill the two perpetrators of this whole mess—Shan Shengling and Mu Ruoyan.

The crowd first went charging toward the general's residence with their torches raised high, but Shan Shengling was already gone, having been escorted away by a few of his men willing to die for the cause. His residence was empty. The crowd searched all over, throwing things around and smashing them. After a moment, someone yelled, "No doubt Shan Shengling has already fled. To the residence of the one named Mu!"

The torches converged together and swarmed out of the general's residence. The people threw a few torches into a side chamber, and the room promptly burst into flames.

With all these delays, Shan Shengling should have already taken Mu Ruoyan out of the residence.

But everyone in the city wanted them dead, and the armies of the Eastern Commandery and the Imperial Court had the city completely surrounded, so how were the two of them going to escape?

I rode the wind and hurried over to the Mu residence. The torches on the streets resembled a meandering fire dragon.

The main entrance to Mu Ruoyan's residence was wide open, but Shan Shengling and Mu Ruoyan were standing in the inner courtyard, facing each other.

This immortal lord let loose a long sigh.

Goodness me, Nanming. At a moment when time is of the essence, what're you doing just standing there? If he's unwilling to leave, just knock him out and hoist him away. The crowd that wants to hack you both to pieces is almost at the door!

I lowered the clouds and heard Nanming say, "… Haha, this is just great. I can't believe even you see me as a tyrant wicked beyond redemption. What else is there for me to say?"

"It's actually me who sowed the seed of this sin." Mu Ruoyan said. "It has nothing to do with you."

Nanming suddenly reached over to grasp Mu Ruoyan by the chin. "Even at this point, are you still regretting killing Li Siming?"

"At this point, you can only get out of this predicament by handing me over," Mu Ruoyan said. "You've been enduring it all in silence for so many years. Do you want to let it all go to waste now?"

The torches had already arrived at the entrance, but the crowd did a double take on seeing the main doors open. "What's this?" someone yelled. "Are they playing us with a fucking Empty Fort Strategy?"

Another voice promptly answered, "Who the hell cares? Let's just storm our way in!" Chimes of agreement rose here and there, but no one dared to move.

Shan Shengling was still grasping Mu Ruoyan's chin as they looked into each other's eyes. He suddenly let go. "Your clan was executed and your family properties were confiscated only because you took me in. Between you and me, who exactly owes whom?"

He suddenly struck out a palm, swift as lightning, that struck Mu Ruoyan's neck before he could react.

Mu Ruoyan went limp and collapsed.

With a clap of his hands, Shan Shengling summoned a few guards in black. Coldly, he commanded, "Send Young Master Mu out of the city, even if you have to risk your lives."

The torches cast a red hue over the sky. Shan Shengling removed his armor and helmet to lean over Mu Ruoyan.

"I, Shan Shengling, will take responsibility for what I have done," he whispered under his breath. "I don't need someone else to shoulder the blame for me."

With that, he took up his longsword and strode toward the door.

Standing there, with his longsword held aloft, he said, "You lot want to kill me, so who has the guts to go first?!"

Torches swarmed forth, and shadows of blades rose. Combat sounds permeated the air.

A guard in black bore Mu Ruoyan on his back, while the others formed a protective barrier around him. They ran for the backyard.

Hengwen said, voice soft, "The time is now if you want to save Tianshu."

"You should go and take a look outside the city," I said. "I'll stay here."

With a laugh, Hengwen said, "With both of us sharing the blame, the punishment may very well be a little lighter." He clapped a palm on my shoulder. The space beneath this immortal lord's feet became empty, and I hit the ground with a heavy thud.

Hengwen landed gracefully behind me. A gust of refreshing air swept past, and before the few guards in black could be shocked, they toppled over like falling eggplants.

Hengwen and I rode the clouds up, this time with Tianshu in tow.

Outside the entrance to Mu Ruoyan's residence, blood splashed like a river. Shan Shengling was soaked in blood from head to toe, still fighting at close quarters amidst the crowd of people. Hengwen flicked a finger, sending a blue light to land on Shan Shengling. "Nanming was once a Dijun, after all. Since we've saved Tianshu, let's shield him with a spiritual barrier for a while."

I suddenly spotted a tiny figure huddled on top of the enclosing wall of Mu Ruoyan's residence. "Isn't that the mountain cat spirit?" I blurted in astonishment.

Hengwen focused his gaze over. "Indeed it is."

Resignedly, I said, "Let's double dip and bring it up here."

As the clouds descended, Mu Ruoyan gave a sudden stir. He woke up.

Perhaps the nourishment from that bowl of jinluo lingzhi had rearranged Mu Ruoyan's constitution so that it was now slightly different from ordinary people. To think he would wake up at this time, even after that blow from Nanming.

This immortal lord watched as he jolted up and surveyed his surroundings, teetering on the clouds.

I had to explain to him, "Don't be afraid. This is this immortal lord's cloud-riding technique. I'll take you out of the city."

Mu Ruoyan stood at the edge of the cloud. "Is this how you two gentlemen mean to save me?"

My silence was my assent, and Mu Ruoyan responded mildly, "You've already said that this is my deserved outcome. The debt that I owe must be repaid. I have no wish to know about what happened in my previous incarnation, but now, I wish to have an ending. Please grant me this."

The silhouette of him moved as he made to throw himself down.

I snatched his arm, and in a moment of desperation, I had no choice but to say, "You don't owe me a thing. Actually... the truth is that I am the one who owes you."

Mu Ruoyan fixed his eyes on me, and I declared, "I'm Li Siming."

Mu Ruoyan looked at me, his expression calm and still.

"Li Siming was a disguise of mine, as was Guangyunzi," I said. "If you don't believe me..." I reached the other hand under the chest of my robes and pulled out a jade pendant. I held it out before him. "This jade pendant of yours is still with me. That day in the Prince of the Eastern Commandery's manor, I fooled you and made a show of throwing it into the pond, but I actually hid it away. I..."

I heaved a sigh and spilled it all. "I descended to the mortal world on orders to set up trials for you. You were originally Tianshu Xingjun of the Heavenly Court, but you violated the laws of Heaven and were banished to the human world together with Nanming Dijun, Shan Shengling. My orders were to set up love trials for you in this life, and many of the unkind deeds I've committed were done deliberately. I deserved that one stab of yours, so you owe me nothing at all."

Mu Ruoyan looked at the jade pendant in silence until he suddenly said, slowly, "This jade pendant... I've had it for as long as I can remember. It was supposedly a gift from an itinerant Daoist priest, who said that this jade pendant and I have an affinity from a past life. Be it past life or present life, or the identity of so-and-so... what does it all matter?" That clear gaze moved until it landed on my face. "Since it's Heaven's punishment, then there exists an outcome."

This immortal lord's heart became flooded, then, with

emotions—innumerable, indescribable.

A blinding flare of lightning suddenly flashed from beneath us. I whipped my head around and looked down to the ground.

"Something's not right," Hengwen remarked.

Shan Shengling was amidst the crowd, slashing and killing left and right, spent and exhausted. The barrier Hengwen had cast on him had already dissipated, slashes riddled his body. More and more people surrounded him, their blades and axes falling in unison. It looked like Shan Shengling was about to meet a violent end under the blades of the crowd.

One long ax hacked down heavily on Shan Shengling's shoulder. Blood spurted and splashed onto the wall of Mu Ruoyan's residence, right beneath where the tiny, dark figure of the mountain cat huddled.

In an instant, a blinding flare of lightning enveloped the wall. This immortal lord stood on the clouds and heard a sharp howl penetrating the skies.

The mountain cat spirit's silhouette loomed against the wall, growing bigger and bigger. The flare of lightning enveloped Shan Shengling, and all those people encircling him let loose bloodcurdling screams. There was a crash—several charred and stiff corpses had toppled to the ground!

When the howl was about to trail off, this immortal lord saw a strange, gargantuan beast leap off the wall amidst the sizzling lightning to land before Shan Shengling. It pounced on the crowd, and blood burst everywhere.

This immortal lord was stunned frozen on the clouds.

"The snowlion..." Hengwen muttered under his breath. "... To think it's the snowlion!"

The legendary ferocious spiritual beast, the snowlion?!

My grip on Tianshu's left arm slackened in spite of myself. I looked at Hengwen, but before I could say a word, my hand turned up empty. My heart went cold, and I whipped my head back. Mu Ruoyan had already leaped off the clouds.

A violent gale rose, instantly sweeping Mu Ruoyan into the clouds. This immortal lord hurriedly jumped off the clouds, only to suddenly bounce off a divine barrier.

A piece of cloud appeared in wisps beneath my feet, buoying me, and a figure flitted past me. "I'm afraid it'd prove hard to deal with the snowlion with your cultivation. I'll go." With these words, his figure disappeared among the wind.

I howled his name and reached out, but my hand grabbed nothing but empty air.

Mu Ruoyan plunged fast. Hengwen, too, moved fast. To my surprise, that cloud fettered my legs, rendering me immobile.

The mythical beast's great sharp claws swiped toward Mu Ruoyan as he was about to fall right before its eyes. Hengwen brandished forth divine light to block the blow, then wrapped a silk sash around Mu Ruoyan to hold him fast.

The mythical beast flew into a violent rage. Several bolts of lightning instantly struck down, and Hengwen warded them all off with a sweep of his sleeve. I struggled, doing everything I could in midair to charge down too, but I could only watch helplessly as the claw of the beast slashed down toward Hengwen's back.

I howled his name again, as a shadow lunged forth and slammed Hengwen out of the way, solidly taking the impact from the beast's blow.

Blood dripped from the beast's claws. It suddenly went still, and the shadow fell over to the ground.

Furball.

The beast howled again. Suddenly swinging its head and whipping its tail, it banged its head repeatedly against the ground. The young and tender voice of a child indistinctly cried, "Great King, Great King, run!"

The beast raised its head to the sky and bellowed, its eyes blazing red.

With Mu Ruoyan under his arm, Hengwen moved to block the beast and save Furball, still on the ground.

I exerted all my strength to shatter my cloud binding, and rushed toward the ground.

The hair of the beast bristled in fury as it lunged at Hengwen. It collided against Hengwen's barrier, sending up a burst of strange light that engulfed all the figures.

Amidst the thunderous noise, I heard what seemed to be an out-of-tone howl from me, "HENGWEN—"

A colossal golden shield dropped from the sky and entirely enveloped the strange light and the ground.

A hand suddenly clapped on this immortal lord's shoulder. "Song Yao, don't worry. This lord is here to subdue this snowlion."

Bihua Lingjun floated over to my side and folded his arms as he watched the glittering golden shield. He sighed, "I *said* you would definitely regret not letting me take that cat away. Alas! Fortunately, this lord has anticipated this scenario, and borrowed Taishang Laojun's Spirit-Suppressing Shield. Without it, how could I have subdued this snowlion?"

The Spirit-Suppressing Shield shrank smaller and smaller under the surge of golden light, even as the golden light gradually dimmed. I saw the ruins of collapsed walls and bodies strewn all over the ground, the sight of which was dreary to behold.

Bihua Lingjun and I made landfall. The golden shield on the vacant land was the size and shape of a small, inverted bowl.

I wasted no time. "Where's Hengwen?" I asked.

"Don't worry, relax. They're all in this shield," Bihua Lingjun said. He then put out his palm; a silvery light emerged from beneath the golden shield, slowly flying into his palm.

"It's inadvisable to remain here," Bihua Lingjun said. "Let's head somewhere secluded first before we talk."

Bihua Lingjun and this immortal lord stepped on a cloud and flew out of Luyang City.

"Song Yao, oh Song Yao, you're really a lucky one," Bihua Lingjun said. "You divulged Heaven's secret and defied the Jade Emperor's decree to save Tianshu. It just so happens that the Jade Emperor is busy with the doctrine dialogue, and Mingge has been called away on an assignment. They are both still unaware of what has transpired. Even more coincidentally, Mingge has entrusted the Mortal Realm Observation Mirror to me and asked me to look out for you. I picked it up for a look the moment he left, just in time to rush over and provide emergency assistance."

Listening half-heartedly, my response came in the form of two dry laughs.

Bihua Lingjun continued with a sigh, "But the commotion this time is so cataclysmic that no doubt some merit emissaries and patrolling deities will report it to the Jade Emperor." His free hand patted me on my shoulder. "It's only a matter of time before Heaven punishes you."

"At most, I'll be sent to the Immortal Execution Terrace," I said.

Once more, Bihua Lingjun gave a long sigh.

Hues of blue washed over the sky in the east; it was already dawn. Bihua Lingjun and I arrived at a desolate mountaintop.

Bihua Lingjun set the golden shield on the ground and recited a chant. The bowl grew in size. Bihua Lingjun carefully pried the shield partially open, and picked out a white figure with his little finger.

Bihua Lingjun laid it into his palm and inspected it. "The snowlion. You've never seen it before, and Hengwen has only seen it in pictures. This lord had the privilege of seeing it once, which was why I could recognize it at a glance the other day. Nanming Dijun had saved its life before, and it snuck into the Heavenly Court to save Nanming after he was imprisoned for his crime. I did not manage to capture it then, and it fled a wounded beast. Seems like it possessed that mountain cat to conceal its tracks after coming to the mortal world. It usually slumbers within the cat, but Nanming's blood scent is capable of awakening it. It should have woken up once before, and that was how this lord was able to recognize it."

So that's how it was. The so-called person in blue who had saved Nanming had never existed. It was the scent of blood on Nanming that day that awakened the beast, who then killed everyone in the fox's lair and let Nanming go. But the mountain cat did not remember this after waking up. In all probability, the beast had created a false dream in its mind, so that the mountain cat would take it as the whole narrative to recount later.

"Bihua," I called out. "Can you stop going on and on? Where is Hengwen... Tianshu and Nanming?"

"Yes, yes, you'll see them soon," Bihua Lingjun answered. He lifted the golden shield, and the mass of silver light on the ground grew larger and larger before gradually dissipating.

An orb of faint golden light materialized in Bihua's palm. "This is Nanming Dijun's immortal soul. A mortal's body cannot hold up against the simultaneous powers of the snowlion, Hengwen Qingjun, and the Spirit-Suppressing Shield all at once, and it has already been obliterated. For the time being, Nanming Dijun's soul will be sealed in this orb of light."

This immortal lord, however, had neither time nor energy to care if Nanming's soul was round or flat. I stared agape at the ground. After the silver light receded, two youths who seemed to be similarly eleven or twelve years of age lay on the ground, their eyes closed. One of them was grasping Hengwen's folding fan, while the other wore Tianshu's jade pendant around his neck.

"This-this-this-this-this-this-this-this-this-this..." this immortal lord heard myself blurt.

A cough. "Well, about *this*..." Bihua Lingjun said, "Hengwen

Qingjun sustained heavy injuries after his barrier collided with the snowlion's beast energy. Fortunately, the Spirit-Suppressing Shield protected him in time, and his immortal energy returned to his body. But this Spirit-Suppressing Shield..." another cough "... also tends to impact immortals in some way... So Qingjun may be like this for the time being and lose some of his memories. He will probably be able to recover after staying in the mortal world for a few days..."

My eyes became unfocused, and my hands trembled slightly.

Bihua Lingjun continued, "On the other hand, it's a tad strange that Tianshu Xingjun did not end up like Nanming Dijun, but this is his real immortal form now. His mortal body should have already been obliterated, just like Nanming Dijun's. Tianshu probably ended up like this because Hengwen Qingjun protected him with a magical barrier, and the jade pendant he always carries on him in the Heavenly Court is a spiritual device, which must have played a part too. He probably... will regress into the appearance and mental capacity of a youth for now, and recover after a few days in the mortal world, just like Hengwen Qingjun."

This immortal lord could only stare blankly at the two youngsters Hengwen and Tianshu had become.

Not far from Hengwen lay the blood-covered Furball who had been beaten back into his original form. It seemed to be still breathing, its belly rising and falling ever so slightly.

Furball was shrouded in a mass of faint, green light. This immortal lord approached it, and that faint light gradually condensed into a tiny ball that nuzzled against the fox's head. Slowly, it faded out and dissipated.

The mountain cat had managed to break its soul free of the snowlion's body after all, and used its soul and meager cultivation to protect the fox, allowing the fox to hang on to its life by that one crucial thread.

Bihua Lingjun joined me to help treat the fox's wounds. He

sighed, "A pity this snow fox's thousands of years of cultivation have been wiped out. It can only be a common fox again."

I fed some of my immortal powers to the fox.

"This lord has to take the snowlion and Nanming Dijun's soul back to the Heavenly Court to report to the Jade Emperor," Bihua Lingjun said. "You—" a sigh "—you will not be able to escape your inevitable punishment by Heaven—"

Another sigh as he gave this immortal lord a pat on the shoulder. "You and I have been fellow immortals for a long time, so I'll do you another favor. Hengwen Qingjun and Tianshu Xingjun shall temporarily remain with you in the mortal world, where you'll keep to their side. By the time I have returned to the Heavenly Court and finished my report, you would have spent a few days in the mortal world. By then, I reckon Hengwen Qingjun and Tianshu should have recovered. When the time comes,"—sigh again—"we'll see how the Jade Emperor's verdict goes."

I cupped my hands. "Thank you!"

"No need to stand on ceremony with me," Bihua Lingjun said. "Donghua, Jinxing, Laojun, and several other fellow immortals will intercede on your behalf, so you might not necessarily be sent to the Immortal Execution Terrace. Once this is over, drinks are on you."

"Definitely, definitely." I cupped my hands again.

Bihua Lingjun then rose in a beam of spiritual light and returned to the Heavenly Court.

Chapter Eighteen

He grabbed the corner of my robe, struggling to get up as he rubbed his bleary eyes. After surveying his surroundings, he asked with uncertainty, "Where is this place? And who are you?"

I flashed my pearly whites and rubbed his head. "This is the mortal world. My name is Song Yao."

"Oh." He cocked his head and looked at me. "I've never seen you before in the Heavenly Court. Are you an immortal lord or an immortal without an official post? Why did I wake up in the mortal world?"

"This humble immortal's celestial title is Guangxu Yuanjun," I responded with a grin. "I'm here on the Heavenly Court's order to bring you to the mortal world for several days to gain experience. When you grow up, you have to take charge of the world's literary ethics, so you have to observe and experience the worldly sentiments and desires in the mortal world."

His black, shining eyes continued to stare at me. "Are you... here to supervise me?"

"Not to supervise, but to take care of you," I said. "If there is anything you wish to eat, play, or want, let me know. There's

no need to address me by my title. You can just call me Song…"
When I spoke to this point, a thought suddenly occurred to me,
If I don't take advantage of this opportunity now, then when?

So I continued in an amicable tone, "You can call me Uncle
Song Yao or Immortal Uncle Song."

A smile gradually blossomed on his little face.

Right at this moment, Tianshu, in the form of a youth,
rubbed his eyes and clambered to his feet in bewilderment.

This immortal lord diverted my attention to look at Tianshu,
and Hengwen looked up at me. "I've never been to the mortal
world, so I don't know what's delicious or fun. Can you show
me around, Song Yao?"

I laughed wryly in my heart. *Hengwen, oh Hengwen. So it turns
out you were never one to be taken advantage of, even as a youngster.*

Tianshu stood on the ground and fixed his clear, bright eyes
on me. "Where is this place? And who are you both?"

You both?

It then dawned on me that Tianshu was born way earlier
than Hengwen. Only heaven knew where Hengwen was when
Tianshu was a youth.

Hengwen blinked. Pointing at Tianshu, he looked up at me
and asked, "Who is he?"

I was still hesitating over my words when Tianshu answered
in a childlike voice, "I am Tianshu of the Beidou Star Palace. I
have never seen either of you in the Heavenly Court before. Are
you both immortals or immortal lords?"

Oh, no, I inwardly bemoaned to myself.

As expected, Hengwen's face scrunched into a frown.
"Tianshu? Tianshu Xingjun is clearly…"

I hurriedly covered Hengwen's mouth and pulled him to
my side. I turned around and bent down to whisper into his
ear, "Something happened to Tianshu Xingjun in Heaven. He's
somewhat similar to you. The Heavenly Court conferred him

the name Tianshu and had me bring the both of you down to experience the mortal world. You'll know why in a few days. Don't say too much for now, all right?"

Hengwen blinked his eyes and scrunched up his nose. Quietly, he whispered back, "All right, but don't watch me as closely as you do him these days."

Solemnly, I acquiesced. "For sure."

I let go of Hengwen, and sure enough, he stood obediently by my side and said nothing further.

To Tianshu, I said, "My name is Song Yao. My humble title, as bestowed by the Jade Emperor, is Guangxu Yuanjun. I'm acting on his orders to bring you and this immortal, Hengwen, to experience the mortal world. You'll know why after returning to the Heavenly Court in a few days' time. For the time being, you'll remain in the mortal world with me."

The present Tianshu did not have the frosty, awe-inspiring aura of an immortal; all he had was an air of juvenile innocence. Furthermore, he was much easier to fool than young Hengwen, who merely nodded his head obediently, believing whatever I said. Hengwen had been raised by the Jade Emperor ever since he was a child, and it was only when he was three hundred years old that he had been granted the title of Qingjun and placed in charge of Wensi Hall. Tianshu, on the other hand, had been born Tianshu Xingjun, the most honorable of all in the Beidou Palace. I had not expected this younger Tianshu to be so easily coaxed. Nor could I imagine how such a sweet-tempered youngster would grow up to become the cold and aloof Tianshu.

Little Tianshu looked at me with his clear, bright eyes. "Please guide me along these few days in the mortal world."

I smiled affably, so much that my face was about to cramp.

Hengwen was all grins as he ran over to Tianshu and took his arm. "My name is Hengwen. Can I call you Tianshu? Is it also your first time coming to the mortal world?"

Tianshu nodded.

Hengwen continued, "Do you live in Beidou Palace? After we return to the Heavenly Court, I'll go over and play with you."

"Sure," Tianshu answered happily.

This old shell of an immortal lord squatted on the side and watched Young Hengwen and Young Tianshu standing together hand-in-hand, finding it as surreal as Donghua Dijun performing a water-sleeve dance right before my eyes.

After a while, I warned Hengwen and Tianshu not to reveal any traces of their immortality before the mortals, even as I prepared to find a city where we could wait for the heavenly envoys to arrive. When that happened, Tianshu would go into his next reincarnation, Hengwen would continue being Qingjun, and I would head up to the Immortal Execution Terrace.

Just as the clouds were about to rise, Hengwen suddenly turned his head and looked at the undergrowth overgrown with weeds at his side. "What's that?"

I followed his gaze. There, amidst the undergrowth, lay a white bundle—the fox.

I was so focused on Hengwen and Tianshu that I had overlooked the fox. It had woken up when Bihua was treating its wounds, but could not move then. It had probably struggled to leave while my attention was on Tianshu and Hengwen, but it could not even shift a few steps given its injuries, so it simply lay flat on the ground.

Hengwen ran over and squatted down to brush aside the long grass. "A white fox. How did it get injured?" He reached out to stroke the fox's back.

The fox buried its head in its fur, its eyes tightly shut.

Tianshu joined them, squatting down. "Its injuries are quite severe."

Hengwen lifted the fox from the grass. Furball, being well-fed, was a tad rotund, and the present Hengwen strained somewhat to carry it. As he held it, he said, "Be good, all right? I'll take you to get your wounds treated."

The fox rested its head against Hengwen's little shoulder. Slowly, drops of tears welled from its shut eyes.

I looked at Furball and heaved a long, long sigh.

"Young Master Song, are these two little young masters your..." My neighbor, Third Granny Huang, stood at the entrance to this immortal lord's small courtyard, staring fixedly at the children behind me.

I laughed dryly without answering. Third Granny Huang was the wife of Third Grandpa Huang, the physician who lived next door to the small courtyard I had just purchased. I had just brought Tianshu and Hengwen to this city, and since it was not very safe or convenient to live in an inn with two youngsters in tow, I had bought a small courtyard.

Having splurged a large sum of silver, the unscrupulous merchant who sold me the house acted swiftly and commandeered dozens of people in and out of the residence. In half a day, the little courtyard was thoroughly cleaned up. Brand new tables, chairs, and beds were all in place, while the beds in the side chambers had been laid out with new, clean bedding. A new, pristine tea set sat on the table, complete with a fresh brew of jasmine tea in the pot.

The crowd then withdrew, their jobs done, leaving behind only a female cook, a young servant, and two maidservants to attend to us for the time being.

I had just been about to close the courtyard doors when an old lady leaned in partially through the frame, and started a conversation with me after exchanging introductions.

Third Granny Huang's old but bright eyes had livened up when they landed on Hengwen and Tianshu.

Seeing as I did not answer, Third Granny Huang continued to wonder with great astonishment, "Young Master Song, you're so young. How could you have two sons this big?!"

"This humble one married early," I answered.

Third Granny Huang clicked her tongue. "Young Master Song, your wife can really give birth. The two little young masters look really…" She stared fixedly at Hengwen and Tianshu, sizing them up and down. "This little young master is really such a looker. My old self can't even begin to draw an analogy for his looks. That other little young master is also so delicately handsome. Tsk, tsk. Given how good-looking the two young masters are, your wife must be a beauty far more ravishing than Xi Shi and Diao Chan of the Four Great Beauties. This old one has not seen your wife yet. The madam, she's…"

"Dead," I answered, slowly.

Third Granny Huang was stunned, then she sighed in lamentation. That evening, she sent over ten freshly steamed buns and a pot of steamed vegetables.

The young Tianshu and Hengwen had never seen steamed buns before.

When the maidservant carried those steamed buns over to the table during dinnertime, Tianshu and Hengwen sat at the table and stared at the novel fare with two pairs of astounded eyes. When the maidservant left, Tianshu put on a contemplative look without making any move, while Hengwen picked up his chopsticks and reached out to poke one of them. "They're soft," he remarked with a face full of curiosity, then he placed the chopsticks in his mouth to taste them. "Hm?" He frowned. "There's no taste."

Tianshu scrutinized the steamed buns, then Hengwen. Following suit, he raised his chopsticks and poked gingerly at a bun.

Hengwen bit down on his chopsticks and asked me, "Eh, what is this thing?"

"This is called a steamed bun," I answered with a serious countenance.

Hengwen blinked his eyes.

"Oh," Tianshu piped up in sudden understanding. "So this is a steamed bun. Taiyin Xingjun once told me there's a kind of food called the steamed bun in the mortal world. It comes in large and small sizes. Then there's another kind that's even smaller than steamed buns, called the stuffed dumplings. So this is a steamed bun."

I initially wanted to say that steamed buns and dumplings were actually very different. One was steamed, the other boiled, and then there was another kind that was made in bamboo steamers. But those two little silly faces were looking up at me, and I feared they would dwell on this topic until tomorrow, so I simply gave a perfunctory answer. "That's right, that's right. This kind is the big steamed bun. The small ones are for breakfast. Then there are the dumplings. You will see them in the future."

I picked up a steamed bun and took a bite, then chewed and swallowed. "This is how you eat it. The skin on the outside is flavorless, but there's filling inside."

Hengwen immediately reached out for the steamed bun he had poked earlier, while Tianshu gently took one and set it down on his plate. Holding the bun in his hand, Hengwen pinched it and looked at it left and right. "But won't it be inelegant to eat it the way you did just now?"

I could only answer, "No. As they say, do as the natives do when you are in a foreign land, and this is how you eat this in the mortal world."

Hengwen lifted the steamed bun to his eyes and looked at it repeatedly, then he nodded and took a bite, after which he held it before his eyes again for a look. Swallowing, he announced, "There's indeed filling in it." Then he simply broke the steamed bun apart and pushed the skin aside with his chopsticks to take a closer look. Choosing a spot with filling, he took a bite.

"Delicious," he declared with a beam.

Tianshu picked up his and ate it daintily, one small mouthful at a time. He had grown up with Hengwen in the Heavenly Court ever since they were young, and even when lifting and biting into the bun, he did so with poise and elegance.

Tianshu ate one, picked up a few handfuls of steamed vegetables with his chopsticks, had a small bowl of porridge, and that concluded his meal.

Hengwen, on the other hand, ate one, blinked, then took another one. Although he ate with refined manners, he was fast, and he had only just finished the second bun when he took the third one. By the time he was starting on his fourth, this immortal lord grew worried that he would bloat, and when he reached for the fifth one, I intercepted his hand to stop him. "Overeat, and you'll get too bloated. Let's see how it goes tomorrow."

Hengwen retracted his hand with a look of reluctance. "All right."

I was about to call for someone to clear the dishes and utensils when Hengwen said, "I'll take one steamed bun for the white fox."

"Foxes don't eat steamed buns," I said.

"Why?" Hengwen asked.

"Foxes only eat meat, and they love chickens best," I replied. "I'll get the kitchen to make its dinner. Why don't you take a bath first?"

Hengwen thought for a moment, then nodded. "All right."

The young servant and maidservants were all quick-witted, having already prepared hot water for bathing in the chamber. Hengwen and Tianshu stood before the doors to the side chamber, politely giving way to each other.

"I'm in no rush," Hengwen said graciously. "You must be tired, right? You go ahead."

Tianshu shook his head. "I'm not tired. You carried the fox today. It's pretty heavy, and you must have caught quite some dirt on you too. You should go first."

The maidservant standing before the doors covered her mouth and smiled. To me, she said, "Master, the two young masters really know more about propriety than adults."

Of course, where do you think the two of them were raised?

Seeing them deferring to each other, I could only think of a way for them to arrive at a compromise. I made two lots for them to draw. Hengwen got priority, so he made his way inside for his bath.

I had already gotten the young servant to call someone from the clothing store over this afternoon to take Tianshu's and Hengwen's measurements, along with a few sets of clothes they could more or less wear first.

Hengwen's and Tianshu's clothes had been conjured and shrunken to fit their bodies by divine magic, and now that Hengwen had changed into the clothing of a mortal youngster with the long sleeves rolled up, he looked even more childlike. A maidservant then accompanied him back to his chamber to retire for the night, a sight that amused me to see.

A short while later, Tianshu stepped out after he was done bathing and changing to a new set of clothes, similarly a picture of childlike charm. I thought of Tianshu, then thought of Mu Ruoyan, and finally looked at the Tianshu before me. It was occurring to me more and more strongly that being able to see this sight, even though I would be sent to the Immortal Execution Terrace in a few days, was all worth it.

While I was washing up, I thought of what Nanming would look like if he had also turned into a youth or a younger child. I wondered if I would be sent to the Immortal Execution Terrace after Nanming and Tianshu re-entered the cycle of reincarnation. If so, would I have the time to ask Mingge for a favor, and borrow his Mortal Realm Observation Mirror to get a glimpse of Nanming in diapers?

Late at night, I drifted into Tianshu's chamber for a look. He was all tucked under the quilt, sleeping soundly, his clothes neatly folded on the chair. He was the very picture of carefree innocence. It was probably rare for Tianshu to have a good night's sleep when he was still Mu Ruoyan.

I entered the other chamber, and Hengwen was sound asleep too. I carefully shifted him inward on the bed, then lifted the quilt and lay down, but I still inadvertently woke him up. Rubbing his bleary eyes, he half propped himself up and looked at me in astonishment. Sounding tired, he asked, "Why are you sleeping in the same bed with me?"

I froze for a moment, still holding up a corner of the quilt. Giving a dry laugh, I said, "It's been busy today, and only two side chambers have been cleared out, so there are only two beds available to sleep in."

I looked at the childlike silhouette before me. The Hengwen of now still did not recognize me. Giving a helpless sigh, I tucked him back in bed and covered him with the quilt.

"Sleep tight."

Then I got off the bed and put on my outer robe, all ready to search for a spot on the ridge of the roof or a tree to squat the night away.

The colors of the night ran deep, with the chilly wind making its presence known. I floated to the ridge of the roof, where I looked up at the sky. The night was so heavily shrouded in clouds, I could not see a thing.

I wondered if Bihua had already arrived in the Heavenly Court.

By all accounts, it was almost winter now. No wonder the wind was so cold; sitting on the ridge just a few days ago had been a marginally warmer experience.

I yawned and lay down on the ridge. Truth be told, it was rough sleeping up there, with all the uneven and uncomfortably hard tiles. Earlier today, the servants who cleared out chambers had even asked me "Is it really enough to just clear out two side chambers?" and I had answered, "Yes, my son lost his mother at a young age and often gets night terrors. He's still in recovery and needs someone to watch over him while he sleeps."

Actually, I was thinking that if the Jade Emperor were to really haul me up to the Immortal Execution Terrace in displeasure, then I would not be able to sleep on the same bed with Hengwen anymore, so I might as well seize the chance to sleep with him for as many days as I could, regardless of whether he was an adult or a youth. To put it in the words of the mortal realm: Even if I die, I have to die a satiated ghost.

But when Hengwen had thrown me that question earlier, it occurred to me just how utterly despicable I was. So being a satiated ghost was out of the question; I was doomed to be a hungry ghost.

Tomorrow, I would get the young servant to clear out another empty side chamber.

I closed my eyes again and yawned when I suddenly heard light footsteps on the roof tiles.

I opened my eyes and gave a start. Hengwen was standing on the tiles looking down at me, wearing just a flimsy inner garment. "I can share my bed with you if you have nowhere to sleep. You left right away just now without waiting for me to respond. It's uncomfortable sleeping here, isn't it?"

I bolted right up and wrapped my outer robe around him. "Why did you come out? Go back and sleep. The wind is cold outside."

If a maidservant or servant were to walk out of the servant quarters right now, only to see Old Master Song and the little young master standing on the roof ridge, they would no doubt be so frightened they would take a tumble.

Hengwen grabbed hold of my sleeves. "All right. You can sleep in my bed. Let's go."

I followed him back to his chamber. Hengwen burrowed

under the quilt; and I thickened my skin and got onto the bed. He even offered me more of the quilt. "You'll need more to cover yourself with, so here you go."

I gave it back to him and tucked him snugly in it. "It's enough for me. You go on ahead and sleep."

"There's no need for you to be so polite with me," Hengwen said. "When I come of age a few more years later and take up an official post, you and I will be fellow immortals in the Heavenly Court. It's only right for us to look out for each other."

"Right, right. You're absolutely right," I answered with a smile.

Hengwen snuggled his head closer to me on the pillow. "But I was told that I'm called Hengwen because I will be Hengwen Qingjun in days to come, so why are you called Song Yao when you are Guangxu Yuanjun?"

"That's because I was originally a mortal who unwittingly ascended to immortality," I explained. "My name in the mortal world is Song Yao."

"Song Yao sounds better than Guangxu Yuanjun," Hengwen commented.

I was going to say that I thought the same, but after thinking about it, I let it drop. I was already about to be sent to the Immortal Execution Terrace, and I would only be adding fuel to the fire if the Heavenly Court were to hear me casting aspersions on the title bestowed upon me at this perilous juncture. Who knows? In a fit of anger, the Venerable One up there might not even let me retain a wisp of my soul for reincarnation.

"If only I had a name that's different from my title," Hengwen said softly.

Many years ago, in the Heavenly Court, Hengwen had said those exact words to me.

At the time, I had only just gotten acquainted with him. A certain heavenly lord had invited over guests, and he did me a favor and brought me, a junior immortal who had just joined the Heavenly Court, along as an accompanying guest. I was still not on familiar terms with the other immortals, but I had a great time drinking to my heart's content, and we enjoyed ourselves till we were tipsy, tottering unsteadily as we each searched for spots to lie down and sober up.

Hengwen pillowed his head on a bluestone and reclined by the Heavenly River, where the merge of waves and mists flowed in an expanse so vast, there seemed to be no end.

He suddenly said to me, "I'd like to take on a mortal name too, but is there anything that would suit me?"

I gushed on and on about the art of naming, from choosing the given name at birth to picking the courtesy name after coming of age, and of selecting a name based on the classics, and of deciding a courtesy name after the virtues one hoped to emulate. There were lots of rules. Once I was done with my little speech, I had said with an embarrassed smile, "Of course, challenges like quoting from the classics would not be a problem at all to Hengwen Qingjun."

"No need for such complications," Hengwen said with a smile. "Just one that's similar to yours—with two characters, catchy, and easy to pronounce."

In truth, it had not been easy coming up with my name. I had heard tell that my old man had called together scores of retainers and invited several renowned erudite scholars from the Hanlin Academy to put their heads together. They had discussed it for several days before a name was finally decided. But I had always been a modest one, so naturally, I would not flaunt this particular story of my birth. I merely said, slowly, "The surname comes first, then the name. My surname comes from my old man. Qingjun, you... what surname would you like to take on?"

Hengwen Qingjun had gazed at the waters of the heavenly river and fell silent for a moment. "Ahem, I guess you can just help me pick one from the mortal world."

After some consideration, I said, "The Jade Emperor's surname as a mortal seemed to be Li, as was Laojun's. Looks like Li is the surname of immortals, so why not take Li as your surname too?"

Hengwen waved his fan. "No, no. It's meaningless if it's all the same."

So I asked, "In that case, do you want a more common surname or a rare one?"

"A common one is fine," Hengwen answered.

So I said, "Wang, Zhang, Li, Zhao, and Wu are the most common names in the mortal world. You aren't keen on Li, so that's left us with Wang, Zhang, Zhao, Wu…"

"The other day, when you introduced yourself to me," Hengwen suddenly said, "you said that your surname is Song from Qi, Chu, Yan, Zhao, Han, Wei, Song. There seems to be a Zhao too among these states' names."

He then tapped his fan on his palm and made up his mind. "In that case, I'll take the surname Zhao."

I had still been drunk then, and when the wind blew against me, I, overcome with intoxication and emotion, blurted, "Zhao Heng—What do you think of this name?"

Hengwen had nodded with a smile. "Excellent. Zhao Heng it is then."

The past from several thousand years ago seemed to be right before my eyes. I turned to my side on the bed and asked little Hengwen, "What kind of name do you want?"

For a moment, he did not make a sound, as if he was thinking about it. Then he said, "More or less similar to your name. Easy to pronounce."

I made a show of thinking about it before saying, "Zhao Heng. Do you like this name?"

Hengwen nodded his head so hard that the quilt shook in tandem. He said in delight, "All right, this name it is then."

I looked at how delighted he was, but I could not say what I felt like deep down.

"Zhao Heng, Zhao Heng…" Hengwen was still joyfully reciting the name.

I tucked the quilt around him again. "You should sleep. You've just arrived in the mortal world; you need to rest and keep yourself in top form."

Hengwen nodded again and turned inward.

When I woke the next morning, Hengwen was leaning against my shoulder, sleeping sweetly. I reached out, wanting to hug him; but fearing my touch may wake him, I shrank my hand back. As of today, I had no more excuses to sleep in this bed. Yesterday was probably the last night, and the thought of it made me duly melancholic.

Just then, Hengwen woke up. Rubbing his eyes and yawning, he got up and very naturally let me attend to him as he got dressed.

He then tugged at the corner of my robe. "Thank you for the name last night."

"It's no big deal," I answered with a straight face. "Consider it my thanks for letting me sleep here."

Hengwen blinked at me and made a sound of acknowledgment, along with a smile.

During breakfast, Hengwen stuffed three steamed buns into his tummy once again. This seemed to stimulate Tianshu's appetite, and he ate two for himself. I was overjoyed. After breakfast, I rose to my feet and was about to head off somewhere for a stroll when Tianshu suddenly asked, "Yuanjun said that the Heavenly Court wanted us to gain experience in the mortal world. Is there any learning topic today?"

This question stumped me. Right. This was not an easy lie to cover up. For a time, I was at a loss what to do, so I could only say, "As we have only just arrived in the city yesterday, we are still not too familiar with the mortal world, so we should use these two days to get acquainted with it. Let's discuss this again in three days."

Tianshu and Hengwen nodded solemnly, and that was how I managed to stall the issue.

Before noontime, I took Tianshu and Hengwen to the marketplace for a stroll, experiencing for ourselves the stores, itinerant peddlers, street vendor stalls, and the pedestrians coming and going.

"It's great here in the mortal world," Hengwen remarked. "It's far livelier than the Heavenly Court."

"But I heard that everyone in the mortal world wants to be an immortal," Tianshu said. "If the mortal world is so good, why do they still want to be immortals?"

I could only answer in all seriousness, "Therein lies a mystery of the universe. You need to contemplate it on your own."

Tianshu cast a respectful glance at me, probably thinking this immortal lord's words to be exceptionally sagely and befitting of an immortal.

Tianshu and Hengwen were both conspicuous, and I was all the more conspicuous, leading them through the market. It might have been a special occasion today, as the marketplace was thronged with plenty of simply dressed married women from poor households and pretty girls of humble births. Every one of them moved to the side of the road and stared incessantly at Tianshu and Hengwen. Tianshu, uncomfortable with the staring, tightened his grip on my hand. Hengwen, on the other hand, was totally unconcerned as his eyes roamed all over. Meanwhile, I felt awkward.

The sides of the street were lined with gaily decorated buildings, quite a number of which were entertainment and pleasure quarters where beautiful women stood against the railings. Had this immortal lord been alone taking a stroll with just a folding fan in hand, I might have made a pass or two at them. But at present, I was laden with two tag-alongs in tow, so I could only dream of romance as I bulldozed through the marketplace, feeling envious with nothing to show for it.

I was sighing when I noticed Tianshu walking and staring at the roadside at the same time. I stopped in my tracks, and followed his gaze to see a stall display of steaming hot cakes fresh from the bamboo steamers. Tianshu seemed to be a little embarrassed when he realized he had been caught, and he turned his head away from the stall.

From the looks of it, Tianshu had never been one to voice out whatever was on his mind even as a youngster.

"Both of you have never tried the cakes this stall is selling, right? Want to try them?" I asked.

Tianshu looked back at me and nodded.

I bought two pieces. This cake was made of rice flour, with some osmanthus and sesame powder sprinkled on top. The peddler wrapped each piece individually in coarse paper. They still felt fairly hot when I held them in my hands. I handed a piece to Tianshu, and peeled back part of the wrapper. "Be careful, don't scald your tongue," I said and gave Hengwen his.

He held it up and took a bite. "A little sweet." With that comment, he looked up at me. "I don't like sweet things, so I'll just taste a little, and you'll eat the rest, okay?"

An old lady weighing walnuts at the dried fruits stall beside us had been stealing glances at Hengwen and Tianshu, and when she heard this, she immediately broke into an affectionate smile.

"Such a filial child," she said to me. "You, sir, are so blessed."

This immortal lord felt very depressed. My appearance should not have changed since my ascension. Tianshu and Hengwen did not look all that young now. At most, I could be considered their older brother, so why was everyone treating me as their father?

They said that immortals live forever in eternal youth. From the looks of it, the vicissitudes of several thousand years had still left its trace on this immortal lord's body, making me look a little weathered and worn.

I smiled at the old lady. Hengwen handed me his nibbled-on cake, and the old lady praised, "What a sensible child!" She scooped some walnuts from her basket and gave them to Hengwen with shaky hands.

Hengwen immediately reached out to accept them. "Thank you, Elder," he said, to which the old lady repeatedly replied, "You're welcome, you're welcome."

Hengwen could not hold so many, so he put them all in his sleeves until he only held one in his hand. He looked it over and over, then opened his mouth to bite it.

"Oh, my." The old lady hurried to stop him. "Don't bite it."

I chimed in too. "You can't bite it. The husk is hard and will give you a toothache."

Hengwen held the walnut in his hand, looking puzzled.

"I'll crack the shells for you when we get home," I said amicably, and Hengwen nodded, blinking his eyes.

"It's a rare sight to see a father bringing his two children to the marketplace," the old lady said to me. "Young Master, you're well dressed, so why are you not taking the sedan chair? You don't even have a servant following you?"

"We just moved here," I said, "so we came to the marketplace for a look."

"Is your esteemed wife at home?" The old lady asked.

"No longer in this world," I said with a wry laugh.

A group of people around us were listening with their ears perked up. On hearing this, every one of them sighed. The old lady sighed the hardest, and filled Tianshu's sleeve full of peanuts. Tianshu said his thanks politely. I dragged him and Hengwen out of the crowd. Even a few steps away, I could still hear the old lady's sympathetic sighs.

"What is an esteemed wife?" Hengwen asked me. "Why are there people giving us food the moment you say you don't have one?"

This immortal lord said with a wooden expression, "They are asking about my wife. In the mortal world, a man has to marry a woman to be his wife."

Realization dawned on Hengwen, "Oh, so when you said you don't have a wife, they all sympathize with you. But why would they give us food?"

I coughed. "Well…"

Nibbling on his hot cake, Tianshu said, "Is it because they find you more pitiable having to take care of us without a wife, so they help you take care of us?"

As expected of a young Tianshu. So thoughtful and considerate!

"That's exactly it!" I nodded.

Tianshu polished off his cake and began studying the secret stash of peanuts. I shelled one for him, and he said in all seriousness, "I've eaten the kernels before, but I never knew that they came with shells." He grabbed a handful from his sleeve and gave it to Hengwen. "Eat these first. They are easy to shell."

Hengwen accepted them. "Thank you. We'll have the walnuts later when we get back."

Sheer silk fluttered a few steps ahead—yet another place of tenderness and many affections. A stunning beauty dressed in a pale rose garment was leaning against the railings on the second floor, seeming to be idly gazing out into the distance, a sight that kept the eyes of all the strong, young men on her.

With my eyes fixed straight ahead, I led Hengwen and Tianshu to the foot of the building. Several simply dressed young girls were picking rouges before the make-up stall by the side of the street. One of them was withdrawing from the store when she suddenly tripped. With a cry of surprise, she fell right into my arms.

I froze, and right at that moment, a light object landed on top of my head too.

Chapter Nineteen

A faint fragrance wafted before my nose. This immortal lord had not had a dalliance in several thousand years, and I had least expected to gain the perk of embracing a tender beauty before being sent to the Immortal Execution Terrace. The young girl struggled out of my arms in a panic. Even her fair neck had turned bright red. She curtsied, then lifted her skirt and fled in a fluster.

I took down the object on my head. To my surprise, it was a pink, sheer handkerchief with a fragrance that assailed my nose, overpowering me.

A person was suddenly standing before me; this person immediately dropped to one knee. "My lord, what a coincidence. Of all people, our Lady Qingxian's handkerchief fell on you. Clearly, this is the work of fate. How about coming over to our building to take a seat?"

Was this not the handkerchief of the maiden who had just bumped into me?

From the building with fluttering sheer curtains and hanging silk, a woman who looked like a procuress sashayed over, waving her handkerchief. "My lord, you picked up Qingxian's handkerchief, so she had this old one come out to welcome you and invite you in for a cup of tea to convey her thanks. Please honor us with your presence, my lord."

As expected, whiling away several thousand years in heaven had worn this immortal lord down, and a scented handkerchief was about to lead me into a trap of the fairer sex. On hearing this, my first reaction was actually to look down at my side.

Hengwen was holding on to my robe, watching with a look of curiosity. Tianshu was also looking around with a perplexed expression. I coughed once and answered with a dry laugh, "I have my sons with me, so it's really inconvenient today. Thank you to the young lady for her kind intentions. Madame, please return this handkerchief to the lady. I'll come again for a visit should I have the time in the future."

The procuress covered her mouth and said with a laugh, "My lord, you are really a prudent man. It just so happened that fate has come knocking today, and besides, it's just a cup of tea. The two young masters are also of an age where they should be aware of the ways of the world and the facts of life. Coincidentally, there's one among my girls who is of similar age to the young masters. She can play with them. Then you can grace us with your presence, go in for a cup of tea and a song to fulfill the wish of that girl of mine to convey her thanks."

The curiosity on Hengwen's face was deepening. My cold sweat trickled down relentlessly. If the Heavenly court were to find out that I brought the young and innocent Hengwen Qingjun and Tianshu Xingjun to the brothel, I would not even need to head up to the Immortal Execution Terrace, for they would outright send a massive bolt of lightning to obliterate me clean.

"Thank you for both of your kindnesses," I said with a stern countenance, "but I'm really not available right now. Please pardon me."

The procuress lamented with deep regret, "My lord is so

insistent on declining the offer. Don't tell me you disdain…"

"Is it because you deem this lowly one to be too vulgar to serve you to your satisfaction?" A woman in rose pink stood gracefully before me. It was the same beautiful woman leaning against the railing staring idly out into the distance. Charming, delicate, finely arched brows; expressive, bright, and seductive eyes. Face as clear and luminous as the moon. Dainty and graceful waist so slender as to grasp. She was like the morning dew, a beauty who far surpassed an entire garden of spring flowers.

With a smile, I said, "It's a blessing to be invited by a beautiful woman, but unfortunately, I do indeed have something on today. I must ask you to treat me to a cup of scented tea should I have the free time another day, and if I could get to hear the sound of your qin too, that'd be my good fortune."

The beautiful woman smiled, her face like the intoxicating rosy clouds drifting in the sky. "Looks like today is indeed inconvenient for the young master. I do not dare to force you to stay, but I hope you will remember our agreement today. I shall be by the window, pining for your visit every day. Since this handkerchief has an affinity with you, please accept it if you don't disdain it. Consider it as a token of our mutual agreement."

I could only take the sheer handkerchief and put it away in my bosom. Beside me, Hengwen suddenly sneezed.

I hurriedly looked down. "What's wrong?"

Hengwen rubbed his nose. "Nothing."

He looked up at Qingxian and smiled, and at the sight of this, Qingxian smiled back sweetly in spite of herself. Then she curtsied and returned to the building with the brothel servant and procuress.

I could not help but think that this handkerchief would not have fallen on my head had I been standing here together with the *usual* Hengwen.

Hengwen tugged at my robe. "When are we going back?"

"Now," I answered.

It was lunchtime by the time we returned to the small courtyard. Hengwen and Tianshu could not stop thinking about Third Granny Huang's steamed buns. Once all the dishes were served, they asked, "Why aren't there any steamed buns?"

"We are out of steamed buns," I said. "I'll get someone to buy some more for dinner tonight."

Only then did Hengwen and Tianshu begin to reach out with their chopsticks.

I made a special point of having the cook fry some scrambled egg for the fox. After lunch, Hengwen took the plate to feed the fox personally.

Furball was temporarily settled down on a soft couch in the small hall. Although I had used my divine powers to help it treat its injuries, its wounds still had not healed. It was weak and feeble, looking very downcast.

Hengwen fed it the egg with a pair of chopsticks, and it ate it one mouthful at a time. Tianshu watched from the side with great interest. Once the egg was gone, Furball smacked its lips and licked Hengwen's hand.

Hengwen stroked its back. "I heard Song Yao calling you Furball. Is your name Furball?"

Furball propped its eyelids open and glared resentfully at me.

"Actually, its name is Xuan Li," I said.

Hengwen immediately petted it and called its name twice, "Xuan Li, Xuan Li."

"Xuan Li sounds like a nice name," Tianshu commented too.

The fox nuzzled against Hengwen's palm, tears reemerging from the corners of its eyes.

I had the maidservants and young servant tidy up another side chamber in the morning, so we each had our respective rooms for our afternoon nap. I sent Tianshu to his chamber, then sent Hengwen back to his. Just as I was about to step out from Hengwen's chamber, however, he piped up from behind me, "Eh, aren't you sleeping? Why did you go out?"

"My chamber is ready," I explained, "so you don't have to squeeze with me in bed anymore. Have a good rest."

"Oh," Hengwen said, "where is your chamber?"

"At the end of the walkway," I replied.

"What's it like?" Hengwen asked.

I could only answer, "Why don't I take you there for a look?"

"Sure," Hengwen responded.

I led Hengwen into the newly tidied side chamber. It was at the end of the covered walkway, so it was not as bright as Hengwen's and Tianshu's rooms. The pond in the backyard was visible from here, and had it been summer, the view would have been a good one. But now, with winter right around the corner, the most the scenery could muster was the occasional leaf or two floating on the pond.

Hengwen walked around my chamber, peered out of the window for a look, then sat on the bed to feel the quilt.

Delicately, I asked him, "If you want to stay here for a bit longer, why don't you take an afternoon nap with me?"

Hengwen thought for a moment before nodding. "Sure."

And so, I earned myself yet another unexpected afternoon. Looking at Hengwen lying on the bed, I felt despicably delighted. As I took off my outer robe and prepared to get in bed, Qingxian's handkerchief sailed out from my chest. I picked it up for a look. Who could have thought I would finally get lucky in the romance department? Could changing my fate of eternal solitude be an actual possibility now?

I looked back at the bed. Hengwen was lying on the pillow, looking at me with black, shining eyes. I tucked the handkerchief away and lay down. Hengwen snuggled up to me, yawned, and closed his eyes. I tucked the quilt around him and closed my eyes too.

This nap took all but two hours. After getting up in the afternoon, I took a stroll in the yard to look at the scenery. The children in the alley, knowing that there were two new youngsters living here, clung to the enclosing wall and craned their necks over it to peek into the yard.

I found Tianshu and Hengwen to be mature in spite of their tender age, having grown up in the heavenly court, and this was a rare trip down to the mortal world, so I urged them to play with the children. In the mortal world, the youth of around their ages would have long found it beneath themselves to play with these children, so this gaggle, upon seeing Hengwen and Tianshu were willing, went wild with joy. Tianshu and Hengwen had never played with children before, so they shared in this delight.

Tianshu and Hengwen returned only when it grew dark. They were, however, perplexed on top of their delight.

"Those children asked what my name was," Hengwen told me. "I said my name was Zhao Heng, and they asked me why my surname is Zhao when yours is Song. I should have the same surname as you. Why is that?"

"They asked for my name too," Tianshu chimed in. "I said my name was Tianshu, and I didn't have a surname. They said I should have the surname Song too."

I rubbed my temples. "Because of this humble immortal's appearance, those mortals thought I was your father. To conceal our identities, I boldly claimed that to be the case. For that, I ask for your pardon. In the mortal world, the son has to take after his father's surname."

Hengwen blinked his eyes like he did not really understand it, while Tianshu added, "Hengwen and I also played chess with a few elders in the afternoon. They couldn't beat us, so they slapped the table and said they'd be our sons and grandsons if they played chess with us again. Is being someone's son a humiliating act in the mortal world? If that's the case, why did you…"

Without batting an eyelid, this immortal lord answered, "Oh, that's because they thought they were a lot older than both of you. In the mortal world, it's very humiliating to say that you'd be the son of someone younger than you and unrelated by blood. I'm much older than both of you, so I can play the part for the time being. That way, we won't expose our identities to the mortals."

Tianshu had always been very easy to coax, and as expected, he looked pensive after hearing these words. With a smile, he said, "We are, in fact, much older than them, so they shouldn't be saying such things, and even if they did, they wouldn't be on the losing end, right?"

"Right," I said, "but you can't tell them, or we'll expose ourselves."

"Okay," Tianshu nodded.

And so the conflict was resolved, and dinner was served without a hitch.

Hengwen and Tianshu did not think much of the steamed buns that we bought, fixated as they were on those made by Third Granny Huang. Hengwen only ate two, and Tianshu, one.

"How about we buy from another stall tomorrow?" I asked. "Or we can make dumplings."

Only then was their interest piqued.

After Hengwen fed Furball, I had them draw bathing lots like they had done the day before. Today, Tianshu drew first dibs, and after he was done bathing, he returned to his chamber as Hengwen started his turn. After my own turn, I went over to Tianshu's chamber for a look; he was already sound asleep. I then went to Hengwen's chamber, but he was nowhere to be seen.

"The little young master has gone to your room," a maidservant told me.

I returned to my chamber, and sure enough, Hengwen was

sitting on the bed, folding a piece of paper. He looked up at me and smiled, and for the briefest flicker of an instant, my eyes played tricks on me under the light: I thought I had been looking at the full-grown Hengwen, smiling at me from the bed.

I walked in. "Why aren't you going back to your room? It's getting late."

"I took a nap at noon today, so I don't really feel like sleeping at night," Hengwen explained. "Tianshu wouldn't play with me, as he has already gone to bed, so here I am."

I sat at the table. "But there's nothing fun to do at night. You should go to bed."

"Song Yao, after our learning experience in the mortal world, will you return to the Heavenly Court with us?" Hengwen asked.

Of course. Of course, we'll return together. Heck, the Immortal Execution Terrace is probably even waiting for me right now.

"If the Heavenly Court lets me," I replied ambiguously.

Hengwen immediately smiled. "That's great. After I return to the Heavenly Court, I'll continue to seek you out for some fun."

I nodded. "Sure."

Sitting on the bed, Hengwen waved the sheet of paper he'd been creasing, a sight that resembled the fully-grown Hengwen when he shook his fan. My heart fluttered again.

Hengwen yawned, and I could not help but ask, "Will you still be sleeping here tonight?"

"Sure," Hengwen said. "It's a hassle to return to my room."

I put out the light, then lay on the bed and pulled up the quilt. Hengwen snuggled up against me. I lay there with my eyes open, thinking of the past and nursing that twinge of regret.

If only I had known it would come to this...

Even if I had known, nothing would change. Having earned all these thousands of years for myself, I should actually be content.

But still, I thought to myself, *If only the one lying beside me now were the usual Hengwen.*

If only the one lying beside me now were the usual Hengwen...

I had only these few days left in the mortal world.

Sorrow welled in my heart, and I felt as despondent as if I were reciting mournful poems and tragic verses again.

A sudden impulse seized me.

I propped myself up, leaned over to my side, and kissed him.

Hengwen was sleeping soundly, but he muttered an *"mn"* and unexpectedly grabbed onto my clothing. My surge of emotions hit boiling point. I reached out to embrace him and sought out his lips. He compliantly parted them, his soft tongue entangling with mine in response. I held him tighter...

I gave a start, suddenly regaining my senses.

I hurriedly released my hold, sat up, and gave myself a slap. *Song Yao, you beast. You wouldn't even spare a youth! You're even worse than an animal! Oh, Jade Emperor, how could I have done such a deed?!*

I stumbled over to the table and downed a mouthful of cold tea.

Hengwen—even if he was Hengwen—was merely just a youngster.

I downed another mouthful and looked over at the bleak color of the night seeping through the window paper.

There were only these few days left, but Hengwen was still a youngster—a youngster who could not recognize Song Yao for what he was.

I let loose a long, dejected sigh. Even if there were only these few days left, we could not continue sleeping like this anymore.

Chapter Twenty

As Hengwen slumbered, I sat alone at the table all night. When the day started to break, I went out to the yard to stand for a moment. Then I retrieved cold water, wiped my face, and strolled around. The young servant and maidservants were all panic-stricken when they stepped out of their rooms to see me staring blankly in the yard. They washed me up again, and I took some mouthfuls of the tea that a maidservant brewed. By now, the sky had brightened, and Tianshu and Hengwen got out of bed.

I had sent young servant out to the street to buy two bamboo steamers of steamed buns beforehand. When they were served during breakfast, Hengwen's and Tianshu's eyes lit up.

Hengwen reached out with his chopsticks and had a bite.

"Delicious," he declared through a muffled voice and a smile.

Tianshu brought one onto his plate.

"You had them buy these, right?" Hengwen said to me. "They taste better than the ones yesterday."

"If you like them, I'll get them to buy again tomorrow morning," I said.

Hengwen immediately smiled in delight.

Tianshu looked at the saucer of chili paste on the table. He tentatively picked up a steamed bun and dipped it in the sauce before taking a small bite.

"So you can even add seasoning," he exclaimed with pleasure.

Hengwen immediately picked up another one and imitated him. His eyes widened. "Whoa, it tastes a little different now."

I could not help feeling amused as I watched them being all so innocent. At that moment, I remembered what had happened last night, and my heart sank once again.

Hengwen looked at me with a frown and asked, "Are you feeling uncomfortable anywhere?"

"No." I crinkled up my face in a smile. Holding a steamed bun with his chopsticks, Tianshu, too, blinked at me.

After breakfast, Hengwen said, "The small steamed buns are delicious, but when it comes to the big ones, the ones from the day before yesterday are better."

Still hung up on Third Granny Huang's steamed buns, I see.

There was really nothing I could do about this. Every shop had their own distinctive flavor. A pity Third Granny Huang did not sell steamed buns.

After voicing his thoughts, Hengwen said nothing further on the subject and went to feed the fox.

I went to the courtyard to bask in the sun. Tianshu had found a book somewhere, and was reading it on the covered walkway. After Hengwen fed the fox, he stepped out of the small hall and made his way down the walkway toward the backyard. From where I was standing, I managed to glimpse Third Granny Huang, leaning against the back door as she chatted with the cook. Hengwen greeted her.

Third Granny Huang was naturally overjoyed, and her hands trembled as she complimented him for being such a sensible young master who did not put on airs.

Hengwen was all grins as he answered, "This junior is flattered. I should thank you instead. None of the steamed buns I've tried thus far can compare to the ones you gave us. My father and brother love them too." As he spoke, there was no covering the insatiable hunger on his face.

Third Granny Huang was so elated she could hardly speak. It was only after a while that she shakily said, "Since the young master loves them, I will bring my old self back and steam some to send over."

"Really?" Hengwen said. "Then I'd be so grateful."

I broke out in a sweat watching from the side. If I were to make my appearance now, Third Granny Huang would no doubt grab me to rain praises and compliments for most of the day, so after another look from my side of the moon gate, I wisely walked away.

Back at the walkway, the young servant announced that there was a guest at the doors requesting to see me, and this guest was an old woman.

An old woman? Was this immortal lord somehow catching the romantic interest of old ladies these days?

I entered the hall to welcome the guest, and the young servant led the old lady in. I fixed my eyes on her; she looked somewhat familiar, perhaps the old woman from the marketplace who had gifted Hengwen and Tianshu their walnuts and peanuts.

The old lady curtsied upon entering and introduced herself. "This old one is from the Lü-Hu household. Greetings to Young Master Song."

I invited her to take a seat with some apprehension. We had only met in the marketplace yesterday, and today, she knew my surname, clearly having asked around. She must have come here for a purpose; just one greeting, and my mind swarmed with suspicions as to what that was.

Madam Lü-Hu sat on the chair and sized up the furnishings

in the hall. With a smile, she said to me, "Your house is so exquisitely decorated. You've only just moved, and yet you've tidied it up so well."

"Not at all," I answered. "This humble one actually has not put in even a fraction of effort. The credit belongs to all the others." Which was the truth.

The old lady continued, "You're really too modest. May I know where you are from?"

I could only make something up. "My hometown is in Jiangzhe."

"Oh, my," the old lady exclaimed. "Jiangnan is a good place. Do you plan to stay in this city for the long term or the short term?"

"We'll see if we can get used to staying here," I answered ambiguously. "If so, we'll stay here for a longer period."

"Actually," Madam Lü-Hu said, "this city may not be big, but it can be considered prosperous. What's most important is that it's stable. The world isn't at peace now, and the Eastern and Southern Commanderies are at war year in, year out. I heard that the Imperial Court even recently deployed troops to join forces with the Eastern Commandery and attack the Southern one, destroying several of the Southern Commandery's cities in the process. The general of the Southern Commandery was even beaten to death by his own soldiers, who revolted. Living in peace is hard when all is not stable in the world. There aren't many cities in the world like ours where you can live a peaceful and stable life. So in this old one's opinion, since you are already here and have bought a house, why not stay longer?"

I followed her lead and nodded. "You're right."

What was the old lady's purpose circling the conversation like this?

The old lady picked up the teacup from the table and took a sip to moisten her throat before setting it down. With her old pair of eyes, she looked at this immortal lord and asked, "As presumptuous as it is of me, may I ask your age?"

What was she asking this for?

This immortal lord was twenty-three years old when I ascended, so I was about to answer twenty-three when I remembered in the nick of time that I still had two exalted lords who looked to be youths in the courtyard—my "sons." So I replied, "Nearly forty."

Madam Lü-Hu shook her head. "You don't look your age at all. If my old self had not seen the two young masters, then even if you said you were in your early twenties, I'd have believed you."

Well, yes, this immortal lord's face is clearly the face of someone in his early twenties!

Madam Lü-Hu covered her mouth and laughed. "You are right in the prime of life, and the two little young masters are still young. Have you never ever thought of... remarrying?"

So. The old lady was here to play matchmaker for this immortal lord.

A marriage proposal knocking on my door the moment this immortal lord came to live in the mortal world. Was it really possible that my fate of eternal solitude could be changed?

Seeing my blank silence, the old lady continued, "This old one has a wonderful potential candidate here to matchmake you with. There is a fabric store to the north of the city. It's not a big shop, but business is good. The fabrics worn by the wealthy and influential households in this city are all from them. Shopkeeper Feng of the fabric store has a daughter who is seventeen this year. Although she's not really a lady from a wealthy and influential household, her dowry is quite generous, and she's a good match for you, looks- and character-wise. This old one isn't just matchmaking you at random. Come to think of it, this young lady has had the affinity of meeting you twice already."

This immortal lord heard rustling from behind the screen and guessed that Hengwen and Tianshu were crouching behind it to listen in.

Madam Lü-Hu continued, "The first is that the clothes the two young masters are wearing are made by the Feng household's fabric shop. There are still several pieces of clothes being rushed. As for the second encounter, you should still remember it. The lady who bumped into you on the streets yesterday before the rouge shop is Young Miss Feng. Is this not a match made in Heaven?!"

I chuckled wryly at that. This matter was quite the curious coincidence, but it was definitely not a match made in Heaven.

I cleared my throat and explained that I was new here and still unfamiliar with the place. Besides, remarriage was such a major event, so I had to consider it seriously. What's more, Young Missy Feng was still young, and I feared I would do her a great wrong if she were to marry into the family to be a stepmother, so we should talk about it again after careful consideration. These were the excuses I used to fob her off.

By the time a decision had been made, this immortal lord would have long been taken to the Immortal Execution Terrace.

Madam Lü-Hu was all smiles as she said, "No rush, no rush. This matter is not urgent. Give it a few days, and my old self will see how it goes after you've mulled it over." After some more prattling, the old lady bade her farewell and left. Before she stepped out, she added, "Shopkeeper Feng also had this old one pass on a message to you. The two young masters' clothes are ready and will be delivered at noon."

I said my thanks again, and the old lady finally left.

I headed back to the hall, and picked up a cup of tea to moisten my throat. The young girl yesterday actually fell in love with this immortal lord at first bump, and her family had sent someone over to propose marriage today. Evidently, I was still as irresistible as I had been in those olden days.

Hengwen and Tianshu stepped out from behind the screen.

Hengwen looked at me with his black, shiny eyes. "Did that old madam come over earlier to tell you that someone wants to be your wife?"

"Yes," I answered.

"Is it the one who threw her handkerchief yesterday?" Tianshu asked.

"Nope." Hengwen wrinkled his nose. "I heard that old woman say that it was the one who bumped into you."

"That's right," I admitted.

"Immortals cannot marry mortals," Hengwen said.

"I know," I replied. "That's why I stalled by saying we'll discuss it again in a few days. By then, it'd be time for us to go back."

A smile spread on Hengwen's face. "Are we going back to the Heavenly Court together?"

I plastered on a smile. "Yes."

Only then did Hengwen stop asking, and ran off to the small hall to visit Furball.

At noon, the Fengs' fabric shop really did send a store assistant over to deliver Hengwen's and Tianshu's clothes. When the assistant collected his reward, he fixed his eyes on me and sized me up like he was buying meat and picking the cuts. Then he looked at Hengwen and Tianshu. In all probability, Shopkeeper Feng had sent him here to appraise his potential future son-in-law. I wondered how he would describe my charms when he returned.

As the maidservant cleared the table after our lunch, the young servant came to report that there was another guest at the back door who insisted on seeing this immortal lord.

I sure was in high demand today.

The young servant ushered the person in. It was a delicate-looking little servant girl, dressed as a study attendant.

"My lady instructed me to deliver an invitation for

tea-tasting," she said crisply, and held out a pink, scented letter with both hands. I reached out to accept it, and the servant girl continued, "Could I ask you to please head over to the back door? The person in the carriage outside would like to invite you for a chat."

Rather off-handedly, I set the scented letter on the small table, and followed the servant girl out of the back door. A horse carriage draped with satin curtains was parked by the door, and another servant girl stood before it. She bowed to me and said, "Young Master Song, please stand before the carriage. Our lady has something to say to you."

So I stood by the carriage curtain.

A sweet, delicate voice floated out from the curtain. "This lowly one has come in person to extend an invitation, in the hope that Young Master Song will come over to Zuiyue Pavilion at dusk today for tea. I wonder if I could possibly ask you to grace me with your presence?"

A breeze surfed past, not at all like the chilly wind of early winter, but the warm breeze of spring.

"Since a beautiful woman has invited me, how would this humble one dare to refuse?" I replied.

The two servant girls covered their mouths and tittered. The charming voice on the other end of the curtain said, "In that case, this lowly one shall return to Zuiyue Pavilion to light the incense and fine tune the qin in silent anticipation of your arrival."

The horse carriage turned around and left at a leisurely pace. I said my farewell as I saw them off.

When I returned to the hall, Hengwen and Tianshu were reading that scented letter together. Hengwen looked up at me. "This says to invite you to Zuiyue Pavilion in the evening for tea. The fragrance is so strong. It's the one who threw her handkerchief yesterday?"

This immortal lord nodded in tacit acknowledgment. I took

the pink letter from their hands and tucked it away under the robes over my chest.

Hengwen and Tianshu were both looking at me. Hengwen asked, "Are you going?"

I yawned. "Time for an afternoon nap."

Tianshu returned to his chamber accordingly. Hengwen, however, followed me, taking one step for every one I took. When we reached the door to his chamber, I opened it for him. "Take a nap."

Hengwen made a noise of acknowledgment and entered, and I returned to my own quarters. Looking at the empty bed, I sighed. Just as I was about to close the doors, Hengwen strode in.

I asked in an affable voice, "Why aren't you sleeping?"

Hengwen blinked and ran over to the bed. He sat on it and flashed a grin. "This bed feels more comfortable to me than the one in my room."

At this moment, I felt like a piece of potsticker suffocating in the wok, sizzling in the oil and stifled by the fumes. It felt terrible. I could only say, "Since you like this room, I'll trade with you. Starting from noon today, you'll stay here, and I'll sleep in yours."

Hengwen, who was pulling the quilt open and nestling into the bed, turned his head to me. "Why? The bed can accommodate both of us, can't it? I can sleep with you here."

I rubbed my forehead. "It's always a little crowded sharing the same bed. Sleep well."

I turned and made to leave. Behind me, I heard Hengwen getting off the bed. "I get it now. You don't actually like sleeping on the same bed as me."

I turned back and looked at his somewhat downcast face, but I held back and said nothing.

Hengwen lowered his head. "I understand. I won't bother you anymore. I'll return to my chamber for my nap." He pushed the quilt back and walked out with his head hanging.

I watched him go. The flame cooking the potsticker was unusually strong, and hot oil bubbled over, searing my heart and insides so that they sizzled.

I closed the door, sat at the table, drank two cups of tea, then took out Miss Qingxian's handkerchief, looking it over. Could peach blossoms really bloom on the old, wizened tree that this immortal lord had been for thousands of years?

When it was close to dusk, I changed into a brand-new set of attire and scented it so that both sleeves gave off a delicate, refreshing fragrance.

Hengwen led a group of children into the yard to play, placing bets on the outcome of the game. Tianshu kept a piece of inkstone and a brush close by—to play referee and draw on the losers' faces. The children, except for Tianshu and Hengwen, more or less all ended up with their faces decorated in ink.

I informed the young servant and maidservants that I would not be eating dinner at home and could possibly be back late, so they were to take good care of the young masters. With that, I made to leave. Tianshu and Hengwen were in the midst of having fun, but Tianshu set down his brush and ran over. "Are you going out?"

"Yes," I answered. "I have something on."

Tianshu made a noise of acknowledgment and asked no further, while Hengwen turned his head aside to look at me, his eyes flickering for the briefest moment before he lowered it again to continue playing chess.

This time, when this immortal lord took to the streets, I was finally a patron taking a leisurely stroll to the brothel, not the baggage-laden person of yesterday. A pity it was getting late. Everywhere on the street, stalls were packing up and shops were shuttering down, while pedestrians came and went in a rush. And at this hour, the young girls from decent families would not be out here wandering around. This made me feel a little lonely.

When I arrived at Zuiyue Pavilion, the rouge stall had yet to wind up for the day. The young lad who set up the stall drew back and looked at me, then at Zuiyue Pavilion.

Zuiyue Pavilion.

An ornate chamber.

A tune of yearning.

Drinking to my heart's content.

"Does Young Master Song find this lowly one's tune to be still acceptable for your ears?" Qingxian pushed aside her qin, inlaid with jade, and smiled at me with tender affection, her ravishing beauty lighting up the entire chamber.

"Excellent," I complimented. "Even better than Chang'e from the Moon Palace."

Qingxian covered her mouth and gave a charming smile. "Young Master sure is an old hand at coaxing others. Your praises leave me at a loss as to how to respond." With dainty steps, she walked gracefully to me, then rolled up her crimson sleeves a little to lift the wine jar and refill my cup.

It was only when the moon was high in the sky that I dragged my half-drunken steps back to the small courtyard. Before leaving, Qingxian called me Song-lang as one would a lover, placed a scented sachet into my hand, and wistfully asked, "Will my husband come again tomorrow?"

This immortal lord heaved a long sigh, held her fair, slender hands, and answered, "With a beautiful woman waiting for me, how could I not?"

That scented sachet was fragrant, and the wind that stirred in my wake seemed to be infused with its fragrance too. With two jars of wine in my arms, I dragged myself back to my room, startling the young servant in the process. He hurried off to prepare hot water, and after stepping out from my bath, I sobered up a little. Although I changed my clothes, the sachet scent still lingered.

I initially meant to return to my room and drink two more

cups of wine to relieve my boredom. Sitting before the bed, I took the scented sachet and handkerchief out together for a look, but without realizing it, I tilted over onto the bed and fell asleep.

I opened my eyes the following day to find myself covered with a quilt. The handkerchief was on my chest, and I was still holding the scented sachet. My clothes that I had worn last night were intact too.

I got up to shout for the young servant to attend to me as I washed up, only to see a small plate with two steamed buns on it set beside the wine jar on the table.

The young servant told me, "Master, you fell asleep last night, and this lowly one did not dare to startle you awake, so I merely covered you with a quilt. The little young master Hengwen left you these two steamed buns while he was having his meal. He refused to sleep and insisted on waiting for you to return to give them to you, but when he brought them over after your bath, you had already fallen asleep. So, he left them on the table and went to bed."

I looked at the two steamed buns, my heart simmering again in hot, searing oil. And still, all I could say was, "All right, understood."

Hengwen only stepped out of his room when it was time for breakfast. He looked at me, but said nothing as he took a seat at the table. This time around, both Hengwen and Tianshu ate quite a lot.

Later that morning, Third Granny Huang came to chat with the cook again. As I happened to be strolling in the backyard, I took the chance to thank her for the steamed buns. Third Granny Huang returned several "You're welcome"s my way, then launched into a conversation.

"Gentleman Song, I heard you intend to marry Shopkeeper Feng's daughter? It's truly a good marriage. Miss Feng is a renowned beauty in our city, and she's able and virtuous. The two of you are a perfect match made in Heaven!"

Baffled, I could not help but ask, "This matter was only briefly brought up to me. The rest is not true at all. Where did you hear these rumors?"

Third Granny Huang sized me up and down. With a smile, she said, "The whole city knows of this. Don't tell me you have still yet to send betrothal gifts to Miss Feng?"

I promptly broke out in a cold sweat. Betrothal gifts? I had only been in this city for a few days. When did I get this far?

After lunch, Tianshu obediently went to take his afternoon nap. I was just about to return to my chamber when I saw Hengwen carrying the fox from the small hall to his room. In his present form, carrying the fox must be quite strenuous. I walked over, and Hengwen looked up at me and smiled.

"It looks quite pitiful sleeping alone in the small hall, so I'm taking it back to my room."

I sighed and stroked a handful of Furball's fluff. "At least it'd be warm with it on the bed."

Hengwen nodded and made a sound of acknowledgment, then gladly busied himself with carrying the fox into his room. I stood for a while outside his closed doors. After all, it was because it had saved Hengwen that Furball had ended up in this state. In any case, there were only a few days left. At least sleeping together would be some sort of comfort for it.

When night descended, I was back in the lady's bedchamber in Zuiyue Pavilion, listening to Qingxian playing a tune.

After a song, Qingxian spoke softly and gently as she sat beside me, pouring me wine. The candlewick burned and crackled. Qingxian pulled out a golden hairpin and picked at the charred snuff. Holding the cup, I looked at the light and could not help but sigh.

Hearing the exhale, Qingxian slowly got up and moved over

to sit by the stand that held her qin. She tuned the strings and played a mellow tune that was bitter and lingering, like a woebegone young maiden in autumn.

When the last of the lingering notes came to an end, Qingxian smiled at me, and made her way back to where I was. As she walked through the shadows cast by light, she turned aside—seemingly without realizing it—and lifted her sleeve, as though wiping away tears. When she turned back, however, her face still wore that same smile. As she bent over to pour the wine, I looked at her and asked, "What has made this beauty before me so heart-stricken?"

Qingxian immediately said with a smile, "Young Master, you jest. I was merely blinded by the candle smoke when I passed under the lamp. On the contrary, it is the young master before me who is courting errant thoughts. For what reason could you be sighing the autumn away?"

I said, "Never destined for each other and yet meeting; meeting though it was never meant to be. High is the bright moon in the sky; within sight but far beyond reach."

Qingxian covered her mouth. "How melancholic and heartbreaking. I wonder which beautiful woman the Young Master is pining for with such anguish. I heard that Young Master Song was still new to the city when love came knocking, and you'll be marrying the young miss of the Feng household. How could you hold such forlorn yearning?"

No doubt the people in this city were all very well-informed.

"Miss Qingxian is a peerless beauty rivaled by none," I said. "All the romantic youths and the rich, distinguished patrons splurge fortunes just to spend a night with you. So why are you still shedding such sorrowful tears?"

Qingxian lowered her head and sighed softly. "Young Master, why tease this lowly one? I make a living by selling my smile and myself. Social status and standing, they are all merely make-believe. I'm just like the merchandise from the stall that belongs to whoever can afford to pay the price, regardless of who he is."

Her voice trembled a little at the end of her words. Qingxian looked up and forced a smile at me. "My momentary lamentation has put a damper on your fun. Young Master, please do not hold it against me. I'll play another tune for you..."

I let loose a long sigh. "If you are in any difficulty, just go ahead and voice it out. It's better than bottling it all up. I may even be able to help you somewhere."

Qingxian was inexpressive as she stared at me, biting her lips. Then all at once, her face was all but obscured by her sleeves. Two trails of tears streamed from behind her hands as she sobbed, "Young Master, please let me play a tune for you. After these few days, I might no longer be able to... The-the nephew of Squire Zhang, who presides over this city, has already told the Madame that he'd redeem my freedom... His uncle's sixty-sixth birthday is in a few days, and when the time comes, he will give me to Squire Zhang as a present... I... I..." At this point, she dissolved into sobs.

And my heart came alive with compassion. There were many things in the world one was powerless to do anything about. When all was said and done, there really was no distinction between heaven and the mortal realm.

I stood at her side with a sigh, and said in a gentle voice, "Don't cry. I'll help you think of a way."

Trembling, Qingxian raised her head to look at me. Then she threw herself into my arms and bawled.

When I left Zuiyue Pavilion, the front of my clothes soaked in tears, the streets were already empty. Somehow, the small stall selling rouge was still open, and the young lad who watched it was sitting at the roadside with his hands in his sleeves, staring blankly at nothing. Presumably, he was waiting for passing Zuiyue Pavilion patrons to buy some boxes for the courtesans inside.

Was there anything easy to do in this world? Not making a living, for sure.

Once more, I returned to the small courtyard at midnight. After helping me wash up, the young servant yawned and went off to bed. Left alone under the lamplight, I did not feel sleepy. I looked at the two jars of wine on the table, took one, made my way to the yard, where I downed several mouthfuls.

It was silent all around, and the cold wind was chilling to the bone. After tonight, I was one day down.

I heard a voice behind me ask, "Why aren't you sleeping?"

A look back revealed a tiny figure standing before me. To my surprise, it was Tianshu.

I was confounded for a while before answering. "I couldn't sleep, so I came out to stretch my legs for a bit."

Tianshu's clear, bright eyes flicked to my hands. I lowered my head and saw the wine jar. Letting out a dry laugh, I said, "Oh, this is fine wine in the mortal world. I fear I won't get to drink it after returning to the Heavenly Court, so I want to drink more while I can."

Tianshu looked quietly at me, apparently taking my word for it. I set the wine jar down by the rockery, then removed my outer robe to wrap around him. "This wind is freezing. You should go back to your room as soon as possible and sleep."

"I… Have I been injured recently?" Tianshu suddenly asked.

I gave a start. Was Tianshu about to recover?

Without thinking, I blurted, "You are now in the mortal world, so this is just a momentary discomfort. Once you return to the Heavenly Court a few days later, it will all come back to you."

Tianshu made a sweet-tempered sound of acknowledgment and returned to his chamber to sleep. Before he left, he looked at me again. "You should rest early too."

I watched his retreating back. These few days, I never saw

little Tianshu without Hengwen at his side; I had sensed nothing different. But the sight of him and him alone tonight, and his retreating figure, I somehow felt a sense of déjà vu. It was as if… I had seen this figure many years before… Perhaps it was because he still bore many similarities with the grown-up Tianshu, and that was what gave me a sense of familiarity.

I scooped up the wine jar again and downed mouthful after mouthful until it was empty. It was still quiet all around, and the night breeze, still as chilly.

I treaded lightly to Hengwen's chamber and ducked in.

As expected, the fox was sleeping under Hengwen's quilt. Sensing my entry, it immediately burrowed out and leaped to the ground. With a flick of my fingers, I put it to sleep and placed it on a chair.

I sat on the edge of the bed and looked down at Hengwen's sleeping face, wondering how many more days I still had left to look at him like this. I tucked him in. Touching his face gently, I could not but whisper, "Hengwen, please recover your original form before I am sent to the Immortal Execution Terrace, even if it's only for one day, or even one night."

I put the fox back in its place, tucked the quilt tightly around Hengwen, and left.

I returned to my chamber, where a lone lamp flickered in the infinite stretch of silence. I fanned out the light and went to bed.

I overslept and woke only when the sun was high in the sky. The young servant told me that the young masters had gone ahead and taken their breakfasts, and were now both in the yard. I acknowledged his words and hurriedly finished my meal before strolling out to join them. Hengwen was rolling dice with a company of youths, and they seemed to be playing for keeps with copper coins at stake. Hengwen had already won a pile that lay before him, and the group looked disgruntled at the loss. Tianshu, on the other hand, was sitting at the stone table, which had been set with a brush, inkstone, and paper. His head was bent as he wrote something.

I went over for a look. Spread out before Tianshu was a book, and beside it stood a stack of paper choked with densely written characters. It looked as if he was copying it.

I picked up a piece of paper for a look.

"The *Analects of Confucius?* This looks like homework the teacher assigned," I blurted in astonishment.

Tianshu raised his face a little and nodded. "Uh-huh. I don't know how to play dice, and I lost earlier. They said they didn't want my money, but then they asked me to help them with their private school homework. Their teacher fell sick a few days ago and paused classes. Once lessons resume the day after tomorrow, they'd have to hand it in, and they can only play with us after their homework is done."

So you just copied everything? I thought. These children really took their teacher for a fool. None of them would get off lightly once they handed in a stack of homework in only one person's handwriting. Seized by impulse, I picked up the stack of paper and flipped through—only to be thunderstruck by what I saw. Of these papers, some were written with skewed and crooked strokes, some were scrawled with a flourish, some were dainty and compacted. They were not written in a single person's handwriting. I looked again at the piece Tianshu was in the midst of completing. It was in yet another kind of handwriting that was squarish and upright, with distinct edges and corners.

"These are all written by you?" I wondered in astonishment.

Tianshu stayed his brush and nodded. "Yeah. I had each of them write a few words for me, but I don't know if my imitation is spot on." Having said that, he lifted his brush and resumed writing.

The page was filled up in no time. Tianshu set down his brush and handed the paper to me so that I could add it to the stack. Taking it, I was struck by this inexplicable sense of familiarity again, as if this scene, too, had occurred before. Perhaps it resembled the sight of Tianshu inscribing books and paintings back in the Heavenly Court?

Perhaps in response to this immortal lord visibly losing myself in my thoughts, Tianshu looked at me questioningly. I replaced the paper in the stack, and strolled away.

Seeing me linger at Tianshu's table probably pricked the consciences of Hengwen's company of youths. As they played, they snuck timid glances at me. Hengwen tossed his newly earned wealth onto the ever-growing pile before him and said, "Don't be afraid. He won't tell your teacher."

The youths' eyes swiveled toward me, and I said with an affable smile, "I won't tell on you."

The youths were promptly delighted, as if they had been granted an amnesty, and shouted "Thank you, Uncle" sweetly, like their mouths were coated with honey. Those few shouts of "uncle," however, really evoked a medley of feelings in this immortal lord's heart.

After several rounds of continued losses, their faces turned a ghastly shade of green. The pile of copper coins before Hengwen became a considerable heap that must have contained the entirety of the boys' snack savings. One of the youths lowered both his head and the dice. "I'm not playing anymore."

Hengwen stretched lazily. "That so? Then let's call it quits." He picked up the dice and returned them to the bowl, then pushed forth the copper coins before him and grinned. "Take your money back quickly. Careful not to get shortchanged."

The youths were all momentarily stunned. Surprisingly enough, they had enough integrity left to remain standing in place. One of them flushed red and stammered, "He who concedes dcfeat when he loses a bet is a real man. Since we've lost to you, then it is how it is."

Hengwen smiled. "It wasn't stated that we would be betting money when we played. We were merely counting copper coins to keep score. These copper coins were always meant to be returned. Since you want to talk about winning and losing, how about this? If I win again after I join the school, all of you will help me copy my homework. Okay?"

The youths blinked and nodded, then immediately swarmed over in delight to return their coins to their pouches. But once that was done, they dawdled, unwilling to leave.

"Want to play something else?" one of them hemmed and hawed.

"Eh? Didn't you say earlier that you weren't going to play anymore?" Hengwen asked.

The youth said with a cough, "I was talking about dice. How about a game of chess?"

Hengwen nodded. "All right then."

So he set up a chess game and slaughtered them all again.

I simply returned to the covered walkway and set up a chair to watch the show from afar.

In the days of my own childhood, I would skip out on homework and play the day away with my classmates or cousins; consequently, I had received my fair share of the rod from my old man. It was all very fascinating to think back on after all these years.

The youths played until lunchtime before reluctantly leaving, their completed homework in hand. The young servant said to me, "Master, the food is ready in the kitchen. Would you like to have it now?"

I nodded, "Serve the lunch."

Hengwen ate quite a lot, especially the fried eggplant. I made to rearrange the dishes and move the plate closer to him, but Hengwen held it down with his chopsticks and said, "No need for that. I can reach it. Or you can also pick some out for me." So I picked up some food from the dish and delivered it to his plate.

He uttered his thanks.

Tianshu, on the other hand, ate less than he had the previous days. In fact, he had eaten less than half of his rice.

"Eat a little more," I urged in a kindly tone. "You haven't tried these stir-fried bamboo shoots the kitchen made today. Try them."

Tianshu picked up his chopsticks and sampled some dishes. To my surprise, he eventually finished his bowl of rice and even drank half a bowl of soup. I was delighted.

After the meal, a maidservant came forth to clear up the table. I knew Hengwen was thinking about feeding the fox, so I bade her bring the scrambled egg over. Hengwen said, "I told the kitchen to replace it with stewed chicken chunks. It should be tired of eggs after being fed the same thing for the past few days, so there'll be a change of taste today."

I petted him on the head. "Then, a change of taste it is," I said.

The stewed chicken chunks came in a large bowl, soup and all. Worried that Hengwen might lose his grip on the bowl and scald himself, I personally helped him carry it to his room. The fox was lying in the chair, squinting as it waited for Hengwen.

I set down the soup bowl. "Once it's done eating, you should rest for a while too."

"Got it," Hengwen answered.

I returned to my chamber and made my plans to visit Zuiyue Pavilion this afternoon. As I did, I gave in to temptation, taking out Qingxian's handkerchief and scented sachet again. A gust of wind blew through the door I had forgotten to close earlier. I looked up in time to see Hengwen striding into the hall, his eyes on the objects in my hands.

I hurriedly set them down. "Why aren't you resting?"

"I thought I'd come over for a look. I'll go back for my nap later." Hengwen walked over to the bed and picked up the scented sachet to heft it in his hand. "How fragrant."

I took it from his hand. "You should go back and sleep."

Hengwen looked at me with a smile. "Are you going to see her again this afternoon?"

I had the self-awareness to know that it was not appropriate to mention this sort of stuff before Young Hengwen, so I gave an ambiguous answer: "I have some urgent matters to attend to."

Hengwen gave an "oh" before following up with a yawn, "Then you should take a nap. I'm sleepy, so I'll head back for one myself." Having said that, he turned and left. I followed him to the door and watched his retreating back. His door closed with a creak, and only then did I close my own with a sigh.

Chapter Twenty-One

When evening came around, I arrived at Zuiyue Pavilion once more.

Except this time, I did not head for Qingxian's room.

I had made a written pact with the procuress yesterday. Seeing as that squire's nephew still had yet to discuss Qingxian's price with the procuress, I had beaten him to the punch, telling her that I wanted to redeem Qingxian's freedom. The procuress had put on a show of hesitating, loath to part with her top earner, and thrown out an exorbitant price. I cooperated by playing the role of a cuckold liberal with his money and gave a candid, ready nod of my head. The procuress was thrilled.

I set the banknotes before her, earning a beam even more radiant than the flowers in spring. "Thank you, my lord. From today onward, Qingxian is all yours."

The ladies from Zuiyue Pavilion crowded around Qingxian as she walked out. With tears glistening in her eyes, she curtsied deeply to me.

At least it could be said that this immortal lord had done a good deed during these few days in the mortal world.

The procuress even went to the special effort of sending a small, pink sedan to send Qingxian off. And so it was in full view of the common folks of this city that this immortal lord led Qingxian's tiny sedan to my humble compound under the darkness of the night.

Qingxian dismounted the sedan and entered the courtyard at the side of this immortal lord. In the courtyard, the maidservants, young servant, and cook all stood still like wooden stakes, and the copper basin in the young servant's hands hit the ground with a noisy clatter.

Qingxian stood beside me, looking like a crabapple blossom adorned with dewdrops as she timidly lowered her head.

I saw Hengwen and Tianshu walk from the doors of the main hall to the covered walkway, where they repeatedly sized the pair of us up.

I said to the crowd, "Miss Qingxian will be temporarily living in the courtyard, so please tidy up a guest room."

The maidservants, young servant, and cook were all very quick-witted. The young servant picked up the copper basin and immediately answered, "Sure, sure, this humble one will go right away."

One of the maidservants came to support Qingxian by the arm. "Miss, please take a rest first in the hall."

The other maidservant said to Hengwen and Tianshu, "It's getting late. Young masters, let this lowly one attend to the two of you while you rest." Hengwen and Tianshu then returned to their rooms with her.

The maidservant helped Qingxian into the small hall, served tea—of which Qingxian sipped a cup—and announced that the hot water was ready, escorting her to the bath.

I instructed the maidservants to serve her well, then strolled over to the side chambers. After a moment's hesitation, I pushed open the door to Tianshu's chamber.

Tianshu was reading a book under the light, but seeing me enter, he set it down.

"Not going to bed yet? You should rest early," I said.

Tianshu uttered an acknowledgment and asked, "That Qingxian…"

"She was being forced into marriage by a wealthy family," I explained, "I took pity on her and redeemed her freedom before they could. Tomorrow, I'll ask her if she still has any relatives she can rely on. In all likelihood, we will have to return to the Heavenly Court in the next few days, so settling her down before returning would be considered a meritorious deed during my trip to the mortal world."

Tianshu nodded his head, albeit with a puzzled expression, then closed his book and obediently went to bed. I went to Hengwen's room next.

Hengwen was sitting on the bed unwrapping Furball's bandage. I moved in for a look. These few days, I had been using my powers to treat its wounds. Hengwen had cast a tiny spell too, and now Furball was completely healed. All that remained were bald spots where the fur had yet to grow back.

"It's getting more and more spirited these days," I commented.

"Yes," Hengwen responded with a smile. "Its injuries have healed." He reached out to stroke the fox's back, and the fox smacked its lips and licked Hengwen's other hand.

I moved Furball aside and took his place on the edge of the bed. "It's getting late. Sleep early."

Hengwen yawned. "Now that you mention it, I'm really a little sleepy."

All I had to say was, "Then sleep. I'll take my leave."

Hengwen smiled. "All right."

I left Hengwen's room and pushed open the door to my own.

Wearing a sheer gown as flimsy as the wings of cicadas, Qingxian sat under the lamp, looking at me with eyes that were bashful, sultry, and enamored all at once.

I gave a genteel smile as I stood outside the door. "Please take a good rest first, Miss Qingxian. If there's anything you feel unaccustomed to, feel free to let me know tomorrow."

I turned to leave when Qingxian said quietly behind me, "Young Master, since you have already redeemed me, I'm yours from today onward. Or do you disdain me for being an unchaste woman past her prime, unworthy of such a virtuous gentleman?"

I had no choice but to turn back to her. "How can you say that, Miss Qingxian? I was merely lending a helping hand by redeeming your freedom; the act in itself is nothing worthy of mention. There's no need for you to beholden yourself to me. You can stay in my humble abode for a couple of days. If you still have any kin or sweetheart whom you can rely on, don't hesitate to tell me. I'll make the arrangements for you."

Not a single thought seemed to cross Qingxian's face, but soon enough, she had covered it with a sob. "In saying this, are you turning me away? Young Master, do you know that when you passed by the building that day, I was taken with your graceful charm. That was why I so boldly used my handkerchief to play matchmaker, hoping to get to know you. I was so delighted when you redeemed my freedom, thinking that Heaven had finally opened its eyes to my plight and Buddha had finally blessed me. But who knew... that Young Master... you... would say such words to me... I... I..."

I heaved a long sigh. "Miss Qingxian, it's not like you don't know that my heart is already spoken for, but I'm doomed to a fate of eternal solitude, with no hope ever of marriage. Wipe your tears and sleep well. I'll figure a way out for you again tomorrow."

I closed the door behind me before I walked to the yard.

Once more, I had nowhere to sleep, and sitting on the roof tiles was chilly, the night breeze growing increasingly colder. I remembered there was another hard couch in the study, so I snuck in and recited a spell to transform it into a large, soft bed. Bolting the door, I turned in.

I had indeed invited a thorny trouble upon myself by bringing Qingxian back. I had two tagalongs in tow, and yet she had still fallen for me at first sight. Apparently, there was no burying this immortal lord's charm.

I closed my eyes, and was about to fall asleep when a plaintive tune rang out from afar. It drifted past the crack of the door and burrowed its way into my ears.

Seeing that Qingxian had hit a roadblock with this immortal lord earlier, she had taken out her bamboo flute to play a tune or two to distract herself. The song was mournful and heart-wrenching; I fell asleep to it.

The next day, all the servants in the courtyard looked listless, their eyes glazed over as they yawned repeatedly. I pretended not to have noticed a thing. Qingxian, meanwhile, had shut herself in her room, and I paid her no mind.

Hengwen and Tianshu could not refrain from letting loose a couple of yawns themselves over breakfast.

To me, Tianshu said, "That one from yesterday—"

"You can call her Miss Qingxian," I said with a cough.

"All right," Tianshu acquiesced. "Why isn't Miss Qingxian coming for breakfast?"

"She probably hasn't gotten up yet," I hazarded. "I'll get someone to deliver breakfast to her later."

Tianshu nodded, and the maidservant serving the dishes lowered her head, hiding a smile behind her sleeve.

In the afternoon, the cook looked at me and said, "Master, it's not our prerogative to speak out of turn when it comes to your affairs, but isn't it a little inappropriate to get the two young masters to call the madam Miss Qingxian? After all… there is hierarchy to consider here. Even if she's only the master's bed-warmer, it's still…"

I wanted to explain the situation at first, but the affairs between men and women were hard to explain, much less in clear-cut terms. So I simply said, "Miss Qingxian is merely staying here for a day or two. All of you should also address her as Miss Qingxian. Just treat her courteously and according to the protocols for a guest."

The cook stole a glance at me, acknowledged my instruction, and left.

I went to Qingxian's room and asked if she still had any kin she could turn to. Qingxian bit her lips and kept her head lowered without saying a word. After a long time, she said, "Young Master, I'm aware that you want to marry Young Miss Feng. My presence here will only make it awkward. I'm already yours, so I have no complaints whether you send me off to the countryside or resell me to another."

I spoke to her for a long length of time without further progress, so I could only leave.

Qingxian took out her qin again and sat in her room, playing and singing several forlorn tunes.

She sang until the cook, maidservants and young servant all fled far away to the backyard, while Hengwen and Tianshu's playmates came for less than a quarter of an hour before they scattered.

I looked on helplessly as a very bored Hengwen carried the fox out from his chamber. The fox sneezed, and its ears trembled. With eyes tightly shut, it burrowed its head deep into Hengwen's bosom.

It all looked very unbecoming to me. The fox was still a demon, after all; it was improper for it to keep sticking to Hengwen, even if Hengwen appeared to be an adolescent.

I said to Hengwen, "If nothing else, put it aside and let it sleep. Isn't it a tad heavy to keep hugging it all the time?"

"Then I'll take it back to the room," Hengwen said, and turned back inside.

As I lingered under the eaves of the roof, the cook and young servant intercepted me.

The young servant bowed and grimaced at me. "Master, aren't you going to comfort Miss Qingxian?"

I said to let her have a quiet moment for the time being and strolled onward.

The cook hurriedly strode a step forward and bowed. "Master, please don't hold it against us servants for speaking out of turn. Ever since last night, Miss Qingxian's tunes have evoked such… heartache in us! Master, you should go and comfort her!"

I sighed in despondency. "I have, in fact, come back from comforting her in the late morning, but it was futile. Since she wants to play, then just let her play."

The cook and the young servant then left, looking rather distressed.

Qingxian took a break during lunchtime, but in the afternoon, when Madam Lü-Hu came calling again, she was greeted by Qingxian's sorrowful tune. After she sat down and exchanged some pleasantries, she got to the point. "Young Master Song, this old one is merely here to pass a message. I hope you don't mind. About the matter this old one spoke to you about the last time—I ask that you please just pretend that I have never mentioned it."

I promptly understood that this was because of Qingxian. It was just as well for me, so I said, "Thank you for passing on the message. May I trouble you to convey another message to them? This humble one understands. It's indeed regrettable, and I'll definitely not bring this up again."

But Madam Lü-Hu changed her tune and said, "Actually, it's not that this old one is speaking out of turn, but you pulled such a stunt just when a marriage was about to be realized. The Fengs find it all very humiliating. They feared that a distinguished person like you did not think much of the young miss of their household, making it seem like they were the ones who had tried to force their young miss onto you. If you send away this courtesan from the brothel, it would not be impossible to turn things around..."

I could not be bothered to expend more energy on this matter, so I gave a perfunctory answer, "It is as you say. This humble one will definitely consider your advice carefully. Let's talk about it again in a few days." Which, at any rate, successfully fobbed off Madam Lü-Hu.

I was just about to return to my room for a drink of water, but Qingxian was waiting at my door, asking to see me. On entering my room, her first words were, "I heard Madame Lü come over in the afternoon. It seems she's here to talk about your marriage. Young Master, there's no need to take me into consideration. If you wish to send me away, then..."

I sighed.

Covering her mouth with her handkerchief, Qingxian sobbed, "But I only love and admire you. Young Master... Just one day, or even one night, let Qingxian serve you once. However you want to deal with me afterward, I..."

I took her in, thinking that she was merely one lovestruck woman in this wide world. I never expected that I would have someone be so besotted with me before I was sent to the Immortal Execution Terrace. Even that bit about my fate of eternal solitude was disproved. I had indeed gained plenty.

I reached out to help her up. In a gentle voice, I said, "I'm not marrying Young Miss Feng. As for you, I'll definitely make the proper arrangements too. Get up first and return to your room."

Qingxian wiped her tears, rose to her feet and curtsied, then did as I asked.

PEACH BLOSSOM DEBT

I was exhausted, having been tormented in turns like a pin-wheel. I could not even stop myself from yawning during dinner.

Initially, I hoped that meant I could get a good night's sleep at night. Then during the second night-watch period, a tune started to waft through the air and linger, sounding like the forlorn cries of the cuckoo and the mournful wails of a widow at her husband's grave. There was even a quiver trailing each note, so much that even I quavered along with it. But as I pricked up my ears to listen, it occurred to me that this sound did not originate from Qingxian's room, but from the backyard.

So I rolled over and lifted my concealed form from my physical body, floating out of the study to investigate. However, the sound of the flute came to an abrupt stop. Under the veil of darkness, a shadowy figure streaked across the moon gate in the backyard.

I followed it into the backyard, only to see a figure leap off the courtyard wall. Under the starlight by the flower clusters, this figure traded gazes with the silhouette of another person here.

The other person had a delicate and lithe figure—Qingxian. As for the other one who had leaped off the courtyard wall, I supposed he was the fellow who had played the flute. Somehow, however, this visitor's form seemed familiar.

I stood beside them. The flute player was grasping Qingxian's hands as he said in an urgent voice, "Qingxian, leave with me. Let's elope somewhere far away."

"Leave?" Qingxian said wistfully. "Where can we go? Why are you here for me again?"

"I—" The flute player had only just said a word when a voice suddenly interrupted from the top of the wall.

"That's right, He Jingxuan, where are you going to take her?"

The flute player and Qingxian both gave a start and whipped their heads up. A figure standing atop the courtyard wall leaped lightly off the wall, walked over to the flute player, and asked again. "He Jingxuan, where are you going to take her?"

That person was dressed in men's attire, but had a sweet, delicate voice and a slender, graceful figure. It was a young girl.

All of a sudden, the script for the *Meeting Between The Butterfly Lovers* turned into *Two Damsels Meet A Hero.*

I stood to the side again and watched as the flustered flute player stammered, "Young Miss Yueying, you, why are you…"

"Jingxuan, you should leave now," Qingxian said softly. "Young Miss Yueying, don't worry. Jingxuan will never come looking for me again. Young Master Song has already bought me, and he said himself that he would not propose marriage to your parents. Young Miss Yueying, you… you can marry Jingxuan with peace of mind. I… Young Master Song redeemed me from a courtesan's life, so I will repay him for all my life. Jingxuan, I-I wish you and Young Miss Yueying a lifetime of conjugal bliss…"

She turned to leave. The flute player grabbed her sleeve, stopping her. "Qingxian, did you deceive that Song man into redeeming you just to bring Young Miss Yueying and me together?! How can you be so foolish?! All this time, my heart only has—"

"Only has Qingxian?" Young Miss Yueying cut him off coldly and took another step toward the flute player. "Well, well, He Jingxuan, you finally speak the truth today."

With a bitter laugh, she continued, "That's right. I should have known that you only have eyes for Qingxian. I should have known the moment you cast aside your dignity as a scholar who'd passed the county imperial examinations to sell rouge at the foot of the brothel. It was just that… just that when we were children, you said you would marry me as your bride, and like a fool, I took it seriously, unwilling to believe that you would end up falling for someone else." She threw an object onto the ground and turned back toward the wall.

So it turned out that the flute player was the young lad selling rouge on the ground floor of Zuiyue Pavilion. No wonder I found the sight of him familiar.

Yueying walked up to the wall, then turned around and continued, "Miss Qingxian, for Jingxuan's sake, you even used yourself to hold back that Song person, so that he could not propose marriage to my parents. You really are foolish. When my parents forced me to marry him, I told them I'd rather die. If they force me into a corner, at most I'll just leave and end this once and for all. You never asked Jingxuan who he liked, and went straight to sacrificing yourself. Didn't you know how it would hurt him?"

This immortal lord realized that this courtyard wall of mine was indeed really low. It did not take Young Miss Feng Yueying much effort at all to climb her way up and jump away.

Meanwhile, Qingxian and He Jingxuan were still gazing at each other.

"Qingxian," He Jingxuan pleaded, "leave with me."

Qingxian shook her head. "It's too late. I've deceived Young Master Song. He has money, so he must have power and influence too. If I leave with you, I will only put you in harm's way. Xuan-lang, leave without me."

I floated over to the moon gate, manifested myself, and coughed.

He Jingxuan was right in the midst of tightly grasping Qingxian's hands. When this pair of star-crossed lovebirds heard my cough, they immediately began trembling like falling leaves in the wind.

"Don't be afraid," I said with an affable smile. "I've seen it all from where I was in the shadows earlier." I fished out a piece of paper from my sleeve and tore it into pieces. To Qingxian, I said, "That was your indenture."

Qingxian looked steadily at me and suddenly fell to her knees with He Jingxuan.

"The love between both of you is so earth-shakingly touching that even a layman like me is deeply moved," I said in all sincerity. "I may not be a virtuous gentleman, but I'm willing to grant you your wish to be together. He Jingxuan, take Miss Qingxian away."

In the middle of the night, when the wind was cold, I stood in the open and spacious backyard and let out a laugh. So this was this immortal lord's fate after all. I thought I had picked up two romances before being sent to the Immortal Execution Terrace, but it turned out I was still a go-between for other couples.

Behind me, a voice said at leisure, "So, how does your recent spate of romantic luck with the ladies feel?"

Chapter Twenty-Two

I looked back and saw him standing close by. He smiled at me.

It felt as if my heart was lifted, and for a moment, I thought my eyes were playing tricks on me. I could not control my legs as I hurried over to him. Even my voice trembled when I spoke.

He simply stood there, smiling as he listened.

"Heng-Hengwen..."

I grabbed hold of his sleeve. I had been longing for this for so long, and now that it was right before my eyes, I suspected it to be all a dream.

He moved in closer to me and whispered into my ears, "Actually, that night when you told me to recover soon, I somehow really did. But then I saw you basking in the love of those peach blossom women, so I wanted to see how your luck would play out this time."

He feigned a sigh. "Looks like there's something to what you've been moping about all this time. Your luck in love truly leaves much to be desired."

I just looked at him, at a loss for words.

"It's late, and the wind is cold," Hengwen said. "It wouldn't be good if someone saw us standing in the yard like this. Let's return to the chamber first."

Embarrassed, I released his sleeve. "All right."

As we re-entered the covered walkway, Hengwen chuckled. "You've been sleeping in the study these two days. Can I enter, though?"

I let out an awkward laugh and pushed the door to the study open.

The room was tiny. I had had someone replace the hard couch with a large bed, leaving only a small gap of free space on all sides. The moonlight just so happened to shine on the table the moment I opened the door. I closed it behind us, and Hengwen erected a magical barrier around us with a wave of his sleeve.

"You've just recovered," I said, "so best not to use your divine powers for now. What if..."

"It's fine," Hengwen said. "Didn't I already use them these past few days?"

I could not help myself, reaching out again to grasp his sleeve. "Still, it's better to use less of it. You..."

Hengwen stood looking at me. He had already recovered. These few days in the mortal world had finally come to an end.

No matter which, there would eventually come a day when it all ended.

I grasped Hengwen by both arms and called him by his name. Before he could react, I kissed him on the lips.

This immortal lord really did admire myself so. How wise was I, to have had someone carry in a large bed this morning.

The peach blossom wood had been an illusion, conjured by Hengwen's divine powers. It had always been unreal—dream-like—and nothing like the vivid realism I was living now.

The tips of Hengwen's brows had furrowed into a frown.

"I'm gentler than I was last time," I whispered into his ear, voice hoarse.

Hengwen opened partially closed eyes, and when he looked at me, there seemed to be a smile in them. Then he bit my neck, hard. "Have at it to your heart's content. Next, *mn*, next time, I won't let you get your way…"

As the harshness of winter neared, drawing well water and warming it in the tub became a more taxing task. The original intention was to wash Hengwen and myself clean, but in the end, we washed until we ended up in bed. So, we changed the water again, heated it up again, and washed up again. Rinse and repeat. By the time this immortal lord was all refreshed and content and taking a nap for real with Hengwen in my arms, it was almost dawn.

"No wonder the mortals love to lament over the 'brevity of conjugal nights,'" Hengwen remarked lazily. "Only tonight do I understand." Then he closed his eyes and drifted into a sound sleep.

I closed my eyes, more than ready for a short rest, but then I had another dream.

In my dream, I was sitting under the lamp in a room, a game of chess laid out before me. The world before my eyes seemed to be shrouded in a veil of fog; I could not see the game clearly, or my opponent for that matter, but I knew viscerally that I had lost.

"I've lost again," I blurted out. "Will I ever get to beat you once this lifetime?" The snuff of the candlewick crackled, although the first light of dawn was already sneaking through the window paper.

The person opposite me waved a hand to extinguish the lamp. He then pushed open the window panel; the morning rays poured across the room.

In the blink of an eye, however, I was standing in a court-yard. It was so foggy I had difficulty seeing, but I seemed to be well acquainted with everything in the courtyard. Ahead of me should be a pond, where the waterlilies had just grown round leaves. At the edge of the bank were a few pieces of decorative taihu rocks and two plantain trees, as well as a pavilion on the opposite bank; in it sat a stone table with a chessboard carved into it. It should be spring at this time. The fragrance of Lady Banks' roses in the morning mist was mentally refreshing. No doubt the vines of climbing Lady Banks' rose branches on the courtyard walls were in full bloom.

He stood right beside me. Behind me was that same window from earlier.

"Perfect is the spring breeze, when the morning dew thins," I said to him. I still could not see his face clearly, but I knew he was smiling with pleasure.

The flowers were fragrant, the morning breeze cool and refreshing. The fog, however, was thickening.

I anxiously looked at his face, wanting to know who he was, but his entire figure was concealed in the fog, invisible and indiscernible. I reached out, wanting to grab hold of him to ask, but the moment my fingers grasped the corner of the slightly cool fabric, I jolted awake.

I was clutching Hengwen's sleeve, and Hengwen was leaning against the headboard, his head tilted aside as he looked at me.

I hurriedly propped myself up. "You... You should sleep a little longer... Lie back down."

"It's not like I'm a mortal," Hengwen said lazily. "I'm not that weak. My fatigue's almost gone after a good sleep."

This immortal lord immediately followed up with a question, "Where... did you learn that mortals are weak?"

"From the books," Hengwen yawned. "When it comes to that sort of book, those with just illustrations are not as good as those with both illustrations and accompanying text."

Hengwen— He— Just how much erotica had he read?!

Hengwen looked down. "What's wrong with your left hand?

It doesn't seem to be very mobile."

I was in the midst of rubbing my little finger. "Maybe I hurt it some time ago. It feels a little out of sorts." Since early morning, I had been feeling stabbing pain at the base of my little finger, like it was being sliced by a knife.

Hengwen raised my hand for a look. All of a sudden, he said, "I'm going to head back first to the Heavenly Court." He laughed at my expression. "Don't panic. I'm not going back to plead guilty. I just think many reasons for your trip down this time are extremely contrived. There's something fishy about this matter, too. I'm thinking of going to the Jade Emperor to clear up all these doubts. As for the confession of guilt," the tips of his hair brushed gently against my shoulder, "we'll go together."

I could never stop Hengwen if he wanted to return to Heaven, so I said, "All right, then."

Following his lead, I draped my clothes around myself and got out of bed. I smoothed the front flaps of his clothes for him, and as Hengwen walked to the door, he turned aside and asked, "Song Yao, who do you think would set up love trials for us the way you did for Tianshu and Nanming?"

With a dry laugh, I answered, "I haven't really thought about that."

Hengwen smiled, then turned around in the morning rays. With a flick of his sleeves, he transformed into a beam of light to depart.

For a moment, I stood blankly in that empty chamber. Then, with a sigh, I reached into my sleeves. I spread a sheet of paper on the table, preparing a brush that I could write with without ink.

In the end, I folded up my work—a sheet chock-full of writing—and recited an incantation. That piece of paper instantaneously transformed into golden light, and vanished without a trace.

When I had initially descended to the mortal world, the Jade

Emperor had bestowed this upon me in secret. It was called a Submission Memorial. No matter where I was, this memorial could make its way to the Jade Emperor's desk in an instant.

I stepped out of the study, rubbing my temples. Hengwen knew nothing of the ways of the mortal world; thus, he still acted without consideration for the consequences.

This morning, the courtyard was missing Qingxian and a little young master. How was this immortal lord going to explain their disappearance to the servants and little Tianshu?

No matter how fast Hengwen was, he would definitely not be as fast as that memorial.

In that memorial, I told the Jade Emperor that the offending immortal Song Yao had failed the Jade Emperor's decree by secretly communicating information to Tianshu Xingjun. On top of that, I had been swayed by secular love. Knowing there was no excuse for this unpardonable sin, I pled guilty of my own accord.

With the memorial submitted, this immortal lord's tragedy of a fate was sealed. I would definitely not escape punishment for my intervention in Tianshu's trials, and since I was already going to be sent to the Immortal Execution Terrace, why drag Hengwen along with me?

The precedent of Tianshu and Nanming was right before my eyes. So, I thought, even if I were to be banished to the mortal world again, it was still better for Hengwen to remain in the Heavenly Court than for the both of us to be exiled.

I made my way to the covered walkway and came face-to-face with a maidservant, who greeted me with a curtsy. I was wondering if I should buy some time by telling her that Miss Qingxian and the little young master were still asleep and not to be disturbed when the young servant suddenly ran over to me in a fluster. "M-Master, the main hall, in the main hall... you should go and take a look, quickly..."

This immortal lord strode swiftly to the main hall, where a man and a woman in the center of the hall fell to their knees on seeing me.

Why had Qingxian and the flute player returned?

They remained on the ground, crying their hearts out to me.

With Qingxian's dainty hand in his, the flute player cried, "Young Master Song, you're this junior and Qing-er's great benefactor. After this junior and Qing-er are married, we will erect a longevity tablet to honor you in our home and offer incense every day..."

The pair cried in tandem. But why in the world had these two not let their tears run their course in the backyard yesterday instead of making a special trip here to cry again?

Resigned, I bent over and helped them up. "I really do not deserve this honor. The unity of a pair of lovers in marriage is the most fulfilling of all in the world. This lowly one—this lowly one is merely acting in accordance with Heaven's wishes."

After seeing Qingxian and the flute player off, I returned to the main hall to see little Tianshu standing by the screen.

Tianshu looked at me with bright, shiny eyes. "Why did Qingxian and that man cry like that just now? Is this the love of mortals?"

I ruffled his hair and took my seat. "That's right."

"Isn't love something that makes mortals happy?" Tianshu asked. "In that case, they should be smiling. Why did they cry?"

"When you get involved in something like this, there will be plenty of tears and smiles," I said.

Tianshu uttered an "oh."

I told the maidservants not to call up the little young master yet, on account of him being a sleepyhead today. I would hold them off for as long as it took. After breakfast, Tianshu asked me in a hushed tone, "Where's Hengwen?"

"He went back to the Heavenly Court first," I answered truthfully.

Tianshu creased his forehead in a frown. I was just about to explain in detail when a bright light suddenly lit up the interior of the chamber. Beiyue Dijun materialized in midair, leading five or six heavenly soldiers. In a loud, clear voice, he announced, "Song Yao Yuanjun, I am here on the Jade Emperor's decree to lead you and Tianshu Xingjun back to the Heavenly Court posthaste."

Tianshu had yet to recover. Confused, he reached out to tightly clutch the front of this immortal lord's clothes.

Beiyue Dijun alighted on the ground and said politely, "Song Yao Yuanjun, this way, please."

The five or six heavenly soldiers moved toward Tianshu, but this immortal took a step to stand before him. "Dijun, if you would be so kind as to allow Tianshu Xingjun to remain by my side for the time being."

Beiyue Dijun looked at Tianshu. "That's fine." With a signal from his eyes, the heavenly soldiers withdrew, and passed through the wall to look around. After a moment, they returned. One of them was carrying the fox in his hands. He said to Beiyue, "To report to Your Eminence, we sent those mortals off into their dreams. When they wake up, they will just assume this household has already moved away."

Beiyue Dijun gave a slight nod of his head. "Let's go."

The scenery in the Heavenly Court was the same as ever, as were the rose-tinted clouds and the few faces guarding the Southern Heavenly Gate.

He Yun, the Jade Emperor's heavenly envoy, stood before the Southern Heavenly Gate and bowed to Beiyue Dijun. "This humble immortal has waited here for a long time on the Jade Emperor's decree. Has Dijun brought back the person the Jade Emperor instructed you to retrieve?"

Little Tianshu stood by my side, while the heavenly soldier holding the fox stood on the other.

"May I trouble Heavenly Envoy He to report back to the Jade Emperor that I've brought them back with no issue?" Beiyue Dijun said.

He Yun looked in my direction, and nodded. "This humble immortal understands." Then he added, "The Jade Emperor has sent instructions that Dijun send Tianshu Xingjun to Yaoguang Palace."

Having received the order, Beiyue Dijun turned to Tianshu. "Please come with me," he said, though he seemed deeply reluctant to do so.

Little Tianshu did not understand what was happening, but he answered in a clear, childlike voice, "Fine. In that case, I shall have to trouble Dijun." He stepped forward beside me, then turned his head again to ask, "Oh, right, where do you live in the Heavenly Court? You've been looking after me these days in the mortal realm. I will call on you again another day to convey my thanks."

I forced a smile. "I live in the Guangxu Manor. If you are able to come over, you can ask the Northern Heavenly King to show you the way."

Tianshu nodded with a smile. "Probably because I haven't been out of the Beidou Palace much, I'm ashamed to say that I've not heard of it before. But after descending to the mortal world these few days, the vista in the Heavenly Court sure has changed some. Farewell for now. Let's go back again when we have free time."

"Sure," I responded and watched as Tianshu walked over to Beiyue Dijun's side.

He Yun replaced him, accompanying this immortal lord. "Please come with me."

I took a step forward, and He Yun reached out a hand to stop me. "Song Yao Yuanjun, this humble immortal wasn't talking about you. The Jade Emperor's verbal instruction was for you to return to your residence, and to rest for now."

He looked at the heavenly soldier carrying Furball. "You, come with me."

Now, I was terrified. He Yun was still very courteous when he spoke to me, and he even continued to address me as Song Yao Yuanjun. Evidently, the Jade Emperor had yet to give the command to strip me of my title and immortal status. This meant that His Venerable Self had a severe punishment in store for me.

This immortal lord watched helplessly as Beiyue led Tianshu and He Yun led the heavenly soldier carrying Furball further and further into the distance. The remaining heavenly soldiers bowed to me and said, "Yuanjun, we have been ordered to escort you back to your residence."

When I looked up, Tianshu's tiny figure had already dissolved into the clouds and mist. Why didn't the Jade Emperor have me hauled to his palace for interrogation? What exactly was His Venerable Self up to?

And Hengwen—how was he now...

Surrounded by the various heavenly soldiers, I returned to my Guangxu Yuanjun's Residence. Come to think of it, I had been in the Heavenly Court for so many years, fumbling for this title of "Yuanjun," without many attendants to show for it. I had been rather envious at the sight of so many escorting Dijun and Hengwen during the morning sessions. Today, sandwiched in the midst of my own escort of heavenly soldiers, it was this immortal lord who came in with pomp and panache for once.

For the first time, I seriously eyed my Guangxu Yuanjun's residence from afar and suddenly found it to be quite imposing with its plastered walls, ink-black tiles, and bright, red-colored main gate. No wonder Hengwen had always loved to wander here, claiming my Yuanjun's residence to be much more comfortable than his Weiyuan Palace. How regrettable that in all these years, I had not treated it with the care it deserved.

When I walked over to the main gate, I felt even more terrified. The words, *Guangxu Yuanjun's Residence*, were still sparkling on the plaque at the top. I sighed in dismay. Looked like His Venerable Self the Jade Emperor was furious. He intended to strip me of my title, tear down my plaque, confiscate my manor, strike off my immortal status, and whatever else to add some variety to my punishment. It was going to be a severe one, merely temporarily deferred.

One of the heavenly soldiers opened the main gate and shoved me inside before shutting it. I heard the clattering sound of chains being wrapped, and then the click of a lock before it clanged against the doors. From the sound of it, this lock was not at all small.

A sturdy, divine dome overhead covered my residence, like a large inverted bowl, detaining me securely in Guangxu Manor.

For the first time, I also realized just how big my Guangxu Yuanjun's residence was.

I strolled to and fro in the various chambers. The residence was empty, and I was its only presence.

The stone bed in the backyard where Hengwen and I had slept together after we got drunk the first time he visited me.

The remnants of the unfinished game of chess was still scattered on the chessboard beneath the magnolia tree.

The two jars of fine wine hidden in the corner of the chamber in the left wing, the ones that he had yet to fleece off me.

The brush on the study table was still the same one Hengwen had offhandedly picked up the last time Lu Jing had hunted him down for an "important" correspondence.

The lotus ink painting hanging on the wall of my bedchamber that he had gifted me the first time he came around.

The glazed screen made with black jade that Hengwen had won in a battle of divine skills with Donghua Dijun, still displayed in the hall. I had unabashedly asked for it after telling him it was at odds with the furnishings in his Weiyuan Palace.

The pillars on the covered walkway were still decorated with the phrases he had offhandedly written during our conversation about matching couplets.

Before we descended to the mortal world, I had sparred with him in the courtyard, and in a moment of inattention, blown up a railing of the wayside pavilion. To date, it still had yet to be repaired.

As I moved from the chamber to the backyard, a voice sounded from beyond the divine barrier overhead, "Song Yao Yuanjun, the Jade Emperor has ordered this humble immortal to bring you to the Peach of Immortality Garden for an audience with him."

For the life of me, I could not figure out why the Jade Emperor had to bring this immortal lord to trial in the Peach of Immortality Garden and not Lingxiao Palace. Of course, if the Jade Emperor's intent was so easily guessed by the likes of me, His Venerable Self would not be the Jade Emperor.

Resigned, I looked up. "He Yun, am I supposed to bring my residence with me to meet the Jade Emperor if you don't open up the divine barrier?"

Radiant were the blooms of peach blossoms in the Peach of Immortality Garden, and glorious were the rosy-tinted clouds.

The Jade Emperor sat upright in the pavilion. This immortal lord, being most discerning of the situation, walked over and fell to my knees with a thud. "This offending immortal, Song Yao, pays his respect to the Jade Emperor."

"You sure are candid when it comes to confessing," the Jade Emperor said, his tone unhurried.

I lowered my head. "This offending immortal has repeatedly violated the rules of Heaven while in the mortal world. I'm aware that there is no hiding the fact from the Jade Emperor's omniscient eyes, and so—"

The Jade Emperor cut me off mid-sentence. "Forget it. Do

you think you can pull the wool over my eyes by being so long-winded and writing a memorial? I have already shown your confession memorial to Hengwen Qingjun, and he has told me everything."

Alarmed, I jerked my head up.

The Jade Emperor smacked his palm on the stone table with an icy expression. "Song Yao, look at what you did in the mortal world!"

My mind was in turmoil as I quickly explained to the Jade Emperor, "Jade Emperor, this is all this offending immortal's fault. You must not listen to the words of Hengwen, Hengwen Qingjun. Qingjun was under my..."

The Jade Emperor jolted abruptly to his feet, flung his sleeves heavily, and said with a grim laugh, "I naturally know the fault is yours. There is no pushing the blame onto someone else even if you want to. You get yourself tied up with Tianshu and now you get Hengwen Qingjun involved too. Song Yao, oh, Song Yao. I sent you down to the mortal world, and you reaped yourself quite the bountiful harvest!!"

I kept silent, and the Jade Emperor continued, "You were a variable to begin with. No one could have expected you to ascend to the Heavenly court that day. I went along with the will of Heaven and let you remain in the Heavenly Court. Sure enough, more complications have arisen with this trip of yours to the mortal world."

I prostrated over the ground. "To begin with, this offending immortal became an immortal through no effort of my own. Tianshu Xingjun was right that day in Lingxiao Palace when he said that I was still sentimentally attached to affairs of the mortal world despite my immortality. Hengwen Qingjun, he... is ignorant of the ways of the secular world. In truth, I have lusted after him for a very long time. In making use of the opportunity accorded to me on this time around, I tantalized and seduced him. Qingjun, he is actually... This offending immortal knows my sins are unpardonable. Whether I am to be sent to the Immortal Execution Terrace or totally obliterated, I deserve it."

The Jade Emperor did not speak again. Following the trail of the cool breeze, a pair of bees flew into the pavilion and chased after each other right before this immortal lord's eyes.

With his hands behind his back, the Jade Emperor stood by the steps of the wayside pavilion, and the pair of bees, chasing after one another, flew over to his side.

"The Dao is, of itself, natural, attained by following one's heart, coming all together in one harmonious whole," the Jade Emperor said. "The Heavenly Court is not like the Western Paradise of Buddha, where one has to be without passion and love, desires and demands. However, the karmic cycle of cause and effect holds true for all living creatures in Heaven and Earth. Immortals might go along with the flow, but they cannot escape reaping what they sow. The rules of the Heavenly Court are, in truth, meant to rectify one's conduct. Case in point, Nanming and Tianshu."

The Jade Emperor strolled back to the stone table and sat down. "Nanming has long developed feelings for Tianshu, yet he was harsh and merciless when he was putting Qingtong and Zhilan on trial with Tathagata Buddha and me. He was already lacking integrity, and yet he was so severe in his treatment of others. If we disregard other karmic causes and effects, it was for this very reason that he and Tianshu must undergo trials and tribulations after their banishment."

This immortal lord suspected that the Jade Emperor's fury was scrambling his senses. No matter how I listened to these few words of his, they were not at all relevant to the topic at hand. Perhaps the Jade Emperor simply wanted to spout some high-sounding words, which was fine by me. There is love in the mortal world, as there is in Heaven. But even in the mortal world, homosexuality was the exception, let alone in the

Heavenly Court. This was the reason the Jade Emperor was omitting by disregarding the other causes and effects.

I heard the Jade Emperor ask me, "Song Yao, do you know what is the gravest of all sins you have committed this time?"

"This offending immortal knows," I answered immediately. "This offending immortal harbored the intent to seduce Hengwen Qingjun with mortal desires, and this sin is unpardonable."

The Jade Emperor rose to his feet again and walked along the wayside pavilion. After a moment, he said, "Go to Mingge Xingjun. Let him inform you of the cause and effect."

I looked up, uncertain, but the Jade Emperor had already made his way down the wayside pavilion. Several heavenly envoys instantly emerged from the peach blossom woods, and followed the Jade Emperor out of the Peach of Immortality Garden.

There were no seventy or eighty heavenly soldiers popping out of the peach blossom woods to detain me after the Jade Emperor left. The Peach of Immortality Garden was silent all around. I could not sense even half a wisp of other immortals' breath. But come to think of it, the entire Heavenly Court was abounded with immortals, and the Heavenly Court was tightly and securely guarded all around. The Jade Emperor did not have to worry about me absconding. Besides, I wanted to know what the so-called "cause and effect" he referred to were.

I took a slow stroll in the Peach of Immortality Garden, thinking about every potential seed of cause before my ascension that would go on to bear the fruit of effect in the Heavenly Court. I ruminated it over, but I could not figure it out.

Exiting the Peach of Immortality Garden from the gate on the other side and walking along a narrow path would lead me to the back door of Mingge Xingjun's Tianming Manor. I walked over to the door. Not far from this door was the lotus pond where I first met Hengwen. The sight of it under such circumstances utterly devastated my little heart.

The clear breeze swept past, and in my daze, I heard Hengwen calling out to me, "Song Yao, Song Yao." I felt more and more melancholy. Hengwen's voice asked right in my ears, "The Jade Emperor ordered you to head over to Mingge Xingjun's residence, so why are you standing motionlessly before the door like a pole?"

I sighed. "I saw the lotus pond and could not help but stop for a look." I realized something amiss the moment the words were out of my mouth, and whipped my head back.

Hengwen was standing right behind me.

I fixed my eyes on him and reached out to touch him.

He was real.

"Why do you look so panic-stricken?" Hengwen asked.

"I thought you were being held in custody by the Jade Emperor," I answered honestly, "so I was a tad startled when I saw you."

Tapping his folding fan, Hengwen said, "Hasn't Song Yao Yuanjun righteously shouldered all the sins committed? So how could the Jade Emperor still hold me in custody?" He raised the tips of his eyebrows and continued, "Since you are dawdling here instead of heading over to Mingge Xingjun's residence, I wonder if you have the time to sit with me by the pond and listen to me preach about cause and effect?"

Hengwen's tone was extremely unfriendly. I went along. "Sure..." I was about to say something else, but Hengwen was already striding vigorous steps toward the lotus pond. I could only catch up with him.

The huge rock from back then—where Hengwen had laid out the paper to draw the lotuses—was still there. Hengwen found a spot to sit without thinking, while I hesitated a little, unsure if I should sit closer or further away. Eventually, I compromised at a spot I gauged to be neither far nor near.

"This lord can't be bothered to speak in a loud voice," Hengwen said, "so come closer a little."

I shifted about three centimeters closer to him.

Hengwen frowned. "Closer."

I shifted another three centimeters.

Hengwen quipped, "Either you head over to Pixiang Palace now and borrow a set of skirts from any of the celestial maidens, upon which you can continue hemming and hawing accordingly, or you come closer still."

I moved so close, I was at Hengwen's shoulder, which finally satisfied him.

I gazed at the lotus pond and said in a soft voice, "Hengwen… Actually, I…"

Hengwen reached out with his folding fan to cut me off. "Since it is so hard for you to speak, don't expend your effort by continuing. Let's leave you aside for the time being. Tianshu has already reverted to his regular self, and at present, he is like a walking corpse being detained in Yaoguang Palace. Let me first share an old story from the past with you."

Even the tips of Hengwen's hair were emanating a chill. Not daring to defy him, I pricked up my ears and listened.

"Of Tianshu Xingjun and Nanming Dijun," Hengwen began, "one was the star of emperors, and the other was in charge of a nation's fortunes and destiny. From birth, they were destined to complement and support each other, to be inextricably connected to one another. After hundreds of years of entanglement, a thread of immortal bond finally formed between the two lords. When the thread of immortal bond first came into being, it was merely just a slipknot on each lord's fingers. In the Heavenly Court, if this thread of immortal bond was formed between two immortals, they must descend to the mortal world to undergo tribulations. This sort of thread was originally formed between a male and a female immortal, since the fusion of pure yang immortal energy and pure yin immortal energy was the natural way of Heaven. Perhaps it occurred in this case because Tianshu and Nanming were too intimately involved with one another, resulting in a thread being unexpectedly formed between them. For that reason, the Jade Emperor sent them to the mortal realm to experience the world's tribulations. Whether the thread of immortal bond is severed or tightened into a dead knot after these calamities is all left to Heaven's will."

So it turned out that Tianshu and Nanming had already underwent tribulations in the mortal world once before. Since there was such a deep, grounded connection to one another, why did the Jade Emperor send me to break up the lovebirds?

Hengwen continued, "Not long after Tianshu Xingjun and Nanming Dijun reincarnated into the mortal world, their thread of immortal bond broke. Tianshu's reincarnation in that life was more or less similar to the Mu Ruoyan of this life. He was the descendant of a family of officials then too, and he was weak and frail by nature. Nanming was the young master of a military family. He grew up with Tianshu, and they were even fellow classmates. The immortals all guessed that Tianshu and Nanming's thread was certain to be unbreakable, that it would turn into a dead knot, but no one could have expected…"

Hengwen paused for a moment before continuing, "No one expected a mortal to barge in between them and break the thread of immortal bond. The thread that was supposed to tether him to Nanming ended up being forcibly bound to that mortal instead."

Huh? Which fellow in the mortal world had this much might?! To think he was able to pull the divine thread off Nanming's hand and secure it to his own finger!

Hengwen proceeded, "That mortal was also a classmate of Tianshu, and he had been considerate and attentive to Tianshu when he was eleven or twelve years of age. There was even a time he protected him during a misunderstanding between Nanming and Tianshu, and it was from then on that the thread was severed.

"At first, the other end of the thread was merely stuck to that mortal's hand, but he showed such care and consideration to Tianshu in every way possible, and the two of them were together all day long from childhood well into their adulthood, reciting poems in the breeze and joining their beds to converse through the night. And so the thread went from merely sticking to that mortal's hand to being bound. Initially, it was a slipknot, but the tribulation Tianshu was destined to undergo in that life was the same as Mu Ruoyan—the execution of his entire clan and the confiscation of his family's properties.

"Tianshu was supposed to return to the Heavenly Court at that time, but no one expected the mortal to actually go against Heaven's will and save Tianshu. He settled down with him in a small courtyard, as inseparable as can be.

"Left with no other alternative, Mingge Xingjun could only make Tianshu gravely ill. That mortal remained by Tianshu's bed, devoting himself to taking meticulous care of him. The day Tianshu finally returned to the Heavenly Court, the slipknot on that mortal's knot had already become a dead knot. The jade pendant that Tianshu has on him was a gift from that mortal, and even after thousands of years, he still carries it with him."

So it turned out that such a story existed in Tianshu's past, one that left listeners sighing helplessly—including me, in that moment.

Hengwen turned his head aside to look at me, and I marveled, "Truly a moving past."

"Don't you find this past familiar after listening to it?" Hengwen asked, tone icy.

Familiar? Why would he suddenly use this of all words to describe it?

Hengwen let out a scornful laugh. "Look into the lotus pond."

With a flick of his sleeve, the lotus flowers and leaves in the pond parted to reveal an unbroken expanse of water. A sudden silver light spread until the surface was a mirror. A scene appeared in this looking glass. In the mirror, there was a hall lined with short tables and chairs; a portrait of Confucius hung in the background of what was apparently a private school.

Two children stood face-to-face with one another, their hands clearly connected by a golden thread. Of these two, one had delicate features, and the face of the other was fierce; these must be the young Tianshu and Nanming.

No matter how I looked, I could not but feel familiar with this scene.

Standing between these two children was another child whom I found intelligent and lovable at first sight. This child was standing before Tianshu, shielding him with his chest puffed out. I felt that I recognized him, but could not place him.

Looking utterly furious, Nanming bellowed, "This is none of your business. Step aside if you know what's good for you."

That child, little big man that he was, retorted, "Do you have the capability to make me step aside? I'm telling you, he's under my protection from now on. Don't even dream of bullying him if you can't get past me!"

Nanming stood, glowering, before resentfully turning his back. As he left, he slammed the table, and the golden thread on his hand slipped off and made contact with the edge of the table.

That child, on the other hand, turned around to pat Tianshu on the shoulder. "Don't you worry. No one will dare to bully you when there's me, Song Yao, to have your back in this private school!"

I gaped, dumbfounded and thunderstruck.

The child in the mirror tugged at Tianshu and pulled him outside. "Let's go out and play." His hand unwittingly pressed down on the tabletop from earlier, and that golden thread stuck to his hand, shining brightly as it connected him and Tianshu—

Hengwen grabbed my left hand and flicked his finger.

Wrapped around the root of my little finger was a piece of dazzling golden thread, and there, at the end, was a dead knot—

How-how could this be?!

The child in the mirror was all grins as he tugged at Tianshu in the courtyard and said, "Du Wanming, you have to do a better job with my homework today."

Du Wanming.

I suddenly recalled the name.

Stars swam before my eyes.

Tianshu, Tianshu actually was Du Wanming!! That, that, Du Wanming—

B-b-but how could Du Wanming and I have had an illicit, homosexual love affair in the mortal world? Clearly—clearly—

"Clearly what? The thread is already tethered to your hand," Hengwen said, with a smile that was not a smile.

I grasped him by his shoulders, not knowing if I should slam my head against the ground or pound my chest and stamp my foot.

Oh, Heaven and deities above, this is a gross injustice—!!!!!

Chapter Twenty-Three

Tianshu was Du Wanming. And Nanming, I remembered him too. He was called Jiang Zongduo.

No wonder he kept staring daggers at me after I ascended to the Heavenly Court.

In truth, I had no grudges against him back then in the mortal world. His father was a second-grade military general, lower than my father's rank, so during the new year and other festivities, his father would often send tributes of respect to my family. But this lad had had a backbone since he was a child, and he never came with his father to come calling at my house.

I remember the name Du Wanming as a nightmare in my childhood. His father and my old man were both successful imperial examination candidates from the same batch of scholars, but his father's road to promotion had not run as smoothly as my father's, and he would later go on to become an imperial censor—a thankless job.

Du Wanming was the same age as me. Even then, he was renowned as a child prodigy, and my father often compared me to him. Du Wanming could recite Mencius backward when he was three years old, yet I would stammer even reading the first two lines of the *Analects of Confucius* at the same age. At five years old, Du Wanming could imitate the strokes of master calligraphers Wang Xizhi and Wang Xianzhi, whereas my handwriting was still chicken scratch. When he was seven, his prose-poetry, *Ode to the Orchids,* was widely read throughout the capital, but at the same age of seven, I was not even sure what a poetic antithesis was.

All day and all night long, my old man was envious of the Du clan's son, and it grieved him bitterly that no matter how he looked at it, his son—that was me—failed to live up to his expectations. When his heartache got too much, he would give me a taste of the rod. My father often lamented with a sigh, "I may have been lucky in my official career, rising above all the others, but several years later, when my son becomes an adult, the Songs would be hard-pressed to match up to the Dus."

All the officials who served in the same administration as my father pooled money together to build a private school where they could send their sons to study. Its true purpose was to give a place for their descendants to build close friendships from youth, so that when they joined the Imperial Court as officials in the future, they could mutually look out for one another and pave the road forward.

When I was ten, Du Wanming enrolled in the private school, and my old man instantly kicked me into the same school.

After I enrolled, I promptly discovered that there were many who were in the same shoes as me. Growing up, everyone had been compared to Du Wanming by their parents and suffered no end of grief. So, seeing the source of their troubles, they would gnash their teeth in resentment, and from time to time, they would find an excuse to take it out on Du Wanming himself.

Du Wanming looked frail and delicate, and he was a pushover to boot. If someone were to bully him, he would endure it in silence, without a single word, which only invoked everyone's desire to do it again. This went on and on, and the bullying he suffered worsened by the day.

The Du clan and the Jiang clan—the latter being the family of the great and mighty general—were neighbors, so Du Wanming and Jiang Zongduo grew up together, and Jiang Zongduo stood up for him. Their relationship was originally quite good.

But one day, when I was passing by under the covered walkway on occasion, I saw a book, all covered in dirty water, lying in a puddle of mud in the yard. I thought someone had dropped it, so I picked it up and wiped off the muddy water with my sleeve. I was still in the midst of wiping it when I looked up and saw Du Wanming standing before me, silently watching. That was how I knew this book was his. Looked like the other children had thrown it into the puddle. I felt that since I had already picked it up and cleaned it, and seeing how pitiful Du Wanming looked, I might as well do him a favor and return it. So, I handed the book to him. He thanked me softly, and I magnanimously said a "you're welcome" before returning to the classroom.

That afternoon, I lost focus and got caught sleeping in the middle of our lessons. As I was a repeat offender, the teacher flew into a rage and sent me to the yard to kneel and copy the *Treatise of Prudent Conduct* ten times as my punishment. My heart was not really in it as I copied, and by the time class was dismissed at dusk, I had only written it four times.

Seeing as everyone had left, I grew anxious that I would never finish. It was at this time that someone walked over to my side and bumped—as if unintentionally—into the pile of papers that I had copied and stacked, sending it scattering to the ground. I looked up. It was Du Wanming. I was just about to curse when he squatted down and helped me to straighten out the pile.

I watched as he slid out a roll of papers from his sleeve. Without even batting an eyelid, he unfurled it and stacked it on top of my barely completed pile. Then he got up and left.

I looked askance at it. To my surprise, those papers were actually copies of the *Treatise of Prudent Conduct,* and the handwriting on it was exactly the same as mine. I counted them; his stack had five copies done. Delighted, I wrote another one to make up the ten, and handed them over to the teacher.

The next day, I pulled Du Wanming over to a secluded corner and asked how he was able to imitate my handwriting.

"I often copy books for my elder brothers at home, so I can imitate other people's handwriting," Du Wanming explained. "You helped me yesterday, so consider those few copies a token of my gratitude."

This was unexpected. He really knew how to repay my kindness. Such an ability was simply too good to be true!

Solemnly, I asked him, "Then, if I help you again the next time, will you thank me again the same way?"

"You've helped me before," Du Wanming said, "so just tell me if there is anything I can help you with."

And that was when I decided to take him under my protection.

As my old man's official rank was higher than the others', the majority of the children in this private school took my lead and did as I said, so when I said I had taken Du Wanming under my protection, the bullying lessened. I also spoke of his ability to a few others who were on good terms with me, and as the news spread to the rest of our school, all at once, no one bullied Du Wanming anymore. They even fawned on him from time to time in order to get off doing a homework assignment.

However, I fended them off, fearing that if he was too swamped with other people's homework, he would not do a good job of mine. Other than myself, he was allowed to help two others at most. The other schoolmates could only twiddle their thumbs, waiting for their scheduled turns, with this one's homework reserved for today and that one's reserved for tomorrow.

Just as everyone was getting along harmoniously with one

another, Jiang Zongduo just had to start stirring up trouble. When he saw Du Wanming playing with me, he found some unreasonable fault with him and reproached him. Since I had already taken Du Wanming under my protection, I naturally could not let Jiang Zongduo bully him, so I shielded him from his tirades every time.

Du Wanming helped me with my homework every day, so of course I would not treat him shabbily. I took him to play with crickets, catch grasshoppers, and fly kites, and I also counted him in when I played guessing games and dice and headed out to the fields in the countryside to steal wheat. I even gifted him a gourd for the crickets, a cage for the grasshopper, and the newest style of kite from Jiangnan that my old man's pupil had brought back to give me.

After we started playing together, I realized that Du Wanming was actually not that bad a person. He was a loyal friend, and quite sweet-tempered.

One time, I took him to an abandoned house on the outskirts of the city to catch crickets, and though he was saved from falling into a well, a piece of jade slipped from the string around his neck and dropped in. There was a plop, and then it was gone. I stole a piece of my mother's precious jade to make it up to him. My mother did not really have that much of a reaction after learning that I was the one who had taken the jade. My father, on the other hand, flew into a rage and gave me such a thrashing with the big rod that I ended up limping for five or six days.

We stayed in the private school together for five years. When I left school five years later, it was just in time for that youthful period of my life where I was fond of cavorting around. Joined by three or five like-minded buddies I knew from the private school, I traversed all over the capital city on horseback, drinking wine, seeking merriment, and visiting courtesans.

I grew more and more distant from Du Wanming. As

someone with great expectations placed on his shoulders, he devoted his time to studying at home behind closed doors. At sixteen years old, the emperor personally appointed him as the top scholar. He was bestowed with a fourth-grade official post and joined the Hanlin Academy. My former schoolmates and I went together to congratulate him, and even though he was wearing the official attire of the Hanlin Academy, his attitude was still as modest and amicable as ever.

This worked my father up so much that he would sigh and groan whenever he saw this face of mine. Fortunately, my mother was rather philosophical about it. "What does it matter if our son can pass the imperial examination or not? All it takes is a word if he wants to be an official. He's still young, and if he joins the official circle, he will only be on the losing end for nothing. Might as well let him enjoy his freedom for a few years. Let's get his marriage arranged first. Once he's married, he'll mature and settle down naturally. It wouldn't be too late for him to be an official then."

My old man, thus convinced by my mother's words, finally took it in his stride. But who knew that things would not work out as expected? His son who was not only incapable of attaining scholarly honor or official rank, but was even doomed to a fate of eternal solitude. The betrothals fell through one after another, and all those who caught my eye fled one after another. For all the flowers whom I courted over several years, I could not get my hands on even a fraction of their pollen.

My reputation as someone doomed to a fate of eternal solitude spread all over the capital, becoming a joke. Even the emperor struggled to fight his laughter whenever the topic of my marriage was broached in my presence.

I was disconsolate.

When I fell out of love the first or second time, that roguish company of friends would comfort me and drink with me to drown my sorrows. But as the frequency of these events grew, their first reaction when I sought them out became a burst of laughter before anything else. And so, I went to drown my sorrows by my lonely, lonesome self.

One day, as I was drinking my heartbreak away in a small wine tavern, I bumped into Du Wanming, who had just been dismissed from a court session. He did not have many words of comfort to say, but he was willing to listen to me pour out my woes, even drank with me. I did not expect him to still treat me as a friend after all these years without contact. So, when I got my heart broken again, utterly crushed, I dragged him out for a couple of drinks. Not once did he ever make fun of me.

It was at the time when the emperor's younger sister finally married her little vice-minister—after an unsuccessful attempt to make me a stand-in father for her unborn child—that something big happened in the Imperial Court. Du Wanming's imperial censor father was implicated in an old case that occurred before the emperor's accession to the throne, and investigations showed that he had connections to the old faction of the prince who had revolted. As such, Du Wanming's family was convicted of treason. His entire clan was executed, and their family properties, confiscated.

That was the day Jiang Zongduo came to call on my house for the very first time ever. Forthright as he was, he got straight to the point as soon as he saw me. "On account of your friendship with Du Wanming over the years, you should save him."

"I don't need you to remind me," I said. "Truth be told, I've already saved him."

The emperor had stolen away the wife I had yet to marry, and his younger sister almost made me a cuckold by making me a stand-in father to her child conceived out of wedlock. By all accounts, he owed me twice. On top of that, the emperor had also once mentioned that Imperial Censor Du's crime was merely a criminal charge, but as it involved the throne, he had no choice but to mete out the punishment. Then he had also lamented—whether wittingly or unwittingly—what a shame it was about Du Wanming. So, I rescued Du Wanming from death row by replacing him with a corpse and saying that he had met with sudden death. To this, the emperor said nothing.

I settled Du Wanming down in a small courtyard on the outskirts of the capital city and often went to visit and play chess with him. I did not really read much of the classics, so I could not discuss those with him, and when it came to chess, I could not beat him either. He was in poor health and often had difficulty sleeping, so there were times we played till daybreak.

The enclosing walls around the courtyard were adorned all over with climbing vines, with a luxuriant bloom of Lady Banks' roses in spring. Sometimes after a night of chess, I would step out of the chamber early in the morning to be greeted with the particularly rich and pleasing fragrance of the roses in the morning mist. The physician said that this fragrance could alleviate the stifling tightness in Du Wanming's chest.

Du Wanming did not weep his gratitude to me for saving him. His entire family had been beheaded, and he was now mostly a shell of his former self. He merely asked me once, with little emotion, if I was not afraid of being implicated in saving him, given the many risks involved.

I thought, *Did you think I would do something I knew was futile?* Of course I had long known that the emperor would not pursue the matter. And besides, we were friends; I would certainly help him if it was in my power and ability to do so.

Perhaps it was true what they say: No good deeds go unrewarded. Not long after settling Du Wanming in, I gave a sudden glance back at the streets and saw Yaoxiang.

I still felt a little heartsick remembering this name now. I fell in love with Yaoxiang at first sight, and was genuinely and whole-heartedly in love with her. I did all I could to please her every day, even going as far as to ask Du Wanming for advice about some lovey-dovey poems and romantic prose to share with her. In order to support and provide for her scholar, she pretended to treat me well. I was basking in the flush of love every day.

However, Du Wanming's health deteriorated by the day. He had been tortured in prison, and the physician said his spleen was injured; to have lived past just a few days was already a feat. Fortunately, he did not suffer much at the end. He passed out from the pain twice and slept it away, and the last time he woke up, he even said thank you to me for taking care of him all these days. When he closed his eyes, he looked rather serene.

He even left me a stack of copied poems so that I could recite them to Yaoxiang.

I buried him by the emerald hillside on the city outskirts and gave special instructions to have someone watch over the grave mound.

After that, Yaoxiang still got together with her poor scholar, and I ended up empty-handed with nothing to show for my efforts. Forlorn, I bought wine to drink myself drunk. There were still two books of poems in the residence that Du Wanming had left behind, and these bitter poems and tragic verses resonated with me. I was heartbroken from the Double Ninth Festival to the next year's Dragon Boat Festival. Then the words Yaoxiang said to me in the temple dealt me such a huge blow that I saw stars.

After that, I crossed the street and asked for a bowl of wonton noodles. And after that, I ascended and became Immortal Song Yao.

Hengwen listened to me without saying a word. I grasped his sleeve. "I have no idea how the Heavenly Court came to twist the story this way, but this is the real story."

"Actually," Hengwen said slowly, "there is really no difference between your version and the Heavenly Court's version."

I looked at the little finger on my left hand, and my heart went cold. "Hengwen, tell me the truth. I always thought it was a coincidence that I could ascend to the Heavenly Court, but in truth, is it related to the fact that Tianshu and I are connected by this thread?"

Tianshu. Du Wanming.

Since Tianshu was Du Wanming, even still keeping the jade I had given him, I would have been a familiar face after my ascension to the Heavenly Court. So why had he always put on a cold, indifferent attitude and pretended not to know me?

"Not quite," Hengwen said. "The thread on both Tianshu's and your hands have turned into dead knots, but you were, after all, a mortal. As long as you undergo five lifetimes of reincarnation in the mortal world without meeting Tianshu, the thread would naturally break off on its own. But—" Hengwen cast a resigned look at me. "You sure are blessed with good fortune. It just so happened that Taishang Laojun's immortal elixir fell into the human world, and you happened to eat it and ascended."

So what if I became an immortal?

Hengwen sighed. "Perhaps this is a fate beyond the control of even immortals. As long as you have become an immortal, and whether or not you remain an immortal after the fact, this thread is said to be unravelable—unless you or Tianshu is obliterated into oblivion."

I looked at that glossy, golden thread and flicked it with a finger.

There was no sensation of having touched it, yet it quivered ever so softly.

"If it can't be undone, then all I can do is leave it bound," I said. "What is the consequence if I leave it on?" They called it a thread of immortal bond, but I had it on for many years having served no particular purpose.

"It's precisely *because* there is a consequence that Tianshu

Xingjun pretended not to recognize you at first and kept his distance from you in the Heavenly Court," Hengwen said. "The time he attempted to have you banished to the mortal realm had also been for the sake of protecting you. I remember telling you before that immortals born in the Heavenly Court, such as Tianshu and myself, have our duties all determined even before we took on forms. That is why I only have a title and not even a name like a mortal would. The same goes for Tianshu. He was born to take charge of the Beidou Palace. As the star of emperors, he is destined to reciprocate and complement Nanming Dijun."

Understanding immediately dawned on me. "I get it now. I butted in between them and severed the thread between Tianshu and Nanming, while getting myself hooked up to Tianshu. As a result, I messed up the mutual reciprocity between these two lords."

But not once had I ever harbored the intent to come between them, so why did this thread have to take it as an interference on my part and insist on securing itself to me?

"And yet you just so happened to pick up an immortal elixir that fell out of the blue. That's quite the luck," Hengwen quipped with a wry smile. "You ascended and became an immortal, and the thread was no longer breakable unless one of you were obliterated. Although Tianshu Xingjun intended to keep his distance from you, both of you were still connected by the thread. Nanming Dijun took this to heart and bore a grudge, and the two lords gradually drifted apart. Calamities and wars became frequent occurrences in the mortal world, and dynasties, unable to achieve stabilization, rose and fell in mere instants... To the Heavenly Court, this thread cannot be retained, but to sever it, it's either you or Tianshu who has to go. If you were the Jade Emperor, who, between yourself and Tianshu, would you retain?"

"Tianshu." My answer was immediate.

Hengwen turned his head aside to look at me.

I sighed. "You can skip the rest of it. I can guess it myself. The Jade Emperor wanted to annihilate me even before that doctrine dialogue, didn't he? That was why Tianshu attempted to find an excuse to send me down to the mortal world. In that case, why did the Jade Emperor design this whole show, saying that Nanming and Tianshu were banished to the mortal world because of their illicit affair and having me set up trials to break the lovebirds apart?"

"This was the part Mingge Xingjun hemmed and hawed over when he told me the whole story earlier," Hengwen said. "It was only when I pressed him further that he told me the truth. Turns out, this whole idea was originally his."

Old Man Mingge! I just knew it! He always has to get himself involved in every single matter!!

Resigned, Hengwen continued, "In this case, Mingge did it out of good intentions to save you. You should thank him instead. The various immortals have developed some friendship with you all these years you have been in the Heavenly Court, and they can't bear to see you obliterated.

"For that reason, Mingge told the Jade Emperor that while a dead knot cannot be undone unless one party is obliterated, you ascended under unusual circumstances and never once developed feelings for Tianshu in all your years. He argued that there may be other ways to resolve this issue.

"Then Yue Lao added that it was a great sin to destroy others' marriage predestined by fate, which would ruin the person's own marriage as a karmic retribution.

"So Mingge came up with this idea, and Tianshu told the Jade Emperor that he was willing to give it a try.

"Besides, Nanming's ruthlessness toward Qingtong and Zhilan meant that there was a debt to be repaid. And that was how you came to descend to the mortal world."

It all made sense now. All the strange occurrences during this descent into the mortal world suddenly had an explanation. In all probability, Mingge Xingjun was the one who had told Shan Shengling about the immortal herb. That was how Shan Shengling, a mere mortal, knew to steal it to save Mu Ruoyan's life.

I looked at the lotus pond, adorned with lotus leaves as green as jade.

Hengwen said, "You really do owe Tianshu a lot."

Du Wanming. Tianshu Xingjun.

Looking back on it now, I still felt that I had not treated Du Wanming the best. I would have done the same for someone else, but this act had indeed severed his bond and reconnected to mine. And by the end of it all, it had become a dead knot.

Du Wanming had lived simply and was sweet-tempered. His appearance differed from Tianshu Xingjun too. No matter how I looked at it, I could not have imagined him to be the cold Tianshu.

I had inflicted Mu Ruoyan with all sorts of abhorrent deeds. To protect me, Tianshu had been willing to descend to the mortal world to undergo tribulations, and yet I treated him in such a way. What was he thinking now? And just how was I supposed to repay him for all I owed him?

Hengwen did not say anything more, and sat side by side with me at the lotus pond. I looked again at my hand. "I wonder if the thread will be gone if I hack off this finger now."

"You wish," Hengwen laughed. "I'd like you to hack it off too. If it worked, the Jade Emperor would have done so long ago. Without your little finger, it can still secure itself elsewhere. Unless..."

Unless I was completely obliterated, and there was nowhere for it to bind itself to.

I let out two quiet, wry laughs. Hengwen and I said nothing more as we remained sitting.

After a while, I said, "The Jade Emperor ordered me to go over to Mingge Xingjun, so I'd better get going." I stood.

"All right," Hengwen said. "I heard Xuan Li has also been brought over to the Heavenly Court. I'll go check in on him."

He rose to his feet, and I looked at him, but I did not know what to say.

"Then, this is farewell, I guess," Hengwen said.

"Farewell," I said.

I watched as Hengwen turned around and left. His back gradually receded into the distance, and for a fleeting moment, it was like I had just ascended to the Heavenly Court for the first time. During that first encounter, I had also watched his back from afar as he gradually walked further and further away from me.

I expelled a sigh of chilly air and entered Mingge Xingjun's residence through the back door.

Chapter Twenty-four

I had just stepped through the back door when the young immortal attendant said to me, "You're finally here, Song Yao Yuanjun. Xingjun has already been waiting for you for half a day." He led me through several roof ridges and doors to a large pond enveloped in mist.

Mingge Xingjun sat cross-legged by the pond, seemingly in repose with his eyes closed. Mist rose from the steaming water in the pond. Could there possibly be hot springs in the Heavenly Court too? Old Man Mingge sure knew how to enjoy life, having a hot spring at home to soak in every now and then.

After the young immortal attendant led me to the side of the pond, he bowed and withdrew.

I approached Mingge Xingjun.

With eyes still tightly shut, Mingge Xingjun suddenly heaved a long sigh and recited, "Alas! Every bite and every drink are all foreordained; cause begets effect, such is the way of the universe—"

He sighed so ominously that my hair stood on end.

There was going to be a doctrine dialogue these days. Don't

tell me Mingge Xingjun has already gone over to the Western Paradise for tea too?

I lifted the corner of my robe and sat down. "Xingjun, you can drop all those subtle Buddhist allegories from the Western Paradise. The Jade Emperor ordered me to come and hear the whole story from you, so please get to the point."

Mingge Xingjun opened his eyes to look at me, then let loose another long sigh.

"This hot spring looks good," I remarked.

"What hot spring?" Mingge Xingjun said. "That's the Fate-gazing Pond. It allows you to see future events."

Caught in mid-reach to stir the water, I immediately retracted my hand in embarrassment.

"Hengwen Qingjun came to me after he returned to the Heavenly Court," Mingge Xingjun said, "and I have already told him the whole story about you and Tianshu. Qingjun should have already told you all about it."

"That's right," I answered. *We sat by the pond for half the day, and he told me everything.*

Mingge Xingjun looked at me with compassion. Slowly, he asked, "Song Yao Yuanjun, do you know what your greatest mistake during your trip to the mortal world was?"

The Jade Emperor had asked me this same thing back at the Peach of Immortality Garden. His Venerable Self seemed to have already told me the answer. At the time, I had been unable to make head or tail of it, but now, I was completely clear.

"I should not have seduced Hengwen Qingjun while I was still bound to Tianshu Xingjun," I replied. "Or seduced him into giving mortal love a try."

Mingge Xingjun still looked at me with compassion. Not fully closing his eyes, he said, "Wrong. You should not have let Hengwen Qingjun know of mortal love, then involve that fox."

What Hengwen told me by the side of the lotus pond about the thread and Du Wanming had been like a bolt out of the blue that left me thunderstruck. But now, my mind was in such an absolute state of primal chaos that I might as well have been literally struck by lightning.

I staggered out of Mingge Xingjun's residence.

Mingge had reached his hands into the Fate-gazing Pond, the spirals of mist that had risen transforming into an image—

Of Hengwen sleeping on the couch, where a snowy-white fox had lowered its head, licking Hengwen's lips.

The mist had changed, producing another image. Hengwen was standing by the heavenly river, and a man was standing beside him. All I could see were his fluttering clothes, not his appearance, but even so, I could tell that I was not that man.

"Back then, when Hengwen Qingjun was just born, the Jade Emperor ordered me to divine his fate for him," Mingge Xingjun had said. "It was foretold that Hengwen Qingjun was destined to undergo a love tribulation in his life. With this snow fox spirit.

"Song Yao Yuanjun," Mingge Xingjun had continued, "That day, you should never have made Hengwen Qingjun understand mortal love, then allowed this fox to get close to Hengwen Qingjun.

"You should never have let this fox risk all its cultivation to save Hengwen Qingjun," Mingge Xingjun had said. "Hengwen Qingjun owes him a thousand years of cultivation and a debt of gratitude for saving his life. And you have to know that a debt owed is a debt to be repaid.

"The Jade Emperor initially thought that your only role was as the variable that had interfered with Tianshu Xingjun's and Nanming Dijun's destined fate," Mingge Xingjun added. "Who would have expected you to also be the go-between for Hengwen Qingjun and that fox?"

A debt owed naturally must be repaid. Tianshu and I were bound by the thread of immortal bond. Mingge Xingjun had said that he owed me a debt from the lifetime when he was Du

Wanming. That was why he had protected me in the Heavenly Court and suffered so much. The fox, enamored with Hengwen, risked its life and a thousand years of cultivation. Hengwen owed the fox, and now, I owed Tianshu again.

So it turned out that all predestined affinities were merely debts to be repaid.

So it turned out that Hengwen's destined lot was the fox.

I staggered on the secluded path I was now walking, and could not help but give a bitter laugh.

I had been an immortal in the Heavenly Court and had seen countless immortals, but in truth, the one who divined my fortune back then was the real immortal.

As expected, I was still doomed to a fate of eternal solitude.

Tianshu Xingjun and Nanming Dijun were made for each other. I was the one who got in the way and messed up their fates.

Hengwen Qingjun was destined to undergo a love tribulation with a fox, and I, acting as the matchmaker, eventually made this a reality.

Each had their own predestined affinity, just not with me.

I was doomed to play supporting roles in these tales. If not a rod to serve as relationship-wrecker, then a bridge to act as go-between.

I walked to Yaoguang Palace, and the heavenly soldiers on duty raised their halberds to intercept me.

"Could you gentlemen please do me a favor?" I said. "I come bearing no intention except to see Tianshu Xingjun."

The heavenly soldiers studied me, their faces giving nothing away. He Yun stepped out from the side. "The Jade Emperor did not prohibit Song Yao Yuanjun from visiting Tianshu Xingjun. Just let him in."

Much obliged, I cupped my hands at He Yun, and he gave me a slight nod of his head in return. I strode into Yaoguang Palace.

It was spacious but empty inside. I saw Tianshu standing before the window.

As I approached him, Tianshu turned around and suddenly said to me, "Everyone in that city died, right?"

I went momentarily blank.

"When the snowlion went berserk," Tianshu repeated, "everyone in Luyang City died, didn't they?"

It then dawned on me the incident he spoke of. Knowing Tianshu's temperament, he would no doubt blame himself for this incident. Thus, I said, "The snowlion suddenly went berserk. If you must blame someone, the responsibility lies on Mingge, who writes the fates. Just have Yanwang arrange a good reincarnation for the people of the city when they arrive in the underworld."

Tianshu merely smiled.

He had now reverted to his true form. As he was awaiting punishment, he simply wore a plain white robe, looking still as cold and indifferent as he always did. I hesitated for a moment before saying, "I never did make you out to be Du Wanming. I'm sorry."

"It is of no consequence," Tianshu said. "I should be the one apologizing to you. It was supposed to be a casual acquaintance between us for one lifetime, nothing more, but you ended up getting implicated and bound to the thread of immortal bond. I'm much obliged to you for taking care of me when I was in the mortal world, so I wanted to see you. I thought I would never get to see you again, but here you are."

I lowered my head. "Don't bring up the mortal world. I feel even more ashamed at the mention of it. I treated you in every rotten way possible while there, and yet you have been helping me all this time I've been in heaven. I... I owe you too much. This is all my fault, and I've dragged you down with me. The Jade Emperor knows the whole story, so he'll surely release you."

Tianshu smiled again. "You sound like you are here to

apologize and beg for forgiveness."

I sputtered out a dry laugh. Tianshu and I were bound by the thread of immortal bond, but for some reason, our conversations were still extremely awkward.

"You feel you have implicated me and got me into trouble," Tianshu said, "and I, too, feel that I have implicated you. The truth is that I actually owe Nanming Dijun a lot. This debt here, and that debt there—who can really say for sure?"

Tianshu turned aside and looked out of the window. "Actually, I've been thinking ever since I returned from my time as Du Wanming that one might as well be a mortal. It is enough just being in the courtyard, watching the change of seasons, and the blooming and wilting of the Lady Banks' roses. It trumps being in the Heavenly Court, embroiled in countless entanglements."

Hearing his words, I sensed something amiss. I had enough experience dealing with Mu Ruoyan in the mortal world to know that these sounded like Tianshu's last words.

I strode a big step forward and grabbed his sleeve. As expected, he was like a flimsy piece of paper that fell limply over. The immortal aura on him was extremely weak, and his divine glow was so faint it had nearly extinguished.

I exclaimed, thunderstruck, "What have you done?!"

"All these years of entanglements, I really am too tired," Tianshu said with a smile. "Let's just forget about who owes whom. I no longer wish to care."

I used a bit of my powers to probe—an expanse of icy coldness.

Tianshu had actually shattered his own immortal essence. To think he would be even more ruthless than when he had been Mu Ruoyan. He wanted to be obliterated, so much that he would not leave even a smidgen of opportunity for anyone to salvage the situation.

Tianshu extended a hand to stuff a piece of jade into mine.

"You have looked out so much for me. In fact, you actually don't owe me a thing. Thank you... for all you did... those childhood days in the mortal world..." His eyes closed as his head drooped.

There seemed to be a stabbing pain on the base of my little finger, followed by a gradual loosening.

Tianshu Xingjun, do you really think you're beyond saving with this one move?

So, the immortal bond between us would prove useful after all. No matter when he sought death, I could always foil his attempts.

I sighed and channeled a stream of immortal energy into his back, then took out something from the front of my robes and stuffed it into Tianshu's mouth.

All at once, light enveloped his body. Not the silver light of Tianshu Xingjun, but the blue light of Song Yao Yuanjun.

I said to the person shrouded in that light, "Xingjun, I'm sorry. You were friends with me when you were Du Wanming, so you should know that what I, Song Yao, fear the most in life is owing a debt. Even if you wouldn't let me repay this debt, I still have to repay it. From now on... when you regain your immortal body, all the past will be wiped clean, and as of this moment onward, you and I do not owe the other anymore."

I looked at that jade pendant in my hand, and with a gentle clench of my fist, crushed it completely into powder.

I left Yaoguang Palace. He Yun was standing right in front of the palace gate. I said, "I've just talked to Tianshu Xingjun, and he has seen the light. May I ask Envoy He to intercede with the Jade Emperor on his behalf? Let him have a moment of quiet these two days, and the rest can be discussed later."

"The Jade Emperor's initial order was to have Tianshu Xingjun meditate for two days," He Yun said. "So, Yuanjun, you may rest assured."

I thanked him and asked in a seemingly off-handed way, "Do

you happen to know where that fox is locked up?"

"The Jade Emperor has ordered Bihua Lingjun to watch over it for the time being," He Yun answered.

I took the walk to Bihua Lingjun's residence. The young immortal attendant informed me that Lingjun was not around, as he had been invited to tea by Hengwen Qingjun.

Needless to say, Hengwen must have asked Bihua to take good care of the fox. Bihua Lingjun's absence suited my purpose—one less sorrowful melodrama of farewells playing out.

"Can I see the fox that the Jade Emperor ordered Lingjun to watch?" I asked.

Put in a spot, the young immortal attendant scrunched up his face.

"The Jade Emperor only gave the order to forbid Hengwen Qingjun from looking at it, didn't he?" I said. "So it doesn't matter if I look at it, right?"

The young immortal attendant thought about it carefully for a moment before acquiescing, "All right."

The young immortal attendant led me to a stone chamber in the backyard and opened the door. "That fox is right in there."

"I'd like to see it alone," I said. "Take your leave first and lock the door."

"All right," the young immortal attendant said, "but be quick."

I entered the stone chamber and heard the door click shut. The fox was lying on a prayer cushion set on a jade bed. Its fur was a dry, disheveled mess, and its head was resting on its front paws. On seeing me, it partially lifted its eyelids.

I sat down on the edge of the bed. "How are you doing, Furball?"

The fox closed its eyes and remained motionless.

"If the Jade Emperor forced you to stop liking Hengwen Qingjun, what would you do?" I asked.

The fox's ears twitched.

"What if the Jade Emperor flayed your skin and crushed your bones into ashes just to force you not to like Hengwen Qingjun?" I probed.

The fox's ears twitched again, its expression dauntless.

Excellent.

"Then remember my words today," I said. "Hengwen prefers his tea mild. When he writes, he often sets his brush in the inkbrush washer and forgets to keep it away. He has to drink himself drunk, or he'll never be done with it, so you can't let him have all the wine he wants. He doesn't have any bad habits when it comes to sleeping, but remember that he has to drink the first brew of Sparrow's Tongue tea when he wakes up.

"He tends to forget the time when he reads official documents, so you have to drag him outdoors from time to time to take a breather. He has someone under his command called Lu Jing who will conjure out a pile of official documents at all hours for him to look over. There's no need for you to pay this immortal any attention.

"Be mindful when Donghua Dijun, Bihua Lingjun, Taibai Xingjun, and the others come looking for him to go drinking. He has a habit of forgetting and losing things. When he leaves his seat, check his table to see if there is a fan or something else that he forgot to take.

"He doesn't really eat sweet stuff, and even when it comes to fruit kernels or nuts, he only eats the salted ones, not the candied ones. His pillow has to be low, and his bedding has to be soft. Take note that his tea water should also be an agreeable temperature."

The fox sat up and looked at me out of the corner of its eyes in puzzlement.

Affably, I petted its head. "Stay by Hengwen's side from now on."

The fox shivered under my palm.

DA FENG GUA GUO

I sighed again and recited an incantation. A blue light materialized in my palm and enveloped the fox, going from a weak glow to a brilliant radiance before gradually diminishing. Eventually, it was all absorbed into the fox's body.

The fox crouched on the cushion and looked at me in astonishment.

"Furball," I said, "you have half of my cultivation in you already. You can now take on human form again. With a little more cultivation, you'll be able to become an immortal."

Furball leaped to the ground and rolled to take on human form. Now that it had my cultivation, it seemed to be a tad more pleasing to the eyes. The fox looked at me. "Why are you doing this?"

"To tell you the truth, my immortal essence and the other half of my cultivation have already been given to someone else as a repayment of my debt," I explained. "I am now being sustained by spells, and in a few days, I'll be reduced to nothing but ashes. This remaining half of my cultivation will be wiped out along with me, so I might as well give it to you. But I'm not giving it for nothing. The debt of gratitude that Hengwen Qingjun owes you for saving this life—I've repaid it for him. From this moment on, he does not owe you anything."

The fox looked at me, befuddled. Gradually, a hint of sorrow washed over his expression.

This immortal lord found myself quite melancholic too. Soon enough, I would fade into oblivion.

"Do me a favor now, won't you?" I said. "I wish to see Hengwen, but I don't want to see him in this state, so I'd like to borrow your appearance. Turn into me and leave this place first. You have my immortal aura on you, so the young immortal attendant can't tell the difference. Come back again after I get to see Hengwen. You and Hengwen have a predestined romantic relationship, so the Jade Emperor will not make things difficult for you. In all probability, you can remain by his side to cultivate. Later, when you become an immortal, remember all that I've told you."

My last words outmatched Tianshu's in emotional impact. The rims of the fox's eyes even reddened just that little bit.

"All right," he answered in a hushed tone, then transformed into this immortal lord. "Let me help you turn into me. You should reduce your use of the immortal arts, then you can... hang on a little longer..."

I turned into the fox and found the world had gotten a lot broader. Even that small prayer cushion had suddenly become bigger.

Furball walked out, and I huddled down on the cushion. Sure enough, an immortal aura approached a moment later. The door to the stone chamber opened, and in came Bihua.

Bihua walked over to the stone couch. He sighed, "What am I to do with you, fox? Hengwen Qingjun insists on seeing you, but he can't come over to my residence. Behave yourself. This lord shall take you to see Hengwen Qingjun."

Before I could nod, a bag swallowed my head, and everything before my eyes turned pitch-black. I heard Bihua Lingjun say, "Stay in the bag and don't move. This lord will take you to see Hengwen Qingjun."

I remained in the bag, sniffing at the scents seeping in through the fabric seam and, from time to time, vaguely determining where I was.

After about a quarter of an hour, Bihua Lingjun seemed to cross over an enclosing wall. That was when I knew we had probably arrived at Weiyuan Palace.

Sure enough, after Bihua Lingjun strode over a threshold, he said, "Qingjun, I've brought the fox over. The Jade Emperor will not put it on trial today, but you have to return it to me tomorrow." He set the bag along with this immortal lord on what seemed to be a board on the tabletop.

"Thank you, thank you," Hengwen said, tones soft.

Bihua Lingjun bade farewell and left. Light appeared overhead from the opening of the bag. I looked up and saw Hengwen.

Looking up like this, Hengwen's face appeared larger than usual, which meant I could also look at him even closer than usual. I tilted my neck up to look, but Hengwen frowned, "You don't seem to be Xuan Li."

I broke out in a cold sweat. Hengwen's eyes were truly sharp. I shamelessly held my head up and wagged my tail.

Hengwen could not help but laugh. "You are not Xuan Li, but you do resemble it. Don't tell me the heavenly soldiers took the wrong one? Who could you possibly be?"

He petted the top of my head, and I turned my head and licked his hand.

I barely had any immortal powers left in my body, so there was no chance of Hengwen sussing out my identity. I licked his hand again, and Hengwen reached behind my two front paws to lift me up. "Well then, we can say it was fated that you were brought to the Heavenly Court, and made it to my residence, no less. I'll play the host and let you stay for a day, then take you to the Jade Emperor tomorrow to have him release you back into the mortal world."

I continued my brazen nodding, and wagged my tail again.

I lay on the chair beside Hengwen to keep him company as he looked over his documents, which he did for quite a while. Then I rested on his lap for the time it took for him to leisurely finish two cups of tea.

Hengwen patted me on the back. "A pity there's nothing you like to eat in the residence. I'll get some fine wine. Do you want some?" He set a dish of the good wine before my paws. I lowered my head and drank it, then shamelessly wagged my tail yet again. Hengwen laughed, the sound quite cheerful.

When it was time to turn in, Hengwen set a cushion on the chair beside the bed for me. I crouched on it, waited for him to lie down himself, then ricocheted myself off the ground and into his bed.

"You want to sleep on the bed too?" Hengwen asked in wonder.

I looked ingratiatingly at him.

Hengwen sighed softly. "Then so be it." He patted the empty spot beside him, and I lay down next to him.

I curled up, sticking to Hengwen with the quilt between us, and closed my eyes. I felt quite fulfilled. No wonder the fox was always designing to get into Hengwen's bed.

Truth be told, if I could accompany him like this even as a beast, I would be willing.

Hengwen seemed to have fallen sound asleep. I rose, shook my fur, and crouched by the pillow to watch him.

Hengwen, Hengwen. Did you know? When I first saw you several thousand years ago, I only saw your back from afar as you left Weiyuan Palace. Just from that, it was from that time onward that I liked you. At that time, you were so high up above the masses and far beyond my reach, I could only gaze at you from a distance. But we would meet again by the lotus pond, and you would come to my residence. For several thousand years thereafter, you and I formed a friendship. But somehow, I always had the feeling that while you were near by my side, you were also so very far apart, and I still could not touch you.

Perhaps, it was just as what Yaoxiang said in the mortal world. The truth is that I had never come to understand what love was throughout all those years. I finally knew of this word after I ascended to the Heavenly Court, but this word would not avail itself to me.

I have gained plenty from all that has transpired in the mortal world, and I think I have more than made up for all of it these few thousands of years. Even if I was only a bridge serving as a go-between, it was all worthwhile.

I wish with all my heart to be a dutiful immortal who knows my place. I wholeheartedly wish to remain in the Heavenly Court, for the days of an immortal are long and never-ending. Even if I could not touch you, I would be content to remain by your side for time eternal.

But here I am, looking at you like this. I'm in no one's debt, just like you. Destiny has decided that I cannot remain by your side, but to watch you and touch you like this now, that in itself already speaks of a deep affinity between us, does it not?

I lowered my head to lick Hengwen's lips, took another look at him, then jumped to the ground and left his chamber.

The Heavenly Court was quiet all around. I wondered where the fox had wandered to in this immortal lord's guise. Let him be. At any rate, I had already told him to make his way back to Bihua Lingjun's residence tomorrow. I reverted to my original form and encountered a few heavenly soldiers on the way, but perhaps the Jade Emperor had already given the instruction to allow me unimpeded access in the Heavenly Court, because heavenly soldiers did not really react when they saw me.

I came before Taibai Xingjun's residence. I did not have the capability to somersault over the wall anymore, so I played by the rules and had the heavenly envoy announce my arrival.

Jinxing, having already fallen asleep, came out to greet me with a disheveled beard and bleary eyes. "Song Yao Yuanjun, what can I do for you?"

"I'd like to sneak out of the Heavenly Court and lie low," I said with an apologetic smile. "Please think of a way for me to slip out of the Heavenly Court."

Jinxing's beard promptly puffed up. "You want to escape to the mortal world? Then what about Tianshu Xingjun? What about Hengwen Qingjun? You drag these two immortal lords through your mess and now you want to flee all by yourself?!"

"I have no choice either," I said. "Think about it, if I remain in the Heavenly Court, the Jade Emperor will go by the book and conduct a public trial in Lingxiao Palace before all the various immortals. Even if I shoulder all the charges, Tianshu Xingjun and Hengwen Qingjun will be punished along with me. So, I might as well escape to the mortal world where I can lie low, and all the charges will be pinned on me. That way, Tianshu and Hengwen will be fine."

"Your gears sure are turning hard." Jinxing gave me a quick glance, and stroked his beard with his hand. "Oh, well. Let's see if I can sneak you out of the Heavenly Court today."

Elated, I said, "Thank you, Xingjun."

"No need to stand on ceremony," Taibai Xingjun said. "But don't blame me if your plan doesn't pan out as you hoped and ended up getting captured back again."

I cupped my hands. "Of course."

Taibai Xingjun covered me in a golden shield and concealed me in his sleeve, then straightened his clothes and stepped out of his residence. Through the slit in the opening of his sleeve, I could make out the Southern Heavenly Gate.

The heavenly soldier standing guard asked, "Xingjun, where are you headed?"

"By order of the Jade Emperor, I'm heading to the mortal world to observe the present state of affairs in the world," Taibai Xingjun answered.

He handed over the gate tally, and the heavenly soldiers let him through.

Taibai Xingjun took me along as he descended to the mortal world and released me from the barrier.

I looked around me—we were on a mountaintop.

"You fled to the mortal world," Taibai Xingjun said. "As to where, this lord does not know."

I reassured him that was the case.

Then Taibai Xingjun rose on the clouds and returned to the Heavenly Court.

I struggled in my journey from the top of the mountain

down to the middle. My immortal powers were exhausted. In an effort to conceal the drain from Taibai Xingjun, I had consumed even more divine spells, and now I was on the verge of giving out.

I found a cave among the shrubbery in the middle of the mountain and made my way in.

It was pretty clean inside the cave, and the soil on the ground was very soft and flat. The entrance faced east, so when I lay down just so, I could see the morning mist and a ray of sunlight.

The immortals of the Heavenly Court should be able to more or less understand what had happened once they saw Tianshu, and the sight of the fox should seal the deal. This was the best outcome. I was a mortal to begin with, so even if I were to be reduced to ashes, I ought to return to the mortal world.

Hengwen would be a little less heartbroken if he did not see this happen with his eyes. He would also be able to get over it sooner.

There was no denying the sadness welling in me as I faced eternal oblivion. I thought, if a wisp of my soul could be retained, even if I was a grass-dwelling bug, that would have been fine too. But when a beam of morning sun shone on me, I was suddenly enlightened.

Whether I was a person doomed to a fate of eternal solitude, a rod meant to wreck relationships, or a bridge to act as go-between—they were all just different facets of a life lived. Think of it from another perspective. All these years Hengwen and I had in Heaven were something no mortal could ever have, even if they had the chance to dream of it over several lifetimes. I got to be together with him, from dawn to dusk, from day to night.

I was about to face eternal oblivion. I would no longer exist in the world and the world, to me. Hengwen and I were together up to the point I turned to dust, and that was already lifetimes together, for time eternal.

A sense of closure draped itself over me all at once. The immortal energy coursing through my body was already exhausted. It felt empty inside, and my vision began to blur. So, this was obliteration.

That's all there is to it.

In my daze, I saw Hengwen standing beside me. Mortals were known to develop hallucinations when they died, so it turned out that one would also hallucinate before being completely wiped from existence.

It was nice to be able to get one more look at him—even if it was but a mere illusion.

Chapter Twenty-five

Depressed, I lay prone on the floor in the middle of the room, wiggling my antennas.

This room had a door, windows, and four walls, but was otherwise empty. It was as if there were some invisible barrier covering it. No matter how I charged and barged, I could not find a crack to burrow into or a small hole in which to hide.

In the middle of the barrier, there was only a table, with a plate of pastries that emanated a faint aroma.

A person stood beside the table. He was all smiles as he waited for me to crawl my way up the table and onto that plate.

A trap to catch me. I would be a fool if I were to crawl in.

I had originally lived in another courtyard, but having gotten tired of eating the kitchen scraps in that house, I crawled all the long journey to this courtyard, wanting to see if there was anything novel to dine on. How was I to know that I would be entrapped inside this room after following the smell over the small hill that was the door threshold? No matter what I did, I could not find my way out.

I saw nothing else in the room other than the table, and

when I saw that person, I knew that was the end of me.

I lay motionless on the ground. That person looked at me, and I, too, looked at him.

Whether he was to crush me or trample me to death, I had absolutely nowhere to flee. But even so, *don't expect me to get into the trap myself.*

He looked at me and said, affably, "Come on up and eat. I won't hurt you. These are for you."

I could understand his words, but I would absolutely not believe him.

I continued to lie prone.

Do it fast if you want to catch or kill me. Don't be so wishy-washy with all these tricks.

I saw the feet under his robe move softly as he walked closer to me. I nonchalantly jiggled my antennas.

Instead of lifting his foot, he crouched down and placed the plate of giant pastries on the ground close to me. The aroma of grease was indeed very tempting, but I would not be so easily swayed.

He said, slowly, "It'd be easy if I wanted to hurt you. Why would I bother giving you food? Then again, if I really want to hurt you, then there would be no escape for you today, so you might as well eat your fill."

I shook my antenna again and thought, *He's right.*

I could not run either way, so I might as well fleece off a decent meal.

I swiftly climbed up the edge of the plate and the enticing mountain of pastries, then dove headfirst into the soft, fluffy crusts.

I ate until I was bloated before I came to a contented stop. I felt like my carapace must be glistening with grease right about now. I found a flat spot on the mountain of pastries, lay on my stomach, and drifted off into a comfortable sleep.

When I woke up, he was still at the table.

I guarded the mountain of pastries, eating and sleeping, sleeping and eating. A day and a night went by, and he was still standing by.

Another morning came around. I was gradually waking up after a comfortable sleep when I heard the door creak, and he went out.

I swiftly made my way down the table and tried to find a crack where I could make my escape, but the barrier I could not see remained securely sealed, and I could not find even a hint of a way out.

Just as I was searching, he returned. I immediately hid myself in the shadows at the foot of the table. The barrier, however, did not work on him, and he simply walked through it.

I heard a thud on the table. He bent over, as if he knew where I was, and said with the same affability as before, "I've brought a plate of new snacks. You can have the latest ones."

Slowly, I crawled up along the leg of the table to the surface, up the edge of the white and icy cool porcelain dish, and into a gap between the pastries. Next to the porcelain dish was a large plate, filled with clear water.

When he swapped it to the fifth plate of new snacks, I lay prone on the table and looked at him. *Don't humans all need to sleep?* He had hardly moved or slept these days; he was even more sturdy than me.

I sprawled over the mountain of pastries, engrossed in nibbling on a gigantic piece of flaky puff pastry.

"Are the snacks I gave you delicious?" he asked.

I jiggled my antennas.

"If you were to search for your own food, would you be able to find stuff as good as this?" he added.

I nibbled on the puff pastry and thought about it, hesitantly, my antennas still.

"Would you be willing to let me give you food if I don't shut you in?" He asked. "In exchange, you won't go anywhere else and will remain living here."

I hugged a corner of the puff pastry and thought about it. This was not something I could guarantee. Who could say for sure that I would not get tired of eating all these things? But this man really was an oddball for wanting to raise a cockroach. Rather than let some other cockroaches benefit from these things, I might as well take them for myself. I supposed I could say yes for the time being.

And thus, I jiggled my antennas.

I never expected him to be really delighted. He immediately broke into a smile. Hugging my puff pastry, I froze for a moment. He looked really good when he smiled. Among the humans, he could be considered one of the more good-looking ones, I guess. And surprisingly enough, that smile was as satisfying as the puff pastries.

Sure enough, he did keep his promise. The barrier was gone, and I could come and go freely. I made a den for myself in a crack in the corner of the room. Every day, I would make my way up the table to feast on the snacks and water he had set there. Once I had eaten my fill, I would cross the threshold and make the long journey to the yard to appreciate the scenery and aid digestion.

A bed was added to this house, and it was on this bed that he slept at night.

He was the only one living in the courtyard, but a man in an apricot-colored long robe often came visiting with a massive cloth bundle in hand. There were also a few in ink-blue robes and dazzling gowns among the frequent visitors. The first time the man in the bedazzling unlined gown came, I was nibbling on sweetened red bean paste atop the mountain of snacks. Always the considerate one, the man who fed me would pry the snacks apart so that I could feast on both the crusts and the fillings. I was very satisfied.

Just as I was contentedly nibbling away, the man in the bedazzling robe moved his gigantic face close to me and immediately let loose a sigh. I did not quite manage to grab on tight to the snack I was hugging, and was blown off to the edge of the plate.

Bedazzling Robe shook his head. "Aye, look at his present circumstances. Truly lamentable."

Not only had he blown me off, he had even made such a hypocritical show of sighing.

I did not like this person.

Ink-blue Robe also sighed the first time he came. He did not say a word but shook his head and left.

All these people came and went, but he always remained in the courtyard. Not once had I ever seen him leave. I found him rather weird. Sometimes, he would sit at the table reading a book. There was a time he set a book on the table, and I crawled onto his book to take a little stroll. He lifted the book along with me, brought me close to look at me at eye level, and smiled. I felt that he was indeed quite the looker when he smiled. I would probably not get tired of the snacks he gave me for quite a while to come.

I did not know how long I lived with him in this courtyard. In any case, the grass in this courtyard had all withered and yellowed, and all these hindrances of leaves were strewn on the ground.

That day, I went to the yard to digest my food and crawled my way to the side of the pond, but unexpectedly, a sudden gust of wind blew me into the water. I paddled, struggling to make my way to the edge of the pond, when a large, gaping mouth of a fish suddenly broke through the surface and enveloped me whole.

Pitch-black all around.

I wondered who else would get lucky with those snacks on his table.

***

I crouched on an old tree branch and shook my pitch-black feathers.

That particular scholar under the tree had still yet to leave. He held a few crumbs of food in his palm, trying to lure me over to peck at his hand. I flapped my wings, craned my neck, and cawed.

I'm such a strong and sturdy one; it's not like I'm a sparrow, so why would I eat off human beings' hands?

The scholar, however, was still standing.

The young monk sweeping the fallen leaves under the tree said, "Benefactor, don't stand anymore. This crow has lived in this tree for several years. No one has ever fed it, and it doesn't eat anything from human hands. On the contrary, those few sparrows under the eaves are obedient and familiar with people."

The scholar finally retracted his hand. "Is that so?" He sprinkled the crumbs under the tree.

Not that I was not giving him face by not eating his food, but his palm probably could not handle my physique. I flapped my wings, flew down to the ground where I crouched next to him, and pecked at the crumbs.

And looked up to see him looking at me with a smile.

I had been living in this old tree in front of the back door of this small temple for a long time.

I used to live on another mountaintop, but there had been a tempest that blew my tree down. My parents and brothers had flown their own respective ways. At first, I had moved to a tree before the door of a household, and I would fly over to the ridge of their roof every morning to caw and remind them of the time. But the mistress of that household insisted I was an inauspicious omen, so she struck off my nest with a bamboo pole and even greeted me with flying stones. I had swapped places, one after another, but was always loathed by all. In the end, I had no choice but to fly to this tree behind this small temple, where

I built a nest overnight.

The next day, the young monk stepped out to sweep the floor. Looking at me, he shouted, "Master, there's a crow on the tree."

The old monk leaned partially out of the back door and looked up at me. "Amitabha. It's a good thing to have a bird settling in here. Let it stay."

The monks in the temple were on a bland, vegetarian diet all year round, while I loved my meat. However, there were a lot of easy-to-catch wild game on this mountaintop. Crouching on the tree every day, I knew everything about when the old monk punished the young monk by making him copy scriptures or when the young monk groused about the abbot bullying him.

After pecking all the crumbs on the ground, I flew back to the branch. From that day on, he came to see me every day, and each time, he would sprinkle food all over the ground for me.

I heard the young monk ask the old monk, "Master, Master, that benefactor comes and goes every day without a trace, and we don't know where he stays either. He can't be a ghost, can he?"

"Amitabha," the old monk said. "That benefactor has an extraordinary bearing. He's definitely not a ghost. As a monk, you must remember not to make wild guesses and cast aspersions on others."

I heard the young monk ask the old monk again, "Master, Master, that benefactor always comes and visits the crow every day. Why is that?"

"Amitabha," the old monk answered. "Everything in the secular world is a web of worldly attachments to begin with. Cause and effect, I'm afraid only he himself knows."

I, too, wanted to know why the scholar came to visit me every day.

He came every day, be it sunny, overcast, windy, raining or snowing.

Later, whenever I saw him coming, I would crouch on a low branch. Sometimes, he would help the young monk sweep the fallen leaves; sometimes, he would teach the young monk how to write, and sometimes, he would hold a book to read. But most times, he would stand or sit under the tree and talk to me frequently. He spoke of how good the mountain view was, how lively the marketplace at the foot of the mountain was, and what had happened in the marketplace today and would occur tomorrow. Everything he spoke of was about humans, but I could understand all of it, so I listened.

Gradually, the young monk came to be on familiar terms with him. He even made the special effort of preparing a stool for him, which he would take out for him to sit on as soon as he came.

The old monk would often play with round black and white stones with him under the tree too. And I would crouch on the branch, sometimes cawing a sound or two.

That day, the weather was abnormally stifling, and he only left in the evening. At night, the wind started howling, thunder started crashing, and the rain started pouring down in torrents.

I was just about to seek shelter under the eaves of the small temple when a bolt of lightning from heaven struck down right on my head.

At the very instant the thunderous crash rang out, I wondered if he would still come from tomorrow onward, now that this tree was no more.

***

I half-floated in the water, my head peeking out. A man in a particularly bedazzling robe at the edge of the pond watched me and sighed. "How truly lamentable. How was he born a cooter?!"

I did not like to hear that. I was clearly a tortoise, why did he call me a cooter?

I knew what a cooter was. They called certain freshwater turtles cooters. Turtle shells are relatively flat and thin without any patterns, while tortoise shells are round and smooth, with well-defined sections and distinct patterns.

I floated back up to the water's surface again and revealed my shell to show him.

Bedazzling Robe continued sighing, "This creature has a long life. Just how many donkey years are you going to have to keep watch over him for this lifetime?!"

"Speaking of which," another person by the pond said, "I was just about to ask you. I asked you to do me some favor and pull some strings so that he could reincarnate into something more decent. Why is he still like this?"

Bedazzling Robe immediately answered, "Qingjun, as you know, each time he reincarnates, it's by stuffing him through any opening we can find. There is no place for him at all in the Book of Reincarnation. He can only fill in for whatever vacancy is available each round." *Sigh!* "How lamentable…"

The other person said nothing. I looked up at his long robe, fluttering in the wind, and nodded to him. So, his name was Qingjun. He was the one who had saved my life, and for that, I was grateful.

***

I originally used to live comfortably in a large lake, but rainfall was high this year, and the lake had overflowed its banks. I was swept away into a river, then swept along the river into a small pond. Someone eventually came along to cast a net, and hauled me up along with a bunch of fishes, shrimps, and crabs. We had been carried to the marketplace to be sold. I crouched in a waterless wooden basin and crawled around a few times. Eventually, I just lay down flat, resigned to my fate.

They said that those like us who were caught would be put into boiling hot water and slowly scalded to death. I had wondered if that was true. I crouched in the basin, watching as people came and went. Those fishes, shrimps, and crabs were all carried away by person after person. I shrank my head and waited, until the corner of some blue-colored attire stood before the wooden basin.

I heard him say, "I'll take this tortoise."

I let him carry me home. He did not put me into boiling hot water, but into this pond, and let me live in it.

He came to the pond every day to scatter some food scraps and talk to me.

Sometimes, I would crawl out of the pond and bask in the sun by the rock at the edge of the pond, listening to him as he spoke of how it was a good day today, of how boisterous the marketplace outside was, and of how he wanted to plant lotuses in the pond next year.

I had been quite happy living in my old lake, but this place was not too bad either.

The weather got colder and colder day after day, and I got lazier and lazier. I dug a hole in the silt at the bottom of the pond. After I was done taking a long sleep, it would be spring-time again, when the flowers bloom.

He said the peach blossoms in spring were the best, and I loved to look at them, but I did not know what peach blossoms were. Perhaps I would get my chance to see them after I emerged from my hibernation.

I burrowed into the hole and started to sleep. Somehow, I kept having the indistinct feeling that he was still talking by the pond, and it woke me up. I was seized with the sudden urge to crawl over and see him.

The pond water was icy cold, and the top was sealed with ice. I struck it with my head for a long time before I broke through, and crawled out with great effort. It was night, and the sky was dark. There was piece after piece of something icy landing on me—snow, I guess. In a moment of inattention as I crawled over a rock, I slipped and, very unluckily, fell on my back.

No matter how I tried to turn over, I failed to do so. The

snow kept falling on my four limbs and head. I struggled and struggled until I could move no more. I lay rigidly on my back and looked at the bright shiny place ahead.

He must be there.

I had never seen peach blossoms, but peach blossoms were surely warmer than snowflakes.

In my semi-conscious daze, I thought, it was actually a fortunate thing that I had been swept out of the lake.

***

A bedazzling robe stood in front of me and sighed. "This is truly lamentable. It's getting more and more outrageous each time!"

I propped up my eyelids and looked at him.

These city folks are so ignorant. Of all the wild boars on the mountain, I'm the most dashing! All the female wild boars melt into a puddle when they see me.

Another man stood behind Bedazzling Robe and looked at me in silence.

I used to have a merry life living on the mountaintop, but in a moment of inattention while dashing in the forest this morning, I had fallen into a trap. These two men immediately descended from the sky and released me. Feeling rather displeased, I snorted, but I could not move my body and could only let these two men size me up and down. I felt even more displeased.

The other man said, "Let it go first. We'll talk about it again when we get back."

Bedazzling Robe said, "Ahem. Or, let me take it back to raise. These atrocious reincarnations can't be helped. In my residence, he could probably become an immortal after several thousand years."

I was shocked. How could I be raised like some domesticated pig? What a great humiliation. The moment my body could move, I took to my hooves and ran.

I ran and ran and ran, running until I saw red. Without realizing it, I had run to the edge of a steep cliff, and in a moment of oversight, I failed to brake in time. My hooves trod on empty air, and then with a *whoosh,* I plunged.

Chapter Twenty-Six

I stood in the streets of the capital, taking in the peonies blooming in the flower market.

Allegedly, crimson peonies were the rarest and most valuable of all. Of all the twenty-plus years I had lived, I had seen bright red ones, white ones, and green ones... but never had I ever seen crimson ones. The day before yesterday, Mudan Xu had sent someone to deliver me an invitation, saying that he had a pot of crimson peony. This was originally a rare treasure in Hongfa Temple's collection, and the abbot had passed it on to him as a gift after he passed away. It bloomed today, so he was hosting a flower appreciation meet before his House of Unsurpassed Beauty and wanted me to attend.

Initially, this young master had no affection for these flowers and plants.

Who cares if it is red or green? It's just a flower, isn't it?

However, I had been frequenting Cuinong Pavilion as of late, and Yingyue said she loved peonies, so I might as well make a trip to this flower appreciation meet and buy a pot of peonies to elicit a smile from her.

The flower appreciation meet started early morning, at the hour of chen. I arrived a little early, so I wandered off for a leisurely walk. By the time I returned, it was nearly at the established hour; the tune of the flute and the melody of a qin had already been performed as an opening beside the flower terrace. A string of firecrackers had been hung beside the flower terrace, and Mudan Xu lit it personally. After the popping noises stopped, he delivered a speech. Then he lifted the veil and revealed that potted peony of his.

The flower was a shade of deep red, and it exuded magnificence in its delicate tenderness.

Indeed a marvelous specimen.

My heart soared at the sight, as I heard someone in the crowd say it aloud: "A marvelous specimen."

What a strange coincidence. Countless people were shouting adulatory praises, and yet out of all of them, I heard this one.

What was more, this voice struck me as inexplicably familiar, as if I had heard it many times before. I looked into the crowd and saw a man all dressed in azure standing among the people.

He turned aside and looked over, and I froze for a moment; it was like the entire marketplace of people and peonies had all faded into nothingness.

For a fleeting instant, I felt as if I had met him before.

I walked into the crowd of people and cupped my hands at him. "This humble one is Qin Yingmu. May I ask for your esteemed name?"

He flashed a candid smile. "My humble surname is Zhao, and my given name is Heng."

After exchanging a couple of pleasantries, he looked like he was going to leave. I hurried up to him and said, "This humble one feels a sense of closeness like that of old friends with you at first meeting, and so I'd like to invite you to the restaurant for a drink. I wonder if you would give me the pleasure of your company?"

He did not turn down the offer, and readily said, "Sure."

It was still the hour of chen, and the restaurant waiter said that it was still too early for them to start selling wine. This young master set a silver ingot on the table, and he immediately changed tune to "We have ready-made fine wine and dishes."

The waiter was all bows as he solicitously led this young master and Zhao Heng into the most exquisite private room, where a few plates of fine cold dishes and a jar of high-grade Shaoxing wine were promptly served.

I raised my cup to the person opposite me. "Here."

"My courtesy name is Hengwen," he said. "You can just call me Hengwen. It feels a tad too constrictive to speak so politely."

Hengwen, Hengwen.

Reciting this name felt somehow familiar.

"In that case," I said, "I shall not stand on ceremony with you. My courtesy name is Nanshan. You can just call me Nanshan too."

He smiled.

Before we knew it, this bout of wine drinking extended well into the evening.

I drank like I had not drunk wine in hundreds of lifetimes—I just wanted to keep drinking. We drank in the restaurant until afternoon, and he said he was staying in an inn on another street. Staggering, I followed him to his inn and entered his room, then shouted again for more wine and dishes to go with it.

I remembered I recited the entire genealogical tree of my Qin clan to him. I told him how my father once had my fortune told when I was a child, and the fortune teller said that I would be lucky in love this life; I was fated to be a ladies' man.

Holding up his wine cup, he looked at me and asked, "Oh, so was it accurate?"

"I didn't believe it at first either," I said immediately, "but it was right on the money. Not that I'm bragging, but I can tell you that countless courtesans in the pleasure quarters of the capital are crying and waiting for me to redeem their freedom."

He said, with the shadow of a smile playing on his lips, "They couldn't have already gotten together with some poor scholar or rouge seller, could they? I hope they are not merely using you as a raft to get across the river?"

I frowned. "How could I be that kind of sucker, not only a scapegoat but also a cuckold?"

He let out an inscrutable laugh and said nothing.

I did not know how long we had been drinking, but at any rate, by the time we finished a whole jar, the candle on the table had already burned out. I drank until I was in a daze, and he, too, drank until he was unsteady on his feet, so we simply lay down on the bed and slept.

I rolled over in bed and said to him, "All these years. And it is only today that I get to drink to my heart's content."

He uttered a sound of acknowledgment and went back to sleep.

The next day when I woke up, the guest room was empty. He was nowhere to be found.

The innkeeper downstairs said that he had not seen that young master go out at all, and the room had not even been paid for yet.

He had disappeared, just like that, and I never managed to find him again over the next couple of days. I searched everywhere I could and paid for that same room in the inn by the day, reserving it for him. The innkeeper told me the young master had not said where he had come from, and no one anywhere else recognized him.

For some inexplicable reason, I just could not stop looking for him. It was clearly a chance meeting, yet I could not forget him.

I searched from the Dragon Boat Festival on the fifth day of the fifth month this year to the Mid-Autumn Festival on the fifteenth day of the eighth month the following year. For more than a year, no matter who I drank with, it all tasted bland to me. I dreamed befuddling dreams when I slept, where I was a wild boar today and a tortoise tomorrow. One day, I dreamed I was in some place enveloped in mist, and he was standing just in front. I called out his name, and he turned around, looking as if he was about to speak, but then I woke up.

This one day, I strolled despondently into a small temple and drew lots to seek divine guidance in my search for him.

The person who interpreted the lot I drew was a bad one, and seeing the person I wanted to see again was as difficult as a monkey trying to pluck the moon off the sky.

The lot interpreter looked at this young master's crestfallen face and comforted me, saying there was actually still a glimmer of hope in this lot, for the monkey plucking the moon was better than the monkey fishing for the moon.

How so? I asked.

The lot interpreter explained, "When the monkey fishes for the moon, it's fishing for the moon in the water. No matter how it fishes for it, it is but a mere reflection. When the monkey plucks the moon, however, the moon it gets would be the real thing."

And I said, "But the monkey can't fly."

Disconsolate, I fished out a silver, placed it on the lot interpreter's table, and walked out of the temple.

The street bustled with a crowd of people coming and going. I strolled to the side of the street, where I heard someone greet me, "Sir, would you like to take a seat?"

So I sat and heard him ask, "What would you like to order?"

"Whatever's on the menu," I said offhandedly.

It did not take long before a large, steaming bowl landed on the table beside me with a thud. The person carrying the bowl said with a solicitous smile, "You seem to be hungry out of your wits, so I took it upon myself to make you a large bowl of wonton noodles."

Wonton noodles?

I perked myself up a little to look at it. I had never eaten this sort of food before. I took a pair of chopsticks to pick up some noodles and deliver them into my mouth—such a unique taste.

An old man slurping noodles beside me looked at me and opened his mouth, revealing half a mouthful of his food.

I gulped down my noodles and asked, "Is something the matter, Elder?"

The old man hesitated for a moment before he said, "Earlier, I saw a big piece of rat dung stuck in the noodles you picked up, but before I could warn you... you had already swallowed it..."

At night, when I returned to my courtyard, that piece of rat dung stirred up a raging storm in my stomach, coursing through my limbs and bones.

This scenario seemed all too familiar to me.

Just like how *he* had seemed familiar to me, how the word Hengwen seemed familiar to me.

And so, stepping on auspicious clouds underfoot, and with my essence, energy, and spirit merged as one, I ascended once more.

I stood before the heavenly envoy receiving newly ascended, unranked immortals outside the Southern Heavenly Gate.

The heavenly envoy did not think much of a newly ascended immortal like me, who became one through no work on my own, so he gave me the cold shoulder as he spread the register of names open, dipped his brush in ink, and asked me, "What is your name in the mortal world?"

"My name is Qin Yingmu in this life," I said.

The heavenly envoy lifted his brush to record it down. "Hold on for a moment. I will have to head over to Lingxiao Palace to report to the Jade Emperor before you step through the Southern Heavenly Gate." He closed the book and continued, "You really have excellent luck. Taishang Laojun's elixirs were ready to be extracted from the furnace today, and the Venerable Elder Mahākāśyapa from the Western Paradise just so happened to call on his residence for a visit. Laojun was discussing the Buddhist doctrines in terms of the Dao with him, and in a moment of inattention while keeping away the elixirs, he dropped one into the mortal world. Who would have thought you'd be the one to pick it up?"

"Having excellent luck is not something I can't help either," I said. "In fact, this is not the first time."

The heavenly envoy lifted his foot and turned around.

"Wait a minute," I called out. "May I trouble you to pass a message to the Jade Emperor on my behalf? Just say that Song Yao has picked up yet another immortal elixir and has, once again, ascended to the Heavenly Court."

The young heavenly envoy suddenly whipped around, his mouth half-agape in astonishment, completely dumbfounded.

I stood at the base of the jade steps in Lingxiao Palace.

The Jade Emperor sat upright on his throne while the Queen Mother sat beside him.

"An aberration!" the Jade Emperor exclaimed. "Truly an aberration!"

"Why say it like that?" the Queen Mother said. "It hasn't been easy for Song Yao. He was nearly obliterated, yet he actually severed the immortal bond and has now returned to the Heavenly Court. If immortals have destinies too, then this is probably it. Since it's Heaven's will, why put him in a spot?"

The Jade Emperor scrutinized my face and sighed after a moment. "Forget it. Just as the Queen Mother has said, this is probably your fate. You were nearly obliterated, and now you have risen from the ashes to be reincarnated and reborn. We will not continue to pursue everything that is now in the past, but you can only be an immortal with no official post in the

Heavenly Court, and the Heavenly Court will also treat you as non-existent. There is an island in the sea in the far east. Make your way there yourself to live out your days!"

I bowed. "Thank you, Jade Emperor." Then I exited Lingxiao Palace.

The young heavenly envoy who had led me into the hall was still outside the door, so I asked him, "Can I just ask where Hengwen Qingjun is now?"

The young heavenly envoy raised his head woodenly. "What Hengwen Qingjun?"

"Hengwen Qingjun of Weiyuan Palace, who is in charge of acclaimed literary figures," I said.

"The one in charge of acclaimed literary figures is the Tianjun, Lu Jing," the young heavenly envoy said. "He lives in Weiyuan Palace. There's no Hengwen Qingjun in the Heavenly Court."

Icy snow crushed down on me.

A voice beside me called out, "Song Yao, Song Yao."

I saw Bihua Lingjun the moment I turned my head. I instantly pounced over and grabbed his shoulders.

"Where is Hengwen?!"

Bihua Lingjun looked at me with eyebrows raised. "You've got some nerve for asking that."

The problem with Bihua Lingjun was that the more you were in a hurry, the slower he would be, and the more anxious you got, the more back he was.

He *slowly* led me to a secluded spot and *slowly* picked a rock to sit on. Only then did he *slowly* say, "That day, you put on such a touching display of crawling to the mortal world to be obliterated, but the truth is that Hengwen knew of it as soon as you left the Southern Heavenly Gate. When he rushed to the mortal world, you were already beyond saving, so he went ballistic and foolishly took out his own immortal essence to save you.

"He had never been a mortal before, and without his

immortal essence, he would have been instantly obliterated. Fortunately, the mortal world could not withstand his powers, and just as he was about to extract his essence, that mountaintop collapsed.

"Donghua and I hurried down and distributed a little of our respective immortal essence to you. Then we asked Laojun for an elixir pill and went to the Western Paradise to beseech Tathagata for some relics. It was with difficulty that we managed to preserve a small wisp of your soul. I asked Yanwang for a favor and stuffed you into the cycle of reincarnation, so that you may nurture and regenerate your soul whole through several lifetimes.

"Hengwen descended to the mortal world in secret to see you reincarnate. The Jade Emperor had him taken back to the Heavenly Court and put Lu Jing in charge of acclaimed literary figures. From then on, Hengwen Qingjun ceased to exist in the Heavenly Court."

"Where is Hengwen now?" I asked.

The scenery in the Heavenly Court was still the same, as if my several lifetimes of reincarnation in the mortal world had been but a mere dream. Prepared to head to the island in the sea to the far east, I stood from afar and gazed at my own Song Yao Yuanjun Residence and Hengwen's Weiyuan Palace of times bygone.

Just as I was turning to leave, a party of immortals walked over from the floating clouds. I retreated to stand by the side of the road. Surrounded by the rest of the Beidou Qixing, an indifferent figure dressed in a plain robe stopped when the party neared.

Having freed himself of the past, Tianshu was no longer as cutting cold. He looked at me, and asked in a soft-spoken voice, "Might you be the new immortal in the Heavenly Court?"

"Yes," I answered. "This humble one is Qin Yingmu, who has

just ascended to the Heavenly Court."

Tianshu nodded and smiled, then proceeded in the other direction.

I looked at his receding figure. The past of years bygone was much like the scent of the Lady Banks' roses in the first rays of yesteryear's morning sun, having faded away into the breeze and mist, leaving not a trace in its wake.

With great haste, I hurried over to the Far East.

The island in the sea was strewn all over with the skewed shapes of divine trees and boulders in disarray.

I weaved my way back and forth among them.

"Where is Hengwen?!" I had asked.

And Bihua Lingjun had said, "The Jade Emperor has exiled him to the Island of the Far East."

He stood under the heavenly tree outside the doors, and smiled softly at me, like the brilliant bloom of three thousand peach blossoms sweeping through the spring breeze.

"I owe you for all of five lifetimes and for restoring my soul," I said. "Coupled with the interest, I might never be able to repay it, ever."

"You repaid my debt to Xuan Li on my behalf. You can offset it," Hengwen said.

"I doubt so," I said. "You'll lose out a lot if I do that."

Hengwen waved his worn folding fan. "I'm not really that bothered about it. So what if it's offset? So what if it isn't?"

I wrapped my arms around his shoulders. "Precisely. You are mine, and I am yours. Between us, there is no such thing as a debt."

【THE END】

Extra: The Living Immortal

The Living Immortal was an ordinary charlatan.

Charlatans were aplenty among all the fortune tellers in the world, and the Living Immortal was just one of the extremely common ones of the lot.

In the words of the Living Immortal, who once lamented to his fellow charlatans, "No fortune-telling in this world is accurate. If fortunes can really be told and fates changed, I'd have long turned my luck around and become the damned prime minister!"

The Living Immortal had originally lived in a small city with an abundance of fish and rice. It was there in the city's Yue Lao temple that he had set up a stall all year round. When the unmarried young women and married old women came to the temple to pray—either for marriage for themselves or their children—they would often head to the stall to have their fortunes told.

The city was small, so the whole city knew which household's miss took a shine to which household's young master, as well as whose daughter was of marriageable age. As such, the

Living Immortal was right on the money every time he told a fortune, and that was how city folks came up with his nickname. They would often invite him for a drink whenever someone took a wife or married off their daughters.

But then, on a certain day of a certain month in a certain year, another fortune teller came to the city. This fortune teller not only could match birthdays, interpret eight characters, divine fortunes and read fortune lots, but was even versed in bone physiognomy and bone weight astrology, invoking deities and spirit writing, capturing demons and subduing evil, as well as restoring peace to a residence and turning its fengshui around.

The Living Immortal did not have as many tricks up his sleeve as the newcomer did, and it did not take long for him to lose the battle. His business dwindled by the day, until it looked like he could not afford to even scrape a meager living. Thus, the Living Immortal decided to try his luck in the wider world. Not only could he receive more business, he could also train and develop his skills.

The Living Immortal thus hoisted on his shoulder a banner with "Ironclad Fortune-telling" written on one side, carried his luggage on his back, and began his journey to the vast world yonder.

On a glorious spring day, he arrived at the capital city.

As he expected, the capital was a goldmine.

Having made his way to a Daoist Temple, the Living Immortal rented a room in the side wing to set down his luggage. Then he walked into the yard to see the scenery, looking up just in time to see a man holding a child by the hand strolling in the yard.

The Living Immortal glanced over, and saw that the person was fair-faced, slightly bearded, and about thirty or so years old. At first glance, his clothes seemed simple and plain, but on closer inspection, they were of high-quality fabric. The child still toddled a little on his feet, and his tiny attire and shoes were all exquisite; there was even a shiny golden longevity lock around his neck.

Simply a fat sheep that has fallen out of the sky, an easy mark for the picking.

Unhurriedly, the Living Immortal walked over, stroked his beard, and smiled. "This little young master has such a distinctive, refined appearance. He's truly a blessed person."

The rich man holding the child's hand looked up at the Living Immortal. "Oh? How can you tell?"

"You have an extraordinary bearing, and the little young master has a noble air to him," the Living Immortal replied. "Those with a discerning eye can tell at a glance that both of you are distinguished people. If this humble one were to say that I divined it, I'd be deceiving you."

He cupped his hands, glanced down at the little one, furrowed his brows in a seemingly unwitting manner, then turned to walk away.

With his hands behind his back, the Living Immortal pretended to look at the horizon as he strolled leisurely and counted inwardly to himself, *one, two, three…*

At the sixth step, he heard the man say from behind him, "Mister, please hold on."

The Living Immortal turned around. "Is there something I can help you with?"

"You seemed a little worried when you looked at my son earlier," the man said. "Might I ask why?"

The Living Immortal walked over slowly as he thought to himself, *What shall this old one use to deceive him? A great calamity in life, a seemingly short life expectancy, adverse to extreme sufferings…*

"A calamity in life" was often overused, and cursing someone with a short life seemed to be bad karma…

The Living Immortal was a charlatan with a conscience.

He walked over to the man and looked down at the child. "May I presume to ask if the little young master was born in the jiazi year, the first year of the sixty-year cycle?"

Peeking out from beneath the longevity lock hanging around the child's neck was a corner of an embroidered pouch, which seemed to be embroidered with a pattern of a mouse rolling money. So the Living Immortal had ventured a bold guess.

The man was awestruck. "That's right. My son was born on the first day of the seventh month in the jiazi year."

The Living Immortal stroked his beard and divined with his fingers. "The little young master was born to riches and honor, and his life is destined to be smooth sailing. In the future, he will get to enjoy a rare blessing that no other can enjoy. However, when it comes to marriage, I'm afraid…"

The Living Immortal mulled it over. He was not really adept at changing the diagram of one's fortune and warding off calamities, but his counterparts in the capital surely knew how, so he might as well pull out his proudest ability and haul in a big, freaking profit.

"What about his marriage?" the man prompted.

The Living Immortal said, "Earlier, when this humble one looked from afar, I saw little young master radiating with brilliant yang energy. Only those born on a yang day of a yang month in a yang year would have such an aura."

Naturally, the man asked, "What do you mean by on a yang day of a yang month in a yang year?"

The Living Immortal explained, "The jiazi year is made up of the first heavenly stem of 'jia' and the first earthly branch of 'zi.' It follows that the first heavenly stem of 'jia' is yang, while the second heavenly stem of 'yi' is yin and so on. The earthly branch of 'zi' is of the same character as 'son' or 'male,' and males are inherently yang, while females are inherently yin. What's more, the jiazi year is the very first year of the Heavenly Stems and Earthly Branches' sixty-year cycle. That makes it yang on top of

yang. Months and days are sorted in accordance with the properties of yin and yang, with odd numbers being yang and even
numbers being yin, so the first day of the seventh month in the
first year of the cycle is doubly yang. To top it up, the marriages
of those born in the seventh month at the peak of summer are
mounted with obstacles to begin with. As the poem goes, 'The
dog days of summer at its height, is when the wild goose alone
flies.' So, a person born on a yang day of a yang month in a yang
year—"

The Living Immortal sighed and shook his head, "—is
doomed to a fate of eternal solitude."

Stunned, the man looked at the child he was holding. "A
fate of eternal solitude… How could that be… Mister, can it be
salvaged?"

The Living Immortal had been waiting for this question.
With a deep frown, he said, "Alas, such a fate is typically beyond
salvation…"

The Living Immortal dragged out the word "beyond salvation," all but ready to add a "however" after it.

But he was only just mid-drawl when the man staggered
back a step. "To think it can't be salvaged!" With that, he turned
his head to gaze at the sky and let loose a heavy-hearted sigh.

The Living Immortal hurriedly strode a step forward.
"However…"

Before he could finish, he stepped on empty air.

As it turned out, the Living Immortal and the man had been
standing by the side of a dry well. A certain royal consort was
coming to the temple to perform a Daoist ritual, so the temple
repaired the grounds, and the fabric they used to lift the soil had
been left behind on the mouth of the well, all but forgotten. With
soil covering the fabric, it looked no different from the usual
ground, other than a slight bulge, and the moment the Living
Immortal stepped on it, he promptly plummeted down right to
the bottom of the well. The back of his head struck against the

wall, and before he could even yell in pain, he fainted.

Once the man was done with his long sigh, he turned back, but it was empty all around, and the fortune teller from earlier was nowhere to be found.

From then on, a new legend that a great master had once appeared here began to make its rounds in the capital.

The Living Immortal broke an arm when he fell to the bottom of the well, and he had to recuperate for more than a month before he got better. His expenses in the capital were high, and his years of savings were almost depleted. The Living Immortal felt that this was just not his time in the capital—his signs possibly clashed with this place—and his fall was an omen that he would not only fail in his endeavor but end up losing money instead. So, the moment his arm recovered, he immediately departed the city and set off for the world at large to ply his trade.

After more than a decade of wandering, the Living Immortal set foot once again in the capital.

The Living Immortal was already in his seventies at this point, and he was no longer mobile enough to lead a wandering life, so he thought of finding a place where he could run a steady business and afford to be comfortable enough to live out his life in retirement.

The Living Immortal was still fascinated by the capital. He found the bustle of the city lively, and there was plenty of business to be done. As they said, "The greater hermit lives in reclusion in the city." The marketplace of the capital was the most thriving of all, which was most suitable for the retired elderly like him.

After more than a decade, that Daoist temple was surprisingly still going strong. The temple master, also nearing seventy years of age, was very warm and cordial when he saw the Living Immortal. The Living Immortal bought two old houses in the alleys of the capital and went to this Daoist Temple to set up his stall during the day.

After the Living Immortal settled in, he first made inquiries about uncommon happenings in the capital, as was his usual practice.

There were countless uncommon happenings in the city, but of them, one stood out as the most uncommon.

The eldest son of the current Prime Minister had a fate of eternal solitude.

Legend had it that Prime Minister Song once met a great master who had told the eldest young master's fortune and said that he, being born on a yang day of a yang month in a yang year, was doomed to be single for life. The fortune told by the great master was right on the mark, and the eldest young master from the Prime Minister's household was now the joke of the capital. Young misses betrothed in marriage to him would definitely elope with someone else, and maidens he took a fancy to would surely get together with another.

Of late, this Young Master Song had his eyes set on a lady from the brothel. Except for his own self, the whole city knew that said courtesan had a lover—a scholar living in a run-down temple.

The Living Immortal received the news with a good amount of astonishment. Never had he expected the fate of eternal solitude to really exist in the world.

If only the one I had met back then was this one.

One certain day, the Living Immortal was sitting behind his stall in the temple when a dispirited young master walked in.

The Living Immortal noted his weak gait, crestfallen demeanor, dejected expression, and lifeless gaze. To his experienced eyes, it was clear at a glance that this youngster was heartbroken.

The Living Immortal thought that since the phrase "fate of eternal solitude" had been used by a great master before and was validated by a person of eminence, he ought to use it often, so he called out, "Young Master."

Said young master pulled himself together a little and turned around. The Living Immortal stroked his snowy-white beard and narrowed his old eyes. "Young master, this old one sees a dark aura over your head, and your Hongluan Star—the star of marriage—is dim. Are you, by any chance, in distress because of love?"

The young master tottered unsteadily to the front of the stall, sat down, and extended his palm without further ado. "Since you can tell, read my palm. I'm asking about my marriage."

"This old one is not versed in the art of palmistry," the Living Immortal said. "Would you take a reading with a character analysis?"

"Oh, well," that young master said, "we'll do that then." He lifted a brush and wrote the character for "pair," 双.

The Living Immortal half closed his eyes. "Break up this character, and it comprises the radical 'again' and 'again,' one after another in a recurring cycle, which implies that there's no escaping from it. Young Master, you asked about your marriage, so forgive this old man for speaking bluntly, but I fear your fate is one of eternal solitude…"

The young master's eyes went blank as he sat in a daze.

The Living Immortal was just about to say, "However…" when the young master suddenly barked out two bleak laughs and mumbled to himself, "As expected. Just as expected. No matter when I have my fortune read, it's always this lousy fate!" He let out another two more laughs and staggered right out the door.

The Living Immortal shouted after him, "Young Master, Young Master, you have not paid me yet!" He chased him to the door, but the young master was long gone.

A crippled beggar outside said with a laugh, "So I see you've also met Young Master Song today. Aye, he's rather pitiful.

Because a great master has verified his fortune before, all the fortune tellers in the city will now come up with 'fate of eternal solitude' whenever they read his fortune in marriage. Aye, he's really unlucky!"

Only then did it dawn on the Living Immortal that the youngster earlier was the famous Young Master Song. Oh well, never mind the money. That lad was indeed quite the pitiful sight.

The second year, the Living Immortal heard that Young Master Song had, for no apparent reason, vanished from home without a trace. This matter stirred up a huge commotion. Even the emperor issued an edict to search all over the world for him, but to no avail. Everyone guessed that Young Master Song, being too heartbroken, had seen through the secular world and had gone to a small temple in an old, virgin forest deep in the mountains to become a monk.

On the contrary, the Living Immortal's business in the capital was smooth sailing. "So many people in the world love to have their fortunes told," the Living Immortal said to his apprentices, "we're not tricking them into spending this sum of money; rather, they are the ones willing to spend."

The Living Immortal's apprentices were all vagrant youths who wandered the streets. Seeing that they did not have enough to eat, he would often share his food with them before eventually coming to accept them as apprentices.

The Living Immortal said, "Just think of it as accumulating merit for the afterlife."

The Living Immortal lived to be more than ninety years old before he passed away peacefully in his sleep.

Sure enough, in accepting those few apprentices of his, he did indeed accumulate merit. Two of the apprentices he had taken in were the only sons of prominent clans who had managed to escape when their family properties were confiscated and their entire clans sentenced to death. Three were the children of starving commoners who had fled to the capital after the Yellow River flooded its banks. Grateful to the Living Immortal, the parents of these apprentices in the underworld had put in a lot of good words for him before Yanwang.

Yanwang summoned the Living Immortal to his palace hall, and said he could arrange for him to be born into riches and honor in the next lifetime. As he still had some merits left, Yanwang also asked if he still had any other wishes.

The Living Immortal said, "Yes, this old man has been called the Living Immortal for a lifetime, and yet I'm not blessed enough to ascend to immortality and see the Heavenly Court. So, I'd like a trip to the Heavenly Court."

And Yanwang said, "That's easy."

He arranged for Judge Lu to deliver an official correspondence to the Jade Emperor, with the request for a heavenly envoy to bring the Living Immortal to the Heavenly Court for a tour.

As the Living Immortal strolled around in the Heavenly Court, he still did not forget to ask about uncommon happenings in the area.

The heavenly envoy guiding him answered, "If you look at it from a mortal's point of view, there are uncommon happenings everywhere in the Heavenly Court. If we were to talk about the most uncommon of all—" the heavenly envoy pointed with a finger, "Immortal Song Yao over there happened to pick up an immortal elixir and ascended; he's pretty much a rarity."

The Living Immortal squinted his eyes and craned his neck to look in the finger's direction.

Only to see a young immortal in a long blue robe and an immortal in a long light-colored gown sitting together under a heavenly tree. The immortal in blue sighed to the immortal in light colors, "Hengwen, I'm telling you, when I was in the mortal world, a great master once told my fortune and said that my fate was one of eternal solitude…"

Afterword

Hello, dear readers. Thank you very much for reading my humble work.

Allow me to introduce myself briefly. I'm an author from China. Many people often ask me the same question when they first get to know me—"Why did you choose such a pen name, 'The Gale Blows By'?"

The reason might actually sound a bit whimsical. Years ago, I was reading a novel on a literary website and got so hooked that I suddenly had the urge to give writing a try as well. It just so happened to be windy and rainy when I registered my pen name, so I spontaneously came up with this name. I didn't expect it to become my official pseudonym that I'd keep on using.

Many authors put much thought into the selection of their pen names, and they would even consult experts to ensure that it'd be an auspicious name. In comparison, mine is admittedly more casually chosen.

I used to submit short stories to magazines in the early days, but it wasn't until after I adopted the pen name, Da Feng Gua Guo, that I started serializing longer novels online. Then I had the fortune of seeing them published as physical books after the novels were completed.

The genres of my humble works are quite diverse, and they include romance novels, adventure novels, detective novels, and so on. However, I mostly write stories set in ancient China or with immortality and fantasy elements. The physical North American releases that I have the honor of seeing published this time, *Peach Blossom Debt* and *The Imperial Uncle*, are both respectively an immortal-fantasy novel and a novel set in fictional ancient China.

It should be noted that most of the settings in my novels are made up. For example, the dynasty in *The Imperial Uncle* is entirely fictional and does not exist in history. *Peach Blossom Debt*, on the other hand, borrows from the settings of traditional Chinese immortals, but the main immortal protagonist of the story, as well as some settings of the Heavenly Court and the mortal realm, are my own creations.

In fact, I was taking the lazy way out by doing this. Writing with a historical dynasty as a background would require me to do rigorous research. Attire, food, architecture, etiquette, and even the words and phrases used would have to be consistent with historical facts; otherwise, I'd make a big fool of myself if there were any errors. It's a lot easier to make things up and borrow information from ancient times like I do...

I'm very grateful to Peach Flower House for their willingness to translate and publish *The Imperial Uncle* and *Peach Blossom Debt* in English. This is also my first time having books published in English.

I am very apprehensive about whether these two novels will be well-received by North American readers.

My humble works are set in ancient China, so the characters' names may be confusing to North American readers. In ancient China, people had a "courtesy name" in addition to their given names. Men would get their courtesy names when they came of age at twenty; in other words, they would hold a "coming of age ceremony" when they were twenty years old and obtain a "courtesy name" which they would then use. The meanings of courtesy names were generally related to those of the given names, and I have retained this custom in my writings. For example, in *The Imperial Uncle*, Jing Weiyi's courtesy name is Chengjun, Liu Tongyi's is Ransi, and Yun Yu's, Suiya. Readers unfamiliar with this cultural background may find the names confusing and perplexing.

In addition, the male protagonist in *The Imperial Uncle* would address others by their courtesy names in his interactions with them to show affection; for instance, calling Liu Tongyi, "Ransi."

In reality, courtesy names were a respectful form of address in ancient China. If the parties weren't on very familiar terms with one another, they couldn't directly call each other by their full names, but rather by courtesy names. By all reason, saying "Liu Tongyi" or "Tongyi" would be more intimate than "Ransi." Yet, due to Jing Weiyi's noble status, it's natural for him to call the others directly by their full names, while "Ransi," "Suiya" conveys a sense of respect with a touch of affection.

This might also be challenging for readers unfamiliar with the background of ancient China to grasp.

On the other hand, in *Peach Blossom Debt*, most of the main characters are referred to by their given names, with rarely any mention of their courtesy names. However, as they are all immortals, they also have an additional immortal title.

As such, I'm worried that my dear readers would find the multitude of names in my works too confusing to remember.

Nonetheless, I personally think that my novels are lighthearted, and I didn't give it too much thought when I wrote them, either. These humble works are ordinary light fiction meant to be relaxing, entertaining reads in your spare leisure time.

What left a deep impression on me during my communication with the publication staff in this collaboration was their professionalism and meticulousness.

Peach Blossom Debt and *The Imperial Uncle* were completed years ago, and I have a habit of revising my works periodically or before each publication of a book.

I'm now self-reflecting on whether this habit is necessarily correct. I myself thought that over time, my writing would perhaps be a little more mature than it was before, and that I might notice some oversights when rereading my past works.

Many readers would also offer me suggestions, especially now that readers can communicate with authors online at any time. For example, a reader once told me after reading *The Imperial Uncle* that they felt Chengjun falls in love too easily, and they hoped I could make him a little more steadfast in his feelings. Or, another reader would feel Jing Weiyi was too mean toward Yun Yu and hope the bond between them could be a little lighter, so that Yun Yu could be a little freer....

There was a period of time when I was more susceptible to influence, so I made numerous revisions to the works when presented with the opportunity to publish physical books.

For this North American version, the staff communicated with me in all earnestness, even doing a word-for-word comparison of the various versions, upon which they expressed their opinion that the earliest version was the most suitable.

I am touched by such thoroughness and meticulousness. To the North American book market, my humble works and I are new, like a blank piece of paper, which subsequently means that sales would be hard to predict. Even so, the staff treated my works with such focus and conscientiousness. Their professionalism is truly admirable.

Upon rereading, I realized that while the earliest versions had more writing flaws, the emotions conveyed were really more complete and robust. For that reason, the earliest versions of these two novels were used. There are many oversights and shortcomings in the content, and I appreciate the efforts of the translators and editors in translating and correcting them.

The North American version of *The Imperial Uncle* not only has the earliest, uncensored content but also the complete collection of four extras, making it the most complete physical edition to date.

This seems to align with the story—for Chengjun, the first is best.

As for *Peach Blossom Debt*, I'm sorry to say there's only one very short extra titled "The Living Immortal;" there are no other special extras. After *Peach Blossom Debt*, I wrote another story set in the same universe, *The Egg of Wishes*. I personally considered this novel to be the extra for *Peach Blossom Debt*, so I didn't write any more.

Over the years, I have written many other novels, and both my state of mind and writing style have changed. I'm worried that if I write another extra, it might not match the style of the original work.

And besides, I do feel that this novel, while not long in length, is already very complete, and I think the existing contents are sufficient.

Am I finding excuses for my laziness?

I'll leave it to you, my dear readers, to decide.

As we reach the end of this afterword, I would like to express my thanks to the editors, translators, designers, and publisher.

Thank you for your love and support for my humble works!

Of course, thank YOU too, dear reader, for your willingness to read and buy this book.

Here's to wishing you the best of luck and fortune! May your endeavors go as your heart desires!

-Da Feng Gua Guo